OASIS

Adèle Blackwood

Oasis

Published 2024 by Stephanie Devlin
Copyright © Stephanie Devlin
ISBN: 978-1-916544-54-3

Printed and bound in Ireland by Lettertec Ireland Ltd.

Publishing Information
Design & publishing services
provided by JM Agency

www.jm.agency
Kerry, Ireland

OASIS

Through the shifting sands she finds herself

MILLIE BLACKWOOD

Contents

To Denis …
for his abiding love.

Book 1

ONE

Flight into Madness

✵

The journey, not the arrival matters.

– T.S. Eliot

Looking out into the blackness, Louise begins to feel unnerved, provoked by the unfathomable void that stares back at her through the porthole. With a growing sense of unease, she pulls the blind down to ignore what is outside and bring her focus back inside the dimly lit cabin.

Recalling her first and only plane journey from Dublin to London with her sister Juliette, it seems so long ago now. This journey is very different, though, not solely because she is travelling alone to another continent but because the reason for her journey is somewhat out of the ordinary.

Only a few hours previously, she had said goodbye to her family and yet it already seems like light years away. Time passes, and she gets wrapped up in her thoughts until suddenly, she becomes aware of the slow, steady descent of the aircraft, which eases itself downwards. It is not long before the plane touches down on the tarmac, thankfully in a smooth landing, leaving the starlit sky far above and below it, a young girl, nervous but eager to embrace what life has in store for her in a foreign land.

Eventually, she stands up, gets out of her seat, stretches and starts gathering her things together. Walking purposefully down the aisle towards the exit, she takes a deep breath, telling herself she is ready for what lies on the other side of the door. The long-awaited journey is at an end and Louise has finally arrived.

Outside, Kareem stands on the boarding bridge, patiently waiting for the door of the plane to open while he chats casually with some of the ground crew. He watches eagerly as each passenger disembarks with a look of expectation on his swarthy face, dark eyes darting from left to right. His expression is one of confidence, a smile playing about his lips. Standing by his side is his older brother Faisal, sporting a rather serious-looking countenance in comparison to his younger brother. In fact, they are not at all alike, in looks. Kareem is handsome of face with a good, solid build that contrasts with his brother whose face is long, made longer than it appears by a bushy beard that reaches well below his chin. Louise notes that his physique is a little too lean for her taste.

Today, her husband looks smart in casual jeans and a short-sleeved shirt, though he appears slightly at odds beside his brother, who is dressed impeccably in a light grey suit, complete with shirt and pale blue tie. His shoes are militarily polished, and it strikes Louise that he cuts quite a suave figure standing amongst his countrymen with a look of authority, self-containment and a style all his own.

Kareem's eyes are still searching amongst the passengers as they disembark until he catches a first glance of his pretty, young wife. Within a few seconds, her eyes come to rest on his, and smiling broadly, she walks briskly towards him, barely able to believe it after months of separation. Instinctively, she wants to throw her arms around him in a great, warm hug but she checks herself just in time, alerted by a deep, primal sensation in her gut. Standing in front of her husband, she looks into his face for reassurance while he simply holds out his hand to his wife. Shaking it, they smile warmly at one another and exchange a few words. The occasion feels regular and nothing special, like they have met for the first time.

Turning immediately to his brother, Kareem introduces his wife. On cue, Faisal offers his hand, smiling broadly. *"Ahlen le Libya, cave-il-halic"* Kareem at once translates.

"It means welcome, Louise, and how are you?"

Louise shakes his hand and, smiling broadly, replies.

"It's so nice to meet you, Faisal. Thanks for coming, I've heard a lot about you from Kareem."

Waiting for Kareem to translate, she is surprised when he answers for himself.

"All good, I hope", he jokes, making the switch seamlessly and without the slightest trace of an accent. "How was your flight over?" he adds. "Was it too long, or did you manage to sleep? I know how boring flying can be sometimes."

Louise hears his deep-throated voice as he asks the question, but more notable is that he delivers it in English, which is clipped and perfectly constructed, without the typical grammar mistakes of a non-native speaker.

She understood from Kareem that his older brother had a few words of English, but she did not expect his command of it to be so advanced. She feels immediately encouraged by that fact alone.

"Actually, it was fine, I read for most of it so it didn't seem too long. Do you fly much yourself, Faisel?" she asks, eager to make an attempt at conversation.

"Yeah, from time to time but not as much as before, when I was in the travel business. Shall we make tracks?"

Without further ado, he turns to address his brother in Arabic, and they set off together, Louise following closely behind the two men.

Despite the couple's first meeting after nearly three months, their reunion feels distant, lacking the warmth that Louise was expecting. Nevertheless, given the constraints of a culture completely alien to Louise, she stretches herself to understand. Evidently, from what she sees, the surroundings and general atmosphere do not appear to lend well to shows of public affection, so they have to comport themselves in a detached, unemotional manner, fitting to the place and its customs.

Once inside the airport building, she has a weird sense of something heavy descending on her, a feeling she cannot understand. Propelled forward in a kind of mechanical motion, everything appears unfamiliar, out of place, literally like nothing she has experienced before. People are staring at her, the women openly from one eye, peeping out from behind their white, floor-length garb, the men less overtly, although she can sense their eyes almost burning into her flesh. The realisation that she looks so out-of-place in the clothes she is wearing is enormously disquieting.

Her linen, knee-length culotte skirt and matching beige-jacket of the same fabric looks great, so she thought when she first put it on. Undeniably, it is stylish and smart in an understated sort of way, except now, she is unsure and self-conscious. Underneath she is wearing a short-sleeved silk blouse with tiny, painted flowers in pastel colours fastened together by a row of pretty pearl buttons that end just below her neckline. On her feet are fawn leather sandals with straps that crisscross delicately over her foot, tying at the ankle in a small gold buckle. Relieved to have chosen ones with low heels; at least she can walk easily if her feet begin to tire. Managing to keep her slim figure has been effortless as a consequence of severe bouts of nausea that always end in a trip to the bathroom. Recently, however, her appetite has returned, and she is more inclined to enjoy her food again.

They move through the building, Louise keeping a steady pace close on their heels. Every now and then, they acknowledge an occasional greeting with a wave or nod of their heads. Evidently, they are well-known and held in some regard, an observation which is shortly to be confirmed.

Presently, they slow down on approaching a group of soldiers dressed in dark-green khakis and displaying an alarming array of weaponry between them, from large Kalashnikovs to smaller handguns. Faisal is immediately hailed by one of the military personnel standing out front and exuding an air of authority. Without losing a single step, Faisal strides directly up to the weathered-looking soldier with a broad smile of recognition. Louise watches in amusement as they embrace, followed by a firm clasping of hands, which they seem reluctant to let go of. Kareem steps forward for an introduction as Louise stands diplomatically to one side, trying awkwardly to feign a look of nonchalance when she actually feels ill at ease, the only Western woman in the building as far as she can make out. Relieved to be spared an introduction, she pretends not to notice when the other soldiers steal a sidelong glance in her direction while the brothers indulge in some friendly banter. Proudly brandishing their firepower in plain sight, the peals of laughter continue for a few more minutes, and just as Louise is feeling increasingly impatient, they bid one another farewell and move on, much to her relief.

Walking a couple of paces ahead of her without uttering a word except for a nod of his head, Kareem beckons her to follow them in the direction of the immigration, an area arranged with a row of three desks that are positioned askew in front of two narrow doors that lead into an open area operating as a baggage-reclaim point.

It appears to Louise that the layout and interior design of *Bab-Al-Aziziyah* Airport does not appeal to the eye or to any aesthetic form. Its appearance is dull, drab and dated, devoid of colour or decoration and lacking in imagination.

Several handshakes later, they walk through the passport control without incident and exit the airport building after what seems like a long time. Throughout the entire episode, nobody addressed Louise at any point during the proceedings, which she is relieved about as she hasn't a single word of Arabic. Most of the people she has seen appear austere and apathetic, giving her reason to believe that the general populace is not very welcoming to foreigners. She figures her arrival in the country signals a fairly rare occurrence, perhaps one that is neither politically nor publicly embraced. Louise has never in her life experienced prejudice or culture shock but now she is on a different continent and has just entered a whole new world.

Stepping outdoors into the night, she is assailed by a heavy blanket of heat and humidity, making it difficult for her to breath. Suddenly, she feels tired, aware that she is sticky and hungry. The atmosphere is oppressive, something she is not used to. Climbing into the back of an old pick-up truck, she braces herself for the journey ahead, beginning to feel overwhelmed. As she sits quietly in the back, it occurs to her that maybe Kareem is also nervous about her arrival.

Very soon, they leave the airport behind and travel along a newly constructed road that is wide and well-lit. They scarcely meet any traffic, except the odd vehicle, similar to the one they are travelling in. Dotted along the way are clumps of date-palms, proudly bearing their fruit and stretching tall into the sky. In a land that values faith and symbolic tradition so highly, the date tree stands above all others. According to Quranic teaching, *Maryam,* revered in Christianity as 'the Virgin Mary,' was instructed to eat dates when she gave birth to *Isa,* or Jesus, because of their nutritional value.

A bemused Louise looks out of the window, lost in her own thoughts, while she tries to register her vision of this new land, so strikingly at odds with what she is accustomed to. Her first impressions of the unfamiliar landscape begin to jar on the surface of her consciousness.

The city of Tripoli is a seaport, lying to the west, along the Tunisian border, literally, on the edge of the desert, on a point of rocky terrain which projects into the Mediterranean, forming a bay. The images passing before her eyes are of a dry, barren environment, with very little vegetation save for the palm trees and an odd spattering of cacti scattered here and there along the route. The soil is sandy, and the land is flat, stretching back across wide expanses. It is desolate and without a hint of green, so parched is the bare and bleak landscape. Louise catches sight of a group of men huddled together around what looks like a small campfire while a single-humped camel stands obstinately overlooking their nocturnal rendezvous; she keeps her young calf close beside her as she forages on date stones strewn about the sandy ground. Bedouins or 'desert dwellers' of Northern Africa are a nomadic people who believe that the curative powers of camel milk are enhanced if the animal's diet consists of certain desert plants. Fortunately for the camel he is not particular in his taste; being highly adaptive, he can manage quite well for long periods without little or any external source of food. The human animal on the other hand, is an entirely different sort of beast.

A hunger gnaws at her stomach as Louise sits silently in the back, feeling slightly irritated now, especially since no word of English has been spoken since they left the airport. In the interests of good manners and social etiquette, she feels offended by her husband and his brother for their lack of graciousness toward her, a newcomer to their country. She wants to say something to remind Kareem about this but decides against it, consoling herself with the thought of mentioning it later when they are alone. As the truck speeds along, all she can think about is food, water, and a visit to the bathroom. It has been a very long day and the thought occurs to her that she has travelled from one continent to another in that time.

Presently, they leave the desert wilderness behind and drive into what looks like a small, dimly lit village. What strikes Louise as they drive through is the lack of human activity and its ghostly atmosphere. She assumes that the residents prefer to be indoors, accustomed to sleeping early; perhaps there is nothing better for them to do in these parts. The infrastructure is makeshift, with no proper road, uneven kerbstones and poorly erected buildings. The only sign of life is a couple of scrawny cats and a mangy dog busy rummaging through some abandoned trash.

Suddenly, they round a corner, and turning off the road, the pick-up slows as it bounces backwards and forwards onto a sandy track flanked on both sides by rows of crude-looking concrete structures, low and flat-roofed. Set unusually high up in the wall are two tiny, barred windows on either side, with scarcely enough space for light to filter through. Louise stares out into the dark shadows, barely managing to make out the shapes, since there are no streetlamps. She is not sure why they are stopping until the truck grinds to an abrupt halt. Surely, they have not arrived, Louise wonders as she looks out in horror!

"Ok Louise, we're here", Kareem announces unceremoniously from the front seat of the truck.

It is only then that it hits her. Shock courses through her veins. Completely disarmed and unsure now of what to expect, she never imagined it to be like this, godforsaken, a ghetto or some forgotten government-project.

Alas, she is here, safely at least but unlike most travellers, she does not feel a sense of elation at her journey's end. Reality strikes her like a flash of lightening, sudden and powerful. A part of her wants to run away, but she gets slowly out of the truck. Floundering, she is seized by a wave of uncertainty and apprehension as her feet connect with the ground beneath. The heels of her shoes sink deep into the sand as she trudges awkwardly towards the door after Kareem. Her abiding memory, as she pauses warily in front of the door, her heart beating fast, is of a band of barefooted children, gabbling and gawking from their surrounding dwellings.

What is it that so piques their curiosity, Louise wonders?

Experiencing a sudden sense of the 'ridiculous', it occurs to her that they have never seen a foreign woman in these parts until now.

How right she is.

TWO

A Strange Arrival

We are such stuff as dreams are made on,
and our little life is rounded with a sleep.

– 'The Tempest', Shakespeare

Standing in front of a wooden door with both brothers on either side of her, Louise feels the adrenalin rush through her body. A weird sound comes from within, slices through the night air, and suddenly, the door is flung open. Louise finds herself face to face with a woman, hand cupped purposefully to her mouth, from which emanates a high-pitched vocal sound that is long, wavering and trill. Louise has never in her life heard a sound quite like it.

"This is my mother, Lou. She's been waiting for us," says a smiling Kareem, standing aside to allow both women space. This mysterious-looking woman standing before her extends a brown, bejewelled hand with fingertips painted a rusty red, after a long steeping in henna. Louise offers her hand with a smile, and she accepts it, not in a firm, solid grip but with barely a touch. She turns and greets her eldest son, Faisal, with a broad smile, revealing a row of even, white teeth that look surprisingly healthy for a woman her age. Suddenly animated, her smile lights up dark eyes and makes no secret of the place he holds in her affections.

Finding her voice, Louise finally speaks.

"Kareem, will you tell your mother that I'm delighted to meet her and all the family. I hope she'll be patient with me until I learn the language."

She utters the words appealingly to her husband, unable to think of anything else to say. He dutifully relays the message to his mother, who nods back, her expression inscrutable.

"Don't worry Lou, she won't bite. Honestly, you two just need time to get to know one another."

Despite his words of reassurance, Louise senses something cold about the woman standing before her. Other family members hover nearby, waiting to greet their brother's new wife. Louise wishes the ground would open and swallow her for a few moments just to allow her some time to rally her strength.

Two young girls come forward, and Kareem introduces them as his sisters, Nuria and Maryam. They appear shy but friendly nonetheless as they hold out their hands to her. She wants to ask her husband to translate for her but is interrupted by the sound of his mother's voice. Whatever she has said to her daughters, they are prompted into immediate action, hurriedly disappearing from view. Presently, a third sister appears carrying a pitcher of water and two glasses.

"Ah, here comes Fatima, my sister, she's the oldest of the three girls," Kareem remarks, before speaking to her. After greeting Louise with a lukewarm smile, the girl pours a glass of water and hands it to her sister-in-law, who drinks thirstily with a new appreciation for its refreshing properties.

In her condition, Louise has developed a heightened sensitivity to smells and odours of all kinds, particularly those relating to food. At the slightest hint, her olfactory system goes into overdrive, triggering all sorts of powerful sensations that usually end in her kneeling over the toilet bowl. Thankfully, it has improved of late, subsiding in time for her journey to North Africa. She is about to enter a whole new world of scents, most of which are pleasant but the more obnoxious ones will rival any she has experienced before.

After exchanging the necessary pleasantries, Louise cannot ignore her need for the toilet any longer, so she asks Kareem to point her in its direction.

Touching the doorknob, she finds it loose and gently pushes open the door to step inside. Instantly, she freezes.

Even before her eyes can adjust, the rest of her body reacts by refusing to move. Transfixed, she begins to look around until her eyes come to rest on the ugly hole in the ground. Something is crawling along its edge.

"Jesus", she whispers instinctively as a shiver runs down the length of her back. Then, she spots another, a black, winged insect making its way stealthily up the wall toward the ceiling. Aghast, her skin begins to prickle and she forces a disturbing thought from her mind. Seized by a paralysing fear, she shudders, wondering how the hell is she going to do anything here. To her dismay, she realises there is no toilet roll, no hand towel, nothing, things you usually take for granted simply because they are there when you need them. Mercifully, Louise only needs to pee but irrespective of the fact, she is adamant not to touch the tiny water-hose lying in a pool of discoloured water on the germ-infested ground.

In the space of a few seconds, an angry thought enters her mind but then flees. It is enough to register a sliver of disappointment with Kareem for neglecting to prepare her for such an ordeal. Tiny beads of perspiration begin to break out on her forehead, and she can feel the urge intensify with the pressure on her bloated stomach. Taking a breath, she lifts her skirt and, gathering it about her, moves warily towards the offensive hole. Trying to prevent the hem of her skirt from trailing in the foul water while at the same time maintaining her balance proves to be the least of her inconveniences.

On bending down, her nostrils are assailed by a vile stench and on impulse, she recoils, almost reeling from the smell. Suddenly, her eyes begin to water, and a wave of nausea rises in her throat. Swallowing hard to stifle it, she takes a deep breath, looks away and tries to shift her focus for a few seconds from the repellent sight and replace it with a positive thought. It works because, presently, the sickness passes.

After hesitating a few seconds, it takes every ounce of her resolve to crouch down a second time. Squatting awkwardly, it strikes her as a decidedly undignified position to be in compared to sitting on a regular toilet seat.

An unlikely thought enters her mind. It is a vision of Joyce's Bloom, savouring a bit of bathroom reading whilst sitting on his porcelain throne at number 7. For Leopold, his toilet practice is one of life's small luxuries, one that combines reading and pooping.

With one hand, she holds a fold of skirt against her face, shielding her nose and mouth against the pong. The other, she uses to free her pants and urinate without completely drenching herself. Because she has held onto it for so long, it feels like a rapid, flowing river that will not stop.

At last, the dreaded deed is done and she steps away from the rotten hole onto the tiled floor and smoothes down her skirt. In the sink, she runs the water over her hands, and giving them a quick shake, she dabs them dry in the folds of her skirt. Before leaving, she steals a glance upwards, noting the changed direction of the creepy cockroach that is scurrying back and forth in a desperate descent to find some dark crevice. Momentarily relieved, Louise pushes open the door and hurries out, her dignity somewhat restored as she walks back to join the family in the balmy night air.

Kareem and his mother are sitting on the open porch at the centre of the house. It is square and simple in its design, with a scullery to its left and, on the right, steps leading onto the roof. Undoubtedly, the most attractive feature is its tiled floor, which looks like marble but is actually coloured stone, hand-carved with a highly polished finish. Crossing the floor barefoot to sit down, Louise feels it cool and refreshing under her tired feet. Maryam appears carrying a large tray with baskets of bread and bowls of watermelon. Nuria follows with another tray, setting it down in front of the couple. It is called *shorba,* a light tomato soup with pieces of chicken and chickpeas. The addition of fresh mint gives it its unique flavour.

Louise tries to forget about the bathroom scene and focuses on getting some sustenance. Dipping a crust of bread into her bowl, she savours its spiciness and the fresh, crispy bread. Despite her recent ordeal, she begins to eat heartily.

"It tastes good, doesn't it?" Kareem looks at her, a grin on his face, "Maryam cooks well, she's better than my mother at some dishes."

"It tastes really good, light and not too spicy so it shouldn't give me heartburn," Louise remarks. "Does your mother agree that her daughter is better at cooking certain dishes?" she asks.

Kareem laughs out loud at the suggestion.

"No way, she would never admit to it, there always has to be some small thing wrong with it."

They both glance across at his mother, who preoccupied, is filling a teapot with water and then puts it on a small lit stove beside her. Before Maryam clears away the trays, she offers them more watermelon, but Louise is full.

"By the way, Lou, you can call my mother 'Hajja' and my father 'Haj', ok?" Kareem suggests before explaining its significance.

"My mother's name is Zohra, my father Abdulla but they have both been to Mecca and done their pilgrimage."

"You mean Mecca, in Saudi Arabia? Louise asks.

"That's the one, a holy city in Islam and you go there to complete a pilgrimage, everyone of the faith is expected to, at least once in their life," Kareem continues, "Haj' is another name for pilgrim."

"Ok, I understand, so it's like a title of honour, in a religious sense, you mean, Louise ventures.

"Exactly and they wear their title proudly."

Louise nods at Kareem, and for the first time since her arrival, she lets her back rest against the cushions, feeling less apprehensive and a little more at ease though still smarting from her nasty bathroom 'surprise'.

When the girls have finished tidying up, they sit down and start chatting amongst themselves. Although Kareem and his mother converse in their own tongue, Louise is glad of the chance to sit quietly and just observe. Only then does she have the opportunity to study the 'Hajja' with a sharper curiosity and to form some impression of the woman who is likely to exert some degree of influence over her life in the near future.

She guesses that the woman sitting opposite her was once very pretty in her youth and has not completely lost her looks despite the hardship involved in bearing and rearing twelve children. There is no doubt she is still active and fresh-looking.

Two plaits, black as coal, reach midway down her back. Only the slightest hint of grey is visible above her ears, the remainder of her head covered with a scarf. She is dressed in a long-sleeved, baggy blouse embellished with coloured embroidery and small sequins sewn along the neckline. Gathered around her middle is a wide, generous garment, part of which she has pulled up and tied at her shoulder; the rest falls loosely to her feet, reminding Louise of a Greek toga. The quality of its cloth looks rich, interwoven with narrow stripes of silver threads worked intricately into the fabric. She notes how the 'dress' is worn and arranged in a way that allows a generous surplus of material to hang, like a hood at her back so she can bring it up easily to cover her head and face whenever she wishes. Such a practice is customary for native women in the vicinity of males who are not of their immediate family. Her feet appear to be the sole area of her body to have suffered the effects of exposure, easily recognisable by their dryness and the condition of her cracked heels.

Turning her attention to Fatima, Louise remembers Kareem saying they are about the same age, which puts her at nineteen. Small in height and plump, she has not inherited her mother's good looks, showing nothing remarkable in her features. Noteworthy, however, is her fine head of hair, the colour of dark ebony and plenty of it. A thick, richly textured plait trails the length of her back, stopping just below her bottom, and to avoid sitting on it, she twists it round her head, holding it in place with a clasp. In contrast with her crowning glory is a rather sullen demeanour, and Louise assumes she may have things on her mind. She imagines it can't be easy being a girl at the centre of a large family, expected to cater for their numerous whims. Already, that much is evident to Louise.

Soon, she is roused from her abstractions by the sound of footsteps approaching and sure enough, a tall, lean man suddenly enters their midst.

He has almost crossed the length of the porch when he stops and looks at Louise, who is sitting quietly and staring back at him. He approaches, with hand outstretched and a welcoming smile on his face. Louise stands up, out of respect, to greet him, having to rely again on her husband to translate. He extends a hand to his daughter-in-law, and when she takes it, he clasps it tightly.

"*Ahlan wa Sahlan, Murhaban, Kafehalak?*" "He welcomes you Lou and asks how you are after the journey?" Kareem translates as he rises to greet his father, and a brief exchange ensues.

Louise sits back down and the 'Haj' comes and sits next to them. When he is settled, Maryam brings him a bowl of water and soap to wash his hands before his tray of food arrives. Drying his hands with a towel, he addresses Kareem with a look of earnestness, asking him to relay a message to his wife.

"Louise, my father says he is sorry that he can't speak to you in English, he only speaks Italian. He learned it in the old days when the Italians were here and he had some business with them."

Between mouthfuls of soup which he scoops adeptly onto chunks of bread, then brings to his mouth without spilling, the old man continues his conversation.

"Tell him its fine, I don't speak Arabic either but I'm determined to learn it," she replies, looking directly at the 'Haj'.

"*Al-hamdu-lillah*", he replies. Praise to God, a warm smile softening his wrinkled face.

It is a phrase not only spoken by Muslims of every background due to Quranic texts but also some Arabic-speaking Christians and Jews.

"He's asking about your family, Lou, he hopes they will come to visit Tripoli one day," Kareem translates.

"Maybe they will," she answers politely, "If they can make the journey", but secretly doubting they would be able to survive such a culture shock.

Meanwhile, his wife is lining up the tea glasses on a tray, ready to pour, and Nuria, already on her feet, is ready to pass them around. Louise takes a sip and winces at the strong-tasting brew.

"I know, it's too strong, even for me," Kareem laughs, noticing her expression. "My father likes it that way, but my mother will make a weak glass for you."

"*Sukran,*" Louise utters, looking across at her mother-in-law.

"Lou, do you want to go with Maryam?" Kareem suggests. "She can show you the bedroom, your luggage is there, if you want to get something, don't be long, the tea will be ready shortly," he adds.

Turning, Kareem speaks to his sister, who gets to her feet and, with an encouraging smile, beckons at Louise to follow her.

When the door opens, the first thing she sees in the middle of the room is a large, old-fashioned bed, standing on thick, brass legs, its headboard boasting a semi-ornate design with a brass finish. It had seen better days and needs a good polishing to restore it to its original shine. On the lefthand side of the room is an Art Deco dressing table made of Italian walnut, finished in veneer. At its centre is a clouded mirror, which needs work to replace the original gleam of its reflective surface. Although an attractive piece of furniture, it is lob-sided, balanced rather precariously on three legs and, sadly, in need of urgent attention. Facing the bed is a small window, its shutters closed to keep the room cool. Maryam stands waiting for Louise until she opens one of her suitcases and takes out two plastic bags containing gifts for the family. It is no time now to consider the bedroom she will occupy for the foreseeable future, with Maryam standing by and the others waiting for her. As they head back to the porch, Louise is left with an impression of a stale, worn-out room, her second disappointment of the evening; she tells herself that she has to make the best of things, that it will only be temporary.

She drinks a glass of tea and distributes the gifts, which they accept rather matter-of-factly but Kareem insists they are genuinely pleased and never expected her to go to any trouble on their behalf. There is a selection of different materials for Kareem's mother, including a variety of fabrics, colours, and patterns, so she can have her own dresses made. There are some lovely headscarves included. For the girls, there are pretty summer dresses, some cotton nightwear, sandals, hair accessories and novel tights in various colours for the cold months, since they tend to be scarce, according to Kareem. He had advised Louise about their sizes and made a few suggestions. For his father, she bought a pair of leather sandals and a sleeveless body-warmer which he can wear over his traditional clothes when temperatures get cool. More than anyone, he appears to be delighted with his gift.

Louise regards her father-in-law with new interest and the vaguest sense that she might get on better with him than his wife. The 'Haj' is typically attired in a loose, cotton Arabic suit, baggy trousers, and a long wide shirt over which he wears a short, maroon waistcoat trimmed with decorative embroidery. The suit is pure white and Louise wonders how on earth it can be kept clean in such a sandy climate. Sitting neatly on his oval-shaped head is a small, black skull cap. Louise is curious about the age difference between him and Zohra, his wife, because he looks considerably older than her, likely the result of many hours spent working under the assault of the sun.

Over the next hour, they continue to chat, Louise making eye contact with the old man who seems eager to talk and willing to engage with her through his son.

"My father had his own vegetable shop and bakery during the time of the Italian occupation. He remembers them as good days, despite the fact that he had to work hard to earn a reasonable living," Kareem explains.

"Oh, I didn't know that, Kareem, you never said," Louise exclaims, looking surprised.

"Most of our customers were Italians," he continues. "They weren't interested in politics, only to get on with their lives."

Louise indicates to the 'Haj' with a nod of her head that she understands.

"They enjoyed life here and we learnt different things from one other; yes, they were good days," the Haj recalls with a deep sigh and a look of regret. "A lot has changed since." Kareem translates.

Looking curiously at her husband, Louise asks, "What does he mean exactly?" Looking past her with a frown, he replies.

"It's a long story, Louise, and a bit complicated. I'll tell you another time." He laughs and the moment passes. Before she can press him further, he picks up where they left off.

"I still remember, as a boy when people came into our 'Suk' and started talking to my father, usually over a glass of tea. Faisal and I used to take advantage and get up to mischief, especially when we were supposed to be studying."

Kareem smiles wistfully and, turning to his father, attempts to jog his memory. The old man points his finger at Kareem and they both laugh.

"He was so strict Lou about our schoolwork you wouldn't believe it, always insisting that we get top marks."

It was unusual for an uneducated man to take such an interest in the education of his sons. Perhaps that was why he was so determined for them to do well. Louise listens as he translates little anecdotes from their past, noting at one point that her husband's face takes on a grave expression, his tone changing slightly. He tells her as a young boy, he was terrified of his father because he meted out severe punishments mercilessly.

"Obviously, he has mellowed now with the passage of time and anyway those memories are in the past."

He changes direction rather abruptly, assuming a lighter tone, yet confirming nevertheless, what Louise already suspects, that there are things she does not know about her husband's life. At least now, she has a context in which to ask questions, but for the time being, she is content to listen.

As thoughts whirl about in her head, it dawns on her how her own childhood had been very different from her husband's, more likely the antithesis of his.

Her mother was always the one she was most frightened of, and still is, but her father is a gentle, retiring sort of man who seems to exist in the shadow of his wife most of the time. Apparently, he has a soft spot for his last-born child, according to her mother and sister.

It is not long before the Haj decides to retire and bidding them 'goodnight' walks a few footsteps to the stairs that lead him to his room overhead. The girls go shortly afterwards, disappearing inside the house. Kareem continues chatting with his mother, and again, Louise retreats into her own private world, feeling a sudden sadness take hold of her. Memories of home begin to flood her thoughts. Her legs feel cramped because she is not used to sitting in the same position for so long.

Realising it is late, she feels tired and wants to lie down and stretch out her body. The journey across two continents was gruelling enough, then reuniting with Kareem and meeting his family, all in the space of one day, seems like an emotional marathon. She might not sleep despite her fatigue, being wound up and overtired. Still, just to lie down and unwind would be restful enough. Pondering as her day draws to a close, she realises that the hardest thing was saying goodbye to her family, much harder than she expected.

Louise looks up into the night sky, its dark immensity illuminated by a constellation of twinkling stars and a half-fluorescent moon grins back at her in a comic absurdity. She finds it hard to credit it is the very same moon that lights the skies above those who are most precious to her but are now so far away.

The hour is late, and Louise feels it is time for Kareem to bid his mother goodnight so he can be alone with his wife.

"Kareem, I'm off to bed now, it's been a long, exhausting day. Say goodnight to your mother for me, will you?"

Louise smiles at the 'Haja' and drops her husband a meaningful glance as she is about to walk away.

Alone in the room, Louise just wants to flop onto the bed, but she dare not lie down without first checking the sheets in case anything creepy is lurking between them. Turning down the blanket, she gives the under-sheet a cursory look, and in spite of its fadedness, it appears fresh enough. The pillows are mismatched; the wool blanket is suitable for winter but too warm for summer. Nothing about the bed is particularly inviting, yet at that moment, Louise doesn't care for luxuries; she only wants to lie down and rest her weary body. Without further ado, she undresses, dons a light nightshirt and ties her hair up in a bobbin before slipping in between the sheets. She stretches her legs down the length of the bed, her body tense and alert as if a predator is lying in wait beneath the covers.

Laying still, her hand placed protectively over her tummy, she wills her body to relax until she feels her breath slowing and her mind becomes still. Apart from a steady beam of light seeping in under the door from outside, the room is in darkness. Kareem pervades her thoughts as her eyelids grow heavier and heavier. Then, alas, a curtain falls and she throws off the cloak of actor and becomes a spectator in a theatre of her own dreams.

In the dimension of 'otherness' beyond the veil, time is not as she knows it; nothing is the same. She finds herself alone in a garden full of exotic trees and flowers, which exude an aromatic perfume, their heady scent pervading the balmy evening air. Up ahead is a gate, and she feels herself drawn towards it with an allure so intense that it feels as if a spell has been cast on her. Someone is beckoning to her from the other side but she has no idea who it is. Stepping lithely across a meandering stream to reach it, her svelte, half-naked body feels free as never before, tingling with untrammelled desire. Unburdened by the realities of the conscious world yet mesmerized by an uncanny familiarity with an unknown world, while the scenes play out in front of her. She is the protagonist and the onlooker simultaneously, her own silent witness to secrets still untold.

In a state of euphoric expectation, she reaches the gate, poised and full of passion. Pushing gently with her hand, it refuses to open and suddenly everything changes. Thrust by the life-affirming hands of eros into the denying grips of Thanatos, Louise enters the realm of death. Looking out beyond the gate, she is seized by a paralysing fear. An invisible enemy, who she cannot see but whose presence captures her in its grip. Within a few seconds, she has fully traversed the emotional spectrum, from a feeling of pure joy to abject despair. Hearing a voice calling to her on the wind, she recognises the words she once resisted, those ominous words. Wanting to turn and run away in desperation, she suddenly forgets what it is that has brought her to this place.

Every step she tries to take is laboured, as if her feet are shackled. Starting to panic, her heart is pounding in her chest, a suffocating sensation grabbing hold of her. Then, to her horror, she sees the bloody cord dangling between her legs, thick and slimy. Screaming, her legs begin to shake uncontrollably. When she cries out for help, nobody hears; the scream just sticks in her throat.

Louise looks on, seeing her distraught self, a body entirely separate from the eyes she is looking through. Yet, she is aware of the persecuting thoughts, the anguish, distress and tortuous fears of her double.

Who or what is being confronted in the dream? Is reality too anxiety-provoking for conscious life to deal with, so the dreamer escapes to a 'different' world in order to process something? Antiquity would interpret it to have a symbolic, even prophetic meaning. Undeniably, the imaginings of a transient, unconstrained mind can surely create its own monster. Whoever claims that a 'sleeping' mind is inactive should think again!

It prompts the question: can one ever really escape the tortures of their own mind?

THREE

An 'Unsettling' In

Be patient and tough, someday this pain will be useful to you.

– Ovid

Louise wakes up with a start, her adrenalin rising. She feels disorientated and confused, suspended between two worlds, the one of her dreams and wakefulness itself. It takes a few seconds for the paralysis of sleep to clear and the fuzziness to abate until, gradually, her eyes adjust to beams of sunlight streaming through narrow slits in the shutters. Looking around for a sense of clarity, she is met by the surreal quality of her surroundings, and slowly it begins to dawn on her that she has had a disturbing dream. Closing her eyes, she tries hard to concentrate but in her efforts to remember the dream images, they start to dissolve and slip away. Still, she is positive it is the dream which has roused her senses and stirred a myriad of emotions. Having felt them so vividly in her sleep, vestiges of their powerful effect stay with her on waking before shortly receding into oblivion. Who can claim that the world of sleep is a passive one? Antiquity interpreted it as having a symbolic, even prophetic meaning. Louise wonders if it is a sign of something to come?

Aware she is alone in bed, Louise wonders where her husband has got to. Trying to bring events into sharp focus, she has a sudden, vague recollection of him whispering something in her ear, probably sometime around dawn. She remembers hearing something strange like a wailing voice, its reverberating echo sounding eerily in the distance, a kind of haunting sound. Was it part of her dream, she wonders?

Totally exhausted, she must have fallen effortlessly back to sleep, back into a partially suspended dream world where what was real and imagined merged seamlessly into one.

Looking at her watch, it is a few minutes past nine, but she is in no hurry to get up and see her in-laws . Lying listlessly in bed, she thinks about everything that has happened since her arrival. Fully awake and alert, she sees a shadow fall in front of the shutter and instinctively draws the sheet up over her naked body. She guesses it is her mother-in-law and such intrusion into her privacy fills her with indignation. Disinclined to move, she closes her eyes and ponders over her situation, the strange inhabitants of the house and how she is going to cope with the formidable woman who lurks outside her bedroom window.

Louise is not expecting to spend her first day alone in the company of Kareem's family. To Louise, it is a perfectly reasonable assumption to make and it never strikes her that Kareem had other ideas. Even before she ventures outside her bedroom that first morning, she realises with bitter disappointment that Kareem is gone, and she regards it as decidedly odd that he is not here with her. Why had he not arranged to take the day off instead of going to work? Is she to spend her very first morning in the house alone with his mother and sisters? The very thought fills her with anxiety.

Feeling an urge to splash cool, refreshing water on her face and brush her teeth, she finally gets out of bed, deciding it is time to shake off the cobwebs in an effort to feel better. Putting all her stuff, including soap, into a toilet bag, not forgetting her facecloth and towel, she makes for the bathroom, hoping it will appear less daunting in the daylight. Pulling on a light, short-sleeved dressing gown, she ties the belt around her waist, opens the door and slips quietly out.

Twenty minutes later, back in her room, she is somewhat rejuvenated, having washed and brushed her hair. Taking a small, purse-sized perfume in her hand, she discharges two quick bursts of spray on either side of her neck, savouring the light, floral freshness of its scent. Pausing a moment, she applies a coat of pale pink lipstick, careful not to choose a glaringly obvious colour. Smiling to herself, she notes how it picks up on the pink, patterned flowers that are the main feature of her pretty summer dress.

She is suddenly startled by the reflection of her mother-in-law staring at her in the mirror. Standing directly behind Louise, she had entered the bedroom unannounced since Louise never heard her knock. Carrying a large velvet box in her hand and judging by the expression of impatience on her face, it is clear that the woman has been waiting for an opportune moment to catch her daughter-in-law's attention.

Immediately, Louise turns round to face her, smiling. There is little else she can do, considering her lack of Arabic vocabulary. The 'Hajja' looks at her for a moment without uttering a word and carefully lifts a royal-blue velvet case, securely closed with a set of gold clasps. Louise stands there, still smiling but unsure of what to do next, so she gestures to her mother-in-law to sit down on a chair in the far corner of the room. Ignoring the invitation, she proceeds to open the jewel case as if she were performing a matter of great but delicate diplomacy.

Louise watches speechless as she places six gold bangles, beautifully handcrafted, on top of the bed. Next there is a beautiful neckpiece with matching drop-earrings that gleam impressively in a shade of yellow-gold. They, too, are laid out on the bed. Louise bends over to take a closer look at the intricately fashioned insets of tiny ruby stones and delicate oriental pearls. She has never seen anything quite like the elaborate pieces that are now spread across her bed. Still not sure why the woman is presenting the jewellery for her to see, she remains silent and waits. Strangely, Kareem said nothing to her about jewellery.

Without asking, this unfamiliar woman lifts up the necklace and, in a swift movement, places it around her daughter-in-law's pale neck. Louise immediately feels its heavy weight but stands still and waits for it to be fastened. Wearing jewellery seems out of place at such an early morning hour when all she can think about is breakfast. It also feels downright uncomfortable, hanging around her neck in the early morning heat. She wants to take it off without causing offence, so she attempts to communicate with facial expressions how much she appreciates the exquisite neckpiece. Without the necessary words, it requires a performance on the part of Louise to get her point across.

With a final gesture, she indicates for assistance to remove it, much to the chagrin of her mother-in-law, who glares at her, clearly displeased. In spite of her best efforts, Louise knows her refusal to wear it is not well received and she begins to feel increasingly frustrated with the whole ordeal.

Again, she thinks of Kareem and feels the anger rise up inside her.

Today, of all days, his presence is needed to explain to his mother what she is unable to, and she intends to let him know as soon as he gets home.

Feeling rather disheartened at how the day has started out, she is distracted by sudden pangs of hunger niggling at her insides. Rubbing her slightly protruding belly, she wishes that the woman before her would quit invading her personal space and simply disappear out of sight. Instead, she lifts the gold bangles, determined not to be deterred from her purpose a second time and indicates to Louise with a steady look in her eye that she means to put all six of them on her arm. Louise eyes them silently with a distinct preference for the bracelets over the necklace and decides to relent. With a nod of agreement and a forced smile, she holds out her arm. Sensing a minor victory, the 'Haja' picks up the earrings and, sitting them in the palm of her hand, she extends it to her daughter-in-law, who takes each one obediently and with an outward show of calmness and resignation, utters the one word she knows, "*Shukran.*" The older woman waits for her to put them on before finally closing the lid on the box. With her matriarchal duty discharged, the two women leave the bedroom and head for the open porch and the bright sunlight.

Louise steps into a hive of activity and her ears are met by a cacophony of sounds, from the clatter of crockery to the clanging of pots and pans.

Glasses clink as they are taken out of their boxes and lined up in readiness for later on. Preparations are already underway for the imminent arrival of visitors who are soon to descend on them from far and near. The girls sweep and scour, moving briskly from one completed chore to the next. Silver teapots are polished to near perfection, cushion covers are changed and urns filled with fresh water to keep it cool.

Louise does not dare venture into the kitchen. The truth is that she feels awkward and unwelcome around Fatima. At least Maryam and Nuria make an effort to look at her and smile as they go about their housework. She sits down on the mattress, not sure of what else to do and within a few minutes, Fatima appears with a small tray and a sullen expression. Placing it down beside her, she barely has time to respond before the girl turns brusquely on her heel and walks away.

Breakfast consists of tepid coffee and half a roll of dry bread. While Louise visualises a plate of scrambled eggs and crispy toast, the butter melting on top, she has no choice but to eat what is put in front of her or else stay hungry.

As she breaks off bits of bread and dips them in the coffee, she hears a door slam inside the house and hears voices approaching. Looking up, she sees the 'Haj' standing at the porch entrance and behind him two young men. As he stands watching, they coax a large, woolly sheep along the outer wall, corralling him up the steps and onto the roof, where Louise guesses he will meet his eventual demise. Though she catches only a brief glimpse of the confused animal, it is enough for her to remember his face long afterwards.

She greets the 'Haj' with a smile and a nod of her head. Sitting down beside her, he lights a cigarette before summoning his daughter, who immediately drops whatever she is doing and heads into the scullery. Meanwhile, the 'Hajja' sits watchfully in the corner, in front of a large wooden board onto which she skins and slices onions in thin strips. Along the outer wall, there are crates of potatoes, pumpkins and courgettes, together with bunches of scallions, parsley, fennel and coriander. More crates filled with tomatoes, lettuce and cucumbers are stacked beside them and their crisp freshness lingers in the air.

Two handsome young men descend the stone steps to join them but before sitting down, they greet Louise for the first time. With broad, friendly smiles, they introduce themselves as Farhat and Jabir. Both are good-looking in different ways, and Louise guesses there is little difference between them in age. Fatima reappears with a pot of steaming coffee and a couple of fresh loaves, delivered with a fake smile that does not quite reach her eyes.

The 'Haj' pours a cup of '*Qahwah*', Arabic for coffee and hands it to Louise. She welcomes the aroma of freshly ground beans, instantly savouring the full, rounded taste of the Arabic blend with its subtle tones of fruit and cardamom. There is the slightest hint of something added, a new taste that leaves behind a pleasant sensation on her palate. After enquiring, she discovers it to be '*ma' alward*' or rose-water, considered important in Arabic culture. Secretly thankful to her father-in-law for appearing, she is able to enjoy a decent cup of coffee at last.

As midday approaches and the hot sun moves higher into the cloudless, blue sky, Louise leaves her in-laws to their own devices. She intends to start unpacking some of her things before lunch. Walking through the house, she passes a large room where Maryam and Nuria are busy. They beckon to her and she joins them, having no idea what to expect once inside.

Thick mattresses line the walls along the carpeted floor, running the length of the room. Others, of equal thickness, are placed upright against the wall behind, serving as a comfortable backing to lean one's body against. Effectively, the general set-up represents a particular kind of seating arrangement, like plush couches but without the legs. It is the classic seating configuration of any traditional-style Arabic sitting room. The mattresses are covered in a rich fabric with matching cushions and can be removed for cleaning, when required. As Louise is about to learn, they are thus organised for special occasions and stored away when all the visitors are finally gone.

Looking around, she sees the girls proudly unfold a huge oriental carpet, covering most of the tiled floor. She can hardly believe her eyes, seeing its bright, elaborate colours, depictions of daily medieval life, ancient hunting scenes and folklore. When she places her bare foot on the luxurious carpet, she feels its soft wool pile, so sensual to the touch.

The art and craft of carpet weaving has long since been regarded as part of a rich and manifold tradition. Aware that it is mentioned in some of the earliest texts of world literature, it reminds Louise of *A Thousand and one nights*. Just looking at the carpet conjures up images of the clever but ill-fated princess Shahrazad who tries desperately to find a way to survive in the court of her husband or else die. Lost in thought, she does not notice Nuria gesturing to her. When she looks up the two girls are standing at the door, smiling. Obviously, their work is done and they are well satisfied. Louise takes a final look around, and with a pronounced gesture, she compliments them on their efforts. Clearly, they are pleased by her signal of encouragement as they close the door behind them.

Leaving the girls, she walks back to her room, glad to have a bit of time to herself before lunch. She takes a long look at the wardrobe trying to figure out where to put her things. At that precise moment, she hears a loud rapping on the front door, followed by a torrent of loud voices mixed with children's laughter. As the procession comes closer, she recognises that unmistakable sound from the evening before.

Without warning, the door swings open and in sweeps a woman, in a cloud of sweet-scented aromatic oil, her loud ululation filling the room. She approaches a bemused Louise who stands on cue with hand outstretched. The woman's genuine pleasure at seeing her brother's wife for the first time is evident in the way she takes hold of her hand in both of hers and, bending forward, plants several kisses on both of her cheeks. Fixing Louise with a steady gaze, she mumbles excitedly to herself while her sisters merely stand and watch. Pointing to herself, she says her name, 'Aisha', and Louise repeats it before introducing herself but Aisha has difficulty pronouncing the name until prompted by Maryam, she smiles and tries again. For some inexplicable reason, Louise takes an instant liking to Kareem's eldest sister.

They all go to sit on the porch, the girls chatting excitedly with their sister while the 'Hajja' keeps a close eye on the cooking. Aisha's two young sons are already planning some mischief, evident from the firm tone of their mother's voice. The 'Haj' has retired to the small sitting room at the front of the house with Aisha's husband, a room reserved for men only.

Louise sits down next to Aisha and at regular intervals the woman turns rather blatantly to observe her sister-in-law, who evidently is a subject of novel enquiry.

Looking restlessly around, Louise's eyes come to rest on a small bundle securely tucked between two large cushions on the opposite side of the porch. As her focus shifts, it is suddenly arrested by the sight of a tiny brown fist. Louise's heart leaps in her chest and an involuntary smile crosses her lips. She immediately goes to investigate, and bending down, she finds, to her delight, the cutest baby she has ever seen. Louise understands, not from the colour of the infant's clothes but from the gold piercings in her delicate, little ears, that the child is a girl. Looking into the face of innocence, Louise whispers softly to her. Stroking the baby's fist, she gently prises it open, and placing her finger in the little palm, the baby grasps it with a surprisingly strong grip. With a widening of her honey-coloured eyes, she attaches her gaze to the unfamiliar face of Louise.

Time passes and Louise is still sitting with the baby, unaware of the surprised reaction of her female relatives. Little do they know what the baby's touch does for her, how a simple act can stir an instant intimacy, an alchemy of two touching hands, one tiny yet powerful enough to reach into the deepest realm, outside of language and transmit a silent human message. In that short space of time, Louise feels she has met a beautiful little angel who has transformed her first day by the purity of her presence. Soon, she learns that the baby is three months old and her name is *Noor*, meaning 'light'.

In her captivation with the baby, Louise does not notice Kareem enter the house. On hearing his voice, she looks up and sees him greet his sister. It strikes her as a rather cold, un-emotive exchange, no hug or kiss, just the usual handshake and a few meaningless words.

Louise wonders how she will find her feet in this new world.

FOUR

Rough Edges

The measure of intelligence is the ability to change.
— Albert Einstein

Lunch with the family is a whole new experience for Louise. The food is already dished out and she watches as Maryam gives Fatima a hand with handing out the trays. Her father is served first; his plate set down in front of him before returning with two separate trays for the couple. They immediately tuck into the food with gusto.

The brothers, Farhat and Jabir, eat together from a large bowl, and the two younger brothers, Arif, who looks around fifteen, and Umar, who is about twelve, share another. Louise had met them for the first time in the morning when they greeted her with a look of painful shyness. Embarrassed and barely able to look her in the eye, she has the impression that unlike their older brothers, who have been exposed to a broader worldview, meeting a modern, Western woman is indeed an unusual experience for them.

"Umm, this couscous is good," Kareem remarks, nodding his head and looking at his wife to gauge what she thinks.

"It's delicious and the meat is so tender," she agrees, clearly enjoying every mouthful.

Smiling to herself, she decides that despite the disappointing breakfast, lunch has at least compensated. Back home, she had sampled the 'Maghrebi' dish, cooked by one of Kareem's friends. It consists of tiny, steamed balls of crushed wheat-semolina topped with a delicious-tasting, spicy tomato-based sauce. In the centre of the bowl are chunks of tender lamb surrounded by fresh Mediterranean vegetables. The sauce is made from fresh tomatoes, crushed and seasoned with salt, garlic and then allowed to marinate in pure, pressed olive oil before finally ending up as a rich, natural puree. The dish can be made with chicken or fish but it is customary on special occasions to have lamb slow-cooked in the sauce, until it becomes so tender that it literally falls off the bone and is served up in generous chunks surrounded by lashings of caramelised onions, slow-cooked in butter ghee over a low heat.

The women eat together from a deep bowl, large and wide enough for them to gather round. It is a strange sight to behold, different to the atmosphere of mealtimes that Louise is accustomed to. The idea of sitting at an attractively set table might seem equally strange to her in-laws.

Louise leaves nothing behind on her plate, and when she gets up to carry her tray into the scullery, Maryam intercepts, taking it from her and indicating that she should sit back down. After a few minutes, the males disperse to take their mid-afternoon nap and the hajja with Aisha and Maryam go upstairs to begin cutting up fresh meat. Kareem informs her it is a lengthy business and they will be kept busy for a while. Already, Louise is forming a broader insight into the domestic activities of native women, who without doubt, do the greater share of work, in addition to bearing lots of children.

Most of the meat is to feed the many visitors due to arrive over the following weeks, and they will partake in a celebratory meal in honour of Louise and Kareem's marriage. A large piece of meat is set aside for 'curing', to make *gueddid,* or dried meat.

The first stage in the process is *kaddada,* which involves slicing the meat into long strips. The second is *charmala,* when the meat is marinated in a salt and spice mixture for about two days. Then it gets hung outdoors under direct exposure to the hot sun in order to dry out completely and change to a darker colour. It can keep for months stored in large jars and used sparingly by the family, usually in the winter months. Regarded as a delicacy in Arab countries because of its strong, unique flavour, *Gueddid* is a favourite dish, eaten particularly during Eid al Adha, the yearly Muslim festival. Kareem informs Louise that he especially likes to eat it with fried eggs for breakfast. She listens attentively while her husband waxes lyrical about the cooking skills of native women, aware that he is enjoying the idea of educating her about his culture and local eating habits.

Louise finds her stomach turning at the preparation of 'sheep's stomach', particularly as Kareem emphasises the importance of thorough cleaning several times over, before being stuffed, steamed and finally left to sit in a pot of spicy tomato-based sauce so the flavours can marinate. Each piece resembles a jumbo sausage, only bigger, longer and thicker. The meat parcel is a combination of finely chopped, fresh spices, lots of them, green scallion, and the lamb, diced into small pieces that produce a hearty, flavoursome meal. Also, they can be trimmed down for serving as smaller portions. Kareem admits it is his favourite dish, but because it takes so much work and preparation, it is only eaten on rare occasions.

"We only eat it once in a while but you will taste it yourself," Kareem insists. "Actually Lou, I only eat it when my mother cooks it, or from someone I know who is very particular because it can't be hurried, you need patience and time," he insists.

"Oh, I don't know if I could eat it, Kareem," Louise sounds wary. "You've rather put me off now," she says with a slight grimace.

"No, its fine," he laughs, "don't worry, you have to taste it, I know you'll like it."

Thinking of the heat and the flies is enough to cancel out any desire she has to sample the dish.

While Kareem is taking the trouble to explain some things, she remembers glimpsing a sheep standing by the door on her arrival. "Kareem why was there a sheep at the door when I arrived?" she asks. Putting the last slice of watermelon in his mouth, he looks at his wife in surprise.

"What, you mean you don't know?" he says, stifling a laugh, when he sees her surprised expression.

"Seriously Kareem, how would I know? Do you think it's a regular thing back in Dublin?" she laughs at the very notion of it.

"That sheep was brought to mark your arrival as a new bride. So, as soon as you stepped inside the house he was….." hesitating to find the right word, Louise jumps in.

"Ok, Ok, I know, you don't need to elaborate Kareem, I'm so glad I never saw that. It sounds horrible."

What she considers to be the sacrificial offering of an animal provokes strong feelings of disgust but she refrains from voicing them.

"Why do it around the house Kareem"? Louise continues. "I mean, why make a spectacle of it?"

"How do you mean?" he asks, making a face.

Trying not to think about the fate of the animal, Louise still wants to know more. "Oh, never mind, surely it can't be a pleasant sight," she cringes, just imagining it.

"It's a religious tradition," her husband explains, "A part of every celebration and for us it's completely normal. Usually, one or two of the men in the family attend to the sheep, its quick and clean, the animal doesn't suffer. Everything is washed and cleaned up afterwards and the meat cut up immediately. Nothing from the animal is wasted, especially the wool. It gets washed and used as a rug to keep warm in colder weather." Despite his tame explanation, Louise remains sceptical but leaves the subject there.

"That's just how it is, that's our culture," he insists, reinforcing his argument.

His words actually echo her thoughts; it must be accepted as a religious and cultural practice.

Louise was so preoccupied with the events of the day that she had barely a moment to talk to her husband about the morning's episode until he asks a question.

"How did it go this morning, Lou? You met my sister, Aisha? He enquires.

"Well actually, it was really awkward, she answers. "I assumed, Kareem, you'd be here, eh, to support me on my first day," blurts Louise.

Ignoring the reference to his sister, she continues.

"It was strange, not to mention embarrassing, being on my own, not able to speak a word to your mother. I wish you had warned me last night. At least I would have been prepared instead of feeling completely helpless," Louise is not finished.

"What a complete embarrassment, insisting I wear all this jewellery, which was the worst," she sighs and waits for a response from her husband.

"I thought it would be a good idea, you know, for you to get used to my family, without me being there. You know, try to get to know them a bit on your own." Seeing his wife's expression, he rushes on.

"Look, don't worry, I'm here now."

Louise frowns as she looks at her husband, thinking it is a rather feeble excuse.

"A good idea for whom, Kareem, she asks, knitting her brows together. "Do you think I'm going to get used to your family in one day? My first day, are you serious? I wasn't happy at all, Kareem."

Looking at his wife, he has no defence, so he keeps silent.

"I just got here after us being two months apart, pregnant and nervous about meeting your family and you decide on your own that it's a good idea. How could you even think it would work, Kareem? Next time you should ask me what I think, before you decide something for both of us." Hurt creeps into her voice.

There is a brief period of silence when neither of them speaks and Louise knows the apology she is expecting is not forthcoming. Although annoyed and disappointed with her husband's lack of consideration, she sees no point in prolonging a negative atmosphere between them at such an early stage.

Changing her tone, she steers the conversation back to the events of the morning, explaining what had transpired with his mother.

"She wants you to wear the gold jewellery, that's all, he says rather casually. It's the custom for a new bride, to show off the gold the groom has given her. Louise immediately wants to interrupt by stating the obvious but instead, she keeps quiet, listening to the rest of what he has to say.

"When the women come to visit you, Lou, they eh," he pauses, "they expect to see jewellery, it's customary and that's why my mother wants you to wear it." His tone is rather matter of fact.

"Ok, I get it, but do I have to?"

"Not if you don't want to," he replies and then digresses.

"It's not a lot of gold actually, I mean, compared with what is normally given to a bride by the groom. It's so expensive to get married in this country, you have to spend a lot of money, and that's even before you find a place to live," he explains. "Apart from the cost of gold, there are other gifts to buy for the bride and for her family too."

Louise listens intently to what he is telling her about their strange customs. Encouraged by her level of attention, he continues.

"Families often ask for something particular which the groom has to provide and if it's not available here, in Tripoli, he has to bring it from outside." He finishes with a sigh of exasperation.

"Gosh Kareem, I had no idea about all that, you never said, how come? She laughs. "Aren't you lucky you didn't have to worry about that? Your family must be relieved that you saved them money and worry, she teases jokingly.

He smiles as Louise is about to ask an important question, her expression now serious.

"What happens if a man can't afford all that?

"Well, the family might not agree to the marriage. If a man really has his heart set on a girl, the union can be delayed but with a promise to her family that he will honour the request within a reasonable period of time."

"Oh, it sounds a bit, umm," Louise hesitates, "like a trade agreement or a business arrangement instead of a marriage", she exclaims.

"Well, that's just how it is," Kareem insists.

"It involves two human beings, though, not just objects that can be bought surely.

Kareem nods in agreement.

"Frankly, Kareem, it sounds outrageous."

Returning to their original conversation, Louise is intent on making a further point.

"I was shocked when your mother appeared with the box, I didn't know what to say," she admits with some regret. "The necklace felt so heavy round my neck, and hot, I just couldn't…" her voice trails off.

Trying to keep her tone light, she goes on.

"If you were here, Kareem, it would have saved me the embarrassment." Afterwards, when I was sitting on the porch, I found Fatima abrupt, she barely looked at me. Why, I don't understand?" She looks at her husband, hoping he might shed some light on things.

"Don't worry about it Louise, I'll speak to my mother and explain things, about Fatima, just ignore her, don't take any notice."

"I'll try, she says, finally relenting but feeling somewhat cheated by the entire episode.

In a lighter vein, Kareem tells her that the 'Haj' had actually brought the jewellery back from Mecca.

"After completing their pilgrimage, they were able to do some shopping. The gold was intended for the next in line to marry, he volunteers.

"Which was you," Louise said. "I bet their purchase was never intended for a foreign wife," she laughs.

Kareem laughs with her, and instantly, their mood lifts. Aware that there are more pressing things to concern her than fretting over a pot of gold and the cost of a traditional marriage, she turns her attention to other things.

Eventually, Kareem stands up, announcing he is going to take a nap.

"Why don't you join the others?" he suggests, but Louise is reluctant, preferring to rest a while in her room, maybe even read for a bit if she can manage to stay awake. Kareem decides to lie down in the adjacent room, which is cooler.

Back in the bedroom, she opens her book, picking up where she had left off. Soon, she forgets about her napping husband and the distant voices of her relatives. Escaping to another world, she finds herself far from the uncertain one she inhabits, the place where at least she knows what she has to do or, where the rhythm of reading calms her senses. .

Later that evening, while the family sit and drink tea Louise finishes her unpacking but not until she thoroughly cleans the interior of her bedroom with warm, soapy water. Every corner, nook and surface is freshened, including the bedpost, which looks so much better after a vigorous rubbing. Earlier that day, the bed was stripped of its light sheets and pillow covers, washed and left to hang in the sunshine before going back on the bed.

Louise wishes she had brought her own bedlinen with her.

She makes no apologies to Kareem about the staleness of their room, which is somewhat improved now, or the insanitary conditions of the bathroom, which is beyond her control. His response is to reassure her that soon they will have a place of their own with all the modern conveniences and luxuries she is used to. She notes in frustration that he has completely missed the point, pleading that his family home is old and needs work. Whilst Louise can accept certain things, she remains unforgiving about others.

Looking around, she wonders how to bring some life to the bedroom and add a bit of lustre. With very little at her disposal, it seems an impossible task. Then, she remembers her trunk standing in the corner, full of books she could not bear to leave behind. There are a few items of sentimental value, including a couple of framed photographs. She opens the trunk, emptying some of its contents and decides to use it as a low table on which to arrange a few of her things. In the wardrobe, she comes across a pretty, embroidered cloth, still folded and new. Spreading it on top of the dressing table, she lines up some of her favourite hardbacks, spines facing outwards so she can see them when she enters the room. They seem to bring her a degree of comfort.

Since early childhood, reading has been a passion, her love of books growing stronger as she grew older, becoming more than just a pastime but a kind of retreat, a portal leading from one world to another where she could indulge her greatest fantasies and allow her imagination to be fired. Between the pages of her beloved books, she experiences new and different worlds, feels the thrill of adventure as if it is her own. She befriends characters only sadly to let them go, and in between, great lessons are learnt, lessons on life and love. Many of them however, she will only fully comprehend as she lives out the experiences and feels the pain on her own terms and in her own time. Yes, one has to feel the pain.

That night, she asks Kareem to pick up some utensils for her the following day so she can do her own cleaning. She suggests a food list that includes instant coffee, tea bags, some plain biscuits, and other provisions necessary to be self-sufficient and make her life easier. She decides it is better to bother her in-laws as little as possible and, moreover, not rely on them for sustenance or anything else.

While she lies awake in bed, restless and alert, her mind unable to cease thinking, Kareem lies next to her, already in the grip of sleep, his breathing deep and soundless. He is due to wake early and be picked up by his driver at six. She wishes to read for a while, hoping it relaxes her enough so that eventually sleep will come but the main light is much too bright and there is no bedside lamp. Had she known before travelling, she could have brought a small one with her. From the little she has seen, she suspects there are no shops nearby that sell lamps so she will have to make enquiries. Then, at least she can read as much as she likes in bed without disturbing him.

At some point, Louise falls asleep because when she opens her eyes, she hears a whisper and feels the caress of a warm hand on her body. The shutters are pulled tightly closed, blocking the first rays of dawn, but the darkness creates an atmosphere of intimacy and calm. Louise welcomes the amorous advances of her husband, his body pressing hard against hers, awakening her desire and triggering a deep libidinous need she has not felt in a while. Given their recent geographical separation and pangs of nausea during the first weeks of pregnancy, being intimate was not a priority.

Suddenly, she wants him with an urgency that surprises her. When their bodies begin to move in a slow, rhythmic motion, a low moan escapes her mouth as she draws him closer, her lustful climax rising to meet his in a sweet, orgasmic moment, a fragment of time that feels all too short.

In rapt silence, they linger a while, their spent bodies hot and soaked in sweat until they separate and lie back on the rumpled sheet. Her eyes close to the world and she drifts calmly into a happy, hormone-induced slumber, her tensions released, emotions satiated.

It is several hours before she wakes again, ready to face a new day and a new life.

FIVE

A Performance

All the world's a stage.

— 'As You Like It', William Shakespeare

Louise awakes to the sound of children's voices outside her bedroom. Blinking, she opens her eyes fully and rubs the sleep from the corners before taking a stretch. Smiling to herself, she remembers the dawn hours and the reason she feels rested and refreshed.

Relieved to have passed through the worst of 'morning sickness' in her first trimester, she remembers those unpleasant bouts of nausea which stretched late into the day and made her feel fatigued. Instead of gaining weight, she lost it, eating less and having an aversion to foods she had previously liked. On entering her third month, it subsided quite suddenly, and according to her gynaecologist, everything was progressing fine, a welcome reassurance for her before she set off. He suggested that she take a letter outlining her general state of health during pregnancy should she wish to pass it on to a new doctor.

After washing, Louise takes her time getting ready, picking out one of her favourite summer dresses. Kareem warns her that relatives will be calling to see her and Louise feels apprehensive but is hoping for the best.

It is mid-morning when they begin to arrive, coming in steady droves throughout the day, usually in cohorts of four or six at a time. Neighbouring women walk the short distance from where they live while others hailing from further afield arrive by car, transported by male relatives. Those closely related to the family generally arrive in the afternoon and stay to eat a hearty supper; some make an earlier appearance and are fed both lunch and supper, so it is late in the evening when they take their leave.

Their arrival is announced by a familiar sound, one which Louise is quickly growing accustomed to. Her mother-in-law, already on her feet with her daughters by her side, greets the women most cordially, with customary handshakes and an abundance of kisses, all the while entreating them to throw off their coverings and sit themselves down.

Louise is poised, ready to offer her hand to the women as they approach her. Once they have greeted her in-laws, they waste no time turning their inquisitive gaze to Louise, who is the reason they are here after all. Fixing their attentions on the shy young girl who stands placidly waiting with hand extended, they advance towards her eagerly. They plant kisses on both her cheeks, muttering in their native tongue, things she has no way of understanding. Whichever way she turns, she catches the strong, earthy scent of their perfume, hanging in the space between them like an exotic cloud, pungent and sweet. Despite feeling awkward and uncomfortable, Louise accepts their salutations with a smile and sits back down, only to repeat the exercise again with another batch of eager visitors. Before long, she starts to feel utterly ridiculous, aware that she is being studied and stared at overtly by groups of women who know nothing about her. Whatever they say or the questions they ask, she is unable to engage in the comments and sentiments they share with her mother-in-law. Finding herself in such a passive, indefensible position irritates her as she watches their faces, how their eyes move back and forth when they look at her and then at her mother-in-law. It is obvious she is the focal topic of conversation, a fact that makes her increasingly discomfited.

Never before has Louise commanded so much attention or been the spectacle of such blatant curiosity. Her green eyes, a shade to rival any feline Mau, sparks much attention and admiration amongst the women and they let her know as much. Studying her face with great intensity, they take in her body, looking pointedly at her now protruding stomach, which appears to mobilise their interest with equal intensity. Being a people who neither understand the art of subtlety nor practice it, they speak their minds bluntly with eyes and hands, gesticulating dramatically, especially when the need to emphasise is greatest. In addition, they are inclined to protest loudly and interrupt, without waiting for one another to finish before bursting in and having their 'say.' It is natural for their conversation and dialogue to include frequent invocations of Allah and his erstwhile prophet, Mohammed, to whom they pay great homage.

Such conversations begin invariably with the words; *'ma sha Allah,* or *'mash allah',* meaning; 'by God's will,' and end with; *'Allah ya-salmik,'*"God keep you safe.' They are among the very first phrases that Louise learns, and it is not long before they roll off her tongue like water.

The women direct all questions concerning Louise to her mother-in-law. She gleans that much easily by the quizzical looks and fixated stares on the faces of her observers. Depending on the nature of those questions, her mother-in-law appears either nonplussed or resigned but at no time does she look jubilant. Louise watches and reads with interest, the expressions that cross her face. Clearly, her mother-in-law finds herself in unfamiliar territory, attempting to answer questions about her daughter-in-law that she is uncertain or hesitant about, yet tradition demands that she oblige her neighbours in an agreeable way.

After a week of lengthy gatherings, Louise grows bored with the constant stream of women, their stares and their unruly children, the increasing noise levels and most of all, having to sit for hours, listening to conversations she can neither understand nor participate in.

Louise finds herself drifting, her thoughts carrying her away while her mother-in-law prepares endless glasses of tea and plays hostess. Every now and then, she smiles and nods to appear polite and present in the proceedings, though most of the time, she is elsewhere, lost in her own thoughts. One keeps recurring, serving only to remind her how big a step she has taken by coming here and embarking on a life that she now feels totally unprepared for.

She is painfully aware it is not an everyday event for a Western bride to set a white, undecorated foot on dry, desert soil. In fact, the rarity of it is a 'cause célèbre' in the wider, neighbouring area where she has settled, for the time being, at least.

In the traditions of Arab relations, the slightest allusion to a possible engagement between two parties is tantamount to a solemn promise. When her mother-in-law's attempt to arrange a marriage between her son and a distant kinswoman was foiled, it left her miffed. Things changed over the years that Kareem was abroad and once his mind was made up, he remained adamant in his refusal of any such arrangement and defended his right to marry independently. He then broke the news to his parents that he was planning to bring a European bride back to settle in their country.

Undoubtedly, the news came as a shock to his parents, especially since Louise is not of their creed. It seems unfair to Louise that a Muslim man is allowed to marry a Christian 'woman of the book', and yet a Muslim woman is prohibited from marrying outside of the faith. Louise's own parents had been outraged at the union for a variety of reasons, religion being the least offending one. They believed their daughter was too young and unworldly to venture out into a world she knew nothing about. Besides, they had aspirations for her that went beyond a university education, and they hoped she would find a good, steady career. Despite their disapproval, she refused to be put off course and rejected all advice against making such a life-changing move. She is beginning to question her decision.

As she sits watching the spectacle unfold before her eyes, she can't help wondering what her parents would think if they were here. Her father's words come echoing back. "Whatever you might think, Louise, it's not a land of milk and honey." What she has seen so far only confirms his misgivings.

It still hurts when she recalls how her mother reacted to the news of her pregnancy. Louise could not have fully understood why, a response stemming from her mother's own deep, unresolved conflict. Marianne, her sister, exacerbated matters by stirring up trouble that was stage-managed to ruffle her mother. As a result, Louise was upset and rather than feeling overjoyed, she felt guilt and shame, plus her mother's stinging measure of disapproval. At the time, she never stopped to ask herself why her sister would be so mean and her mother cold. The answer mightcome in the fullness of time.

Louise knows her mother is undemonstrative; at least, that had been her experience growing up. From an early age, she struck fear into her youngest daughter with just a scowl or a look of displeasure, seldom, if ever, raising her voice. She had a sense of her mother's formidable personality, which formed in the young girl an apprehension that became firmly ingrained in her psyche. That fear followed her into adolescence, even adulthood.

Her father, on the other hand, is a retiring, mild-mannered man who insists on reverting to his wife about most things. Her relationship with him is a simple one, uncomplicated in many ways. Like so many fathers of a particular generation, there are certain things, like sex, for instance, they never openly discuss with their daughters. Yet, she has felt a close bond between them since childhood. His company feels like an easy place to be compared to her mother, whose energy field she can find provocative.

Her meanderings of memory are soon interrupted by the sound of a kerfuffle beside her. Looking up, she sees a woman preparing to leave, 'hijab' in one hand, the other pressing a wad of money into the hand of her mildly protesting hostess. A comical exchange follows between the two women, ending with the *Hajja* accepting the gift of money, which now nestles safely against her bosom, inside the folds of her blouse. She gives one of her rare smiles as she sees the woman to the door. According to Kareem, gifts of money, usually handsome sums, are customarily given to the mother of the Groom.

The male relatives are accommodated in a large tent erected in the street outside, close to the house, and comfortable enough to accommodate the men so they can eat, relax, and drink tea. Food gets dispatched from the kitchen inside the house but the tea is generally made by the men themselves because they are in the habit of staying late into the night, often playing cards.

It is approaching the end of her second week and Louise has seen very little of her husband during these days. When he arrives home from work, the house is full of women, so he eats lunch with the men and then slips surreptitiously inside the house to grab a nap, after which he returns to the tent and the male company until close to bedtime when the female visitors have all left.

Both men and women are free and comfortable in the company of their own society. The women, in particular, when outside their own houses, occupy spaces reserved exclusively for them, spaces where no man would dare venture or impose on once a party of women is in attendance. The code of contact is strict in this respect, but the onus lies chiefly upon the male members of society to 'keep out of the ways' of women unless they are of a familial or lawful association.

When finally they are alone one night, Louise tackles her husband. "Kareem, I was thinking, you never told me things would be the way they are. Why is that? It's like you landed me in the deep end," she says, looking at him squarely.

"You wouldn't have understood," he replies, too quickly, adopting a jovial tone. "It's hard to explain the way things are here unless you see for yourself, you'll get used to it, after a bit of time."

If Kareem intends his remarks to be consoling, they have the opposite effect on his wife.

"Seriously, Kareem, you know very well what I mean, don't pretend you don't know what I'm talking about. You never gave me even the most basic bits of information, stuff that could have helped. I mean, did you honestly think I would find things easy? You really left me in the dark. What were you thinking?"

Pausing a moment to assemble her thoughts, she continues.

"I feel really ignorant about lots of things and there's so much to take in all at one time, it's a struggle." She tries to keep the annoyance she feels out of her tone.

He listens but makes no response.

"You can go to work, Kareem but I need to get out of the house, do something different, us together, I mean." Forcing a smile, she tries to keep her voice light.

"The sooner all these women are finished visiting, the better for me."

Kareem nods his head, indicating to his wife that he takes her point on that, at least.

"It won't be for much longer; I know it's frustrating for you but what can I do? If I told you about all this from the beginning, you might not have come."

He looks at Louise with a question in his eyes, waiting for her to say something.

"I never said that, Kareem; you know that's not what I meant."

She is not about to console her husband when she is the one in need of consolation.

Tapping his hand on the bed, he gestures for her to come and sit beside him. Looking past her husband to a spot on the far wall, she suddenly stops speaking, trying to avoid pursuing a negative trajectory and realising it is a pointless exercise anyway. The die has been cast, and she will simply have to get on with it for now.

Walking over to where he sits on the bed, she stands in front of him and looks into his dark, seductive eyes. He pulls her gently onto his lap and she doesn't resist. Finding her lips soft and moist, he forces on them a hungry kiss. When she presses hungrily back, he stretches back on the bed and pulls her gently down beside him.

In a moment of fierce abandon, Louise forgets about everything and gives in to the ardent advances of her husband. Soon, they move as one, heedless to the world outside, as if nothing can come between them.

SIX

À Chink in the Looking Glass

Man is not what he thinks he is - he is what he hides.

– Andre Malraux

I f the prince of Arabia dropped in for an impromptu visit, it is doubtful he would receive a greater welcome from his loyal subjects than the one Faisal gets from his mother. Louise is highly amused at her mother-in-law's change of attitude at the sight of her eldest son, clearly evident in her radiant smile and all the fussing and fawning over him. The last time Louise saw that smile was when she accepted gifts of money from the visiting women.

Brothers and sisters look sharp as soon as Faisel appears at the door, his wife following close on his heels. He cuts a dashing figure in a light, airforce-blue suit with a white open-neck shirt. His attire contrasts with the surroundings but Louise assumes he has somewhere important to go. The scent of his cologne hangs lightly in the air and she inhales its fresh notes as he bends to shake her hand. Speaking in English, he immediately introduces his wife, Zanib, who greets her with a beaming smile. Turning, she sees an elderly woman approach with a young girl at her side. "Meet Ameera, my daughter and 'Haja' Salma," her grandmother. Faisal cheerfully makes the introductions as his mother jumps immediately to her feet, leaving the tea gently brewing while she affably receives them. After a few minutes, once her gaze settles upon her son's wife, her smile appears rather diluted. Louise is almost sure she has seen a hint of something unpleasant in her mother-in-law's expression. She senses a slight tension in the air.

Much to her surprise, Louise receives an enthusiastic welcome from Salma, the 'grandmother' who meets her eyes directly with a wide, genuine smile. "*Mabrook, Mabrook, Mashallah.*" She repeats her congratulations several times as she gesticulates approvingly with one hand, the other still clasping Louise's. Speaking utterances that are incomprehensible to her, she manages to communicate an unmistakably positive and heart-warming energy. It feels neither fake nor forced, unlike others she has experienced in recent days. Louise finds herself responding to the woman's geniality with a natural fluidity.

From the far corner, she observes her mother-in-law eyeing the cordial exchange between the three women with a peevish glance, assuming that nobody has noticed.

Zanib and Salma both turn to Kareem and, with loud exclamations, extend their congratulations and good wishes. Looking pleased with himself, he reciprocates, and they continue to engage in light-hearted banter. Judging by the peals of laughter that follow, they appear to be at ease in each other's company.

Having accepted a large box of cakes brought by the visitors, Maryam soon returns with them arranged on a tray to be served with tea.

"You have an invitation, Lou, to visit Zanib and her mother anytime you like."

Kareem addresses his wife with a laugh.

"You've impressed them already," he says jokingly.

A blushing Louise replies with a promise to accept their kind invitation.

In the corner, the Haja busies herself with tea-making, lining up all the glasses on a silver tray. Her beloved son lounges casually beside her and dismissing his mother's attentions, he addresses Louise, curious to know how she is getting on. She suspects he enjoys speaking her language and is more than happy to indulge him since speaking her native tongue feels comforting. After some small talk, he decides to take his leave, the scent of aftershave lingering behind, woody notes of sandal and cedar contrasting sharply with the scent of body heat and stuffiness in the surrounding air.

"Faisal must have a special appointment," Louise remarks to Kareem.

"Oh, that's not unusual for Faisal; he likes to dress up." Kareem speaks the words with a hint of evasiveness that sounds a little odd to his wife.

Over the next hour, until tea is finished, they sit and converse with their visitors, Kareem facilitating the conversation by acting as translator between his sister-in-law, her mother and Louise. He has a chance to converse with his niece Ameera, although she is shy around her uncle. In spite of this, she has a pleasant manner and a kindliness that emanates from her personality. Regarding her with a sharp but subtle alertness, Louise decides there is something unusual about the young girl sitting opposite her; apart from having keen attention, her eyes sparkle with intelligence.

Then, Kareem provides an unexpected answer to her ruminations on the pretty young girl.

"You know Ameera lives with her grandmother Lou, actually, since she was a baby."

She raises an eyebrow in surprise but waits for him to continue.

"We have a custom here that when a daughter is born and her grandmother is without help in old age, the child goes to live with her who, in a manner of speaking, brings her up".

Sensing a slight hesitation, Kareem looks at his wife, waiting for her reaction. To Louise, it immediately sounds like giving your daughter away but she stays silent. Instead, she is struck by the obvious pride and delight that the old woman takes in her granddaughter and she senses a strong bond between them. Evidently, in this instance, the situation worked out well, maybe best of all for the young girl.

"Yes, I can see that Ameera is her grandmother's daughter," Louise smiles.

Although the notion of 'giving' one's first-born daughter to a grandmother to rear, whatever the circumstances, seems odd, Louise speaks the words sincerely. Kareem looks at his niece with pride as she smiles radiantly back at Louise, a smile that illuminates her delicate features, just like those of her mother.

From the first moment Louise sees Zanib, she regards her as different from any native women she has met, mainly because of her patrician looks. Skin that is pale and unblemished covers a delicate nose and small heart-shaped lips. When the light catches her eyes, it accentuates their amber tone, her iris casting them a near translucent, golden colour. Her hair is light brown with honey tones and is wound loosely into a bun that sits at the nape of her neck, shiny and smooth-finished like ornamental wood. Whenever she smiles, it reveals a row of healthy, white teeth that light up her whole face, giving an overall impression of softness and youthful vivacity to her handsome exterior. Apart from the obvious difference in appearance, there is something more that Louise observes about her bearing and general aspect, which is also different, not unlike her daughter, who appears to have taken after her. Principally, it is her demeanour that sets her apart from other women Louise has met.

Underneath her manner of friendly sociability, there is a reserve and dignity that endears this woman to Louise; perhaps she is too dignified a person for the family she has married into.

Curiously, Kareem's sisters, Aisha and Zanib, are similar in age, yet they strike Louise as being miles apart by comparison.

Aisha's skin is weathered for her age, her eyes beset with premature lines and the stray wisps of greasy hair that seem to frequently escape from underneath her headscarf are pushed carelessly back inside. The soles of her feet are dry, her heels cracked, from over-exposure to water and walking barefoot. There is an air of neglect and staleness to everything she possesses, including poor, beautiful little Noor, who could benefit from a bath and some freshly laundered garments. Still, when Louise felt her soft, downy hair, damp with sweat, she felt pitiful compassion for the innocent baby and her mother.

Louise regards her sister-in-law as being innocent of the wider world, a world that stretches far beyond her limited view. Nevertheless, Louise acknowledges to herself that perhaps her pity is unjustified if Aisha is content with her humble lot and, to a degree, remains untroubled by a world that, despite its advantages and freedoms, is challenging.

According to Kareem, the two women married within months of one another. Aisha looks older and worn out compared to her sister-in-law, but then her marriage has not ended well. Considering the glaring disparities between their situations, it may be that neither one is living the life they anticipated when they married, albeit for different reasons.

Soon enough, the evening steals upon them, and it is time for the visitors to say 'goodbye.' Khalid, Zanib's seven-year-old son, comes rushing in from the street outside to announce that 'Uncle Mansour' is waiting to take them home. While Kareem goes out to greet Zanib's brother, the women stand to put on their burkas, but not without first pressing gifts of money into the hands of their hostess, who forces a smile as she prepares to see them out. To Louise, Zanib holds out a tiny, heart-shaped box, a wedding gift, she proclaims.

No sooner have they gone than Louise opens the lid to find a beautiful leaf filigree ring in yellow gold with an amethyst, oval-shaped stone at its centre.

Slipping it onto her finger, she holds it out for Kareem to admire.

"That's so kind of her, I wasn't expecting anything like this," Louise exclaims excitedly.

The Haja comes immediately to examine it at close range.

"It fits you perfectly," Kareem smiles distractedly at his wife before picking up his car keys and pausing in front of the door.

"Lou, I'm just popping out for a bit to see someone about a work issue, I won't be long," he says.

Louise looks at him but does not answer straightaway, still in a state of surprise and well-pleased with her unexpected gift.

After a long, mentally exhausting day, she wants nothing more than to relax with her husband for what remains of the night. Resisting the temptation to object, she reminds Kareem that she has not spoken to her parents since her arrival.

"Kareem, I really need to speak to my parents as soon as possible, at least to let them know that I'm ok, otherwise they'll be worried," she insists.

"We have to go into the city to call them, to the main post office," he replies, with a slight note of impatience.

Louise is suddenly irritated. "Well, that's not a problem surely, whatever happens tomorrow, Kareem, I have to call home." Her inference is to let him know that irrespective of visitors who may be due to call, her parents are the priority.

She has already had to wait three weeks for an opportunity to speak with them, which is far too long. The consequences of such a delay will put her at considerable pains to find a plausible explanation without raising their eyebrows. She can only hope they will understand it was not her intention.

"After we go to the post office, can we have a look around the city, Kareem, I could do with a walk, some fresh air and a change of atmosphere," she suggests, with a note of determination in her voice.

He responds with a nod of his head but lacks the enthusiastic reply she is expecting.

As her husband heads out into the warm summer evening, she senses he has other things on his mind but consoles herself with the thought that tomorrow is a new day.

In her bedroom, she decides to read for a while, until her eyes grow heavy and she can no longer keep them open. Before succumbing to sleep, she ponders on the events of the afternoon and is pretty certain there is some bad blood between Zanib and her mother-in-law; she had picked up on the energy between them. She is convinced there are strange family dynamics at play. The fact that Zanib is a native and cannot get along with her mother-in-law provides her with food for thought.

Turning her thoughts to Salma, she finds herself comparing the old woman's kindness and warmth to her mother-in-law's lack of it. Having seen enough already of her sour temper, it makes her wary and not entirely at ease in the house. She will have to be careful if she wants to avoid conflict between Kareem's mother and herself in the months ahead, until she is no longer living under her roof.

SEVEN

The Root of All Things

All things must come to the soul from its roots, from where it is planted.
— Teresa of Avila

As the weeks pass, Louise constructs a historical landscape, a narrative of Kareem's family background, by asking him a few obvious questions. Some he is unable to answer owing to shortfalls in memory, lack of access or simply ignorance, but nevertheless, she endeavours to fill in some of the missing gaps in his narrative.

Louise has a love and fascination for history and the past. Anything possessing a special historical value, articles of character, family heirlooms that speak of a particular period, including houses and places, all capture her interest. Most of all, she has an appreciation for narrative, for the stories people tell about themselves and other people's lives.

It is most likely inspired, in part, by all the reading she had done as a child since many of her favourite books were set in circumstances and inhabited by colourful and provocative characters. They created a landscape of imagination as powerful and vivid as the physical one outside Louise's window. There were the stories, too, narrated by family members and relatives at numerous gatherings. They were storytellers in their own right, their tales by times every bit as rich, entertaining and mysterious as those that graced the pages of her books. Hence, the beginnings of her love of history were formed long ago amongst her own kin in the house where she was reared.

It is evident that her mother-in-law's pregnancies had occurred within relatively short spaces of each other. That fact is easily worked out. Kareem tells her his mother was only fourteen years old when his father, eight years her senior, first cast his eyes on her. Being part of a trading family whose ancestors had plied the Silk Road and later travelled from Tunisia in the northwest during the late twenties, they eventually came to settle in a rural province of Libya amongst relatives.

It was during the years of the Italian occupation when most of the natives led an impoverished life, remaining subservient to their colonial neighbours.

By all accounts, the young Abdulla was a hard worker, toiling from dawn to dusk in the fields, turning his hand to farming and whatever else he could do, determined to make enough money to open a small market where he could sell his fresh produce. Around that time, a marriage was arranged between two fathers, and Abdullah took the teenage Zohra for his wife. Some years later, they moved from the rural outpost to the city with their young family, hoping to make a new life and prosper.

There, he eventually opened a small bakery and began delivering bread and other provisions to the residences of Italian expats who would account for a lot of his custom. Kareem remembers, as children, how he and Faisal had accompanied their father on deliveries before they went to school in the mornings and in the evenings when they returned and completed their homework by candlelight. They had their various chores to do before settling down to sleep, no doubt exhausted after their long days with little or no time for play. Despite the fact that their father is illiterate, he exacted strict, even cruel demands on both his son's school performances, expecting them to excel and achieve top results. His persistence and their endurance paid off because they both made it to university and did extremely well in their chosen subjects. Kareem studied engineering and was accepted as part of a highly selected team to continue his studies and qualify abroad, while Faisal entered the business sector and, within a few years, rose to a senior management position in his country's national airline.

After the birth of Faisal, Kareem and Aisha, two more sons followed close on their heels. They were named Mourad and Sharif, with only a bare year between them. According to tradition, they are next in line for marriage, after Kareem. However, since Mourad is abroad on a tour of duty with the Libyan Navy, this means that, effectively, any matrimonial plans have had to be shelved pending his return, whereupon the intention is to find brides for them both so they can wed in a joint nuptial celebration.

Sharif is tall and of average build, with a mop of black frizzy hair and a beard that is equally frizzy. One eye is set in a permanent squint, and he has a tendency to angle his head to one side, which lends an overall impression of awkwardness to his general gait. From the moment Louise first lays eyes on him, she understands he is a curious character, displaying a kind of brooding ill-humour with a permanently sullen expression. Keeping mainly to himself, he speaks very little except to his mother or to scold his sisters about some trivial thing. When he does speak, it is one of two extremities, either a barely audible mumble or a raised angry shout. At times, his speech is slightly slurred, reminding Louise of someone who has recently imbibed. She wonders what it is that occupies his thoughts so intensely. He may have good reason to be preoccupied if his world lacks beauty and life feels dull and pointless.

Then Louise learns that he had been shipped off to fight a war in Chad, a bitter conflict in which the Libyan army suffered a terrible defeat, due to a lack of leadership and military incompetence despite being well-equipped and having numerical superiority. She realises that Sharif undoubtedly experienced trauma, which has left him looking much older than his twenty-four years. If a large proportion of his days are spent attempting to extinguish ghosts of the battlefield, this is a good enough reason for his 'down-at-heel' look.

As for Mourad, she has yet to meet him on his return; hopefully, he has not suffered the same fate as his brother.

At the opposite end of the family line come the two youngest sons, Arif, who is about fourteen and still at secondary school and Umar, the youngest, aged eleven. He appears to be greatly favoured by his mother but still no competition, Louise reckons for Faisal When she enquired about his age, Kareem merely guessed it. Give or take a year, what does it matter? Certain subjects are taboo and making enquiries about the timing of pregnancies seems to fall into that category.

In any event, Kareem insists his youngest brother's upbringing has been very different, much more lenient and softer than his own and the other siblings. His father, according to Kareem, has mellowed considerably, affording his last-born more freedom, part of which includes more time in the ambit of his mother's shelter. Kareem believes his young brother is spoilt, certainly compared to the severe rearing he and Faisal had received. Speaking his thoughts aloud, he remarks reminiscently, how things in the family only began to relax after his sisters came along.

Nevertheless, Abdullah, the 'Haj', is clearly looked upon as father and master of the house. Nobody, including his wife, is formidable as she is, feels inclined to challenge his authority.

Being the eldest daughter, Louise concludes that Aisha had no say in the shaping of her own destiny. Having received no schooling, her childhood consisted of helping her mother with domestic chores and tending to her brother's needs. At seventeen, a marriage was arranged for her, but after a period of two childless years, it ended in divorce. Louise is surprised to learn from Kareem that very quickly, another suitor was procured, this time to an older man whose wife had died and left him with two young boys. In Arab culture, it is perfectly acceptable for a widowed man to remarry at the first opportunity, especially if there are children to be looked after. For a divorced woman, however, the situation is a little more complex.

Having surrendered her virginal status, she is deemed not as desirable as she once was and, therefore, not as negotiable on the wedding market. Acquiring a second husband may be subject to a woman's acceptance of a particular circumstance, which often means taking on the children of a previous marriage. Generally, it tends to be a union of mutual convenience.

In Aisha's case, because she was so young, it was considered only proper that she should not remain husbandless. The fact that her new husband was a few years her senior was of little consequence, once she was newly married and could bear children of her own. So, a suitor was duly found who needed a wife for himself and a mother for his two children. For Aisha, her fall from marital grace, along with the stigma of returning to her father's house, was disgrace enough but remaining there indefinitely was likely to be the greater of two evils.

The uncertain hands of fate determine the outcome of these situations and if the couple are fortunate, it will smile kindly on them, enabling them to carve out a new life together, the second relationship possibly bringing a blessing that the first had not. Having seen little Noor, the fruit of Aisha's second marriage, Louise considers her to be one such blessing.

The new arrangement has taken her far from her father's house to a remote part of the Mediterranean coast, around seventy kilometres west of Tripoli. There, in a humble, three-room dwelling with a tiny kitchen that was not much bigger than a mud hut, she settled into family life. Her husband eked out a living by farming a small tract of land, otherwise taking on odd jobs to supplement their frugal existence.

Sabratha, the largest of three ancient Roman cities, once a Phoenician trading post, became her new home—a vast, sprawling archaeological edifice that in 1982 was declared a UNESCO World Heritage site. There is an entire history surrounding the region, a long and rich chronicle of Roman Amphitheatres, including a Justinian Basilica and temples dedicated to Isis and Serapis. The sights on her doorstep are impressive structures of sandstone, stucco and marble brought over from ancient Greece. The preserved mosaic floors of the seaward or *Forum* baths, directly overlooking the shore, where emperors, philosophers and great warriors once bathed, can still be seen.

During the 1940s, the Mallowans, Lord and Lady, spent long evenings on the patio of their Italian villa that looks out over the sea at Sabratha. Better known as the legendary Agatha Christie and her second husband, Max, an archaeologist, they created fond memories of the place. Christie's biographer later described it as a "glorious attachment." Yet, in all of antiquity's glory and past splendour, towering high under the hot sun, old-world riches meet the new developing world. There, Aisha continues to pass a quiet, limited existence in her modest abode, leaving only to visit her family once in a while.

Sadly, she has little appreciation of her surroundings and its precious legacy, since she had received no real education about its past or indeed, its historical value.

Louise, on the other hand, has a great appreciation for the wonders of the past and could have strolled amongst the ruins for hours, marvelling at the wondrous sights while enjoying the sea breeze. Despite her keen intentions, she is not free to do as she pleases, and Kareem is not eager to accompany her on long walks through the ruins. They visited once, not long after her arrival, and since it is not safe for her to go alone, she has to be content with a brief walk about before heading back to sit in his sister's stiflingly warm and cramped dwelling, listening to idle conversation which she neither understands nor has an interest in.

Her thoughts drift back to Zohra, her mother-in-law and the world into which she had been born. How must it have been for her, as a young girl, to be married so early and become a mother? How difficult it would be, she imagines, to spread your affections between offspring whose numbers and demands require a lot of self-sacrifice and patience. Not surprisingly, the woman that Louise comes to know is tough and formidable, attributes which are necessary to survive the harsh climate of her youth.

Kareem had barely spoken to her about his country, and certainly not in any great detail, except to say that life was different compared to her country. Kareem had left Ireland and Louise behind, not knowing if they would ever meet again.

Several months passed before she heard from him again, in which time she had practically erased him from memory. When she did see him again, something inexplicable happened between them, that to this day she still tries to fathom. Perhaps it was the way he looked at her, or the way he spoke, she still tries to put a finger on it.

In truth, Kareem told Louise shortly after they met that his upbringing had been different from hers: very religious and less privileged. It really did not mean that much to her at the time, though. During their brief courtship, when he got the summons to return home, Louise recalls her feeling of amusement at his reply to her question.

"Can I write to you?"

With a smile, he replied, "I don't have an address."

She laughed, thinking he was joking or, at worst, he was being disingenuous.

He was adamant that there was neither a postman nor a delivery service where he lived. Disbelievingly, she let it slide, feeling disinclined to pursue it until finally, she forgot about it altogether.

EIGHT

A Fading Empire

Colours fade, temples crumble, empires fall, but wise words endure.
— **Edward Thorndike**

The country to be Louise's new home was once a powerful seat of the Roman Empire, sharing its borders with Egypt, Sudan, Algeria and Tunisia. Being no country for tourists, she has the overall impression that the natives are slow to accept strangers into their midst.

Prior to her arrival, she knew nothing about her immediate neighbourhood on the outskirts of a city named Tarabulu-Al-Gharb, meaning 'Tripoli of the West' nestled between the expansive shores of the Mediterranean Sea and the vast plains of the Sahara Desert.

In the weeks following her arrival, Louise looks forward to exploring the new city and learning as much as she can about her new surroundings. That, at least, was her intention.

The country she has come to inhabit has a long, eventful history, rich and diverse, and a history of tribes, conquests, and religious fervour. Its name alone derives from a single Berber tribe, which was known to the ancient Egyptians, and so the name came to be attributed to most of Northern Africa and its Libyan inhabitants, who are Berbers. Their origin is somewhat shrouded in mystery, inviting much academic speculation but failing to yield anything definitive.

According to ancient Egyptian records, a Berber tribe, Levu, or 'Libyans', were moving eastwards as far as the Nile Delta to settle there. Many Berbers served in the army of the pharaohs, one of which reached a powerful position as a ruling pharaoh. His successors of the twenty-second and twenty-third dynasties, named the 'Libyan-dynasties' (ca.945-730

B.C.), were believed to have been Berbers. They were present throughout the entire history of the country, spanning different periods of colonisation and power in the surrounding regions.

Herodotus, the fifth-century Greek historian known as 'the Father of History', described the inhabitants of Libya as two peoples: Libyans in the north and Ethiopians in the south. Libya began where Ancient Egypt ended and extended to Cape Spartel, south of Tangier on the Atlantic coast, just below the caves of Hercules.

In ancient times, the Phoenicians, Carthaginians, Persian Empire, Romans and Byzantine representatives ruled all or parts of Libya. The mighty armies of Alexander the Great crossed the vast deserts of eastern Libya to where the great and ancient city of Cyrene still lies today. Its classical name owes its origin to a Greek Princess of mythology, much loved by Apollo, who took her to Africa and founded the city of Cyrene in her name. In 631, the ancient Greeks founded the city, later to become one of the greatest intellectual and artistic centres of the Greek world, famous also for its medical school, academies of learning and architecture. It was also an early centre of Christianity, home to over 100,000 Judean Jews forced to settle in the Cyrenaica province under the rule of Ptolemy.

In the early part of the sixteenth century, the Spanish Habsburgs and the knights of Saint John occupied Tripoli until the Ottomans arrived in 1551 and claimed the city from the knights. Libya, under the Turks, was heavily involved in the Barbary wars during the nineteenth century, and the slave trade was flourishing in both black and European slavery, mainly from Sudan and other parts of Africa. In fact, it was an active part of life alongside other forms of trade and commerce at the time. The Island of Malta, located roughly 685 miles north of Libya, was also implicated in the lucrative practice, seeing the entire population of one of its nearby islands, Gozo, numbering 6,300 inhabitants, enslaved and sent to Libya by a Turkish navigator, Admiral Reis.

In the early part of the twentieth century, the Ottoman decline and eventual removal from Libya were not the result of antagonism within the country itself but rather due to Italy's imperialist ambitions to take its stake in Africa and expand its empire in the region. So, in 1911, the country was invaded by the Italians, beginning a colonisation which lasted over thirty-five years, culminating in the arrival of Mussolini and fascism to Libya. As a result, the country played a significant role in the region during World War II.

Despite the influences of the long, convoluted but distinct histories of the country's regions, Libya, post-1951, with its newly found independence, was essentially a developing country struggling to emerge from an underdeveloped backwater to establish some form of unified national consciousness.

Very few Westerners had any real knowledge of Libya as a country, a fact Louise discovered when she first mentioned it at home in Ireland. In actuality, many in the West were entirely unaware of its existence until the October Revolution of 1969, led by Colonel Muammar Gaddafi. Then, quite suddenly, the country made a dramatic entrance onto the world stage.

Preceding this, there was a significant discovery of petroleum by research prospectors, which constituted a major turning point for the economic situation in Libya. As a result of these explorations, Libya went from being an impoverished nation to being extremely wealthy. However, the daily lives and living standards of a large section of the population remained backward, uneducated, and primitive in some ways.

So, it was to a country in transition that Louise made her journey in May of 1979, a journey undertaken in good faith but in complete ignorance of a land and its people, which was so totally alien to anything she had experienced in her life. Louise had no idea of the capital city's historical background before her arrival. She discovered that Tripoli is a city renowned for being the centre of Greek and Roman civilisations, of great learning and scholarship, a melting pot of multi-cultural diversity and belief systems that contributed to and influenced its inhabitants in a multitude of ways.

For centuries it was also a base for plying the Saharan trade routes and a port for harbouring pirates and slave traders.

Eventually, with the arrival of the twentieth century and the removal of a dysfunctional monarchy followed immediately by a swift and silent revolution, Libya, despite the long and distinct histories of its territories, was in many respects a new country still developing as a nation and also its 'people' along with systems of government, institutions and infrastructure.

Louise's first tour of the city is at night by car, with Kareem skirting the main areas of the city, pointing out various sights and places of interest. On first impression, Louise feels it possesses much real character and old-world charm with a touch of elegance despite some of its crumbling structures. Immediately, her appetite is whet, and she is curious to explore its ancient walls. Though her observations are fleeting, she notices that preservation and the subject of heritage have been somewhat neglected in the city's urban planning. She firmly believes that without history and the value of memory, the present becomes devoid of context and can exist only in a vacuum. Yet, here is an instinctive sense that the old town harbours much of historic value beneath some of its decaying ruins.

The centre of Tripoli itself is named *Medina* from the Arabic translation for 'city'. Being the oldest quarter, a lot of its architecture dates back to the Ottoman era. There, one can find a society of artisans, shopkeepers, merchants, and religious scholars, all comprising a traditionally structured community of people. The streets around the medina itself feature wide avenues, piazzas, small parks, and residential areas where the elite of the military once lived.

It is late in the evening when they drive around the city, but Louise can smell freshly baked bread coming from the kilns dotted around the medina's streets. Eager to explore and with time on her hands, she needs only an English-speaking guide willing to accompany her. In theory, the obvious and ideal candidate for the task is her husband; however, in practice, he is not up for the task, citing various reasons, except the one she fears is the real one, a complete lack of interest and resistance at the notion of his wife walking about and the commentary it might generate. Regrettably, she cannot go alone.

Louise was only nine years old when Gaddafi came to power, and it is exactly nine years later when she arrives in a recently converted republic of Libya, ruled by his revolutionary command and a homespun version of Islamic socialism. As a leader, he is determined to break with the old social order with its privileged heredity and patronage and make way for a new, supposedly egalitarian climate of governance. Within a few short years, he set about implementing his first set of principles towards the remaking of Libyan society. According to the accounts of friends and family, the country's great transition had reached its peak in the mid-seventies with the appearance of Gaddafi's 'Green Book'. In it, he formulated his ideas and prescription for what he termed a 'popular and cultural revolution, giving birth to the popularised term *Jamahiriya,* a slogan which became ubiquitous at every level and grouping of Libyan society. Louise read a piece by the American scholar, Lisa Anderson, in which she attempted to ascribe a correct translation to a difficult term. Her approximation was "people-dom' or "state of the masses."

At the age of 19, Louise is largely ignorant of politics outside of her own country. Although she had excelled as a student of history at school and that involved a keen academic interest in political systems of the periods she studied, particularly Ireland, she does not consider herself a politically minded person, in the strict sense of the word. There are areas of study which appeal to her sense of enquiry far more than the pursuit of political ideologies.

More important for her is the study of human psychology, and she has always had a fascination for whatever driving force propels the human condition forward or backwards, as the case might be.

Essentially, politics seems to Louise to be both a precarious and multifarious occupation, spanning a myriad of ideas, styles of leadership, and power relations. The cynic in her is convinced that most politicians are largely self-serving, appearing to love the public and scorn the people. They are in the business of making promises which often, in the final analysis, are delivered by the people themselves. Her belief is that traditionally, politicians have always sought to structure and organise societies of people into communities of so-called, well-functioning groups with a unified ideal, espousing to create a common good for all.

There are all kinds of societal and emotional deprivations, ideologies, hierarchies and class privilege, distinctions of which lead ultimately to human conflict and it seems to Louise that while the notion of achieving equality of opportunity and outcome in the world is entirely noble in theory, in reality it may be little more than a fallacious ambition.

She has read widely and studied the dictators and ideologues of the early to mid-twentieth century, names which continue to haunt people's cultural imaginations, such as Mussolini, Hitler, Stalin and Mao-Tse-Tung. By the age of sixteen, she had read Tolstoy, Dostoyevsky, Leon Uris and in particularly Alexander Solzhenitsyn, who, in his masterful work, *The*

Gulag Archipelago, shocked her at the depth and scale of human depravity, suffering and endurance she discovered between its pages.

When Louise reads great works of literature, she feels like a whole new world opens up. She is moved by new understandings and insights gleaned from the pages of narratives, nothing less than epic stories of humanity at their best and worst. As a young girl with a thirst for knowledge, they had made a lasting impression on her.

At twenty-seven, Muammar Gaddafi, the son of Bedouin parents, led a successful and bloodless coup, ousting King Idris and taking control of the vast and rich oil fields before declaring a new Libyan Arab Republic. At first, he must have appeared to the Libyan people to be a saviour who had risen up to rescue them from what had become a greedy and corrupt monarchy, self-serving and intent on furthering their own interests, in a country with a long history of colonisation and usurpation. For a large swathe of uneducated people who thought of him as 'a man of the people, for the people,' he wasted no time in telling them what they needed to hear.

In the early years, he built roads and introduced free, accessible medical care with increased life expectancy and improved the quality of life for many people. Lending support and direct financial aid to higher education became a priority of governance, and thousands of young people benefitted as a result.

On the flip side, a percentage of others who comprised a cross-section of the population, already well-educated, skilled and worldly-wise, soon began to regard him with suspicion. Those dissenters who spoke out against his regime soon either disappeared or found themselves thrown into gaol, to be dealt with accordingly and their families, merely by association.

Initially, the country's university students appeared to support the new regime. Yet it was only a matter of time before they, too, realised that their autonomy was severely threatened. The alteration of curricula and the dismissal of professors and deans angered many intellectuals, not least of all the imposition of curtailed study time to facilitate military training for students. From time to time, there were periods of unrest at Benghazi University, located in Libya's second-biggest city, but security forces were deployed to quell any further expressions of opposition. Over time, reports leaked out that several students were shot and killed, but it was vehemently denied by the governing forces.

In every walk of life, people were loath to speak freely, and in the universities particularly, traditionally breeding grounds for free expression and uncensored opinions. They came under silent but strict surveillance. Secret police were dispatched to find and root out any hint of unrest or persons who constituted a direct threat to the political status quo.

Notwithstanding the totalitarian state of Gaddafi's rule and an ever increasing rate of political oppression, there was also a marked increase in the country's prosperity. This was supported by the fact that he had inherited one of the poorest nations and transformed it over time into the wealthiest in Africa. Life expectancy increased and so did its GDP per capita. For the poorer, uneducated people, daily life improved, providing new opportunities in the sphere of housing, free education and medical care. For the most part, life for women under the Gaddafi administration also improved, affording educational opportunities and independence. Whether that was a genuine attempt to curry favour with a female electorate by a government genuinely eager to encourage their emancipation or to rally them as a vital source of labour in a limited workforce remains debatable. Alternatively, their leader likely wished to be seen differently internationally, as forward-thinking and liberal whilst still managing to remain within traditional and religious boundaries at home.

Louise is delighted to see some native women driving about in cars, unaccompanied by their men folk. Ironically, she has already run into a problem whenever she raises the prospect of herself taking up driving. After mentioning it to Kareem a few times, he immediately comes up with some half-baked excuses, why it might not be such a good idea, as opposed to encouraging her. She refuses to argue the point but is quietly determined to revisit the subject later, amongst other things. Besides, there are more important issues to address first. Nevertheless, as a mature, adult woman, prevented from organising things for herself and by herself, she finds it all really irritating. She learns that practically everything for a woman needs to be endorsed by a male relation, according to the laws of the land, something she was totally unaware of until she began living there.

In her first year, the implications of living in a country run by a dictator present no imposition on Louise's daily life, at least not in any concrete way.

Wherever you go, it is impossible to avoid the ubiquitous gaze of the country's leader as giant-sized posters of him are everywhere. On street corners, at traffic intersections, on rooftops and entrances to public buildings, his dark eyes follow you wherever you are. His broad, grinning face shows a seemingly benign exterior, yet it appears strangely at odds with a portraiture that screams pomposity and pretentiousness at every turn.

Louise is unsurprised at how his humble beginnings have not immunised him against a lust for power, corruption and evil deeds, just as the line of dictators before him. It reminds her of Narcissus, who eventually meets with a deathly fate as he stares adoringly into a water pool at his own reflection.

In time, his provocative activities and associations with radical groups, together with war-mongering rhetoric, seem ever more likely to implode.

Against such a precarious background, Louise is preoccupied with her own personal struggles, trying to adjust to a new life. Between learning a new language, grappling with reluctant in-laws and confronting a self-absorbed husband determined that his 'single' lifestyle should continue as usual, Louise is already overwhelmed. Her immediate environment and close relations present a much greater challenge than the ever-shifting position of a country in transition.

NINE

Cracks Appear

It is not the strength of the body that counts, but the strength of the spirit.
– J.R.R. Tolkien

The weeks drag and time plods along, with temperatures soaring and Louise's stomach swelling with each week that passes. Life becomes a daily and nightly battle between the heat and humidity, fitful sleep, the scourge of insects and Kareem's family.

Louise grows weary of spoilt children who scream and demand constant attention from their mothers. Sensing the mother's attention elsewhere, they persistently look for a breast to soothe them, though they are long past the need for the nourishment of the mother's milk. Such loud infantile frustrations make her feel terse and tense, when she is subjected to it all day and every day. The same toothed toddlers are able to bite into a crust of crispy bread, but it is no substitute for suckling on a breast, the best antidote to a child's woes, and their mothers are always ready to silence them by thrusting a swollen nipple into their impatient mouths.

It never seems to occur to them that perhaps the child needs stimulation of a different kind. Great emphasis is placed on having lots of children, but once they appear, it seems they are left more or less to their own devices. In Louise's opinion, many of the children she sees are neglected in various ways, seen but not heard in the way they deserve to be. They do not possess such luxuries as toys and playthings, and lacking a healthy model of socialisation, they resort to mischievous ways of obtaining attention. With no consistent and reasonable model of correction, children have a tendency to be spoilt in the wrong way. On rare occasions when discipline is applied, it tends to be too rough and sometimes inappropriate, so there are no clear boundaries for a child to follow. As a result, nearly all the children Louise meets are little people who are frustrated and aggressive.

Observing their behaviour is her first experience of what unhealthy parenting looks like, making her wonder who gains the most comfort from a symbiotic relation; it appears not to be the child.

Despite maternal attempts to pacify restless children, they appear to be frequently disturbed and anxious during their play, fighting and unwilling to share with peers. Other times, they are completely out of control, displaying a general lack of sociability. There are temper tantrums and angry outbursts, mostly from male offspring, which does not surprise Louise because they are overly indulged by their mothers, unlike the girls, who are generally more placid and compliant. They seem groomed to take instruction from an early age, to serve rather than be served, something Louise is horrified at.

As time goes on and she sees more, Louise realises just how much the women she meets are defined entirely by their maternal role. It affords them a certain comfort, a gratification which they may not find in their marital relationships. In the role of mother, they are needed, made to feel important, but as a wife, more dispensable and less fulfilled.

The social, cultural and religious milieu in which they exist is limiting for many women, thus curtailing future possibilities and potential since their roles have already been assigned to them by a dominant and domineering patriarchy. Most of the women Louise meets just seem to accept how it is. In truth, they have very little choice. If one is fortunate enough to receive a fairly decent education, and even that has to be encouraged by the family, it increases the chance of securing a good husband. That is generally the most important development in a woman's life because he can either encourage her to grow or shut her down.

One small boy, barely more than five or six, attempts to bite his mother, while another spits in his mother's face. Louise looks on in horror as she laughs and roughly pushes her child away, completely dismissing his unruly behaviour. This goes on for a few minutes, the child growing angrier and his mother becoming increasingly irritated. Eventually, giving up, he throws himself down and begins to howl pitifully, an avalanche of tears streaming down his face, while his mother sits there, continuing to laugh and ignore his loud protests. An older woman, obviously a relative, goes to try and comfort him, but he is inconsolable and looks across the room to meet his mother's gaze. She has already turned away.

On another occasion, a young boy pulls down his pants and begins to pee in a corner of the room where they are sitting in a desperate attempt to gain his mother's attention. It strikes Louise as a kind of 'comedy of errors' and she notes with a degree of sadness that what is playing out before her eyes is a theatre of tragic misbehaviour, of 'acting out' because a great many of the children's emotional needs are unmet; they do not possess the language to express their frustrations. As long as mothers suffer from their own very real deprivations and re-enact their unconscious maternal experiences, how can their children be at ease? Negative attention is preferable to none at all.

Just as Louise begins to feel that she cannot bear to smile at one more woman, the visits taper off and eventually cease, much to her relief. She realises with some annoyance that over a period of four weeks, she has held court to scores of women, indulging their curiosity by becoming a site of display for strangers who know nothing about her except that one of their menfolk had chosen her as his bride. At least she no longer has to endure their intrusive stares and listen to their collective voices, speaking over each other like a group of cackling hens.

While enduring the visits, she has been thinking about the things she would like to do. Chief among them is for herself and Kareem to spend some quality time outside the house, away from the smothering company of his family. Sadly, as she will soon find out, her wishes are not reciprocated.

Louise's days are long and arduous, with little by way of amusement other than her books. To kill the boredom she reads voraciously, retreating into other worlds, her books supplying her with the comfort and stimulation that her husband fails to provide. At times, it is hard to concentrate on her reading, owing to the presence of high-pitched, boisterous voices both in and outside the house.

Her mother-in-law's voice is frequently raised, either to scold her daughters or to reprimand her teenage son. He seems to get under his mother's skin like no one else. Whenever Louise witnesses a disagreement between them, it invariably has the same outcome: he gets angry, which sets off a vicious attack of stuttering and stammering, sending him into a visible rage. For the most part, his mother remains unmoved, and it seems to Louise, on such occasions, that she does nothing to alleviate the situation. Eventually, in a state of complete rage, he removes himself from her presence altogether for fear of an even greater outburst.

A repetitive word is often bandied about in relation to her son and Louise is curious about its meaning. Something in the way it is said makes her wonder if it might have a negative connotation.

"Kareem, what does the word '*mahboul*' mean because I have been hearing it a lot. Is it a 'nasty' word? Louise asks. Her husband, laughing loudly, looks at her and is even more amused at the serious look on her face.

"What's so funny, Kareem," she enquires.

"It means 'mad', 'crazy', he answers, finally maintaining a straight face.

Louise thinks about it for a moment before answering.

"I was right," she says, nodding her head.

"It is offensive. I'm glad I know now what the word means."

"Why do you ask? He enquires.

"Oh, nothing, just something I heard," she dismisses it, not inclined to share her thoughts with him. In any case, she doubts he would understand her reasoning on the point, as is often the case. Changing the subject, Louise makes a suggestion.

"Kareem, why don't I pop round to visit Zanib tomorrow afternoon? It's well over a month since I saw her."

"Yeah, I can send one of the kids round to let her know you're coming in case she plans to visit her mother." Apart from a genuine desire to get to know her sister-in-law better, Louise needs a change of scenery.

Zanib's house is close enough to walk to, but Kareem insists on dropping her off at the door. It is similar to the structure of the family house except with a tiled frontal porch and three steps, which give the entrance an impression of being larger than it is. Set in from the sandy track, it is slightly removed from the street outside.

Zanib, expecting Louise, appears at the door, waves at Kareem, and steps forward to greet Louise with a warm, welcoming smile before ushering her inside. Leading her to a small seating area in the centre of the house, the two women sit down, and Zanib wastes no time lighting the small stove, filling the silver teapot with water, and setting it on the ring.

Jumping up, she fusses about with some cushions, singling out a large, soft one, which she places behind Louise's back and gestures for her to lean back and relax. Immediately, her guest feels at ease in the new surroundings.

For the first time in many weeks, Louise actually enjoys drinking tea. It is infused with a pure mint herb that Zanib had picked from a tree in her mother's garden. In anticipation of Louise's visit, her brother made sure to bring it earlier. It is such a refreshing taste, known in Arabic as *Shay naenae*. With it, she serves a plate of delicious sweets called *Baklava*, light, flaky layers of filo pastry filled with chopped nuts and drenched in honey syrup with almonds on top. Louise has never tasted anything quite like them before, and she savours the new, sweet-tasting pleasure characteristic of the Levant and the broader Maghrebi regions.

Because of the language barrier, conversation between the women is limited, but despite a scant vocabulary, they manage to do well enough by employing a mixture of signs and body language. Louise has by now acquired some basic rudiments, which help a little. She is pleased to find that Zanib also has a few simple words of English, taught to her, she tells Louise, by her brother, who studied medicine. During their conversation, she learns that Zanib is a teacher but had to give up teaching after marriage because Faisal prefers that she stay at home. Louise listens, keeping silent on her opinion, but there is an unmistakable note of resentment in Zanib's voice, clearly intended for her husband.

When the conversation turns inevitably, to their in-laws, Louise notes an instant change in the woman's expression and knows for sure that what she had sensed at their first meeting was not imagined and relations between them are indeed strained. In truth, Louise cannot help but identify with her sister-in-law after being treated to a measure of unfriendly hospitality herself. She guesses that whatever is at the root of Zanib's grievance is well-founded and moreover more than she can hope to understand in a single afternoon. Suspecting that her visit will cause a ripple of displeasure with her mother-in-law, she has no control over it, nor does she care. So far, Kareem has mentioned nothing to enlighten her on the subject but she intends to ask him about it.

During her visit, Zanib points to her stomach and utters the word "baby" with a grin, to which Louise replies, "*Mabrook*" understanding instantly what she is telling her. Her pregnancy is in its early stages because Louise would not have guessed without Zanib telling her.

For most of the afternoon, her young sons have been playing in the street outside, and as dusk begins to settle, she goes to the door and summons them inside to eat supper. They sit down together to eat a light but hearty dish of eggs poached in a delicious tomato sauce of tomatoes, olive oil, onion and garlic with small cubes of potatoes added. Louise eats with enthusiasm, dipping soft, crusty bread into the bowl and scooping up the tasty sauce. Zanib names it *Shakshouka* and Louise is determined to get the recipe before she leaves.

When they have finished, Zanib beckons to Louise and she follows her into the kitchen, where she takes out the spices she used to prepare the dish. Louise thinks that it may be a while before she can put any culinary skills into practice, not in her mother-in-law's kitchen, at any rate.

Zanib seems to have read her thoughts and pausing, she puts the jars down on the counter.

Struggling to make some sense and be understood, she manages to get her message across. Louise nods decisively to show her that she understands.

"Tell Kareem to find a house for you, now-don't stay with them for long time, you understand? There are many, always problems." With a grave face, she delivers the cautionary words.

"*Ana aerif,*" I know, "*Sukran*". Placing her hand lightly on Zanib's arm, Louise acknowledges her advice with a solemn nod of her head, aware that she can do little else because of the language barrier between them. For all that, she intends to take heed of the warning.

TEN

A Bitter Moon

And think not you can direct the course of love, for love,
if it finds you worthy, directs your course.

– Kahlil Gibran

Kareem works for the national airline and returns home most days by around two if he is working the early shift. Alternatively, he leaves around three and works until late at night. Irrespective of his schedule, he generally goes out in the mornings, citing various errands or business that need attending. His wife knows little about the exact nature of it because he tends to keep his own counsel, especially if he has reason to think she might disapprove. In any event, it turns out that Louise sees far less of her husband than she would like.

On his arrival home in the early afternoon, he is promptly served lunch by his mother or sister. Afterwards, it is his unfailing routine to take a long nap, lasting over two hours, during which time his wife has to find a way to keep amused. While he is physically active and working, she is indoors, lacking regular exercise and fresh air.

Napping during the day is not something Louise is used to, especially having lived in a cold climate. Fortunately, her love affair with books ensures she is mentally stimulated, and when she wants to put her wits to the test, she pulls out a book of crosswords. Without them, she would be in a constant state of boredom.

Louise comes to dislike the moment her husband wakes or is awoken rather, usually roused by a car horn sounding outside, followed by one of his many acquaintances loudly calling his name. He is usually rushing to get out, leaving practically no time to speak to his wife, reluctant to keep anybody waiting too long. Following the summons, he has just enough time to splash water on his face and change clothes before heading for the door. If Louise speaks to him to enquire where he is going or when he will return, he frequently snaps at her, partly because he is cranky, having just woken but she also suspects he resents being asked questions about his movements.

Louise begins to realise that she is simply not a priority. Through his behaviour, she gradually understands that he feels entitled to go about his life and see friends when he chooses. The fact that he is aware of her inability to go beyond the four walls of his family home is annoying her. Why should she have to stay in the house with his unaccommodating family and take care of their son when he is free to explore and enjoy himself as a single man? It seems grossly unfair.

It is often late at night before Louise sees her husband again and she wonders what on earth her purpose is in being here. In the evenings, there are endless rounds of card games and a never-ending spate of weddings and engagement-parties he feels compelled to attend at the supposed behest of a wide circle of friends and acquaintances all over the city. He never misses an occasion or an opportunity. It only leaves the mornings, prior to working afternoon shifts, free for house-hunting, so he tells his wife. Louise soon becomes fed up with his constant outings whilst she stays at home, under virtual house arrest. It strikes her that she has made the wrong choice if this is the life he wants. The stark realisation, and one which she has no control over, is that the cultural milieu she finds herself in is predicated on a system of unadulterated male authority. No matter how much one might attempt to dress it up in clever, subtle arguments, she is not for convincing otherwise. The fact is she lives in a patriarchal society that privileges a toxic social construct of masculinity. She sees that now and the realisation is crushing. Part of that masculine identity is so embedded in the national psyche that it has to be preserved as part of an old-world order, under threat of crumbling in a fast-changing world.

The wives of Kareem's friends are not at home alone while their husbands merrily pass their hours, nor are they left to the uncertain mercy of their in-laws, far from home in an alien culture, unaccustomed to the sweltering heat and pregnant on their first child. On the contrary, they are secure within the bosom of their protective families.

Moreover, it is a culture shock of immense proportions for Louise, not helped by the fact that her new husband kept her virtually in the dark by failing to offer enough information about the country he has brought her to. Worse still is the inherent suggestion and unfair expectation, demonstrated by selfish behaviour that she should make the necessary adjustments, a transition he appears to expect her to do totally unsupported.

Louise feels alone in the marriage, and even when Kareem is not absent, she feels he is not present for her in the way she would like him to be.

So, the rounds of parties and celebrations continue without due thought to how she manages herself in partial isolation. In a stubborn refusal to adjust his lifestyle, even minimally, to include her, seeds of doubt are sown in her mind. Gradually, as the months go by, she begins to perceive her husband in another light entirely.

There are places he could take her, drives they could go on along the coast, and see some of the country. Before the weather gets too hot, they could grab some food and eat outdoors once in a while, but it seems to be too much of a bother for him. That at least is how it looks to Louise, leading her to acknowledge, rather reluctantly, that she doesn't really know her husband or his character at a deep level. She recognises that he likes control, reflected in his passive-aggressive behaviour.

On the other hand, Louise knows that she cannot and will not be controlled.

ELEVEN

Lost For Words

All we have are words.

— **Samuel Beckett**

In the months after her arrival, Louise makes a pact with herself to learn the native tongue, although she knows it will not be an easy task. It occurs to her that time does not afford her the luxury of picking the language up at a leisurely pace because her need to communicate is immediate, a question of survival. It is a choice between being heard or ignored, and she cannot depend on her husband to represent her indefinitely, both from a pragmatic and a personal standpoint. The notion of him being her voice is not appealing to her.

Sooner rather than later, she has to integrate herself into the society where she has come to reside, so why procrastinate? With this thought in mind, she grows determined in her resolve not to be put off and sets about devising a system for herself whereby she learns to hone a sharp listening ear, gradually growing accustomed to the sounds and patterns of the new language, its unusual vowel shifts, consonant clusters and lexical meanings.

Her patience is sorely tested, trying to get her tongue around the Arabic pronunciation with its raspy 'Ch' and rolled 'R' sound that is absent in her native speech. Some of the vocals she attempts to master have no equivalent in English and are produced by contracting the throat muscles to mimic a choking-like sound. Likewise, shifting vowels and strong intonations are also new to her, and she begins drilling herself in the hope that practice will eventually make not perfection necessarily but understanding and competency.

Despite the difficulties that learning the language presents, she perseveres, and little by little, she begins to make progress, surprising everybody, including herself.

She comes to understand the power of motivation and what one can achieve with real determination. Apart from her love affair with books, how else is she to fill her lonesome days except with something that will stimulate and challenge her intellect and benefit her life practically?

So, she carries her notebook with her everywhere, and when she encounters new words and expressions, she tries to match them to particular sounds and intonations. When she does not manage to translate something immediately, she catches up later and reviews what she has learnt that day.

She rarely asks her husband for help whenever he is home; instead, it is Farhat, his brother, she relies on, and he seems genuinely glad to help. One day, he arrives home from university and hands her a small leather-bound, English-Arabic dictionary. It proves to be a valuable little asset in the acquisition of her new language.

Her commitment to learning soon pays off, and much to her delight, she becomes quite adept at transcribing single words into whole sentences, eventually progressing to longer linguistic units of conversation. She also builds familiarity with a discourse exclusive to coteries of women and their favourite topics of chat. Starting to feel that the fruits of her linguistic labours might soon be rewarded, she is hopeful that, before long, she might be confident enough to conduct a proper conversation in Arabic.

To Louise's ear, English is a much softer sounding language than Arabic, more restrained in its style, muted and less obtrusive, while Arabic has a higher pitch pattern, a louder intonation, which seems to serve the general attitude and emotions of its speakers quite well. She becomes attuned to the mood-swings and mannerisms of those whose company she is regularly part of. Often, they are prone to change without warning, and over time, she weighs what she observes of their simmering passions against the language of their bodies.

Native speakers tend to use their hands when they speak, the women in particular being more emotive. Between displays of histrionic gesturing, mixed with a sing-song musicality of tone and a slight rotation of the head for additional emphasis, their communicative style is a real spectacle to watch, especially when in groups.

Louise learns that when verbal speech fails, the body speaks instead, saying more than words ever could. On the lips of a seasoned liar, words tend to ooze effortlessly from the mouth, but the eyes and body cannot betray what lies in the heart and mind - that easily. Louise keenly observes the facial expressions, gestures and emotionality of the speakers, soon deciphering what those around her are saying without their realising it. She becomes aware not just of gesturing and intonation but also of body posturing and the eyes, the eyes that rarely lie but rather tell their own story. There is no doubt that, with all of the body reading and the varying dialects, Louise is sometimes overwhelmed.

'Maghrebi' Arabic, based on a Berber substratum, is chiefly a spoken vernacular language used throughout Northern Africa and the one that Louise first grows accustomed to. It contains a mixture of influences shaped by the regional diversity of its people and administrators during the course of its long history, such as Latin, Ottoman, Turkish, Italian, Spanish, French and Arabic, of course. The form of Arabic Louise hears has its own specific dialect and is colloquial rather than formal. Because there are principal subcategories of Arabic, colloquial and standard, it can present learners with some difficulty. In written and formal settings throughout the Arab world, the standard or 'pure', 'al-fusha' version is widespread and mainly used, in addition to being the language of learning and literature.

In the Arab world, little distinction is made between the more ancient form of classical Arabic and its more modern version, since the morphology and syntax have remained basically the same.

As time passes, Louise becomes exposed to a diverse range of Arabic speakers who can adjust their speech in various ways according to the person they are speaking with. That does not happen, though, until she finally separates from her in-laws and the narrow confines of her initial environment. She notices that how the people manipulate and draw on the authority of the language reveals their level of education and social standing, so substantial differences exist between Bedouin people, men and women, those who live active or sedentary lifestyles and those who reside in villages or major cities and are university educated.

One morning, Louise enters the small kitchen at the back of the house to make herself a cup of tea and finds Fatima alone there, soaking beans. Louise hesitates on the threshold, pausing momentarily to catch the girl's eye and smile, but her sister-in-law does not turn around to acknowledge Louise's entrance; instead, she is dismissive and cold. She feels instantly uncomfortable in the small space with her sister-in-law.

It is not the first time she has raised an eyebrow privately concerning Fatima's sourness. Continuing with her purpose, she goes to the stove and notices the matches to light the stove are missing from their usual place, so she glances around but cannot locate them anywhere. Feeling disinclined to search further, she gives up and returns in a while, hoping to find someone else in the kitchen. Vowing to get a lighter for convenience's sake and not have to depend on anyone, she makes a mental note to ask Kareem to bring one. The house is unusually quiet for mid-morning, and she wonders where her mother-in-law and the two younger girls have gotten to.

Just as she is walking out of the kitchen, Louise hears a light thud on the stone floor behind her and Fatima's irritated voice. Turning to look, she sees and hears the box of matches hit the ground in front of her, deliberately thrown down for her to pick up. On impulse, Louise bends to retrieve them but stops short in mid-motion. Straightening up, she looks at Fatima to qualify there has been no mistake or indeed a misunderstanding on her part, but seeing her expression, Louise immediately understands the girl's ill-intention.

Suddenly, Louise feels hot; her cheeks begin to flush red, and droplets of perspiration form on her forehead. Finding her voice, she fixes her eyes firmly on Fatima's angry face. The words come in a rush, spoken instinctively in her mother tongue without thinking or caring whether the girl understands. No doubt her sister-in-law is capable of deciphering body language even though the words mean nothing.

Louise looks down at the matches pointedly and back at the girl standing in front of her, still mumbling under her breath.

"Who do you think you are, and who do you think I am?" The words tumble out of her mouth, loud and forceful.

"How dare you," she continues angrily. Picking up the box of matches, she slams them down on the kitchen bench next to Fatima and as she turns for the second time to leave, she hears the word again, unmistakably clear and though she hasn't a clue what it means, it is said with such venom that she is convinced of its malign meaning.

Refusing to listen to another word, Louise flees the kitchen, away from the vindictive girl and into her bedroom, determined not to leave it until she sees Kareem, remembering that he is due home within a few hours. Taking up her notebook and opening it on the last page, she carefully writes down the word she has heard, repeating it to herself as she writes it down. '*Ga-ba.*' Even as she says it aloud, it sounds rough, noting that the first syllable, 'ga' is stressed for emphasis. Louise remembers to affect the desired intonation or intentionality of the word itself.

Feeling rather dispirited, she lies down on her bed in a foetal position and with one hand placed protectively on her large belly, she eventually falls into a troubled sleep, escaping briefly the vicissitudes of a busy mind and an eventful morning. The world of sleep, into which she escapes, offers a chance to mollify her thoughts so when she wakes, she might be better able to cope with the parallel world in which she finds herself.

TWELVE

Moments of Madness

Don't tell me the moon is shining;
show me the glint of light on broken glass.

– Anton Chekhov

The unpleasant scene with Kareem's sister represents a turning point for Louise, a much-needed wake-up call to jolt her out of a semi-passive state. It leads her to adopt a more assertive and firmer stance towards her husband and his family.

Slowly but surely, she becomes more confident in speaking the language, feeling that she is gaining ground whenever she manages a successful communication, however simple. She knows the family have underestimated her ambition to learn their native tongue, having clearly mistaken her quiet but conscientious observations for apathy and indifference.

With that consideration, Fatima must have been shocked when her very own words exposed her, the mention and context of which is excruciatingly shameful for her in front of her older brother and the rest of the family.

When Kareem first hears what has transpired between his wife and sister, his eyes open wide, and he does not react well to the grave insult that his sister has levelled at his wife and, by extension, at him. Of course, Louise does not realise at the time what the repercussions will be.

It all begins when Louise asks Kareem to buy her a box of matches. Looking at her quizzically, he wonders at the strange request.

"Look, Kareem, if I could get them myself, I wouldn't be asking you, would I?" she points out, a slight note of irritation creeping into her tone. "Actually, there are a few other things I need as well, like a jar of coffee, tea bags and crackers for snacks, if you don't mind picking them up."

He nods his head. "Yeah, ok, I'll have some stuff for you tomorrow when I come home from work," he promises.

Luckily for Louise, Kareem has contacts in the airline's catering department, and as a favour, they supply him with items that are scarce or unavailable to buy in the shops.

Hesitating for a moment, on the brink of indecision, Louise is not sure whether to confide her fears in him about the incident earlier that day. In truth, there have been a few other minor things with his mother over the past few days, but nothing as upsetting as the episode with his sister. On that basis, she decides she ought to tell him.

"Kareem, I think Fatima has some problem with me and I don't understand what it is or why," she says, jumping straight in. Opening his mouth to say something, she gestures for him to hold onto his thought. Rather than lose momentum, she keeps going, recounting the brief events of the morning, including his sister's rudeness and hostile attitude towards her. Completely unaware of what is about to unfold and its impending impact, she keeps going, finally speaking the offending word to her husband, remembering it well because it was said more than once and with such forceful conviction.

"I don't know what it means she explains, repeating the word '*gaba*' again and without pausing for breath, she presses on but is suddenly silenced, halted by the forceful interruption of Kareem's loud and angry voice.

"You don't need to say it again," he shouts chillingly, his voice ringing in her ears as she draws back in total surprise. She has never before seen her husband so angry.

Momentarily disconcerted, she watches as his eyes take on a fierce look, nostrils flaring and his facial expression full of rage, the like of which she has not witnessed before. She opens her mouth to say something, but before the words form on her lips, he is already on his feet, arms flailing, his hands sweeping the air, and his temper growing more ferocious by the second as he exits the room and makes for the front porch.

Only then does she sense something nasty is afoot, though she does not understand what. Unable to stay still any longer, she stands up, feeling her legs a little shaky, and taking a deep breath, she follows her husband out of the room. Why does he not just say what is bothering him, she wonders, with a degree of irritation.

Lunch is long over, and for some reason, Kareem has broken his usual pattern of taking an afternoon nap before heading out for the evening. Ironically, Louise had thought to seize the opportunity to engage her husband, hoping to talk him into spending the following day with her, since he is off work and she wants them to do something together.

It is just another late afternoon, quiet in the open courtyard, the sun beginning to succumb to the first hint of evening, its shadows still remote but promising to usher in a night whose atmosphere is cool and light. Except this one is different.

Inside the house, Kareem's father and brothers are still napping and are due to wake soon from their afternoon slumber. Her mother-in-law and Fatima are sitting side by side under the stairway, sifting flour through large sieves before transferring it into waiting containers. The younger girls have been dispatched upstairs by their mother to tend to other chores, the faint murmur of their voices audible from the rooftop.

With a suddenness that feels surreal and nonsensical, the peace of the moment is shattered by a loud, angry voice. It is Kareem, and as Louise reaches the double doors that open onto the back porch, she hesitates on the threshold, incredulous, not daring to venture further, for she can barely take in what is taking place before her eyes.

At the sight and sound of her brother and his enflamed temper, Fatima immediately jumps to her feet like a terrified animal, knocking over the large bowl, its contents spilling across the stone tiles. In her desperate haste to cross the short distance to the stairs, she falters, misses her footing and nearly falls. Emitting a desperate cry, she manages to catch hold of the rail, pulling herself awkwardly onto the steep steps but it is too late. Kareem has already closed the short gap between them, and lunging forward, he thrusts his hand out, grabbing hold of his sister's long plait, restricting any movement she tries to make. Louise hears their mother's screams, mingled with Fathima's own, as Kareem grabs her arm tightly, holding her in a firm grip. His voice is loud but the sound of Fatima's wild and primal screeches practically drowns out any other, her breath coming in short gasps. Unintelligible words tumble from her mouth, words that Louise does not understand.

She hears her own voice sound, clear and distinct.

"Kareem, what the hell do you think you're doing? Let go of her, NOW, do you hear me." Another hysterical scream from his mother.

"*La, ya Karem, la, ukht, haram.*" Reminding Kareem that Fatima is his sister.

Standing beside her son at the foot of the stairs, she repeats it over in a desperate, panic-stricken plea.

Repeating her protestations beseechingly, she tries to intercept, calling on 'Allah' and his prophet to make her son desist and to leave well enough alone.

"Kareem, listen to your mother and stop this craziness," Louise says, her voice raised.

A lengthy verbal exchange ensues between mother and son, he gesticulating, still in a rage, his mother blocking his path until several entreaties later and much persistence on the part of his wife, he finally releases his tight hold on the snivelling girl but not without threats and a stern admonishment as she stumbles up the steps to escape the wrath of her brother.

A shocked, ashen-faced Louise is left standing helpless by the door, unable to move, her legs wobbling uncontrollably. Trying to regain her composure, she sits down on the nearest 'mendar' relieved that such a shockingly unpleasant situation has been averted, but she is left shaken by the unexpected turn of events. Never in her life has she witnessed such a scene, and it will take her a while to process it.

Aware that both Farhat and Jabir are awake, no doubt roused by the noisy racket, they appear on the porch and quietly take stock of the situation. Finding the matter resolved, they head immediately back inside, undoubtedly reluctant to meddle in the somewhat delicate matter concerning their older brother.

Their mother has retreated to the top of the house, mainly to check on her disgraced daughter and to send the younger ones down in case their brothers or father should need anything. Ever the pragmatist, when it comes to her male offspring, she decides it is wise to avoid her husband and stay invisible until supper time, lest he call her to account for the unbefitting behaviour of their daughter, supposedly of good character and soon eligible for marriage. It would not do for her father to hear about the incident because it would most certainly incur his wrath, and his wife knows it.

Louise decides it is prudent to stay silent and allow the tension in the air some time to settle before tackling her husband. Besides, she needs to gather her thoughts and return to a state of partial calm.

Just as Louise exits the porch, she spots the 'Haj' quietly leaving the house without saying a word. He has decided to take tea elsewhere this evening rather than in the company of his wife.

Later in the evening, there is finally a chance to discuss the earlier events.

"Kareem, will you please tell me what is going on," she asks him. It takes a few moments for him to reply, then, taking a deep breath, he finally speaks.

"Fatima said something she shouldn't have and disgraced herself," he admits, anger beginning to rise in him again.

"Well, surely, it can't be that bad. What has it got to do with us or me?" Louise presses him, and suddenly, a bad feeling descends on her.

Looking away from her, he continues to nod his head from side to side in disbelief.

"What did she do?" Louise is growing impatient.

Finally, he spits it out.

"She called you a prostitute."

Louise's initial reaction is to laugh because it sounds so ridiculous. Abruptly, she stops, hilarity turning to distaste as she regards her husband seriously.

"The word you heard is the Arabic word for…it," he explains, visibly struggling to keep his temper in check.

It takes a few seconds for the word and its associations to enter her field of cognition. As its full implication settles, it is met with an entirely different response in Louise than in her husband. As such, their disparate responses serve only as a marker for a monumental division in their personalities, mannerisms and belief systems.

Eyeing her husband intently, she utters not a single word for what seems like a long interval.

Instead of placing culpability at the feet of a misguided and misinformed young girl, Louise believes the disgrace belongs as much to her husband and his parents as to the girl herself. Therefore, Kareem has to take responsibility for contributing to his sister's behaviour. She wonders if, as her older brother, he has expressed an opinion about the importance of his sister having an education. Without this, the result will surely be that uneducated women like Fatima stay trapped in a society of men whose perception of women is seriously skewed. In any event, his sister has shown a grave lack of respect towards both of them.

When Louise is ready to speak, she surprises even herself with the calmness of her tone, though she is inwardly in turmoil.

"I have to say, Kareem. I feel very let down by your family, not to mention downright unwelcome and as for your sister, I have to wonder about her ideas, I mean, where they originate from. "

"What a thing to say to anyone," she reinforces. "Do your family have any idea of what respect means or what my life was like before I came here?"

She pauses a moment before going on.

"I don't know what you said out there; it was all a bit crazy and by the way, I never knew you had such a temper."

Ignoring his wife's reference to his bad temper, he tries to reassure her.

"Look, Lou, I spoke to my mother. She is upset about what happened. Nothing like that will ever happen again," he insists, trying to sound reassuring.

"Well, she ought to be," Louise bounces back at him. She secretly wonders whether Kareem is more put out about what he regards as an affront to him personally or the awful treatment of his wife.

"You're absolutely right, Kareem. Nothing like it will ever be repeated simply because I won't allow it to be. I'll depend on myself for that rather than on your mother."

Suddenly, the very sound of Kareem's voice is irritating and she just wants to lie down and not talk any more about it. Yet, she realises something more needs to be said while the opportunity is present.

"Listen, Kareem, I think you should speak to your sister, not your mother. I mean talk to her, not roar at her."

As Louise speaks, she knows her husband will never do as she suggests.

"Someone needs to explain to her, Kareem, that there is a world beyond this place."

She stops talking, expecting her husband to respond with a meaningful comment, even a crumb that might at least turn the whole sorry experience into an opportunity for change.

He just hums and haws without saying anything useful, just as she expects. Louise wonders if he is dismissive or needs time to think about it.

"Ok, since you're not convinced, Kareem, there is absolutely no point in defending my honour just because I happen to be your wife."

"What," he says, with a look of exasperation, "What do you mean?"

"Well, don't you think you have a responsibility as Fatima's older brother to set her straight about certain things in life, for the sake of all women?" He looks at his wife but says nothing.

"Well, your parents obviously don't think it important enough that their daughters have schooling. It's disgusting, actually."

Louise stretches out on the bed, placing a tired head on the pillow.

"The whole thing has been shocking, to be honest but enough said on it for now," she tells him, turning over to face in the opposite direction.

"We'll talk later about it, Lou," he says as he crosses the room to the door.

Louise has no intention of picking up where they left off because, as far as she is concerned, there is nothing more to add. For now, she just wants to be alone with her thoughts and rest a while. Soon enough, her eyelids grow heavy and sleep eventually claims her.

Nobody disturbs her until much later when she is already awake and reading on her bed. The 'Haj' sends Maryam to ask her to join him for tea.

Over the next few days, it comes as no surprise to Louise that Fatima fails to appear and, when she eventually does, is slow to circulate in their company. Louise senses that her original attitude has been altered, and it looks as if she is going about her business with a renewed resignation. Metaphorically, Louise likens it to a water channel that has been blocked and is temporarily cleared of detritus, allowing for the build-up of inner, toxic material to be released. Perhaps in the angry episode, her role was merely that of a conduit for something much greater.

In a larger context, the appalling slight to Louise, Kareem's wife, is not only an insult but is considered a social taboo, especially when delivered by an unmarried girl who is expected to be shy of such baser things in life.

Fatima's scornful remarks generate a level of outrage which is considered unheard of in a decent Muslim family. Actually, what angers Louise more than the 'name-calling' is the intentional action of throwing the matches on the ground for her to pick up, a deliberate act of rudeness on Fatima's part, which says a lot about her upbringing and the family, in general.

Her behaviour contravenes a social and religious order. If it were to be known outside close family quarters, it might be regarded as blasphemous, bringing disrepute to the family name and even affecting their daughter's reputation in the marriage stakes.

By the end, Louise almost regrets that she ever mentioned the incident; the whole episode has proved to be extremely dramatic and unpleasant. On the other hand, she discovers something very disturbing about the mentality of Kareem's family and the broader culture in general. The entire debacle leaves Louise with the haunting impression of a ruthless predator in pursuit of his frightened prey.

It seems that just as she is discovering new things about the man she married, he, too, is beginning to wonder about the girl he has brought to his country.

This educated and assertive Western woman may yet prove to be a challenge for him unless he can find a way to mould her into something more pliable.

THIRTEEN

An Awakening

You must be ready to burn in your own flame;
how could you rise anew if you have not first become ashes?

– Friedrich Nietzsche

Louise awakes with a start, struggling to sit upright in the tired, old bed. Looking slowly around the room, she is gripped by an overwhelming sense of fear and dread. In the near distance, she hears the *Adhan,* an Islamic call to prayer, the root of which means 'to listen'. The solemn but insistent cry of the Imam, calling his flock to the first prayer at dawn, is a beautifully haunting sound, eerie and yet distinctive, shattering the lingering stillness of first light.

The temperature in the bedroom is hot and humid, the atmosphere heavy, a different quality of heaviness to the one she feels in her stomach. Now it is time for her to listen to that deeper voice that speaks to her from the depths of her being. As she throws off the cloak of sleep and reality begins to solidify into a wakeful state, Louise finds little comfort in it, her agitation only increasing.

Struggling to regain her composure, she tells herself that she must have been dreaming, but the sense of relief one feels in the wake of a bad dream is strangely absent. Everything seems frozen in time and obscured in a way that feels alien and unsettling.

Tired and groggy, she tries to shake off the uncanny residues her dream has left behind but there is a lingering sense of impending doom that hangs over her and it feels scary. There is nothing for it except to muster pleasant memories of home to create a distraction and chase away the effects of her nightmare.

Sitting up, propped against her pillow, surrounded by shadows that shift in the half-light, dawn begins to break gently and with it arrives a shocking epiphany. Sudden and powerful, it strikes her with incredible force. A startling and terrifying realisation that she has made a great mistake in marrying Kareem and coming to his country. Sitting still in the bed, she allows the truth to wash over her, slowly and measured, without resisting it.

Ironically, as the first faint rays of sunshine peep through the shutter alongside the debilitating thought, there comes a feeling of relief. The recognition of her poor choice, as she now sees it, the acceptance that things are not as she had imagined and likely never will be, provide a degree of emotional transparency and relief. Rather than suppress the thoughts that invade her consciousness, she allows them to sit with her. Fantasy has given way to reality.

It is a reality that crushes Louise's expectations into smithereens, shattering her naïve, unsullied dreams into a million fragmented pieces, leaving her with a state of things as they actually exist, stripping away the outer layer and laying bare her imaginative longings.

Louise knows that a mistake of such proportions cannot be reversed easily, and she begins to slowly consider its manifold implications. Ultimately, it is her problem and her predicament, so she will have to find a way to deal with it.

Remembering how determined she was to leave her home and say goodbye to everything she knew, an entire life, she is saddened and lonely. Struggling now to accept her past choices, she thinks about the well-intentioned advice of her parents, based on the little they actually knew about this part of the world and Kareem. In their wildest dreams, they could never have imagined what life is like here, for she can hardly get her own head around it. Louise is suddenly consumed with guilt for not listening to them but it is too late for that now. At the time, she was obsessed with a blind certainty, holding fast to her decision, and she proceeded obstinately towards the abyss.

Why were her actions so reckless? Was it a case of pure infatuation? A form of escapism? Or maybe a combination of all three? She starts to delve into what had prompted her to take such an ill-advised step. What unknown force was at work in her mind that compelled her to follow the path she did? She finds it hard to find answers, however.

Thoughts whirl and reel about in her head, like the west wind, waking her from a summer dream and delaying the moment when she will have to rise and face another day with her in-laws. Thoughts of her unborn baby spring to mind, and she is already looking ahead to the day she will finally give birth. It is with a degree of trepidation that she prepares for the event, but ignorance can be blissful in certain situations.

Placing a hand on her tummy, she feels a rush of warmth and an indescribable feeling takes hold of her. There is not only herself to think about now but a tiny, innocent human being, a little person created from her own desire, who would shortly enter the world and be entirely dependent on her for everything.

Louise tries to visualise herself as a mother, and reverting to her own childhood, she attempts to visualise scenes and bring forth memories of her own mother. A few come to mind, but she suspects there are more that are buried deep and lost within the folds of memory, creating little gaps of amnesia.

She can see her sister towering over her, taking charge of things like she always does. Arleen, her sister, is there, a permanent fixture, always present in her mind's eye. She holds Louise's long, plaited hair tightly in one hand whilst she adroitly manoeuvres a ribbon in the other. They are the pleasant memories surrounding her childhood until suddenly, one day, Arleen leaves in a cloud of secrecy, leaving behind an atmosphere of clandestine whisperings. Although Louise is too young to understand what is happening, she is able, nevertheless, to pick up, as only children can, that something serious is afoot in the house, involving her beloved older sister and their parents.

However, like a lot of things, it is never explained to her in any child-friendly or graspable way, and so it left an imprint on her young, developing mind. Her parents felt it best not to tell Louise the truth, as they thought a child has no need to know or understand things. Louise always felt that this was a mistake.

Louise feels ill-prepared for motherhood. Ironically, her only experience of it has been through watching Arleen and how devotedly she cares for her two babies. To Louise, she represents a kind of maternal goddess, and from the outset of her pregnancy, she had fortunately picked up some invaluable tips from just observing her.

Naturally, being the last-born child with four much older siblings does not equip you or provide the necessary tools to help with the neonatal needs of newborns. She will have to rely on her instincts and hope they can see them both through.

Louise knows little about pregnancy, let alone the immediate aftermath of childbirth and feeding regimes. How she will find the initial mothering experience is not something that enters her head because she simply knows nothing about it. Since it is an entirely subjective experience, the meaning that childbearing brings to the internal world of each individual woman is different. Louise is only now beginning to wonder about the prospect of a living, breathing person under her skin. She wonders if a woman is even allowed to explore that notion, or is it just an accepted fact of common culture that a woman must embrace jubilantly without hesitation? Yet, there is nothing common about it at all.

Louise has no idea or expectation about feelings of maternal ambivalence and how they infuse a woman's pregnant life. They cross an entire spectrum of fluctuating emotions, eventually paving the way for a relationship with a real child and not a product of any idealised expectations.

Eventually, she gets up and sits on the side of the bed. Time has passed along with her thoughts, and the glow of morning sunlight spills into the room, scattering the light, enough to illuminate the tiny speckles of dust particles floating and dancing vibrantly in the warm, stuffiness of her bedroom. Louise reaches for her book and a carton of apple juice she had placed conveniently on a bedside table. Pouring its contents into a glass, she drinks thirstily. Before opening her book, she hesitates, putting it back down on the bed. Still in a contemplative mood, she pauses to evaluate her life so far. Other than learning a new language, she is unconvinced that her life has yielded anything fruitful.

One looming thought makes its way to the surface of her consciousness and has become a source of anxiety for her. Since she is 'persona non-grata' in her mother-in-law's home, she expects to find little support from them when the baby is born. Sadly, her own family are a continent away. What about Kareem? Will he prove to be a better father than husband?

She is really unsure about him since she already feels let down by him. Pushing such unsettling thoughts from her mind, she wants to stay positive for the birth of her baby.

Louise wonders about coincidences and if everything happens according to its own design. In her situation, whether an accident of fate or the result of some horrible mistake, it matters little because the 'here and now' is what must count for her. A nightmare has become a reality which no amount of mental processing can remove her from unless she finds a way to adapt to her inhospitable environment or until her husband finds a place for them to live. Perhaps then she will feel more confident to confront his personality and consider how to move forward in her life.

Still pondering the past, she considers rather derisively, the brief relationship between Kareem and herself, lasting barely a year before being abruptly cut short, the result of an urgent summons from his government to report for duty without delay. His departure was swift. Louise was upset, but quickly got over it and life continued. He returned a year later in somewhat deceptive circumstances with a proposal of marriage. By that time, Louise had almost completely forgotten him. Why and how then was their courtship reignited?

Feeling hot and clammy, little beads of perspiration begin to appear on her brow. Reaching for her sundress, she emits a sigh of resignation, contemplating another long day flavoured with boredom.

Leaving the privacy of her modest room, she takes her book with her, grateful for the distraction it provides while she struggles to keep her emotions in check.

Stepping into the sunlit courtyard, she sits down under the shade of a lemon tree overhanging the iron balustrade above. There she settles on a thick, spongy *mendar,* a soft mattress, and opens her book, disappearing into a world of storytelling.

FOURTEEN

À Mother Is Born

Youth fades, love drops, the leaves of friendship fall;
a mother's secret love outlives them all.

– Oliver Wendell Holmes

Louise is quiet and subdued on the bumpy truck ride that eventually takes her to the hospital where she is to deliver their baby. Kareem is in a ferocious rage and has driven the pick-up recklessly across the uneven, dusty track for about two miles until it finally meets the main road. All the while, Louise is full of fear, holding her stomach as she lurches from side to side, thinking the journey will never end. Words rise in her throat but die, leaving nothing but an unpleasant taste behind. Not wishing to inflame his ill-temper further, she knows instinctively it is in her own interests and her baby's to stay silent.

Hot and drained, she is physically and emotionally spent from the day's exertions when, finally, they reach the hospital. Lifting out her small suitcase, she steps down from the truck and walks solemnly to the hospital entrance without looking back. Hearing the truck pull off, she hesitates a few seconds in front of the door to gather her wits and prepare to face one of the most important journeys of her life.

Now that the time has finally arrived, what is she to expect? How is a mother-to–be supposed to feel? Trying to cope with everything else is more than enough for her without dwelling on the vagaries of childbirth in a still-developing third-world country. Fortunately, youth and good health have rewarded her with an uncomplicated pregnancy thus far.

She and Kareem had argued again before leaving the house, and this, more than anything else, preoccupies her thoughts. Since earlier that day, her husband has been moody and distracted. Whenever she tried to talk to him, he reacted aggressively, rudely swearing at her in Arabic, his tone dogmatic and insensitive. At one point in the afternoon, she could feel the blood rushing to her face, with both embarrassment and anger, made worse by the fact that his family were within earshot and could hear everything he said. Looking at him directly in the eye, she addressed him in a voice struggling to contain her anger and remain steady.

"Don't speak to me like that, Kareem. I've already told you, have some respect. If this keeps happening, we're going to have real problems, I can promise you that."

Having dropped the barb, she looked away unflinchingly, throwing aside the cushion, and stood up, hardly believing the steady sound of her own voice. While inside, she was ready to crumble. A shameless Kareem took no notice, and registering his increasingly angry tone, Louise hesitated.

"That's enough," she hears a note of warning in his tone, shutting her down as if she were a naughty child. Knowing him well enough, she expected a further barrage of abuse. Still smarting from his humiliating display, she felt an angry frustration rise up in her chest. This time, she was not to be silenced.

At that precise moment, she was interrupted by the sight of her father-in-law appearing at the door, his finger pointed at Kareem.

"What are you doing?" he asks, his tone sharp and direct. Without waiting for a reply from his son, he walked over to where Kareem stood, eyeing him intensely.

"Leave it now, do you hear me, Kareem? Leave it," he warned his son in a stern voice.

Turning, he addressed Louise by the name he had adopted for her.

"Sit down now and rest a bit, Isa. Don't mind about anything."

He indicated with his hand and a smile, for her to sit next to his usual place.

Slowly and reluctantly, she followed his advice, secretly glad of his intervention and also not wishing to offend her father-in-law's attempts to defuse the tension. Stealing a sidelong glance at Kareem, she noted with some satisfaction that he had been suitably silenced by his father. After a short while, she retreated to her room, leaving her husband to think about what she said. It occurred to her that he probably loathed being challenged in front of his family and by a woman at that, even though the woman in question was his wife. An admonishment from his father had made a point and Louise was grateful for it.

It is late in the afternoon when Kareem leaves his pregnant wife outside the hospital entrance, a parting with no soft words of comfort, no reassuring smile that might serve to put her at ease and help quell her feeling of nervous anticipation.

Once inside, a young woman's sour, unsmiling face looks out at Louise from her *hijab* and issues a brief instruction, her shiny, white teeth chewing vigorously on gum as she barks out the words. No surprises, Louise thinks because she has seen plenty of it and notes for the umpteenth time how unbecoming it looks.

Stepping inside the stuffy lift, she is suddenly overwhelmed by a delayed emotional response. The simmering anger she feels occludes thoughts of her husband and the cold look she had seen on his face. Louise knows there is something terribly wrong about all of it. The journey to the hospital in her condition is a scene she will never forget.

The city's only public maternity hospital does not permit men to accompany their wives to the delivery area. Native women are usually accompanied by a female relative who remains for a while, but Louise will face the birth alone. As she makes her way to the lift, she registers the dull, austere surroundings, taking in the absence of nursing staff, which one would expect to see amid the hustle and bustle intrinsic to a busy maternity hospital. Here, there is little sign of any activity.

A fetid smell hangs about the place, and it reeks of sweaty odours and stale body fluids, most probably for the want of a thorough scouring. On the third floor, she emerges from the crepuscular lift to be nearly blinded by a strong but welcome stream of sunlight filtering through the partially closed blinds from a corridor facing her. She looks up, half expecting to see a sign that will direct her to the birthing room, but there is none. Ahead of her, a short distance away, she sees two women disappear around a corner, tall, ghost-like figures draped in white. She follows them into a long room with some narrow beds positioned haphazardly along its back wall. The so-called beds are more like low-lying cots, some without pillows and others with no over sheets at all. Louise claims a bed and sits, setting her case down beside her. She has no idea what will happen next or what to expect.

All she knows is that a close friend of Kareem's is a nephew of the resident gynaecologist and he has promised to alert his uncle about her imminent arrival. Nothing is certain, however, because it was mentioned some time before, and Louise wonders if they even remember. Having already met 'the uncle' for a check-up shortly after her arrival, she found him friendly enough and they chatted for a bit about his time working abroad.

Owing to the turn of events earlier that day, Louise can only hope that the doctor in question or one of his team will come through for her.

Two native women, one enormously pregnant, eyes Louise inquiringly as she approaches, but the subject of their curiosity is oblivious because, once again, she is distracted by her own thoughts. Even if Kareem had been permitted to stay, she does not desire his company now for reasons which have little to do with the birth itself. At such a significant moment in time, any thoughts of her husband simply repulse her.

Presently, one of the women lets out a low moan; her face contorted as she crouches over, feeling the first pains of childbirth, her labour advancing rapidly. Louise, visibly alarmed, looks over and realises that despite their differences, they share a common unity of purpose, a humanity that makes their pain a necessary conduit to the gift of life. She manages to smile at the other woman, who immediately returns it with a question.

"Have you other children?" she enquires, her breathing laboured. "No, this is the first," Louise answers, stroking her belly. "And you?" she asks, eager to keep the conversation going. The older woman answers, pointing to the other, attempting to settle rather awkwardly on a nearby chair.

"She's my daughter, her first baby, like you," she informs her proudly, nodding her head several times.

"*Insha Allah*", if God wills it, she repeats before being abruptly interrupted by an even louder moan, followed by words that Louise cannot understand but can only guess. The girl's mother speaks reassuringly to her daughter, "*Allah maak, Al-hamdu lil-lah,*" and then to herself, in a half-whispered prayer, "*bismillah*", 'in the name of God'. Louise is able to understand the sacred words, enshrined in their holy Koran but adopted as part of common parlance.

With the passing of the years, Louise finds that she is unable to remember an ordered sequence of events surrounding the birth of her first child; rather, she snatches scenes here and there, scattered and somewhat disconnected. No matter how she concentrates on summoning certain things to memory, with the exception of some isolated images that seem frozen in time, they enter and flee her mind in milliseconds. What has remained is remarkably vivid, whilst others are scant and blurred. It is as if her mind only allows her to glimpse briefly, a phantasmagoria of images, before dissolving into oblivion, barring all coherent traces of the past.

What Louise can remember is her loneliness and feeling of isolation, restless and afraid as she lies on a bed and waits. She remembers a popping sensation, a sound that alarms her, a gush of water spilling onto the floor beside her, then the dreaded realisation that it is coming from her own body. Nobody had told her what to expect, and speaking loudly to herself, beseechingly, to anyone who could hear, she felt a distant ache which turned into a sharp, insistent pain. It is the sudden onset of labour, pain which comes in rapid, spasms, searing and intense.

At some point, a white coat materialised, a figure attached to an unfamiliar-sounding voice, garbled and broken, but the word *pethidine* registers at some level of her consciousness.

Her memories of giving birth, limited as they are, seem like a battleground of smells, sensations and fluids, an altogether bloody business, something primordial and raw. In the painful aftermath, she figures it is not for nothing it has been named 'labour'. It strikes Louise as a bittersweet task that ends in the birth of a mother as well as a baby. The bringing forth of a new life is indeed a labour of pain and love from which two future identities will be powerfully formed.

The moment she first saw her son was a surreal, ephemeral moment, which no amount of eloquently constructed words can fully capture. She recalls having to convince herself that this little human being is her baby and he has literally come out of her body. She cries silently as the smiling doctor holds him up for her to see, reassuring her that she has delivered a healthy boy who exceeds the average weight of a newborn.

Things become hazy after that because there is a sharp break in the continuity of her thought, due perhaps to the possibility that she had fallen into a state of exhausted sleep, made drowsy by the effects of sedation, physical exertion and the relief she experiences after giving birth in such challenging circumstances.

One thing is clear and trumps all else: on a bright autumn day, a fine baby boy enters the world, healthy and strong, with not a blade of hair on his innocent head, perfect in every way.

The following day, Kareem makes his appearance accompanied by his mother and Saoirse. Louise remembers sitting in bed, the curtain drawn around her bed waiting, waiting for what seems like a very long time before her husband finally appears. Watching the door through a slit in the curtain, she observes lots of visitors filing past her door and she begins to feel deflated, wondering if anyone will come. What is keeping them?

When Kareem finally arrives, his greeting is almost as cool as his farewell from the previous day.

"How are you feeling, Lou? Everything ok?" he asks, as if nothing had happened, from a respectable distance at the foot of her bed.

Louise has to swallow hard to answer her husband, feeling herself filling up, eyes watering. She is pleased at least to have a small room for herself and a tiny bit of privacy. Fighting hard to chase away the tears, she slowly finds her voice.

"Now we have a beautiful little boy and he's worth all the sacrifice."

Kareem looks at his wife from across the room, nodding his head in agreement. There are no displays of affection and Louise feels a stab of resentment when she looks at him, but it soon dissolves, replaced by a determination that nothing will overshadow or mar the unique occasion.

Smiling, Kareem approaches the cot gingerly as if something might jump out and attack him. After looking at his son for a few moments, he eventually turns to look at the three women.

"He's sleeping," a surprised voice announces, and he stays looking into the cot for a few minutes as if he cannot quite believe that there is a living baby inside it.

Louise is truly delighted to see her new-found friend and the fact that she is knowledgeable about 'baby' matters only adds to her joy. Saoirse, the second eldest of nine children, has a lot of experience around children. Her youngest brother had just turned three when she left Ireland to follow her heart. Saoirse, also from Dublin, had arrived ahead of Louise, and once they had settled in, Saoirse was the first to call. Delighted, Louise welcomed her with open arms, overjoyed to see one of her own in a foreign land. From that day forward, a deep friendship was forged between the two women.

"Congratulations, Louise, I'm thrilled for you. Gosh, he's such a fine baby. He could easily be mistaken for two months old." She laughs, moving across the room to stand beside Kareem, who is looking admiringly at the sleeping Sami.

"Isn't he beautiful, a fine baby. You must be delighted. *Mabrook, Mabrook*," she says, looking round at Kareem's mother, who stands scowling in the corner of the room.

"I can't wait to get out of here," Louise admits, and Saoirse responds with a wink.

"Don't worry, Louise. If you like, I can get Sadik to bring me over to you as soon as you arrive home."

The reply is immediate, with a hint of desperation in her tone. "Oh, would you Saoirse? That'd be great. I could do with your help."

Louise feels instantly relieved and not nearly as apprehensive about handling her new son with a little support from her friend.

"Stop worrying, it'll all be fine. You'll be a natural in no time," she says, smiling reassuringly.

"It means a lot to me, Saoirse. Thanks so much." The expression of gratitude obvious on her worried face.

Louise had never thought about what it would mean to become a mother, to carry a human being inside her and live together under one skin. She was shocked when she discovered she was pregnant, her overall feeling being one of unpreparedness, but fortunately, she had Arleen, her older sister, for practical and emotional support since other family members were less welcoming of her news when she told them. Louise was really hurt, but without realising it at the time, the origin of their feelings stemmed more from their own internal conflicts rather than anything involving her.

Little Sami lies sleeping beside his mother's bed in a cot devoid of frills, a basic hospital issue but functional, nonetheless. It appears at odds with the exquisite blue and white eiderdown covering the precious bundle that lies on the thin mattress. A gift from Louise's parents, it had reached her rather circuitously via contacts of her sister, who were returning to Tripoli from Dublin. Her family had gone to great trouble to organise a large parcel and make contact with the expats. It meant so much to Louise when she opened it and lots of tears were shed as she read the letters and cards they had written. Such a beautiful gift for their new grandson, and it gladdens her heart whenever she tucks her little body inside its soft folds.

Still smiling, she looks into the sour face of her mother-in-law, who is speaking to her son animatedly. Looking at her husband with eyebrows raised, Louise is not sure what their conversation is about but senses it concerns something about the baby or herself. Unbeknownst to Louise, her mother-in-law has spied two feeding bottles standing on the bedside locker and decides to tackle her son.

"My mother is just asking. Why you're not feeding the baby yourself, Louise? It's better for Sami, your own breast milk, you know."

While Kareem is translating the message, his mother regards Louise with a look of unabashed disapproval. Looking back into the woman's scowling face, something shifts in Louise, and in her mind, she can hear her own words even before she speaks them. Being in a foreign country, with no guidance on the challenges of breastfeeding, she has decided to bottle-feed Sami.

"I'm going to bottle-feed, Kareem. I have all the equipment, the steriliser, my mother sent over, remember?"

In the background, the bickering continues, her mother-in-law openly voicing her criticism to Kareem as if his wife were not present in the room. He tries to reason with his mother, but it is clear she is doing everything to exert her influence and gain the upper hand.

Louise feels the tender, reassuring pat of Saoirse's hand on hers as she is hailed by a barrage of protest.

"*La, La, haram,*" comes the loud accusation amidst other words that Louise does not understand. Something about bringing bad luck and misfortune or that folk might think she is a bad mother. On and on her mother-in-law wrangles, her unpleasant voice and sourness of face jarring with Louise's attempt at happy thoughts. Suddenly, Saoirse intervenes.

"Louise is tired, you know. She's only recently given birth and I think she should be allowed to rest."

She looks pointedly at Kareem and then into the face of his tiresome, insensitive mother.

"All this talk is upsetting Louise, and I think enough has been said for now, don't you?" she continues, smiling while driving her point home.

Though Saoirse is polite, there is no mistaking the intention of her words or her expression of quiet disgust. Any reservation she feels is overridden by her concern for her friend. Because her Arabic is reasonably good, she uses it to address Kareem's mother, whom she glares at unwaveringly before reverting to her son in English.

"Maybe Kareem, you could explain to your mother that Louise has just had a baby and all this talk is not good."

In the meantime, the expression on Louise's face has changed from one of good humour to one of gloom. Inwardly, she feels tired and disappointed, but drawing on a stoic reserve that surprises her, she finds a gathering strength. Before anyone can respond, she draws herself upright in the bed and delivers a measured and decisive reply.

"I'm going to be bottle-feeding my baby," she announces confidently.

Sensing that Saoirse has scored a point, Louise decides to push on determinedly, her voice rising slightly.

"Kareem, will you thank your mother for her advice? But I won't be breastfeeding. That is a decision for me only, and I believe I know what is best for my baby and me," she adds with a hint of sarcasm. Now, I'm feeling tired and need to rest so thank you all for coming."

He looks at his wife in silence before turning to face his contentious mother. Nothing more is mentioned on the subject of breastfeeding, and soon, it is time for them to leave. Louise is bid a lukewarm farewell by her mother-in-law, whose presence she can hardly wait to be rid of.

No sooner have they walked out the door than tears begin to gather in her eyes, but she holds them back, not wanting to give them free reign because once they flow unchecked, Louise fears she will not be able to stop them. She wants to stay focused for her baby, and right now, that means staying strong.

Late in the evening when Sami is settled and sleeping soundly in his cot, Louise lays out a new bath-towel and long, cotton nightshirt on the bed. Slipping out of her room, she ventures along the corridor to find a shower room, but first, she stops at the toilet.

A dreadful sight greets her eyes and nostrils, with used sanitary pads strewn about the floor and the disposal bin full to overflowing. Stale blood spatter soils the toilet seats and splashes are visible on practically every surface. On the floors, drops of congealed blood mix with dust and dirt, hardening into little lumps of stubborn grime. The air is hot and stuffy, with no adequate ventilation, but Louise has no choice but to use the disgusting toilet. Out of her light dressing gown pocket, she takes a fresh sanitary pad, tears off the paper, dampens it under the nearby faucet and wipes the toilet seat vigorously until it looks passable enough to sit on. Balancing herself carefully, she can feel the tight pull of her stitches, reminding her of the birth experience. Carefully, she tries to avoid touching anything with her bare hands, but there is no toilet tissue and the soap dispensers are empty. Luckily, she has wipes in her toilet bag, a last-minute thought.

As luck has it, on exiting the filthy toilets, she catches sight of a nurse and she tries to walk a little quicker to catch up before she turns the corner. Coughing loudly to attract her attention, the woman turns, and Louise puts up her hand to indicate she needs assistance.

"Is there a shower? Louise gestures, and the woman, eyeing her up and down, points rather disinterestedly down the corridor.

"Shukran," Louise doesn't hesitate a second longer but takes off in the said direction. When she enters the room, there is a row of showers against one wall, and surprisingly, none of them are occupied. At a glance, she takes in the soiled plastic curtains and the general aspect of the place. It is a little better than the toilets but no matter once there is water and soap to wash. Taking out her shower gel and shampoo, she steps under the hose and waits for the refreshing sensation of water to pour over her body. Reluctant to delay, she towel-dries hurriedly and, feeling somewhat better, hurries back to her room, eager not to leave Sami unattended for too long.

On her way back, she sees a ghostly woman in her white garb disappear into one of the rooms. Apart from that, there is no sign of activity.

All is quiet when she enters the room, Sami still sleeping peacefully, his tiny fists tightly closed, touching against his cute, chubby cheeks. When she is satisfied that all is well with him, she turns her attention back to herself. Deciding to put on her new nightshirt, she turns to lift it off the bed and to her horror, it is gone. Wait a moment, she pauses, second-guessing. Flustered, she scans the room, but it is nowhere to be seen. It dawned on her then that somebody had taken, no, stolen it in the short time she was gone.

Feeling instant panic, a shiver runs down her spine and real fear creeps up on her. The suitcase, God no, she suddenly remembers all her new stuff from home. She drops to her knees, momentarily halted by a sharp pain in her lower abdomen but she pauses only for a couple of seconds to take a breath before reaching underneath the bed. With enormous relief, her fingers tighten around the handles, her precious case is still concealed where she had left it. Starting to cry with a mixture of relief and fear, she suddenly feels a gratitude so total that she slumps down onto the floor before retrieving it, not daring to imagine what might have happened had it disappeared with her nightshirt. It has all Sami's new clothes and hers to go home in. Holding her toilet bag appreciatively, Louise is so happy to have found it intact with all her irreplaceable bits and bobs inside. Taking out a bottle of body cologne, she sprays it generously on herself, savouring its notes of lemon verbena and lavender. Lying on the bed, feeling revived, she waits for Sami to wake, and it is not long before he begins to stir.

Getting up, she goes to the cot and looks in, observing him closely, noting his every movement until he becomes fidgety and lets out the unmistakable cry of a newborn. Carefully, she gathers him up in her arms, half afraid that she will not handle him correctly but instinctively, she rests his small, precious head on the inside of her folded arm, where she cradles him for a long moment, feeling the gentle pressure of his small body pressing warmly against her own.

Louise feels a sudden deluge of emotion, overwhelmed, as tears well in her eyes to overflowing, slowly trickling down her face, leaving a rivulet of wetness, tiny drops dripping down onto her baby's bare head. It feels like a dam has been opened, its floodgates releasing a myriad of pent-up energies and dispersing them onto the surface. She sits for a while with Sami nestling in her arms, allowing the feelings to flood her thoughts until the shadows of evening lengthen. Being alone with her baby amid thoughts that someone might snatch him away from her only adds to her fears. Unwittingly, she may have transmitted those feelings to Sami because suddenly, he becomes restless and starts to cry, as if sensing his mother's anxiety.

Despite all that has transpired during the day, Louise manages to sleep that night until the early morning hours when she rises to attend to Sami's demanding cries.

She does not have long to wait for Kareem to arrive and take them home, away from the hospital and its lasting, inhospitable impression that will be forever etched into her memory.

She also takes an infinitely more positive memory structured around an initial, wobbly but later solid foundation, built with painstaking, tender care and fashioned from pure love. It is a love cemented by a maternal bond deeply moulded within the confines of dull, forbidding walls, erected against all the odds but nevertheless has the power to endure.

The next day, Louise leaves the hospital with her precious baby son and a new-found purpose in her life.

FIFTEEN

Beginning of the End

Trust is a delicate flower,
once broken, it takes ardent care to make it blossom again.

– Olivia Anderson

Sami is only one month old when Kareem delivers his hammer blow. Taking his wife by complete surprise, he causes her great upset at a time when she should have been recovering from childbirth and adjusting to a new person in her life. The days and weeks immediately after Sami's birth are tough for Louise, battling symptoms of painful mastitis, sleep deprivation and lack of familial support, topped by her husband's general ineptitude around his baby son. Emotionally absent and disengaged, Louise sees how he makes little or no effort to be actively involved in the care of his baby son.

He is content to come and go as he pleases, assuming his wife is happy enough to fill her days caring for and meeting the demands of a new infant without considering that she, too, has needs of her own.

The fact that Louise is a young mother, unpractised in postnatal skills, puts her in a vulnerable position, and her living conditions do not help to improve things. Life is tolerable for Louise only because of Saoirse's regular visits, her invaluable support in handling a new baby and most of all, her friendship.

In the immediate weeks following Sami's birth, Louise ponders long and deeply over who she is in relation to her baby and, ironically, her own 'baby self.' She believes these prescient considerations need to be addressed for any new mother; but seldom are. Perhaps this reflection is too provocative and ends up drawing a woman, whether young or older, into the depths of her psychic space, a space where many women do not wish to go.

To embrace a new life or a new love is like shedding an old skin. We give up something old, familiar and tested for something completely unfamiliar. Over time, we infuse the new with substance and construct our own meanings around it, allowing it to be influenced by the climate of our psychic realities. Nonetheless, we always erect it upon our individual subjectivities and personal ambivalence.

Little Sami is not long after his bath, and Louise is settling him down for his mid-morning nap when she looks up and, to her surprise, sees Kareem entering the bedroom. Immediately, she puts her finger to her lips to shush him, indicating that Sami is going asleep. Oddly, her husband has only been gone a couple of hours.

Within a few minutes, they are alone in the small sitting room having left Sami peacefully having his nap. The house is unusually quiet since her mother-in-law is out and the girls are occupied with a mountain of laundry to tackle. Louise makes coffee, and they settle down to drink it, but the brief moments of peace are shattered by her husband's untimely news.

"Louise, the airline is sending us on a training course to the US." he begins.

Initially, she hears the word 'us' as meaning he, Sami and herself but something tells her she is mistaken. Instantly, her smile turns to a frown and she regards her husband with evident confusion on her face, unable to string any words together, unable to express herself.

On the other hand, Kareem, if he has any concerns about how his wife might respond to the news, is mindful not to make it obvious from his outward manner. While Louise needs a few seconds to register what she has heard, Kareem picks up his coffee cup and takes a sip. Suddenly, her heart sinks into the pit of her stomach and a lump forms in her throat. It takes her a few minutes to find her voice.

"What do you mean? You're going on your own, Kareem and leaving us here. You can't be serious. Are you joking?" Even as she asks the question, she knows what his answer will be.

"I only found out yesterday, Lou, and there was no point in saying anything before the trip was confirmed, and then we had a meeting this morning."

"So, what are you saying? You're going alone?"

Louise persists, though she knows it is pointless. Fear and dread rise up in her body and, with it, a sense of disbelief. It's as if events are conspiring against her to make life harder than it already is.

"The training course is in Washington for nineteen days and a group of us have been selected to go," he explains, avoiding her actual question.

She listens, trying desperately to assemble her thoughts into a coherent state.

"What about me and Sami if we can't go with you? Louise can feel the anger simmering inside, but she understands it has to be contained for the sake of little Sami. Kareem will go ahead with his plans in any event and she will be the one left to deal with her emotions. Still, she wishes to let him know how she feels about his upcoming trip.

"Kareem, how do you expect us to manage while you're away?"

With great difficulty, Louise avoids raising her voice, so she lowers her tone, trying to keep it steady. A plethora of thoughts come rushing into her mind at breakneck speed like a swarm of ravaging locusts coming to strip the crops bare. What vestiges of hope and positivity she has are being inexplicably stripped away.

Oh God, she thinks, what if Sami gets sick or needs to see a doctor, or what if…? Suddenly, the thought is overtaken by another, equally unsettling one. What if the family is horrible to her and takes advantage of Kareem's absence? A lump is stuck in her throat, preventing her from speaking, but she swallows it, pushing against a desire to give way and reveal her vulnerable state by allowing the tears to flow unchecked.

Her heart begins to pound in her chest, and a fear unlike anything she has ever experienced grips her. Her husband is speaking, but she is only half listening. Louise is not one for public displays of emotion, preferring to keep her sorrow private, but her inner turmoil feels overwhelming. Suddenly, Louise feels the stinging heat of suppressed tears behind her eyes and is powerless to halt their flow.

"It's work, Louise, what can I do? I would take you both if I could, I really would. Your residency papers are not complete and my job will not allow family to accompany us on training programmes." He hesitates before going on.

"Don't worry, I'll make sure you and Sami have everything you and I need before I go, Lou, I promise."

Wiping her eyes, an unrelenting Louise manages to regain a degree of composure, enough to think a little straighter. Ignoring her husband's reassurances, she addresses him, not caring what she says or how it sounds as the words pour out of her mouth.

"Why don't you think about what you just said, Kareem, about my needs, simple as they are and ask yourself a question?"

Somewhat confused, he looks at her quizzically, emitting a barely audible sigh of exasperation.

"What's this now that you're saying, Louise?" he asks in a condescending tone.

"Kareem, don't pretend to be stupid because you're far from it. Since when exactly have you been thinking about my needs?

Holding his gaze, she intends it to be more of a statement than a question.

He begins to speak, but she carries on dismissively, speaking over his voice. "I'll tell you exactly what I'm saying, Kareem. The truth is you haven't been doing well as a husband; in fact, up to now, you've done nothing for me to make my life easier or more enjoyable. That's not to mention the bad temper and your behaviour, how you speak to me in front of your family."

"What do you want from me, Louise?"

"That's a silly question, Kareem and you know it."

"I haven't been a priority for you since I arrived. I'm still not; you make that obvious nearly every day. Now, you tell me you're taking off, just like that."

He puts up his hand in a gesture of annoyance.

"It's my work, you know that."

While Louise is speaking, he looks all around him but not at her.

She pauses deliberately to punctuate the conversation and give him the space to say something, though he appears to have nothing useful to add.

"I feel like a prisoner in your country, Kareem, no, actually, in your house," she corrects. "I'm beginning to think that I don't belong here and maybe I should never have come in the first place."

She can tell he is angry now, that she has struck a chord, but surprisingly, he manages to hold his temper, which is out of character.

The conversation is interrupted by Sami's crying coming from the bedroom that he shares with his parents. Waking up in the darkened room, he is already searching for his mother's face and has begun sucking his tiny fist in an attempt to self-sooth. Feeling disheartened, Louise rises and goes to attend to their baby son.

Lifting him from his pram, she feels the instant weight of responsibility amid the chaos, a reminder of how much he depends on her for his life.

His pram is an old-fashioned but attractive contraption that she liked as soon as she set eyes on it. She had spotted it on display in the window of 'Chicco', an Italian baby-shop in the city, driving by in the car. Along with a blue, shiny bath and a few other essentials, they were the only purchases she made on her return from the shop the following day on an excursion of necessity.

Rather than follow Louise into the bedroom, Kareem stays sulking in the other room.

When she returns in a while with Sami, her mother-in-law is sitting down with the tea-tray arranged in front of her. She passes some incidental remark to Louise, who answers politely, though she is not in the mood for small talk. Putting Sami down beside his father, she goes to the kitchen to prepare his bottle. Having drunk his fill, Sami is content to sit on his mother's lap while she turns the earlier events over in her mind.

Bored with listening to her in-laws, she takes Sami and retires to her room for the remainder of the afternoon. She settles on her bed with Sami lying contentedly beside her. Every now and then, she pauses to talk to him and stroke his plump, little hand. Assuming her maternal instinct has been satisfactorily activated, she still worries about being a 'good enough' mother, but Saoirse has reassured her, telling her not to worry because an unbidden bond will form of its own accord. Such assurances have made all the difference, and sure enough, as the days roll into weeks, Louise grows more confident as a mother, able to interpret baby language and how to decipher its various meanings. Presently, she sets about getting Sami ready for his bath, a nightly ritual she looks forward to.

The sight of those chubby, little arms and his gentle wriggling in the water never fails to delight his mother, a welcome proof she has not lost her sense of wonderment. He appears to like the water and tends to sleep really peacefully after his warm bath. Once he has been carefully dried, Louise delights in sprinkling some fresh-scented powder on her son's soft, velvet skin, marvelling at how he is growing by the day and beginning to make smoother movements with his legs.

It is a couple of days before the subject of Kareem's upcoming trip is revisited and Louise has had a couple of days to think about everything by the time they speak to one another again.

Undoubtedly, her husband is hoping the time-lapse might serve to quieten his wife, and if he is lucky, she might even have come to terms with his imminent trip. That would allow him an opportunity to focus on his preparations and not on her.

However, Kareem fails to realise that his trip to the US acts as a catalyst, sparking a greater fall-out than either of them is prepared for.

SIXTEEN

A December Deception

Deceit is the false road to happiness, and all the joys we travel through to vice, like fairy banquets, vanish when we touch them.

— Aaron Hill

The door to Louise's bedroom remains shut. The 25th of December is drawing to a close, and soon, Christmas will have passed unnoticed. In faraway places, the festive season and good cheer are in full swing. Not here, though. Before long, the year, too, will be over, endings making way for new beginnings. Louise, ordinarily full of optimism at this time of year, feels no joy on the eve of St. Stephen, after whom she is named.

The temperature has cooled considerably, averaging around twenty degrees by midday in the winter sun. The previous days have been dull with grey skies and a gathering wind has signalled a sandstorm due to blow in from the desert. Eventually it hits but leaves almost as quickly, depositing a film of rust-coloured sand and dust behind on every surface. The rising storm seems to stir up a tide of emotion from deep inside Louise and she wishes for the day, of all days, to end so she can commit it to the past.

Feigning a sick stomach, Louise tells her in-laws she is resting and not to bother with lunch for her, having not the slightest intention of leaving her room until night falls. As much as she dislikes her dull surroundings, in some strange way, she has managed to make them her own, apart from which she has no desire to spend the day in the company of her in-laws.

The lock on her bedroom door was broken for a long time, but she insisted before Kareem left that it be repaired. It at least has put a stop to the unannounced intrusions of her sister-in-law's and ensured a little privacy for herself.

Two weeks have passed since Kareem set off for the US, leaving his anxious wife and six-week-old baby behind. On the morning he left, there were tears, plenty of them, followed by hours of contemplation and soul-searching within the confines of her sparse surroundings, the place she spends her hours alone with Sami.

The days are long and arduous, and her baby son either sleeps in his pram or lies beside her on the bed. To combat her boredom, she continues to immerse herself in books, reading voraciously, which helps to keep her distracted and calm.

During dull December days, Louise is weighed down by the cruel, raw touch of despair. It hangs heavily on her shoulders, like a cloak, bearing down on her spirit in a way that feels alien to her. The one thing that brings a smile to her lips is her infant son as he begins to smile and has an abundant supply for his mother. The sight of those chubby, little cheeks and bright eyes breaks the spell of gloom.

There are surreal moments when she questions who she is, barely recognising herself, conflicted between the person of a few months ago whom she knew so well or thought she did and, alas, the one that has falsely imposed itself on her. Overwhelmed by the inconsistencies between her profound personal beliefs and newly acquired situation, she struggles to cope with the nuances of contradiction and ideas presented to her on a daily basis.

At night, she lies awake, alive and alert to every single noise, her body tense, her mind reactive. Not a creak or rustle sounds inside the house but she hears it; nothing goes unnoticed. She knows an army of roaches, those horrible things she hates and fears most, lurk despicably in the darkest corners, scurrying noiselessly across the tiled floors, but she is ready in case one of a winged variety decides to settle on her person. It happened once already, shortly after her arrival and she was so traumatised that her screams had woken up the household.

At a rational level, she knows the infernal insect will do her no harm, but at another less innocuous level, the mere sight of one sends her headlong into the grip of an inexplicable panic that sets her heart racing and sends shivers down the length of her spine.

Inside her bedroom, a tiny, shuttered window positioned high in the wall is kept shut at night to keep out nocturnal offenders. Outside, a world of nightly activity is thriving when she should be sleeping. The smallest of creatures seem to make the loudest, most disturbing noises, ignorant to the fact that they trouble the nightly stillness of her room. It could be the chirping of a male cricket in search of his mate or a green desert frog calling to attract a female with his equally seductive song. Sometimes, it is the deep, throaty croak of a toad foraging for insects and small lizards. A clowder of feral cats trumps all with their tuneless caterwauling throughout the night, but as dawn approaches, they slink furtively away to seek out their crepuscular prey before the rest of the world begins to stir.

Between hunting and courtship rituals, Louise is alone with nature, a silent listener in the dark room, except for a broad flood of moonlight streaming in. Lying there, she is reminded of the lonely traveller in de La Mare's poem, who finds himself in an eerie, unknown place, waiting by the door for an answer to his urgent knocking. Eventually, he has to go away without an answer.

Sudden, uninvited thoughts of death enter her mind, like demons, striking fear into her where, before, none had existed. They seem only to flirt with her sanity and jar indiscriminately on some inherent sense of safety, thereby arousing wild and unpleasant apprehensions of the imagination. Surely, there is no better time for a fanciful notion to influence an impressionable part of the mind than when its owner is thrust into isolation.

Louise chases the morbid thoughts from her mind, though it means sometimes having to get quietly out of bed so as not to wake Sami. To break the chain of thought, she might switch on the night lamp and tiptoe about the room before sitting back in bed.

What if she becomes ill or, worse, her baby boy? Who will look after them? How would she contact Kareem urgently? What about her family? If something were to happen to one of them? Round and round, the thoughts swirl in her head, one leading provocatively to another until she finally falls into a fitful sleep.

She rises early, and by mid-morning, having washed, dressed and attended to Sami, she sits with her in-laws on the outer porch until it is time for lunch. The fresh air is a poor substitute for actually being outdoors, but nevertheless, Louise is glad of it; it is better than none at all.

Because there are no proper footpaths in the surrounding area where she lives, only uneven, sandy tracts, it is impossible to wheel a pram. She had tried venturing out alone once in the early days, and it turned out to be a total disaster. Kareem was at work, and she felt like some fresh air. As she headed for the door, her mother-in-law fell into a panic, blocking her exit and thereupon, quite a drama ensued. On the morning in question, Sharif happened to be home and heard the furore. After much wrangling between him and his mother in front of the hall door while a helpless Louise looked on, he decided to accompany her, mainly to appease his mother.

Within ten minutes, they were back in the house, only this time it was Louise who decided to return, with an understanding of why her mother-in-law was so against her going out in the first place. Apart from being the only woman in the street and uncovered, to make matters worse, she felt like a pariah, some sort of target, since all eyes were locked on her as she moved uncomfortably and self-consciously along. Walking beside her, Sharif undoubtedly felt the discomfort too, aware of the attention she was attracting, but as long as he was there, they could only risk a sly, lascivious glance. Louise never again ventured out in the area and her mother-in-law was saved the embarrassment.

She misses Saoirse desperately, as she knew she would. Two hours spent in the company of her in-laws usually passes quickly, and once she has picked at some food, she retreats to her room, beset with an attack of tiredness that is likely the result of sleepless nights. When she emerges again, it is early evening, time to make a cup of tea and prepare Sami's night-time bottles. She looks forward to bathing him because it usually settles him for the night. Fortunately, he is placid; otherwise, life would be more taxing for her than it already is.

Later on, when Sami is finally settled for the night and sleeping soundly, Louise thinks back to the day she called on Saoirse to break the news of Kareem's trip. What a day to remember; it is unlikely she will ever forget it. Struggling to get used to the idea of her husband's looming trip, she was not expecting to be treated to a further, unwelcome surprise.

After the two girls had their mid-morning tea and 'twabaa' with Azisa, they retired upstairs to Saoirse's quarters to have a chat, leaving Azisa to do her household chores.

Louise could hardly wait to tell her friend about Kareem's trip and how disappointed and upset she was at the prospect of staying alone with her infant son. She felt grateful though to have a friend with whom she could talk about things.

When they had settled, and Sami was put down for a nap, Louise recounted the circumstances surrounding Kareem's imminent trip to the US and the fact that she would not be going with him. According to Kareem, her documents were incomplete and she could not travel, and baby Sami seemed to be an added complication. Ending on a note of resignation, she begrudgingly accepted the explanation her husband had given. However, Louise failed to notice the subtle change of expression that crossed Saoirse's face while she listened attentively.

"Anyway, I can spend the odd day with you, Saoirse. If I ask Kareem, I'm sure he can arrange for one of his brothers to drop me off and return later. It's the least he can do."

As she listened to her friend, alarm bells immediately sounded in Saoirse's head, especially at this suggestion. With a sinking feeling in her stomach, she quietly deliberated how on earth she would respond to her friend without causing more upset.

"Did Kareem say anything else, Louise? Has he mentioned that Sadeek is not going by himself on the trip?"

Saoirse was careful how she framed the question, sensing something was amiss and hating the idea of unintentionally hurting her friend. At the same time, she had to be honest.

"What, no, he never said," Louise faltered a second, a look of surprised confusion on her face.

Saoirse crossed the room to where a large jug stood on a side table. In an attempt to stall and gather her thoughts, she poured out two glasses of water, handing one to Louise. Avoiding going into too much detail about the trip, she knew that Louise would eventually work it all out for herself.

"I'm going myself, with Sadeek, to the US and then home to Dublin for a holiday."

Saoirse threw her friend a quick glance before rushing on.

"I know Louise, that's not what you were expecting to hear. Seeing her friend's stricken expression, she felt guilty for having to tell her at all but she had no choice. Guilt was soon replaced by annoyance towards Kareem, but she dared not show it or risk making things worse. Yet, she felt a deep concern for her friend and tried to explain things for the sake of clarity.

"Initially, I thought yourself and little Sami would be going. Actually, I hoped we might be together on the trip, and now I'm so sorry you're not going, Louise, for whatever reason. I really don't know what else to say to you."

She added in a desperate attempt to smooth over the rough-sounding edges. Saoirse felt uncomfortable and hated being the bearer of such unpleasant news. Louise needed understanding, the best she could offer in the situation. Suspicious of Kareem's motives, she was reminded again that there was something about him she had never liked.

On the bed, Louise sat silent and motionless, her eyes watering as she tried to absorb the impact of Saoirse's words, but it was hard. A little time and thought were needed to soak up all the minute but significant details that were attendant upon her friend's revelation. Saoirse stepped out onto the balcony to allow her friend a few moments of space to gather her thoughts.

When she returned, Louise saw her discomfiture and forced a smile. "Saoirse, don't worry about anything you said, please, it's not your problem, honestly, why should you feel bad? Look, I won't lie, I envy you heading away, especially being reunited with family over the New Year, but at the same time, I'm genuinely glad for you, though I'm really going to miss you." She tried to steady her trembling voice.

"I know you will, Louise. Obviously, you had no idea I was planning on going away. It's a bit of a shock."

Louise nodded vigorously at her friend.

"I hated being the one to tell you but you understand why I thought it best to wait and say nothing, don't you?"

"Of course, I get it, Saoirse. I can't imagine, though, why Kareem never told me; he should have."

Louise had a strange feeling in her stomach, a familiar gut instinct telling her that something was not right with the story. It occurred to her that it was not the first time her husband had lied to her, but it would not be easy to prove. She recognised it as one of those situations where you felt a certainty about something but were powerless to substantiate it. Though furious, she tried hard to keep a lid on it for the sake of her friend, not to make her feel awkward. Besides her anger, Louise experienced a deep sense of betrayal and the very fact that Kareem withheld the information about Saoirse was, as she saw it, an admission of guilt in itself.

"It occurred to me, Louise, that if Kareem were to see me as interfering, it might only annoy him and ultimately affect our friendship and neither of us wants that."

"Yeah, no, of course not, you're right, I hear you," Louise responded with a genuine note of understanding, relieved they had cleared things up.

Weeks before, Sadeek had already begun making plans for himself and his wife to travel together. They intended to spend Christmas in the US and then travel to Ireland, where Sadeek would stay a week, leaving his wife behind for an extended holiday, before returning alone. Sadeek had earlier shared his intentions with Kareem, assuming he would have similar plans, but he was taken aback when there was no mention of Louise and the baby accompanying him. From the outset, Sadeek had a sense that Kareem was being deliberately vague, so he was reluctant to press him further. A little later, his suspicions were confirmed and he then confided in his wife. They agreed it was better to remain silent about the trip and wait for Louise to mention it since neither of them understood what exactly was going on.

As the weeks passed, Saoirse, to her great surprise, realised that her friend knew nothing about the imminent trip. She felt it was not her business, nor was it appropriate to break the news to her friend as long as her husband was silent on the matter. So, she decided to hold fast until Louise spoke to her first, and sure enough, it came to pass.

The time soon arrived when they had to say their goodbyes. Beforehand, Saoirse suggested taking letters back to Louise's family, so she set about writing them in readiness for her friend's departure.

"Thanks, Saoirse, for everything you've done for Sami and me over the past weeks. I don't think I could have managed without you."

"Of course you could, don't be silly, I enjoyed it. Taking Sami in her arms she hugged him close and planted a kiss on both cheeks before handing him back to his mother. Saoirse knew that Louise was hurting badly and sensed the silent disapproval of her husband, but neither of them said anything further about the matter.

"Look after yourself, Louise and little Sami, until I see you again soon."

On that parting note, the two friends hugged, and Saoirse walked briskly away, disappearing into Sadeek's waiting car.

The following morning, a driver came to pick Kareem up just after dawn to take him to the airport, where he would board a flight to Germany in transit to the US. His mother was already up, true to habit, rising at dawn, for the *al –fajr* prayer, before sunrise. They both said their goodbyes to him at the front door. Louise, neither amorously nor kindly disposed toward her husband, was content to cooly wish him a safe journey. A heated argument had flared between them a couple of days before and Louise accused him of being disingenuous. She was convinced he did not want to take them because it was simply too inconvenient, so to avoid the hassle, he spun a story that would get him off the hook. When she put it to him, he denied it, secure in the knowledge that she was powerless to do anything about it.

Going back inside, she got back into bed, unable to curb the unstoppable tears that flowed freely until there were none left to spill. With the departure of her husband and her friend, she felt utterly bereft.

Sometime later and rather inexplicably, a sense of calm descended on her, likely due to a tumultuous release of pent-up tensions and frustrations which needed to be discharged. She felt the purgative affects of a long, overdue catharsis,however, it took a bit of time for her thoughts to cohere in a clear, intelligible way.

Something died inside Louise the day Kareem left. She reflected on the quality of their relationship, and more than ever, it felt like she was married to a stranger. Could a union of two people be sustainable when the intentions for pursuing the relationship may be propitious for one but at odds with the intentions of the other? Could you make someone a priority when all you really are is an option?

Louise had witnessed her husband's temper, grown sick of his moodiness and disagreeable manner. She came to recognise an arrogance that he brought to bear on much of what came within his ambit. If she was being really honest, she had caught a glimpse of it in the early days of their brief courtship.

However, now that the scales have fallen from her eyes, she has to confront the fact that she is only latterly coming to know the person of her husband.

She knows he has let her down badly, and despite the realisation, it is better to know it sooner than later.

At the end of a painful foray into uncertain territory, she concludes that her life now is incompatible with her internal beliefs. How she is going to resolve the dissonance between her deep-rooted principles and daily realities, she does not yet know. A clash of two opposing positions is difficult to negotiate.

Louise is growing weary of the mental gymnastics, of turning things over again and again, in her mind, trying to make sense of things where there is none. For the time being, though, she must wait with great forbearance for her husband to return.

SEVENTEEN

A Test of Strength

In the depth of winter, I finally learned that within me,
there lay an invincible summer.

— Albert Camus

By the time Kareem returns from his American trip, Louise's spirit is close to broken. Yet, despite everything, she is relieved to see her husband. In those first hours and days following his arrival, having been starved of social interaction, she almost forgets the cause of her despair, almost but not quite.

She is vulnerable, craving tactile stimulation and intimacy with the man she married and longs for a chance to reaffirm that she is alive and sentient. It feels like the right thing to do, to welcome him home and put aside any negative thoughts.

Louise has been through so much in Kareem's absence that she is loath to spark an argument so soon after his return. So, heeding her internal voice, she knows that once the lid lifts on her emotions, there is no containing them. The explosion likely to ensue could be ugly, so she decides to leave it for another day. Despite that, it is to a different woman Kareem returns.

Sadly for Louise, it is not long before Kareem lapses into his old habits. There are renewed rounds of cards, meetings and reasons for him to be away in the evenings while she is home alone with Sami once again.

Late one night, Kareem returns home to find Louise sitting on the bed waiting for him. Her mind is made up. She can no longer endure her life as it is, tired of his lame excuses. In her head, it feels like a switch has been turned on and she is prepared for confrontation.

As usual, her husband strolls into the house as if nothing is wrong, mistaking his wife's cool, calm exterior for something else. She knows meeting him with blunt anger will serve no constructive purpose for her except to escalate into another useless row. Without preamble, she tells him in a firm, measured tone that she has made a huge mistake by marrying him and she has no intention of staying with him as he is. The relationship is over. It is to be her final word on the subject of their marriage.

Louise is not surprised by his reaction to her words. His face becomes sullen, and like so many times before, he starts swearing, a litany of profanities and insults spewing angrily from his mouth. Glaring at his wife with contempt, he levels all sorts of ugly and unfair accusations at her, but she holds her tongue, mindful that Sami is asleep in his pram; she wants to avoid a ruckus.

Determined to listen to no more of her husband's vitriol, Louise sweeps out of the room without another word, leaving him to consider the ultimatum she has given.

A couple of hours later, after he has had time to settle down and fall asleep Louise returns to the bed she shares with him. There is nowhere else for her to go, so she slides delicately in and settles on her side for fear he might waken. If only there was another place for her to sleep.

Repelled by the sight and sound of her husband but having no other choice, she has to lie beside him.

EIGHTEEN

A Family of Things

Friendship is a sheltering tree.

– **Samuel Taylor Coleridge**

Azisa sits cross-legged, in typical Arab fashion, gently rocking a four-month-old Sami on her lap. Saoirse, her daughter-in-law, and Louise chat warmly with her as they sip tea with fresh mint from her garden. The weather for the time of year is mild and the morning sunshine filters into the room from the courtyard outside, lending a pleasant aspect to their gathering. Louise is feeling particularly pleased with life because it is her first visit to the house after a long spell, and she has missed both women a lot, in different ways.

Since Sami was born, Louise has become a frequent visitor to the home of the Jebelli woman who is speaking to her baby son as if he understands her every word. Curiously, he responds to the words by shifting his gaze and softly babbling, a hint of a smile playing about his small mouth. Fortunately, his mother has discovered in Azisa, and Salma, her daughter, the substitute family that she hasn't found in Kareem's.

The relationship has evolved accidentally but organically through her regular visits to Saoirse. It all began with Sadeek inviting them over for dinner at his family home. After that first visit, Louise never looked back, having found Saoirse's in-laws warm and welcoming towards her, the atmosphere contrasting sharply with that of her own in-laws.

Naturally, Kareem is happy enough to drop his wife and son off at Saoirse's house whenever she wants to spend the day and returns to pick them up in the evenings. It gets him off the hook and lessens his sense of responsibility, making life easier for him and keeping his wife occupied.

On first meeting Azisa, Louise instantly liked her, sensing a kind, wholesome earthiness about the woman. As she got to know Azisa, she grew comfortable in the company of the tribal woman whose efforts at hospitality far exceed those of her own in-laws. Azisa is unsparing in the kindness and warmth she shows Louise and Sami, making her feel privileged to be accepted into the bosom of her family.

When she visits, she finds a calm atmosphere strikingly at odds with the space she leaves behind, which is always tense, noisy and dramatic, not to mention its complete lack of privacy. Kareem's teenage brothers are loud, the older ones spoilt, and the grandchildren, not surprisingly, are wild and out of control. Of course, her mother-in-law presides over the mayhem, spending a lot of time giving out about one thing or another. As for the *Haj,* Kareem's father, who is head of the household in name at least, he is absent most of the day, seldom concerning himself with domestic issues except when absolutely necessary, usually in an attempt to chastise his wife and rein in the considerable influence she exerts over their offspring.

It is no surprise, therefore, that Louise feels relaxed and relieved at the opportunity to spend time in the company of the *Jebelli,* 'mountain' woman and her family. Apart from Salma and Sadeek, there is only one other son, so their family is considered small by usual standards. Because women congregate separately from men, Louise had little contact with Azisa's husband initially, except when crossing the courtyard. He would acknowledge her presence with a broad smile and enquire after the *walad,* or 'boy' in Arabic, checking on his progress. Although he is considered a scholar of Islamic doctrine and law in the surrounding community, it seems to Louise that he wears the title lightly with as much dignity as his wife is generous-spirited.

Azisa is a great cook and she finds a most appreciative fan in Louise who looks forward to the delicious dishes she prepares with such care and attention.

Most afternoons, she is to be found kneading dough for her bread before laying it out on large trays, too large to fit in her own oven, so they are dispatched to one of the local bakeries to be cooked in a giant oven before arriving back in time for supper. The evening meal frequently consists of a tasty soup or sauce served with beans or eggs. In addition, there is an abundant supply of home-pickled olives, chilli, capers, figs and other delicacies prepared by Azisa.

The water sourced from a nearby well is sweet, so-called to distinguish it from the tap water which is salty and undrinkable. Actually, it is a task entrusted to men a lot of the time - to fetch water and keep several filled containers stored in the house. At intervals throughout the day, water is transferred from a container and poured into urns, where it stays at a cool temperature for drinking.

Today is a bright, sunny morning in early February. It is the first day in a long time that Louise has felt her mood lighter, and she is beginning to recognise herself again. After enjoying the brew, Azisa rises to clear away the tea things, and Saoirse slips upstairs to check on something, leaving Louise in the company of her own thoughts to soak up the atmosphere of the morning.

Louise can smell the fresh mint from a tree in the far corner of the courtyard garden, perfectly positioned to perform best in full sun whilst sending out its pungent, pleasant perfume. It is customary to drink it in Azisa's house, and Louise loves the cool effect it leaves behind, lingering long on her tongue. Traditionally, the tea is served three times; the amount of time left steeping gives each glass a unique flavour, so aptly described by the native *Maghrebi* proverb; '*The first glass as gentle as life, the second as strong as love, the third is as bitter as death.*'

Carrying Sami in her arms, she exits the small sitting room whose doors open onto the courtyard beyond. Breathing in the fresh morning air, she imagines early spring in her home country, the green, lush grassland strewn with newborn lambs or ewes waiting to give birth. She visualises daffodils and tulips popping up everywhere and hedgerows bursting into life, heralding the arrival of spring.

Unlike European gardens, often designed for walking in, traditional Arabic gardens are intended for rest and contemplation. After ambling around for a bit, she sits down in the open shaded porch that forms part of the spacious courtyard. Setting her son down on his blanket beside her, she looks around for a few moments and listens to Sami gurgling happily. And it seems to Louise like the perfect place to be alone with one's private thoughts. She is so delighted to be back in this house after spending weeks virtually alone in her room except for Sami, waiting for Kareem to return and then Saoirse.

On such a glorious morning, the past few weeks feel almost like a distant memory, to think that she had been so unhappy and in such a dark space. Fortunately, the tempest passed, skies cleared, and she was able to witness the dawning of a new day. Ironically, she feels stronger as a result, certainly changed. Such resilience can only be appreciated retrospectively and with a degree of incredulity on her part.

Looking up, she takes in the clear sky, a giant, blue canopy, high above the enclosed garden where she sits, protected by the shade of a tall, elegant date palm, its glossy spread gently tipping against the modest *mashrabiya* that forms the outer façade of Saoirse's upper quarters. It is a typical architectural feature of an Arabic house, a type of projecting window that looks down on the courtyard below. Without doubt, it is an attractive sight enclosed with carved latticework and fashioned in wood. Louise loves its ornamental, artistic style, and the design serves as an effective device to allow for the passage of cool air to pass through the house.

In the far corners of the courtyard stand clumps of small fruit trees, lemon, fig and pomegranate. The olive or 'sacred' trees, two of them, stand together, small and squat in a large, soil-filled square, which has been purposely dug out at some point to plant them. They are likely to have been there long before Azisa acquired the house. Their presence is more symbolic than anything else, she suspects. The tree and its precious fruit boast a long and prestigious history, referenced in all the holy books, dating as far back as the Bronze Age and Greek antiquity. Scattered about the courtyard are numerous evergreen shrubs, growing in their own area of dug-out soil, acacia, myrtle santolina and exotic Arabian jasmine, while others thrive in huge earthenware pots; aloe vera and bougainvillea, its vigorous spread barely contained, adding splashes of flowering colour to the surrounding glossy foliage.

In the centre, a small marble fountain breathes life into the garden; its circular bowl is finished with hand-painted ceramic tiles, most likely sourced from neighbouring Tunisia. Standing dormant, having long ceased to perform its sprinkling function, Louise can imagine how it was in its former glory, the gentle sound of cascading water, since it is still aesthetically pleasing to the eye, even though it is now silent. For Louise, it amounts to a sensory experience, the water, shade, exotic plants, and aromatic herbs providing fond and treasured memories of a beautiful Arabic garden, a place of stillness and peace in an imperfect world.

Louise feels at ease in Azisa's Garden, grateful to have come through the trials of the past weeks, surprising even herself. At one point, she thought that she might lose her mind because she felt trapped and alienated, her very identity threatened, but hope alone had kept her sanity intact. Now, she feels as if she has grown up rather suddenly. The things she has recently seen and done have wrought profound changes, causing her to evaluate most things in her life, particularly the first lessons of love and loss.

Louise hadn't thought before about how life's losses and innocence are related, and that once something has been irretrievably lost, as with innocence, it cannot return in the same form. Remaining ignorant, and there is a multitude of reasons to stay so, leaves a person unable to imaginatively grasp the perils of life and death, along with a tendency to view the human condition through a rose-tinted lens. It seems then that innocence, like loss, goes deep, deeper into the psyche, creating a somewhat mysterious functioning of the imagination. In their wake are hope and the pursuit of meaning, two inseparable entities, which, lead us to a greater agency and self-knowledge.

Louise has lost her innocence but discovered hope and the liberating power of truth. As for meaning itself, it would come later.

Indeed, she feels different, that much is certain. There seems to be little left of the person she was several months previously compared with the person she has become.

Startled out of her reverie by Saoirse appearing in front of her with a large bag, she perks up.

"A penny for them, Louise. You're lost in thought."

"Oh, nothing important, just enjoying the fresh air and thinking how nice it is to be back," she admits, laughing.

"Well, I guess that's important enough, after all, isn't it?" Saoirse replies as she sits down next to her friend and smiles down at Sami. "He's really come on since I last saw him. You must be dying to open the bag and see what's inside," she teases.

Louise smiles back and leans over to move the bag closer so she can open it, but she pauses for a second.

"You're so good to bring this back. It's heavy. You didn't have to," Louise replies excitedly.

"Look, it was no trouble. I knew how much it would mean to you and especially your mother, to bring it. You can do the same for me sometime. Now open it and have a quick look. There are letters, too; I put them in my handbag, let me go and get them."

Louise opens the bag, barely able to contain herself with excitement, like a child filled with wonder when opening a bag of candy or a stocking full of toys. She is not disappointed, for her mother had filled the bag full of treats and surprises for her and Sami. Overwhelmed, Louise takes everything out one by one. There are little summer suits for Sami with matching hats, vests, shoes, sets of dribblers and other bits and pieces. Folded carefully and wrapped in white tissue paper, separate from the other baby clothes, are little cardigans, instantly recognisable as the flawless work of her mother's own hands. Louise's eyes water when she lifts them up, feeling the soft, fine merino wool between her fingers. They are exquisite, in lemon and light blue, with a slip-stitch pattern and a row of tiny pearl buttons.

"Your mother is a fantastic knitter. She showed me some of her work, what a finish," Saoirse remarks.

"Yeah, she loves it. She knits for all the family and even made things for my dolls when I was a child. She can do anything with a pair of needles," Louise proudly insists.

They sit a while until Louise empties the bag and looks at the things her mother has sent, amongst them some summer tops, a sundress, cotton nightdresses, a pair of pretty sandals and other useful things. Well, secured in bubble-wrap at the bottom of the bag, her mother had packed a box of teabags, some different flavoured jellies and custard, tins of sardines in tomato sauce, Irish crisps and biscuits, some of her favourites. Arleen hadn't forgotten about her either. Being aware of her sister's love of reading, she included two carefully chosen books that she knew Louise would enjoy. A thick letter and a belated birthday card are resting just inside the front cover. She is so grateful to them both and over the moon with everything, unable to remember a time in her entire life when she had felt so pleased to receive a gift.

At Saoirse's suggestion, they go upstairs and once inside the bedroom, she hesitates in front of a new wooden closet. It occurs to Louise that there is something else to be pleased about besides a new wardrobe. Clasping her hands together excitedly, Saoirse looks at Louise with a big smile.

"I've got some news for you, Louise." After a tiny pause, she announces it with pride.

"I'm pregnant."

Before she has time to add anything, Louise throws her arms around her friend in genuine delight. "That's fantastic news, Saoirse. I'm so thrilled for you. Have you told Azisa yet?"

"I told her when we arrived and they were delighted, of course, their first grandchild. Azisa wanted to tell you this morning as soon as you arrived, you can imagine, but I asked her to wait until you and Sami were relaxed and to give you a chance to open your parcel. I didn't want to hijack your moment, after waiting for so long."

"Well, I'm so happy for you and Sadeek".

All the while, Sami follows them with his eyes in his propped-up position and nestling securely between two cushions. It is almost time for lunch, and they are reminded of it by the tempting aroma of herbs and spices that reach their nostrils in Azisa's kitchen below. They know she is cooking up a delicious storm since it is a celebratory occasion.

No sooner have they finished looking at some of Saoirse's purchases than Salma's voice can be heard from below, summoning them to eat. Taking Sami with them, the two friends head downstairs to find a fine spread awaiting them. Putting Sami in his bouncer, Louise walks over to Azisa and offers her congratulations.

"*Alf Mabrouk Azisa, Mubarak.*" Shaking the woman's hand, she kisses her on both cheeks. The older woman replies with a wide smile, showing her genuine elation.

"*Barak Allah fik,*" she says, invoking God's blessing.

As they sit down to eat, a loud and joyous ululation is heard ringing out over the courtyard walls, to the outer reaches of the nearby minaret. High on a balcony, the muezzin raises his head in silent contemplation, a book of surahs open on his lap. There, he will wait to call the faithful to prayer, where they will face the *quibla* before leading them in the '*salat al-asr*', or afternoon prayer.

The *Adhan*, which translates as 'call to prayer', is without doubt the most distinctive and soulful soundscape Louise has ever heard. The rendering of its sweet, melodious timbre produces a beautifully haunting effect that feels instantly arresting.

As the small gathering waits for Azisa to finish her silent prayer, they have much to be grateful for on such a glorious spring day.

NINETEEN

The Winds of Change

The fault, dear Brutus, is not in our stars,
but in ourselves that we are underlings.

– 'Julius Ceasar', William Shakespeare

Louise stands on her veranda, overlooking the quiet street as the sun sets over the city and twilight fast approaches. Just below the horizon, a diffusion of wondrous colour, shades of pink and fuchsia, scatter their brilliant rays of light across the evening sky. She can hardly believe it is the same sky she looked at two days ago because, like her world, it appears to have suddenly expanded. That is how it feels after a long spell in virtual seclusion and being cramped into close quarters with Kareem's family. As she looks at the sky, she feels like she has been given a new lease of life, and it is so liberating.

Kareem has gone to pick up some provisions, and Sami is sleeping soundly, a little earlier than usual, having missed his afternoon nap with all the upheaval. It has been a busy day with plenty to do, between giving all of the tiled floors a thorough washing, dusting surfaces and scouring the bathroom and kitchen from top to bottom.

That is just the downstairs part of the house. Louise is not too bothered, content to finally clean her own home, especially since it was beginning to feel like she was doomed to be dependent upon the hospitality of others.

When Kareem finally announces the long-awaited news that he has found a place, she can barely contain her excitement. Two days later, he tells her that her official documents are complete, and she can travel home for a holiday within a few weeks. Louise can hardly believe it, after a long and tiresome journey, things are starting to come together.

Their new apartment comprises the entire top storey of a very large house, once the city residence of a Turkish dignitary and his family who had lived there for many years.

Looking directly across the street from her position on the balcony, it occurs to her that she might as well be in another world marvellously different to the one she has left behind. Admiring the villas, some two-storey residences, and other larger but altogether impressive-looking structures, she is struck by the contrast. They all appear to share some common architectural features, such as flat roofs and spacious courtyard gardens. However, unlike most Western houses, they possess an introverted aspect and are generally surrounded by high walls with gated enclosures to ensure family privacy, an integral element influencing their layout and design. Each house has its own buzzer system to announce the arrival of visitors and ensure extra security, especially since some of the residents are ambassadorial representatives from various countries.

Climate is an additional factor that affects building style. Due to the scorching temperatures, one immediately senses the need to erect as much shelter as possible to shield the inhabitants from the harshness of the environment.

Some houses resemble small castles, with charming outer facades and attractive mashrabiya-style windows, especially on the upper floors. They are characteristic of traditional architecture with a distinctly Islamic twist and are enhanced with the most colourful stained glass.

At the other side of Louise and Kareem's apartment, in what is to become their bedroom, another veranda faces onto a long, leafy street, largely embassy territory, boasting imposing edifices that stand proud, shaded by tall palm trees. Amongst them are a few 'old money' family residences, the elders of which comprise the upper echelons of Libyan society. Generally, the younger occupants are either temporarily in residence or abroad being educated in foreign universities. According to Kareem and other sources, they are living in a prestigious area. However, Louise is not really concerned with prestige or status, caring more for the things in life that cannot be secured with either position or wealth.

An elderly man and his two daughters live close to Louise. They are both pretty and appear quite modern compared to other young women she has seen around the district. On the other side lives a family of three children and their parents; the mother is Egyptian, married to a native man. They have already bumped into one another on the footpath outside and had the opportunity of introducing themselves. Louise is immediately struck by their friendliness, especially the woman who wears an expression of warmth and benevolence that strikes a chord with Louise. When she speaks, her voice is intoned with a wonderfully musical lilt, a kind of sing-song sound interspersed with a series of rising, falling inflexions. Later, Kareem explains it is characteristic of colloquial Egyptian-speak. After welcoming her new neighbours, she extends an invitation to call and drink a coffee with them as soon as they are settled. At that point, Louise could not have imagined how her life would become intertwined with this woman from Alexandria.

The physical move is easy simply because there is not that much to remove. The sum of Louise's belongings are the things she had brought with her, and since she has added very little to that, apart from Sami's clothes, a new cot and a few other possessions, it takes just a few hours and a couple of trips.

The house is empty of any furnishings or conveniences, which lends it an air of spaciousness, emphasised by the high ceilings and the faint echo of their voices. The entrance opens into a large sitting room off which a long hall runs the length of the house, until it turns a corner and ends with a kitchen off to the right. Midway along the hall, there are narrow stairs that lead to the upper floor. At the top, a double glass door opens onto a very large, open porch, enclosed by a high, stone-cladded wall with a decorative white finish. The floor resembles white marble but is actually covered in ceramic tiles with a porcelain finish in grey matt. She thinks how nice it would be to sit up there in the coolness of an evening with Saoirse and enjoy the privacy.

While she cleans and arranges their belongings, Kareem is out, mainly to purchase new crockery, pots and pans for cooking, along with some other kitchen utensils. Their sleeping arrangements for the moment are less than ideal. Louise, not being used to sleeping so close to the ground, will have to make do with two thick mattresses borrowed from Zanib's house, and Sami will sleep beside them in his cot. Within the first few days of their move, Kareem orders a bedroom suite, complete with wardrobes, dressing table and other furnishings, but because Italy is the main supplier of quality, they have to wait a few weeks for it to be dispatched.

Louise makes some mint tea and takes it back to the veranda. She opens out a folding chair and sits down to enjoy the night air. The street below is quiet and peaceful, except for the gentle rustling of trees on the avenue below. In the distance, the sound of a car is barely audible as it slows to a halt, followed by the door slamming shut. She can make out the deep, ethereal hoot of an owl perched further away somewhere in the invisible treetops. A mate responds with a series of warbling hoots, equally distinctive, filling the nocturnal ambience with their soulful duet.

Sitting alone beneath a black, terrestrial sky, Louise looks up to see a sprinkling of glowing celestial bodies scattered here and there. She wonders if the brightest one might be Sirius, the 'Dog Star', known for its bluish-white luminosity. Louise reckons she has never seen it shine quite so bright before. Maybe there is something in the numerous mythologies and beliefs surrounding the 'supposed' sacred star and its connection with ancient civilisations.

Suddenly, a pensive mood captures her, and her thoughts turn to the events of the previous week. Because things are happening so fast, there has been little time to process them adequately. Almost overnight, she has a new home in this strange city and within a week she will be on the move again, going back to her 'real' home, as she regards it still. After almost a year, she is finally to be reunited with her family and is counting down the days.

Smiling to herself, she has reason to feel good. Apart from her imminent trip, her relationship with Kareem appears to have taken a positive turn. For a while, she was pessimistic, fearing the worst, but they are now in a better place. Their relationship is much less fraught with tension these days, and she can only hope that her husband has taken her words and concerns to heart. Faced with the possibility of their marriage ending, he seems to have heard the alarm bells sounding.

Despite the trials and despair Louise experienced, she has come through by her own sheer tenaciousness. Her traumatic experiences had driven her to ask piercing questions in an attempt to find meaning. Although her pain may not be entirely vanquished, she is able to transform it into something useful and creative.

A lot has happened and closing her eyes in brief reflection, she finds it surreal to be sitting here on the balcony thinking about their new place, eager to get going with plans for refurbishment. They have already discussed the work, which is due to begin as soon as they leave and is set to continue over the summer while she is away. Everything should be complete by the time they return, Kareem has assured her.

She is distracted by the low purring sound of a car, and looking over the balcony, she sees Kareem pull into his parking space. Presently, he joins her on the balcony, where they drink tea and chat for a while until it gets late.

Inside, the bedroom is dark save for a gleam of ghostly light. As Louise pulls her t-shirt over her head, she senses Kareem behind her, his warm breath on her neck, and she can feel herself stiffen. With a slow determination, his hands move slowly down her sides and rest on her tummy. She feels his body pressing closer to hers, and with his hand, he opens the button on her jeans. Reaching down, with searching fingers, he finds what he is looking for, his desire peaked. With a silent act of resignation, Louise turns to face her husband to perform her wifely duty.

Kareem is in a lustful mood after a dry spell that has continued for weeks, his appetite now whet. Louise is more interested in 'make-up' words rather than 'make-up' sex, in that order. Nonetheless, they make out for the first time in their new home with the mellow light of a pale moon bathing them in its soft, mysterious light.

For Louise, it is a performance of tremendous will.

Book II

TWENTY

No Place Like Home

The end of all exploring will be to arrive where we started.

– T. S. Eliot

Louise is giddy and lightheaded with excitement, barely able to sit still in her seat with anticipation. The voice of the captain comes over the intercom, his words like music to her ears. Outside, the weather is unusually clement and as the plane begins its descent, the very first sight that comes into view is the great, many hues of green below. Her eyes fill with tears, and she feels her heart swell with pride, overjoyed to finally lay sight of her beloved homeland.

Sinking lower now, she sees the rolling, fertile fields and forests dense with native oak, birch and pine dotted everywhere along the landscape. Louise is truly in love with this lush, emerald land and its fertile soil in a precious and personal way. If she could physically embrace it in her arms, she would. Instead, she holds it in her heart amid tender thoughts and silent words of love.

Louise has a great appreciation of the natural world, especially its beauty and restorative power. It seems to her a sacred thing, a wellspring of restoration that can heal a wayward mind and soothe a troubled soul, its power as deep and perennial as the grass itself.

Butterflies turn over in her stomach while she gazes out at the wonders of her approaching world. Bright rays of late afternoon sunshine are dancing on the waters of Dublin Bay, like diamonds rippling on the surface in a dazzling show of optical brilliance. Suddenly, the aircraft lurches, its whole body beginning to shake, and it starts to descend more quickly. Cruising over the eastern coastline, its engines on idle power, the giant bird glides steadily towards the earth, merging seamlessly into the surrounding lands. Louise holds Sami close, and he sits contentedly on her lap, examining the colourful buttons on her blouse. With every second that passes, Louise feels the heady excitement more intensely, imagining the expectant faces of her nearest and dearest converging in the airport building, waiting to greet her and little Sami, whom they will meet for the first time.

They disembark and move quickly through passport control; before she knows it, there is a barrier separating them. She spots her mother's headscarf, her father's eager face, watching, waiting to lay eyes on their prodigal daughter. Standing tall between them is Arleen, her hand raised in a frantic wave, moving closer, her steps quickening towards them.

"There she is," Arleen exclaims in delight and in a flash, Sami is scooped up by her sister. Louise's arms are free to wrap around her mother first and then her father, who stands affably by, his familiar, genial smile almost melting her heart. Louise senses they are as happy to be reunited with her as she is with them. Sami is unquestionably the one who steals the show and, ironically, as if he knows he is the star act, becomes more animated, smiling and making endless silly noises. Much to Arleen's delight, her attempts at 'peekaboo' are soon rewarded with lively giggles, making certain to elicit their undivided attention on the short journey home.

The first week passes in the blink of an eyelid, and Louise is well and truly settled in her parent's house. They immediately take Sami under their wing, urging her to take some time for herself. Likewise, Sami has no problem adjusting to his grandparents; if anything, he appears to relish all the new-found attention he receives. Louise thinks that having a baby around them brings new colour, adding a sparkle to their otherwise predictable lives, perhaps making them feel youthful again.

She spends a few afternoons going around the shops, has her hair done and catches up with friends. The greatest novelty of all though is to sit in Bewley's coffee house on Grafton Street, where she sips tea and sinks her teeth into one of their delectable buns. It may be one of life's simple pleasures but for her, it's an indulgence she has not had in a year. Lingering there, she watches the world go by from her seat by the window, the atmosphere warm and cosy. Nobody bothers with anyone's business except to drop an occasional friendly smile. It is such a different world from the one she has left.

Louise feels liberated, like herself again, and it feels good. At the same time, she is aware, in her own quiet way, to take nothing in life for granted, ever again.

In tripolitan society, women's movements are restricted, and most of them never venture out unaccompanied by a male relative. The city's cafés are dingy, poky affairs intended for male custom only. Not that she has visited any, having spied them only from a passing car. She remembers them as spaces commandeered by hordes of men drinking strong coffee and engaging in idle chat by day and endless card games by night.

Foreign women, in particular, seem to be easy prey for groups of males whose favourite pastime is to cast leering glances at females, making life very uncomfortable, even dangerous. Louise and her friends had been subjected to plenty of lewd remarks when they ventured out, especially beyond their own locality where they are generally known.

What they failed to understand in words was made clear to them by ogling stares, lecherous looks and even hand signals. There were times they could barely wait to get safely home, having decided to say nothing to their husbands about their unpleasant experiences. In the beginning, they were often angry, feeling slighted and affronted as Western women, something they were not used to in their home countries. In time, they became impervious to remarks passed and simply moved on. There were, however, rare occasions when they retorted in the local tongue and ruffled a lot of feathers since the notion of chastisement by a woman was not well-received.

A fortnight after her arrival, Louise's father organises a trip to the southeast, where they will spend a week on the Hook peninsula. The surrounding countryside is the home of his maternal relations, and much of his early life was spent there. Not surprisingly, he holds a deep attachment to the place where his fondest memories were formed.

Louise's older siblings were fortunate to have spent time there. As children, they had escaped the crowded city to spend their summer holidays walking the meadows and pastures that skirted the farms of their aunts and uncles.

On the way to their destination, they stop for a picnic in a quiet lay-by, cut off from the main road. They find a wooden table to lay out their picnic on and a long bench where they can sit. It is a glorious morning with an azure sky, the sun warm on their faces and only the slightest hint of a breeze. Louise has never regarded herself as a 'city girl', and she is looking forward to spending time in the countryside again. It reminds her of the feeling she had as a child when they would set off, just the three of them. Now they have Sami, and her parents seem well pleased with the new addition. Her mother did no end of fussing before they left with all the paraphernalia she insisted they would need while her father prepared egg mayonnaise sandwiches because he knew they were his daughter's favourite.

It's not long before they arrive at their quaint accommodation, a pretty cottage perched on the side of a low hill facing the sea. They reach the red, painted door by walking under an archway and exit down a narrow path flanked on both sides by a charming little garden, vibrant with the assorted colours of summer flowers in early bloom. Within a half mile along the twisty, narrow road, not far from the lighthouse, is the beach itself. Louise views the overall setting as idyllic, surrounded by verdant fields and high, rocky cliffs that sweep down to the golden sands of Dollar Bay.

"Wow, what a setting. This is what I miss." She says it out loud, forgetting for a moment that she is not alone.

"It's a grand place, alright, and you enjoy it, love." Her father shouts across at her from the far corner.

Looking back over her shoulder, she sees him smile and instinctively knows he understands. She walks round to the rear of the car and helps him unload the luggage. When the last of it is done, he turns to his daughter.

"C'mon in love, and we'll all have a cuppa, then you can go for a nice, quiet walk while the little man has a nap."

"Thanks, Dad, you and Mam are very good. I really appreciate all your help."

"Sure, aren't we glad to have the two of ye? That's what parents are for. Enjoy it while it lasts." He winks at her jokingly.

No sooner have they finished their tea and biscuits but Louise is away down the path, leaving her mother with her knitting and her father reading his paper. With all the excitement and fresh air, Sami is ready for his afternoon nap.

She heads straight for Dollar Bay, the name given to the secluded anchorage that earns its name from the buried treasure of pirates and their ill-fated expedition in the year 1765. It was here that the robbers came ashore under a stormy midnight sky, as historical records would have it and hid their fortune before making haste to Dublin, intending to return at a later stage. However, their escape was scuttled, and after being apprehended in a tavern somewhere along Dublin port, they were finally hanged and later disposed of on Bull Island, off the East Coast. According to local legend, not all of the vast fortune was ever recovered.

Here, in a beautiful little cove, one of Louise's clearest memories was formed. When she looks out to the open sea and along the shoreline, memories come flooding back of times she had dipped in the warm waters of the bay. On one occasion, in particular, she had proudly launched her big, inflatable boat on the water, her father guiding it along so as not to drift too far. She can still see it now, red and white with the enormous face of a tiger in its centre. On a deckchair, with the shelter of the rocks behind her, sits her mother, knitting. Every now and then, she raises her head to look out at them, and they wave back at her.

During these days, Louise falls in love with the places of her childhood, places that hold a special meaning for her. Now she rediscovers them with new eyes, eyes that measure their beauty as one who has been long absent and, on returning, realises with a sense of nostalgia just how special they are. These places bring beauty and brightness to dark corners and help heal her spirit, restoring it to a lighter state of equilibrium.

After a week, they decide to stay on because Louise is reluctant to leave. Each morning after breakfast, she leaves Sami with his grandparents and takes a leisurely stroll down to the beach, where she spends an hour walking from one end to the far stretch of shore, stepping along the low rock pools and collecting seashells. Walking between the rocks, she bathes her feet in the cool, lapping water before sitting on the rocks, the warmth of the early morning sun on her face and shoulders. Early morning stillness steals its way across calm waters where gulls cry and rise proudly above the water. Warm mists break over green hills, lush flower-filled fields where bumble bees dance and butterflies bounce. Fresh forest ferns tower gracefully into clear, blue skies, forming a kaleidoscope of colourful perfection blending harmoniously into the sights and sounds of summer.

In the distance, Louise hears the sound of a dog barking playfully, the whirring of a motorcycle and the far-off drone of a plane, its sound carrying on the wind. There are no other sounds to disturb her early morning solitude, the feeling of being alone with her thoughts, away from the noise and commotion of everyday life. She wishes she could stay here forever, but she knows it is temporary. Nevertheless, she feels refreshed, the cobwebs blown away, her mind cleared of unwanted detritus. At the close of these wonderful days, having cried a few secret tears, walked a lot and ruminated over existential quandaries, home beckons, and she responds with a renewed sense of purpose and a shred of fresh hope for future days.

Being with her parents offers a sense of security. She is also genuinely glad to have the chance to spend quality time with them and do stuff together. Even now, she feels guilty about causing them so much worry, although it was unintentional. Taking off to the other side of the world really was a big deal, and everything about it must have been abhorrent to them. She can see it all now, and what is more, they have spoken about it and ironed out a few issues. Things are smoothed over, possibly helped by the presence of Sami in their lives. In some strange way, he represents for her parents, the son they never had, the one who did not survive.

Louise has spoken to Kareem a few times on the phone, short conversations, mainly about the progress he is making in their new home. Surprisingly, she is not missing her husband, telling herself it is completely normal, rationalising about the novelty of being home and distracted, having no time to think of anything else. She imagines how it might be, just her and Sami, living with her parents, but she chases the notion from her thoughts. Kareem encourages her to prolong her stay for the entire summer to allow him to finish the refurbishments. Louise never questions him but is only too happy to go with his suggestion.

In Louise's dreams these nights, the houses are bright, orderly and full of light compared with the physical elements of dreams in her recent past, which had dark, shadowy interiors with non-descript features. The atmosphere was regularly one of chaos and gloom. In them, she had seen herself surrounded by people but felt a sense of estrangement, which she now finds unsurprising given the state of her emotions at the time. Clearly, in the inner recesses of her mind, something is being processed.

She recalls the famous statement made by Sigmund Freud, the famous Austrian psychoanalyst.

"We are not masters in our own house."

Yet, we do not have to be slaves to our emotions.

On her many walks, during blissful moments of peaceful solitude, Louise realises that home connotes for her so much more than just a house with a roof over her head. Instead, it is closely associated with who she is and with her sense of self. She has figured out that aside from establishing a primary connection between her and the rest of the world, it functions to orient her properly in space and time, amongst other things. However, after lengthy reflection, she recognises that home might not hold a similar meaning for everyone. In fact, depending on how they perceive it, it may symbolise several different things: a relentless battle between fantasy and reality, of bonds forged and then broken, or a place both empty and full.

If home is where the heart is, she wonders, as many people believe, is it then synonymous with the place they feel most comfortable? Is it a uniquely special place they construct with equally significant others, therefore existing as a pure state of mind? For many people, it is the abiding place of their affections, a place where they have built their precious memories. Despite certain doubts, there is one thing Louise feels quite certain about. Without a feeling of belonging, of rootedness centring people in an inhospitable world, a familiar place from where one starts out, then what can one hope to come back to?

Alas, she settles on the belief that there is nothing quite like the sweet taste, the eternal call of belonging.

In the end, everyone has to find their own Oz.

TWENTY ONE

Through Their Eyes

I will comfort you there in Jerusalem as a mother comforts her child.
— Isaiah 66:13

Louise's period is late by a few days. Although accustomed to menstruating like clockwork, she is convinced the delay is most probably due to hormonal issues. A casual mention to Arleen causes her to immediately stop what she is doing and raise her eyebrows in alarm, and Louise tries to play it down in an attempt to rescue the situation and avoid causing concern. Then, Seeing the worried look on the face of her younger sister, Arleen moves to allay her fears, telling her not to be alarmed that it may indeed be the body reacting to a change in circumstances.

Louise and Sami are spending a few days with Arleen and her husband, whose house stands at the foot of the Dublin Mountains. Built on an elevation with stunning views of Dublin Bay and city, it is a lofty sight, particularly of an evening. Her living room, the dimensions of which could rival the reception area of a large hotel, faces outwards through a floor-to-ceiling window wall. Installed with perfect fusion is a sliding door that opens onto a wide veranda and runs along the entire front-facing aspect of the big house. Positioned in the centre of this generous room is a long, curvaceous sofa in camel-coloured velvet, which can easily seat eight people or more, adding a focal point of definition to the spacious room.

It seems like yesterday, though in fact nearly two years have passed since this very room was buzzing convivially with the chat and laughter of guests. They had sat or stood about in small groups, there to celebrate with the young bride and groom. Arleen was the consummate hostess, opening up her home and showing her hospitality for the occasion of her youngest sister's wedding.

It was a cold, crisp morning in January, the day Louise was married. She stood alone on the veranda, looking out at the breathtaking vista of snowcapped mountains, the pearly-white peak of *Lugnaquilla*, 'Hollow of the wood' towering majestically over the green valleys, frosty glens and lonely loughs of the Wicklow hills.

Later that evening, some of the guests stepped outside into the chilliness of the night air to see the city skyline from a remote distance and marvel at the twinkling lights that spread out across Dublin.

It was an unusual wedding party, more of an intimate gathering for family and friends, in the days when elaborate church weddings were very much the norm in Ireland. A mere nine years previously, Louise had been flower girl at her sister Juliette's wedding, bursting with excitement to play her part on the day. Compared to hers, it was a lavish affair, from the ceremony in the local parish church and afterwards to an imposing castle overlooking the sea for the reception. Yet, for Louise, her special day seemed perfectly adequate.

In the morning, there were two brief ceremonies in different locations: one, a civil marriage in Kildare Street, the other, at the city Mosque, presided over by an Imam. It occurs to Louise now that both events passed over her head as if in a dream. Even now, she lacks clarity, her memory arrested by some form of partial amnesia, it seems.

Louise is delighted to visit the house again and spend time with her sister. They have lots to catch up on and inevitably their conversations stray to family stuff. Arleen tells her sister how much their parents missed her when she left and how excited they are at the prospect of having her and Sami for longer.

Louise confides in Arleen about the culture shock and the difficulties she experienced with Kareem's family. What she declines to tell her sister, though, is about the behaviour of her husband and all the unnecessary pain she has been through. She decides to keep it all to herself rather than worrying her family unduly. Besides, how would it sound, especially to her parents, for her to be so soon having regrets about the action they had strongly advised her against?

It was Arleen who eventually intervened between Louise and her distraught parents when the shocking bombshell, a marriage between their youngest daughter and the most unsuitable husband they could have imagined, was dropped unexpectedly on them.

Louise is convinced that things would have been much more difficult for her had it not been for Arleen. She suspects that her parents, especially her mother, took comfort in the knowledge that her eldest daughter was there to share in their burden and steer things in a particular direction. She had helped alleviate a really problematic situation, making it less upsetting for their parents in the end. It strikes Louise also as deeply ironic, in light of certain past events which involved Arleen and her parents, when she was still too young to understand.

Arleen and her husband seem to be rather fond of Kareem. They believe they know him but they have never seen the other side of his personality. Louise is reluctant to paint them a negative picture of her husband, partly to save herself the embarrassment and also because she wants to avoid letting him down

Fortunately for Kareem, he managed to talk his way out of a potential reprimand from Arleen when she challenged him about the delay in contacting them after Sami was born. Her sister is not easily fooled, so whatever excuse he procured, it must have been good because she never made an issue of it.

Louise's attachment to Arleen has always been strong. As a child, she remembers waiting for her to come home from work in the evenings. Then one day, without warning, she disappears for a long time. Louise suspects that her unexplained absence profoundly affected her childish world, being the rather sensitive child she was. Eventually, she reappeared, coming back into Louise's life in a meaningful way, offering her support when she most needed it.

She knows that Arleen and their mother are close. For as long as she can remember, it has been that way, and it seems natural since she is the eldest, her first-born child. She sets great store by having Arleen's opinions on things and Louise knows that her mother is an equally abiding influence in her sister's life. It is no surprise that Arleen's first-born child is called after their mother, proving that there is something profound at work in the names we choose, charged as they can be with our unconscious desires.

She gets to thinking about a time before she was born. Not quite understanding why, she doubts that Arleen's impressions of her parents have much in common with her own. For one thing, they had lived half their lives before Louise came along. How could their stories be the same?

When her parents first met, they were in their late teenage years. By the time they reached twenty, they had married, and Arleen was born. It would be another twenty years before she intruded upon the cusp of her mother's mid-life after a respite of eleven years.

Louise finds it hard to describe her mother. Even if she had all the time at her disposal and the precise words to hand, she would scarcely be able to achieve a comprehensive portrayal of her character, every nuance and quirk. True to the ancient Greek idiom meaning "one's own", she is not without her idiosyncrasies, a woman who likes to do things her own way.

She senses something different in her mother of late, something she never expected, a slight softening around the edges of her character, and the effect is surprisingly comforting. She feels the faint but familiar fear dissipating and the guilt that felt disproportionate to anything she might have done wrong beginning to fade. What does it matter now, she asks herself because the love she feels for this woman is silent and unstinting if only time will allow it to open its folds.

During one of their chats, her mother confides that the day she had left for Africa, her father sat on the side of the bed and shed tears for his youngest daughter, whom she feared he might not see for a long time.

The very thought of it pains her still, triggering childhood memories of walking through country fields holding his hand, taking care to avoid stepping on cowpats. As a child, she was intrigued by the round, flat pancakes of dung with their hard outer crusts forming a skin that looked to her like a giant oat biscuit. Then, there was the litter of tiny puppies, the cutest creatures she had ever seen. There are some old photographs knocking about of her with all six of them huddled together, one in particular where she is cradling a puppy on her lap while their gentle-natured mother sits at her heels, keeping a watchful eye on her young. She cried the day she had to leave them, pleading with her father to let her have one, but he explained in his own unassuming way that it wouldn't be right to take a pup so young away from its mother.

Louise wonders why so many of her memories are centred around her father. Memories of her mother are more transient, seeming to hint at absence, vague images that flit inexplicably in and out of her consciousness.

Her father is not the type of man to shy away from domestic tasks like cooking and cleaning up. Throughout her teenage years, Saturday mornings were a real treat because she would awaken to the delicious aroma of bacon wafting upstairs from the kitchen below. Her father would stick his head around the bedroom door she shared with her sister Marianne to ensure they were awake before returning with their breakfast tray. Aside from his culinary efforts, it was made with kind and tender care.

All through the years, she remembers her father kneeling modestly at the end of the bed that he and her mother share. Crossing himself, he would rest his arms on the eiderdown and join his hands in silent prayer. Despite his quiet devotion, Louise never really regarded her father as a religious man because he is quiet and reserved about his faith, the way he is about most things. The years have passed, he is now an older man; Louise a young woman and still he kneels at the foot of their bed. To Louise, there is poetry in that act.

His passions in life are drinking tea, copious amounts of it and horses, his great love of horses. Being the son of a farrier, he had been in the company of horses from an early age. One of his earliest memories as a young boy is being given the gift of a pony by his father. Later in life, he cultivated a keen interest in the 'sport of kings', a hobby he still pursues with great gusto. In his retirement, there is more time to study their form, and nothing pleases him more than when his efforts are rewarded with a winner.

Louise believes her father needs a distraction in life, something to take his mind off her mother, whose moods are sometimes broody, unlike him with his cheerful, outgoing disposition.

Her father is a man of simple pleasures, her mother complex. He is outgoing, but she prefers to be indoors. While he is trusting, she is suspicious by nature. He is compliant, her mother insistent. She dominates and he accommodates. Louise experiences her mother as having a mercurial temperament, and her degree of friendliness depends on the way the wind blows. She can be a social butterfly, commanding great attention from those she regales with her wit and charm. If she likes you, you may be a friend for life; otherwise, you will have to work hard to earn her favour and even harder to keep it. She never suffers fools gladly. For the most part, she leads, and her husband follows. For all that, he is the string to her bow, the sweet to her sour, notes to her melody and a beacon of light in her more saturnine moments.

Louise sometimes wonders if her mother is too much for him, he too little for her. On deeper reflection, she comes to the conclusion that many of us are drawn unconsciously to the differences of those significant others we choose to be with. Does this not, therefore, make for a greater balance? Louise is not so sure.

What is most heartening is the truth of her father's devotion to this woman, pure and simple. He knows her spirit well, its highs and low points, and even though he might not experience things quite the way she does, they have nonetheless discovered a common ground between them. They both have known pain in their lives and they hide their feelings in different ways.

Her mother's people did not have much money, unlike her father's, whose family were well-to-do. It must have raised some eyebrows when they got together, though clearly, he was smitten since she was a real beauty, as Louise had seen for herself from old photographs.

Her maternal grandfather had been raised in a rather salubrious suburb of Dublin by his two unmarried aunts, who ran a small but thriving business. There were whispers they were not altogether happy when their nephew became entangled with a city girl of simpler means. Apparently, he was well-educated and was training to be a teacher when they met. He never finished, however, and most likely had to find a job to make money, since he could no longer depend on his aunts for his livelihood. So, they went on to have four children, Louise's mother being the last born after a ten-year gap. It strikes Louise as a coincidence that both her mother and grandmother were past their fortieth year when they gave birth to baby girls, each with a significant gap between them and their siblings.

According to accounts Louise had heard from her parents, the reality of Dublin's working-class population, who inhabited the heart of the city in the early twentieth century, was increasingly impoverished. Tenement life was stark and Dublin had some of the worst slums on record in contemporary

Europe and the highest rate of prostitution. By the 1920s, the situation was worse and the inner city was in urgent need of a rehousing plan. For the ordinary people of Dublin, life was hard and notoriously unhealthy. Louise's parents were born at the turn of the century during those times.

In fact, Louise knew very little about their former lives, if the truth be told, or the relationships they formed with their other children before she began to take shape in her mother's body and her father's thoughts. What of their dreams and desires? Louise thinks it a bit irreverent of her to admit that she hardly knows them, at least not in the same way perhaps that her older siblings do.

Louise does not rightly know how or why she is thinking about these things. Yet such a plethora of questions and curiosities may in time shed light on her parent's precious lives leading to insights undiluted by personal bias and surface impressions.

Louise spots her father's car turning into the driveway and immediately goes to the front door with Sami in her arms.

"Oh look, is that Nana and Granddad?" she whispers into his ear excitedly, and he responds with a smile, beginning to wiggle and stretch his arms out rather cutely. Arleen and Louise are standing together, waiting to greet their parents as they step into the hall. They look really pleased to see their young granddaughters, who greet them with warm smiles and hugs.

Louise has a soft spot for her six-year-old niece, who is such a sweet child. Her grandmother regards her namesake with a special pride, her face lighting up when she comes to the door. Taking her by the hand, they head into the kitchen to sit at the large table and wait for Arleen to serve lunch. The aroma of freshly baked bread fills the kitchen.

After a short but enjoyable stay, it's time to head home with her parents, who are looking forward to having Sami back again. Louise promises Arleen that she will come back shortly and stay for longer. Perhaps next time, she might even leave Sami with his grandparents. Hugging her sister tightly, she thanks her for everything, promising to let her know straight away if she has any news to tell her. Sami's cousins kiss him on both cheeks before they depart. As the car winds its way down the drive, Arleen waves from the veranda until they finally disappear and are swallowed into the groves of trees.

A week has passed since Louise visited Arleen and she is no longer in suspense about her condition. She rises early, bringing her mother a cup of tea in bed before setting off for the coastal village she is so fond of. Her father is already up, preparing breakfast for Sami as she lets herself out through the back door, having arranged to meet him and Sami later on. Waiting at the bus stop, Louise notices that the rest of the world has barely emerged. Reminding herself it is Sunday, she finds herself alone on the bus except for a few day-trippers.

The upper pier is partially deserted at this hour, and Louise prefers it that way rather than running into crowds. The bottom pier is flanked by a marina where rows of softly bobbing boats and small yachts are moored on the shimmering water, their fenders sounding like jangling bells bumping gently together in time with the rhythm of the lapping water. The islands, a sanctuary for birds, loom large and clear ahead as if their form has risen out of the water for no other reason than to evoke a visually dramatic effect. Louise absorbs the sounds and smells of summer, being in no particular hurry to get anywhere or do anything except enjoy the morning and be alone with her thoughts. Soon enough, her father and Sami will join her, and they will find a nice spot to have an early lunch.

For now, she needs to digest her recent news, take a bit of time to feel her emotions, connect with them and adjust before she can even contemplate the future or tell Arleen.

The opposite side of the pier looks out beyond the harbour to the vastness of the open sea. Where the beams of sunlight hit the shimmering water, it sparkles like blue diamonds. Overlooking the sea, the tumbling green hills and brown rocky cliffs of *Eadair* rise rugged and proud in a steep headland above. To Louise, it is a place of beautiful contrasts, wildness and charm, enveloping the best of what nature has to offer in one place.

In all the years she has been coming here, Louise has never tired of its natural beauty, always freshly enchanted with every visit, as if seeing it for the first time. She gets a coffee and walks up the steep hill to pause at the top of the cliff walk. From there, she looks down on the Baily Lighthouse, positioned at the southern edge of the jutting pier. Built in 1817, it bears witness to a number of vessels wrecked against the rocks and cliffs around Howth Head in heavy fog, the *Queen Victoria* being the most notable in the year 1853. Enclosed within its circular wall is the tall granite tower with a white lantern and red tail standing aloof above a keeper dwelling. Louise has always been fascinated by the long trail of history left behind in the small harbour village, stories of invasion and conquest, piracy, seafaring and maritime adventure.

The peninsula itself is a place of great mythological significance in both legend and folklore, the small but charming village occupying a place in the history of Ireland that is long and proud. It is prominent in ancient tales of *Cuchulainn, Fionn MacCumhaill,* the *Fianna* and several branches of prestigious knights, since they used the lands as hunting grounds and convenient points of entry and exit to the open seas. As far back as the ninth century, Vikings ruled on Lambay Island, five miles north of the village, until the arrival of the Normans in the twelfth.

Legend holds that a bloody battle was fought, and one Sir Almeric Tristram led his army to victory on a day of religious significance. As a mark of respect and thanksgiving, he adopted the patronymic, Lawrence or St. Laurent of Normandy, whose heritage and namesake survive still and prominently into the twenty-first century, the events of which are recorded in the *Book of Howth,* a sixteenth-century manuscript compiled by the seventh Baron of Howth himself.

From an elevated position on the hill, Louise gets to thinking about her own early life, realising that much of her history is entwined with this place. Her mind then comes to rest on her childhood, her former days of yore. It is here her parents had brought her as a child, usually stopping at a tearoom run by a local lady. She remembers her parents drinking tea and her lemonade and delicious homemade scones dripping with sweet-tasting raspberry jam. She enjoyed those little excursions, always ending in the purchase of fish on the pier so carefully chosen by her father. Remarkably, she can still see, in her mind's eye, a red-lipped, dark-haired woman named Annie, tall with porcelain-like skin. She always wore Wellington boots and a long, white apron. They engaged enthusiastically in friendly banter whilst she bagged up the fish her father had selected.

It was also here, in this charming, little village, in the early flush of youth, that she encountered her first brush with the opposite sex and romance, landed her first weekend job, earned her pocket-money, congregated with friends and celebrated her graduation. They strike Louise now as exciting days, though at the time, they probably felt ordinary. Now, she returns, older with lived experience, to seek space and solace so she might imbue this new life that is growing inside her with the spirit of this special place.

In the afternoon, after eating lunch at a cosy, little seafood café, they decide to take a walk among the rhododendrons. Driving through the open gates of Howth Castle and up the long avenue of trees, they reach a clearing that overlooks the city. Louise knows how spectacular the view is once twilight descends and below becomes a sea of twinkling lights. The afternoon is bright and they have time enough to explore before going back home.

Holding Sami by each hand, they take to the path, a beautiful trail of purples and pinks, of yellows, whites and reds, their voluptuous flowers surrounded by rich, exotic-looking greenery. They remind Louise of bougainvillea, so typical of the Mediterranean. Forest ferns and palm fronds are scattered numerously in the undergrowth, prominent amid the shrubbery and occasional clump of wild garlic growing in the turfy soil. Trees of various species are dense in certain places, towering high overhead, creating a deep shade where only narrow rays of sunshine filter through, creating an atmosphere of calm and stillness. They walk slowly, allowing Sami to keep up at his ease while they amble along a series of meandering pathways through thick foliage that winds around the hill, eventually leading them out onto the top so they can look directly across at Ireland's Eye, in the distance. Pausing for a few moments, Louise experiences a kind of silent relief, a calm that seems to rise up from deep inside and surround her.

The very next day, Louise breaks the good news to her sister. Now Arleen can look forward to being an aunt again, and her three daughters to welcoming a new cousin.

TWENTY TWO

A Fresh Start

*A cynic is someone who knows the price of everything
but the value of nothing.*

– Oscar Wilde

Louise has found it really hard to settle back into a new routine, more challenging than she had imagined. Several weeks have passed, and she is only just beginning to acclimatise herself after being away for over a year and a half. Leaving Dublin and her parents was about the hardest thing she ever had to do. Even walking into a fresh, newly refurbished house did not dispel her feelings of loneliness and nostalgia at having to leave them. She tried hard to hide her emotions for the sake of the children since they had grown even more attached to their grandparents during that time. Naturally, they, too, were feeling the effects of the sudden separation.

Tara was born in the month of February, two weeks after her due date. In April of that same year, Kareem had to return to the US for two months on another training programme. Louise considered it a lucky twist of fortune that she had a legitimate reason to stay on and spend the summer in Dublin with her family. Though Kareem was due back in Tripoli in early July, he insisted she stay on. Louise suspected it suited Kareem very well for her and the children to be abroad for the remainder of the summer. It was, after all, the season for weddings and there were surely plenty of occasions for him to partake of. Being free to come and go as he pleased was undoubtedly an attractive option for Kareem, but before heading back to Tripoli, he flew to Dublin for a few days to see his infant daughter.

She smiles now, her mind skipping back to the day her father drove the short journey to the maternity hospital and accompanied her inside, waiting with her until the nurse appeared. Later that evening, she delivered a fine baby girl. Her crowning glory was an abundance of black, silky hair, which could easily be tucked behind her tiny ears, much to the delight of everyone. The nurses were pleasantly preoccupied with combing and attaching pink bows to it as if she were a novelty doll. Early next morning, her mother appeared, eager to hold her baby granddaughter, whom she insisted on naming there and then. She chose the name Tara, which Louise liked, so it was settled, and no more was said about the matter. Sami had been named by Kareem's father, and Louise figured her mother should have the same privilege.

At nearly two and a half, Sami is a busy, precocious toddler with a mop of brown curls. Everyone remarks on how handsome a child he is. Louise is mindful that he misses his grandad since practically all his days were spent in his company. Some nights, he woke from sleep restless, having been put to bed earlier that evening. It was grandad he looked for, no one else would do. After securing a seat on his lap, he would settle down in the warmth and eventually doze off to sleep. Louise was reluctant to protest because her father always had a legitimate sounding reason for the child's disturbances, urging her to be patient and leave him be. Looking back, Louise accepts that he was probably correct in his assumptions.

Taking stock of everything, Louise can see that Kareem has worked hard to transform the house to its current style. He refitted both bathrooms, extended their living room, installed a spiral staircase fashioned in beautiful wood, and added new furnishings to the rest of the house. It looks nothing like its former self, having been totally modernised. Even the old hall door has been replaced. Therenow stands a heavy, panelled door of solid wood, polished to a fine finish with a gleaming brass knocker in the shape of a lion's head mounted in the centre.

It seems like the time has arrived when they are finally together as a family and Louise wants to do her best to make it a home for all of them. She is relieved that Kareem seems a little more settled since their arrival. One new development, however, is how much he is occupied with his new job promotion. It carries more responsibilities and involves him being away for a couple of days on domestic business from time to time. He had known for some time that he was in line for the new posting but never mentioned it, a fact that did not surprise Louise. Kareem, being his own man, is not likely to consider a career change to be a concern for his wife, much less merit an input from her. By the same token, he avoids talking to her about his financial earnings or other perks of his job, except only to mention it in the vaguest of terms.

Once Louise had pressed him on it in a perfectly matter-of-fact way, but she came away as wise as she was at the outset. Instead of answering, he redirected the question back to her. In a semi-jovial manner, he questioned why she needed to know at all; it was nothing she needed to bother herself with.

"If I have left you short of anything, Louise or the children, you just tell me," he insists.

Louise decides to let his remark slide for the time being rather than challenge him on it.

As he speaks, he looks at her with a pained expression whilst skilfully diverting her original point and turning it on its head.

"Kareem, I think you've completely misunderstood the question I'm asking."

It feels like she is trying to humour a sulking child, she notes.

"Kareem, I don't understand why we're even talking about this…. I only asked you a simple question about your salary in this new position. Look, if you asked me the same question, I'd simply answer it. Can it be that complicated?"

Louise decides to say no more on the subject because he is beginning to irritate her, and she knows that if they continue, she is likely to say something that will really annoy him. Already, it has escalated into a superfluous dialogue, and clearly, her husband believes that what he earns is his own business. That in itself raises further questions for her to consider. With that in mind, she is resigned to let it go for now. She smiles wryly to herself, changes the subject and moves on to something else.

There is a lot yet to learn about her husband, she reminds herself, looking askance as she goes about her chores. She suspects the conversation they had about finances will be the first of many and they are probably always destined to disagree about money matters. Louise has already experienced some reluctance from Kareem to part with money, even when necessary.

While still in Dublin, she asked him to send on money because of her extended stay. He grumbled about it even though he was earning plenty and could well afford it, and only moderated his attitude after she reminded him that her parents were already doing enough and that supporting her and the children was not their responsibility. He didn't seem to realise that without her parents' support and generosity, it would have cost him a lot more. There are things that money cannot repay, and these cannot even be measured in monetary terms.

Her marriage to Kareem has been a rather steep learning curve. Does she really know the man she married? She smiles at her own question, prompted by a prevailing thought that has taken root lately.

TWENTY THREE

A Charming Wolf

Beware of false prophets who come to you in sheep's clothing,
but inwardly they are ravenous wolves.

– Matthew 7:15

Six weeks have passed since their return from Ireland. After breakfast one morning, Louise is in the living room with the children, settling them down to play. Looking admiringly at the bookshelves Kareem had installed while she was away, Louise decides to rearrange some of the books to accommodate new ones.

All Kareem's large aviation manuals are stacked rather disorderly on the bottom shelves and need to be organised into some kind of a system. Fortunately, there is plenty of space to house all Louise's books, including those due to arrive soon. Whilst in Dublin, she had arranged to have them shipped to Tripoli, including large volumes and anthologies, some of which were gifts from Arleen and her parents. She intends her modest library to grace the room with pride and become a focal point only a devoted reader can appreciate.

She sets about taking all the larger manuals down and stacking them carefully on the floor in order to thoroughly dust the shelves before replacing them. After a brief deliberation, she assigns all of Kareem's manuals their own place on the bottom two shelves, since they are large and thick. Stepping back to take another look and feeling pleased with her efforts, she picks up another manual at the end of the pile. As she goes to stand it on its end, something slips out, dropping onto the rug at her feet. Bending down to pick it up, Louise realises it is a piece of folded paper, and automatically, she turns it over in her hand.

Carefully unfolding it, she sees a photo placed in the centre. She stares at it for several moments before reading the message so clearly written in pencil below it.

Seattle, November Thanksgiving. Continuing to stare at the picture, she can hardly believe her own eyes, but it is indeed her husband that she sees and a woman.

Snow is thick on the ground where they are standing. Behind them, a spectacular backdrop of forest and mountains is visible in the winter sunlight. What a perfect snowscape. Unless the camera is lying, the image of Kareem, looking so comfortably at ease with the woman, whoever she is, tells its own story. With her arm firmly entwined in his, they appear to be no strangers.

The woman's face is turned invitingly to meet his lips, and leaning in close to one another, they both seem unperturbed by the camera and absorbed in the moment. The adage: 'A picture is worth a thousand words,' springs to her mind. Alas, the still photograph had captured something outside the locale of a harmless flirtation. That much Louise is certain of without rational explanation; she can feel it in her body as if the photo has an energy field of its own.

With nobody to hear her sardonic laugh but the children, preoccupied in play, Louise returns the picture to the book and places it back on the shelf.

Kareem knew how to make good use of his time between training and periods of study, which, according to his account, were long and intense. Louise now knows that his hours were not all spent studying. She also knows her husband is a liar, and it was not her imagination at work when she sensed he was being deliberately vague. Whenever she asked him about his trip, he gave her nothing except to speak sparingly about his time there and how it was spent studying.

The full impact of her discovery does not initially register with Louise and when it does, the effect will be long-lasting. She says nothing about it to Kareem when she sees him later that day, although she is quieter than usual. He notices she is quiet, asking her if anything is wrong, but she fobs him off, allowing her time to think further about it in the following days.

Eventually, four days later, in the evening, when the children are finally in bed, she broaches the subject. Having schooled herself to stay calm and say what she needs to without giving him the opportunity to manipulate things like he usually does, she comes into the living room where he is sitting watching television.

Smiling when he sees her, he assumes she is ready to relax for the evening, to come and sit next to him on the couch. Suddenly, she produces a photo from her pocket and places it on his lap.

He says nothing for a moment and looks at her quizzically, feigning ignorance.

"Kareem, don't pretend to be a fool; we both know what this is."

Speaking quietly, she points at the photo, still on his lap. He starts to say something, but she holds up her hand to silence him.

"Kareem, don't tell me any more of your lies. It's better if you say nothing because you're just digging a bigger hole for yourself. It won't make any difference."

He starts to say something, but she waves a dismissive hand in his direction, cutting him off.

"First, you took off to America after Sami was born, leaving us alone, insisting there was no way we could go: the first lie. You spent all your time there working and studying: another lie. You neglected to say that you met someone and had a little romance while you were there and, no doubt, plenty of hot sex as well."

Straightening up, he tries to protest, but Louise presses on, leaving no space for her husband to interject.

"Conveniently, the airline sent you back to the US for more training when Tara was born, lucky you." She laughs.

"Was it the same woman you hooked up with the second time round or a different one?" Now, she looks at him with contempt before laughing bitterly.

He nods vigorously, assuming a pained expression, and Louise knows he is preparing a defence as she speaks.

"You won't let me explain, Louise." He begins, before letting out a big sigh.

Immediately, she is on her feet, determined not to listen to any tale he is about to weave.

"Kareem, Kareem," she repeats quietly but with a note of anger creeping into her voice. She decides to halt the tirade before it turns into what she wants to avoid.

"I don't believe you; whatever you say now, whatever story you tell me, I don't believe it, so don't waste your breath talking." Her tone is cold, and she cannot bear to look at him for a moment longer.

She turns suddenly and walks swiftly from the room, leaving him mumbling under his breath. Stealing quietly upstairs, she is careful to avoid making any noise that might wake the children.

In the days that follow, Louise gets on with life, keeping herself busy with the children, tending to the house and going through the motions of daily living. They only talk at a superficial level. She is careful to assume an outward show of normality and to avoid an atmosphere in the house, which the children are sure to pick up on. She says as much to Kareem, so between them, they have an understanding. For Louise, there are distractions of her own, friends and study, the same as Kareem has his. And so, life goes on.

After that first night, she returns to their bedroom, mainly because she doesn't want to confuse the children or arouse their curiosity. Louise also believes a long absence from their bed will only further jeopardise the relationship on a purely symbolic level, even though it has already been compromised.

She knows that Kareem will doubtless interpret it only one way, so she tells him she is not ready to have close physical contact and asks him to respect her boundaries.

Confiding in Saoirse about her personal stuff helps, especially as she is sensible and mature. Louise knows she can be trusted and at the same time be honest with her advice. When Louise tells her about finding the photograph, Saoirse listens silently without showing any surprise.

"Saoirse, you were there at the time. Is there anything I should know?" Louise immediately senses something in her friend, in her facial expression.

"Well, I never saw them together, Louise. We asked Kareem to join us a couple of evenings at the local pizzeria, but he said he was tired and needed an early night. I thought it slightly odd."

Louise can only laugh derisively.

"I think you and I both know how he was spending his evenings."

"Honestly Louise, I don't have anything to add and if Sadeek knows something he never said, for obvious reasons. You know Louise, how these men are."

"Oh, I completely understand. Nobody wants to get involved in a marriage or come between two people."

"Who knows, Louise? Maybe you were meant to stumble across that picture, upsetting as it is."

"Yeah, you may be right. Time will tell," she agrees.

After that, Louise never mentions the subject of her husband's infidelity to Saoirse again.

Life goes on, as does their friendship, both women seeing each other regularly. Adil, Saoirse's son and Sami, with roughly a year between them, make good playmates, and they usually take the two toddlers to a small playground near Saoirse's house and then for ice cream or pizza. Tara is a placid, good-humoured child, always pleasant, and loves being outdoors, observing everything around her. Louise takes the buggy so she can sit in it when she gets tired after walking about in the park. Already, she is showing signs of being an independent child, capable of amusing herself.

When Louise looks at her two children, she is reminded regularly of how they have grown and blossomed into two beautiful little people. They also serve as a daily reminder that despite all else, she has accomplished something of inestimable value in her life. The other less pleasant aspects of her existence seem to pale into partial insignificance.

TWENTY FOUR

Turning Lead into Gold

When fishermen cannot go to sea, they repair nets.
– Nabil Azadi

Fortunately for Louise, she likes cooking and did a bit at home before moving to North Africa. A real inconvenience, however, is that lots of things are scarce, unavailable or not at all easily found. That means some things just cannot be done without the necessary ingredients. Nevertheless, Louise is fast learning to be resourceful with what she has at her disposal and tries to be creative with whatever is the nearest equivalent she can find. It's rather like a game of substitution.

There are plenty of certain commodities, such as flour, rice, and sugar. Oil is in abundance and can be used instead of butter, which is often scarce. Oranges and lemons are plentiful and ridiculously cheap, as are tomatoes and certain vegetables.

Louise follows Arleen's recipe for marmalade, and although there is a bit of work involved, she is getting better at it. For lemon curd, she uses an easy recipe, and Sami loves to spread it on his bread.

When they first moved in, Kareem mentioned their neighbours, a Scottish woman and her husband, who live a minute's walk away. There had been no time for introductions because Louise was about to leave for Dublin within a week of their move.

Soon after they arrived back, Kareem arranged for an introduction with the couple. Marleen called with a housewarming gift for Louise, and they hit it off right away from the first meeting. Several years older than Louise, she is attractive and stylish with a lovely head of auburn hair.

With a genuine, upbeat personality and a warm, friendly disposition, she is the opposite of her native husband, who is quiet and reserved.

They have two older children, a son of eleven and a daughter of nine. Louise cannot help but be intrigued by how fate has brought them together. They have been living on the street for over ten years.

Days before Kareem had finally closed the agreement on their new house, there was a falling out between his mother and himself. It seems so long ago now. Louise had stopped asking about it, as once, when she asked Kareem about it, he became crabby and reluctant to talk about it.

It comes as a big surprise to her, therefore, when Kareem announces out of the blue that his mother and sisters are coming to see her the following afternoon. Of course, she realises they have not seen Tara or Sami since he was six months. That fact alone may be a good enough reason for them to mend bridges. So be it; she would be ready to welcome them to their home.

Saoirse and Marleen are also due to call the same afternoon, and Louise decides to invite her Egyptian neighbour Safar, who Louise believes will diffuse any tension and add a good balance to the occasion.

On the morning in question, Louise finishes kneading the dough for her pizza and puts it aside to rise. Preparing the tomato sauce is the easy part because tomatoes are plentiful and cheap.

Before the pizza goes in the oven, she scatters some green olives and fresh oregano on top, essential when making a classic Napoli pizza. For something sweet, she bakes a lemon sponge cake, putting the mixture in a deep, rounded tin with a hole in the centre. Later, when it cools, she tops it with a zesty glaze.

Although it feels strange to see her in-laws after such a long spell, they appear genuinely pleased to see her, notably her mother-in-law, whose manner seems to have undergone a thawing. Kareem's brother Jabir drops them off at the house, and when he returns to pick them up, Louise invites him to sample some of her pizza. She is surprised when he makes a point of asking after her parents and making a real effort to chat with her about Ireland and other general things. She is glad that Safar joined them because she made a great effort with everyone, and it really made a difference. Saoirse and Marleen stay on for a while after the in-laws and Safar leave.

For the first time since arriving in the country, Louise begins to feel she is not entirely alone.

Often, the most endurable friendships are forged in the most unexpected, even adverse circumstances, founded upon common and shared human experiences.

TWENTY FIVE

A Time to Mourn

Only people who are capable of loving can also suffer great sorrow, but this same necessity of loving serves to counteract their grief and heals them.

— Leo Tolstoy

L ouise wakes from a dream in a state of fear, feeling rattled and shaken, her mind consumed with thoughts of Bella, her dead sister. It's November, and though the nights are still mild, she feels a chill as she gets out of bed and pulls on a cardigan. Looking at her watch, she realises it is only half past midnight and the night is still young. It was approaching eleven when she had closed her eyes, tired as they were from reading. Now, she opens the veranda door and steps outside for a breath of air, eager to break the spell of emotional intensity she is feeling. All is eerily quiet; not even a cat stirs in the deserted street below. After standing in mild contemplation for a few minutes, she goes inside and climbs back into bed, eventually falling asleep, but not for long.

She wakes the second time to a similar scenario, except this time more fraught with nervous tension. Without understanding why, she feels the strong presence of her dead sister in the room. It seems to pervade the shadowy spaces around her as if her spirit has come to give her a message, but Louise immediately dismisses the thought as ridiculous. Distressed, she gets up for the second time and walks barefoot along the cool marble hall to the kitchen, where the wall clock tells her it is almost three. She feels no inclination to return to her bed tonight. Instead, she hits the switch on the kettle to try and revive herself with a cup of tea, resolving to stay awake until the hour of the wolf has passed.

Suddenly, she turns and finds Jabir standing hesitantly by the threshold of her kitchen, with an expression of relief on his face. There is an awkward silence between them when both become aware that she is scantily clad in a revealing nightshirt. Embarrassed, she tries to detract from the moment by speaking while he looks discreetly away.

"Jabir, sorry if I woke you. I… I just had a bad dream and I couldn't get back to sleep," she smiles at him, feeling exposed and a trifle silly.

"No, no, I wasn't sleeping…I heard a noise and decided to come down…. just checking, so I'll leave you in peace." He moves to walk away but stops on a second thought, looking back at her with a smile.

"I'll see you in the morning."

The next day dawns early and Louise is up to see Sami off to school. He walks the short distance with Safar's son of the same age, Ahab, and his two older sisters. When Tara turns four, she, too, will join them. They attend school every day except Friday, the Muslim day of rest and prayer but the school day finishes before two in the afternoon. Kareem is away in another city working and is not due back for two days, now a regular occurrence twice or three times a month. Louise has grown accustomed to these trips, though at first it was a bit scary, and Louise felt isolated with just her and the children alone at night. Until Kareem asked his two brothers to check in on them while he was away or, if need be, to stay over when he was absent for longer periods.

At the start, both his brothers dutifully took turns bringing shopping and other things she might need or sometimes just stopping to drink a cup of tea and chat. After a while, Farhat was made assistant to the dean of his university, and due to pressing academic responsibilities, he found himself with no time to spare. At around the same time, he began a relationship with a girl in the law faculty, but since their meetings were clandestine, he became increasingly preoccupied and unavailable.

In Islamic culture, it is not permissible for a couple to be seen in public unless they are officially engaged. Even then, their meetings have to take place sparingly, with a chaperone or in the company of the family. As for the more traditional ones, it is out of the question for a couple to meet except on the day of their official engagement and maybe once again before the actual wedding day. Certainly, Kareem's family is among the more traditional ones.

Jabir, on the other hand, has more time on his hands, having already graduated. There is a compulsory requirement for all young men to serve a yearlong military service or more, in some cases, before beginning a career. Most men are not happy to do it, but since it is not optional, they must resign themselves. Jabir is fortunate that he has only to report on certain mornings for four or five hours, which leaves him free to call on them whenever Kareem is out of town. Recently, his trips away are becoming more and more frequent.

Most evenings when the children are in bed, Jabir and Louise just sit and drink tea. There are endless things for them to talk about, and they never appear to notice the time passing. Louise often speaks about her family back home and Ireland, which he always seems interested in hearing about. He in turn, confides in her about many things, from local politics to more personal stuff, expressing his deep frustration with some of the customs, his countrymen and the closed society in which he has grown up.

Fortunately, Louise has managed over time to achieve a good command of Arabic, which enables her to converse easily enough. Safar has been instrumental in her progress, having taught her a lot, not just about the language but also about Egyptian cooking and Arabic culture in general. Louise is fortunate to have this interesting woman from Alexandria as her friend.

Jabir is eager to know why Louise had woken from her sleep and asks her the next time he calls. Surprised he even remembers, she tries to conceal her anxiety, but Jabir manages to see through it. Struggling to explain what for the most part is ineffable, she does her best to explain, even more difficult in a foreign tongue. Some thoughts she prefers to forget, and they remain hidden. Besides, Louise doubts that Jabir would understand, assuming he has no personal experience of loss.

Saoirse had understood Louise because she was no stranger to death herself, having lost her brother only a few years before they met. He was the eldest of her family and they had a really close bond. They spoke about their personal responses to grief a few times and how it affects everyone differently and in very particular ways.

Bella was the second in the birth order, with a significant gap of eighteen years between them. Sadly, Louise feels she hardly knew her sister, although people often comment on their physical likeness. She married when Louise was only four and moved to the west of Ireland. One enduring memory in Louise's thoughts is the morning of Bella's wedding. Only four or five years old at the time, she remembers sitting on the stairs and being aware of all the fuss around her. Sensing that she was not part of it seemed to upset her greatly; at least, that is how Louise feels whenever she thinks back. It was compounded by the prospect of being looked after by a relative, someone she obviously did not like, for whatever reason she cannot recall. What is certain is that it seemed to upset her no end; otherwise, why would it remain unchanged and so prominent in her memory?

In the following years, their paths barely crossed, except for brief visits whenever Bella was in Dublin with her husband and children. Her first child, a boy, was born when Louise was only five years old, making her a very young aunt. They visited for the first couple of years at Christmas and Louise can still picture the warm and cosy traditional scenes, the glimmer of tinsel, reds, greens and gold, classic poinsettias, laughter and the scent of spices. Potatoes roasting, golden-skinned turkey resting, sprouts jostling, wine breathing and champagne fizzing. The festive dinner was always a hearty gathering of family, all sitting around her mother's handsomely dressed dining table with pinecones and candelabra.

Assigned a special place by itself on a side table would sit her mother's signature Christmas cake, a particularly masterful production, the icing an elaborate affair in itself. Thick white peaks of snow covered its marzipan top whilst minute sleighs, pulled by tiny reindeer, carried Santa on his way. A good old robin-redbreast perched proudly on a low branch, partially covered in sweet snow and surrounded by sprigs of frosted holly. Around its rich, fruity perimeter, her mother had wound a thick, red satin ribbon with painstaking precision before the cake was placed on a silver base and allowed to stand on display in preparation for the Christmas cutting ceremony.

There was plenty of jollity, wine and song, eating and merrymaking that continued late into the night. At some point, Bella's husband would take his place at the piano and entertain everyone with musical renditions and lashings of charm. Suddenly, Louise finds herself reaching into the vast reservoir of nostalgia, into the lost property box of distant memories.

She remembers the journey made in haste, but nonetheless, one that accommodated her swift departure. It was Faisal who took them out to the airstrip and helped them board the cargo plane after introducing Louise to the captain and his first officer. Once they were securely seated at the rear of the cockpit, Kareem climbed into the aircraft to bid them adieu. From behind her seat, she heard the sudden, unmistakably characteristic whinnying of a horse. A reply followed in the form of a soft nicker and a series of snorts before finally settling. For some unknown reason, it was a welcome sound for Louise and she began preparing the children, who were still small at the time, for take-off.

She never imagined, in her wildest dreams, that she would be travelling with a cargo of equines en route to Shannon from Northern Africa, and moreover, the reason for such a journey would be to say a final goodbye to her older, beautiful sister. She was stunning, so easy on the eye, tall, slim and blond with striking, pale, green eyes. She seemed to have it all: talent, personality and a quiet charm. Louise was somewhat in awe of her older sister, though in truth, she knew little about her. Louise imagined that Bella received admiring glances wherever she went.

An accomplished artist, many of her paintings featured scenes from the 'heart' of Connemara with its rocky, mountainous landscape, the twelve pins on one side and the wild Atlantic on the other. Her work was displayed in various places throughout the Western province, and although a true Dublin city girl, born and reared, she felt entirely at home in her beloved West of Ireland. Over the years, she earned herself the reputation of being a great hostess, charming and fun to be with. Louise had heard it first-hand, through others, in the most unexpected places and circumstances, her name frequently mentioned in wide circles long after she had passed away.

Louise remembers the day she got the fatal call that summoned her home, the look on Arleen's face when she greeted her at Shannon airport. Louise went straight to her sister's home, not knowing what to expect. Entering the garden through a side gate, she saw Bella, only a shadow of her former self, lying on a sun-lounger. It was the last time she saw her sister alive. The image is an enduring one that has never faded over time. Later, Louise returned to Dublin with Sami and Tara to her parents' home while they kept vigilant at their daughter's bedside, waiting for the inevitable to happen. When it did, it was swift.

She made the surreal journey back to the West to attend her sister's funeral.

In a cold, impersonal funeral parlour, Louise looked for the last time on Bella's face, a face that had once been so lovely. It was the first time Louise had ever stood at a coffin and looked inside; the trauma of seeing her dead sister would register only later. She remembers the numbness that followed afterwards but not the details that refuse recall to conscious memory.

Now, more than three months have passed, and Louise tries to explain to Jabir that she was visited by her sister in a dream. She recounts how she felt when she woke up, though the details of the dream itself are not accessible to her lost memory, except that she felt her sister's strong presence in the room. Strangely, though, she feels more peaceful since the dream, and she wonders if something in her internal world is trying to resolve itself.

"If Kareem was here, I mean, I could talk to him about it, maybe," she falters, suddenly overcome by a wave of emotion. She has to stop herself speaking, swallowing hard because the words that begin to form make no sense at all and only stick in her throat. Even if her husband were here, she would be just as upset because he appears to have not the slightest inkling about her grief, nor does he seem to care. He never asks anything about how she feels and never seems interested.

"I know Kareem is away and I understand how hard it is not having your family close by. It's a big sacrifice." Jabir tries to offer some compassion. Louise is grateful for his concern.

"Even when he's here and not working, he... he goes out a lot. He doesn't spend his time with me and the children but always has something to do, somewhere to go."

She sighs, immediately regretting her words, wondering why she had spoken her thoughts at all. She smiles apologetically at Jabir who is listening attentively to her every word.

"Sorry, I shouldn't have," she begins, but he stops her from saying anything further.

"Louise, listen, you don't have to worry about anything you say to me, ok?"

He looks across the room and holds her gaze for a few seconds, long enough to assure her that his words are sincere.

"Don't worry about anything, as long as I'm here to help." Louise acknowledges his kind words with a nod, grateful for his support. She looks away but he continues speaking.

"Anything you or the children need, just ask me, or if you want to talk, nobody has to know."

Louise nods at him for the second time and smiles.

"I will, and thanks, Jabir, for everything."

He smiles back, and Louise gets the feeling he is as relieved as she is that they have made a simple pact by attaching words to something that previously existed only tacitly. They say their goodnights and part as two companions are wont to do.

TWENTY SIX

The Body Remembers

What does not kill me, makes me stronger.

– Friedrich Nietzsche

After the first few pages, Louise puts down her book. It is useless trying to read because her mind won't stop wandering, so busy with scattered thoughts, leaving her with no inclination to sleep. Thinking about Kareem and their relationship, lots of thoughts come rushing into her mind all at once. Leaning back on the pillows to rest her head, she folds her hands, takes a deep breath and lets the thoughts go where they will.

In her mind's eye, she can see herself as clearly as if it happened only yesterday. Struck dumb with shock and suddenly very frightened, she is unable to speak in those initial seconds after Kareem had head-butted her in the nose. She can feel drops of blood trickling down onto the collar of her beige trench coat, the one she had bought just the week before, delighted with her new purchase.

It feels like her body has not forgotten the sharp stab of pain she felt when the offending blow landed on bone, a sharp sensation having stayed with her. The sweet taste of blood on her lips still lingers somewhere on the frontier between body and mind, her body keeping the record.

Fortunately for Louise, the bleeding did not persist once she held the scarf firmly to her nose. Yet, it felt sore and tender for days afterwards, leaving a tiny scar on the bridge of her nose, which eventually faded after a long time, never completely disappearing. The emotional scar, however, is deeper and takes much longer to heal, if ever.

They were in Germany when it happened. Kareem was posted in Frankfurt for two months with his job, and Louise joined him for a week there, having left the children in the care of her parents. She was hoping that a break away would be good for both of them, but it was becoming clearer that no matter where they were, things never remained good between them for long. Louise was thankful and relieved that the children were spared the unpleasantness of witnessing such an incident.

The assault happened in a flash, coming totally without warning. Seeing her own blood, tasting it and attempting, in a matter of mere seconds, to grasp what happened and that it was her husband who inflicted the injury was overwhelming. One minute, she was standing in a bakery shop, the next, she was outside on the footpath, holding a scarf to her bloody, aching nose. The memory is so clear. She remembers asking Kareem to get her a pastry as he was buying some bread. For some unfathomable reason, he scowled, muttering something inaudible under his breath. Once outside, Louise simply asked him if he had forgotten it, and he flew into a rage, which ended in a violent assault on his innocent wife.

She has never understood why Kareem reacted in such a bizarre way. As there is no justifiable reason that could condone his nefarious behaviour, Louise is left perplexed. What he did was apparently without rhyme or reason and no clever use of words or soft talking could diminish it in her estimation. No sooner had he struck his wife than he realised he had gone too far. It may have been the initial fear of serious injury to her nose, requiring possible hospitalisation, explanations and the repercussions which might follow that stirred him. All of a sudden, he pleaded concern, insisting it was a mistake and that he had never meant to hurt her. Despite her shock, Louise felt his words were ridiculous but was too scared to contradict him.

Louise remembers feeling like a chastised child in a candy shop, except that she was a grown woman who had been degraded. In truth, she had been troubled for a while by dark surmises about the true nature of her husband's character, and after the incident, she was haunted by them. She should have walked away then, for good, told her family, even sought professional advice when she returned to Dublin.

Two days later, she got on a plane to Dublin and flew home, telling her husband at the airport that she would be spending the next month in Dublin with her family and not to bother calling her. Of course, he appeared contrite, but whether it was genuine or not is a matter of conjecture. At that point, his words were utterly meaningless to Louise as she walked silently away from him without looking back.

Once in Dublin, she had plenty of time to think about everything, about where her life was going. She was scared, afraid to make the drastic changes that would turn her life around. There was a fear of failure and a feeling of shame associated with breaking up a family and taking the children away from their father. Leaving them behind was never an option, not in her wildest dreams. There was also a deep sense of embarrassment for not heeding her parents' advice, for having to admit that their concerns were justified after all. She could imagine her sister Marianne, triumphant, gloating at her younger sister's misfortune.

Everything rushed headlong at her in a great flurry of negative thoughts. Teetering on the edge of reason, it felt as if her mind had been taken over by an angry mob spewing vitriol at her whilst she struggled to push them back. The prospect of rebuilding a new life for her and the children felt daunting, but what she dreaded most was how Kareem would react. Each scenario carried a particular obstacle, a bridge which had to be crossed. She felt neither prepared nor emotionally strong enough to face the unknown. Unsatisfied with life as it was, it somehow felt less anxiety-provoking to stick with the familiar, with what she had come to expect from her husband, awful as it was, rather than confront a new day without him.

TWENTY SEVEN

In Search of Better Days

Friends are the family we choose for ourselves.

– Edna Buchanan

Louise stands in the lovely, landscaped gardens of the British Residency in Tripoli. Looking around her, she is struck by the calmness and tranquillity inside its high walls, despite the urban surroundings beyond. Nobody, except those well-informed, would ever dream that relations between the two countries had been strained for some time and were about to get worse.

Nonetheless, it is a beautiful morning, the first day of spring, pleasantly warm with blue skies and the soothing sound of water sprinklers can be heard spraying the lawns at the far end of the walled garden.

Everything is set up outside in readiness for a lavish party scheduled to begin with a barbecue at 1 pm in the afternoon. Typical afternoon tea with all sorts of homemade delights is to be served from three. Louise has spent the previous two days baking dozens of fairy cakes, with icing on top, her personal contribution to the annual spring event. It is intended as a 'thank you' to her friend Shelley for inviting her and a couple of other friends along. Louise is also grateful for her vote of confidence in putting some teaching work her way. Only recently, Shelley recommended that Louise give private tuition to the children of foreign dignitaries and non-native work colleagues attached to the British and Italian embassies stationed in Tripoli. Eager for their children to be taught English by a native speaker, they consider themselves fortunate to have found the person they are looking for in Louise.

Shelley herself works at the embassy, and her husband is a Libyan pilot employed by the national airline, so Kareem is naturally acquainted with him. It was not through her husband, however, that Louise had come to know Shelley. She had been introduced by another English friend at a 'coffee afternoon' in her house. After that, they met several times and a friendship slowly evolved.

Though invited, Kareem is not with her, which is no big surprise. Sami and Tara are there, already enjoying themselves outdoors, hitting a ball around the tennis courts. Tara is excited about the fancy dress competition that is being put on at about five in the evening after tea is finished.

Louise is convinced that children need plenty of social interaction to develop their personalities. Unfortunately, the Libyan model of early education is proving too rigid to allow children to express themselves adequately. A distinctly religious and political flavour drives the school programme and curriculum. Whoever it serves, it is certainly not the student, falling between two idols, an omnipotent deity and a powerful sovereign. Children have a natural right to be exposed to an education which is open and imbued with the true philosophy of learning instead of closing down the art of enquiry. Louise is determined that both her children will be literate in English, apart from being orally fluent.

So, she reads with them, mainly when their school homework is done. It is hard work as keeping Sami focused is a task in itself because he always has an eye and ear on some possible adventure that may be happening outside the window, wishing he is a part of it rather than reading about it in a book. Typically, boys will behave as boys do, though at times, Louise gets quite frustrated in her efforts to teach him what she believes will be useful for him later on.

She is thankful though for the awareness of difference and cultural diversity their lifestyle offers, not least because of exposure to it by their upbringing but also in the wider contacts with her close friends, their interesting backgrounds and being able to mix with children from different cultural backgrounds apart from their native schoolmates. Louise now belongs to a small community of women, English, Scottish, Maltese, Greek and Polish, who all have one thing in common: the nationality of their husbands.

Looking up, she sees Shelley walking towards her along the flagstone pathway, with Martha and Marleen following close on her heels. Louise is thinking how nice it is for the friends to be together today for a little celebration of springtime. When she arrived first, she never imagined that she would meet such interesting people, much less build lasting friendships with them. Shelley had met the girls previously at Louise's house on several occasions and made a point of inviting them to the garden party.

After they greet one another, Shelley accepts a large tray of fluffy scotch pancakes from Marleen and a basket from Martha full of freshly baked 'pastizzi', a popular Maltese snack with a sweet or savoury filling. Today half are filled with mincemeat and the rest with apple, enough to feed a small army. A delighted Shelley carries them off to the embassy kitchen to be carefully put away until later.

Martha is Maltese and has become a really close friend and, coincidentally, happens to be married to a cousin of Kareem's. They met in Valetta, where Omar was a partner in a travel agency. After a few years, they decided to return to Tripoli with their two young daughters, Sabrina and Samantha, who are good playmates with Tara, being of the same age.

Martha is strikingly pretty with short black hair and dark eyes. She is petite with a well-shaped figure, and when she moves, her person seems to glide smoothly across the floor with natural poise and elegance. Her character and general disposition are gentle and reserved but not in a stand-offish way. A conscientious person, you can always rely on her to give an honest opinion tactfully, and Louise particularly loves this about her. She possesses a kind of 'open' sincerity with nothing concealed. People seem to sense that and are immediately at ease in her company. Amused, Louise thinks of a saying that her mother would often use about someone with 'good breeding." If ever she meets Martha, Louise knows it is exactly what she would say! Louise has to admit Martha possesses a graciousness that is a rare commodity in the world of people she has met so far.

Marleen, her Scottish friend, is about twelve years her senior with a bubbly personality. Practically always smiling, she appears to be in perpetual good spirits, one of those people who, when worried, anxious or annoyed, tends to cover her inner thoughts and emotions with an outward show of jollity and light-heartedness. Appearances, however, can be deceptive, as Louise learns over time. One thing is certain, though: she has a big heart and a generous spirit, and she is always kind and inoffensive. Perhaps, a little too soft by times when the situation calls for a firmness of purpose. On the other hand, every individual has their unique way of being in the world.

Marleen, like Martha, met her husband outside Libya, in Edinburgh, Scotland, where he was studying Aviation. They got married, moved to Tripoli and had two children. The house they live in belongs to Marleen's brother-in-law and his wife, who now reside in the US. Years ago, they decided to emigrate, and since both their parents are dead, they have no plans to return. Fortunately for Marleen, they eventually handed over their original home to her husband so they could live there indefinitely. Marleen is in a unique position amongst her friends, being entirely free from the interferences of in-laws.

Notwithstanding that, she confided in Louise how alone and isolated she felt for quite a while after she first arrived in Tripoli. She keeps saying she is truly delighted to have met Louise, and her daily life has suddenly expanded beyond belief.

They do not need a car because the friends live within minutes walking distance away. It surely is a life-changer, and Louise, like Marleen, is grateful to have a new-found friend. Early in the morning, they often meet and walk to the *suk* before the sun gets too strong. Later in the afternoons, Jabir is usually on hand to take Louise and the children wherever they need. It relieves Kareem of the task.

People have already begun to arrive, small groups and couples, standing about admiring the gardens and flowers that have been tended to so carefully by the resident gardener who is here with his wife and children. Shelley points them out to Louise, and glancing towards the far end of the garden, she spots him wandering about, proudly showing some of his more exotic shrubs to a small company of devotees. They walk over so Shelley can introduce him to Louise. Everywhere you look, there are various species of acacia, mostly white and shades of deep pink; some are large, having grown to full height, others are smaller shrubs, all beautiful to look at. Gerry the gardener, explains to Louise the many health benefits of the acacia tree before insisting on showing her around the gardens, including a commentary on the array of herbs in a secluded patch at the rear, but closely situated to the embassy kitchen.

Strains of music begin to waft across the lawn, where the musicians are set up on a slightly elevated bandstand, positioned to provide shade between a grove of palms at one end and a copse of beech trees at the other. The unmistakable sound of a violin reaches their ears, its sweetness and high vocal quality lifting their spirits as soon as they hear it. The party is finally underway.

The musicians, all attached to the embassy in some way, have volunteered to play for them today, only too pleased to give their instruments an airing and exercise their considerable talents. Shelley whispers that one of the three musicians is quite an accomplished guitarist and will treat them later to some amazing Spanish guitar.

Louise recognises a few of her English pupils who insist on bringing their parents over to engage her in conversation for a few minutes.

People move about, mingling and soaking up the relaxed atmosphere, enjoying the sunshine and music.

By six, most of the guests have left, with only a few dwindlers taking time to say their goodbyes as they amble reluctantly towards the exit gate. Louise can hardly blame them and is slow to leave, but the children are tired after a long, exciting day. Spent from playing, they prefer to sit under a large, low-hanging willow and tell each other stories. Tara's wish has been granted, and if she never wins another prize in her life, she will remember this one forever, Louise smiles to herself.

The three women sit together and savour the last shreds of fading sunlight as evening shadows begin to creep gradually across the residency lawns. Having overindulged in the delights of afternoon tea, they laughingly attest to being so full they can hardly move and gather up their belongings.

Just as Louise is about to rise off her seat, she is suddenly distracted by the appearance of a tall man emerging out of the shadows in the near distance, walking towards them, smiling with a casual wave of his hand. Shelley's voice rings clear as a bell over the gardens in the evening stillness.

"Hey Jeff, is it you, I don't believe it." Now, off her chair and walking toward him, they connect in a warm hug, clearly pleased to see each other.

"Shelley, it's great to see you. It's been a while, how is everything?"

"Fine, all good, how about you? I wasn't expecting to see you back yet. When did you arrive?"

"Actually, only yesterday, a bit of a story, too long for now," he says, laughing. "Where are the little rascals?"

"They're here. Come and say hello to Uncle Jeff." She calls to her twin boys, Hassan and Hussein, who come bounding over to 'high-five' their affable, good-humoured friend.

Then, Shelley turns, remembering her friends are about to leave, waiting to bid her adieu. She makes the necessary introductions, and Louise is momentarily struck by Jeff's arresting voice and manners, even the way he speaks. She also sees probing blue eyes that seem to sparkle with intelligence and wit. Suddenly, an intense curiosity seizes her, and she finds herself drawn to this ruggedly attractive man, wondering and wishing to know more about him while thinking how impossibly ridiculous this feeling is.

Shelley motions to Jeff to sit down and he grabs hold of a nearby chair, draping his linen jacket over the edge. Casual but stylishly attired, he cuts a sharp picture in chinos, striped shirt and suede loafers, a shade of moss green. Illuminated by the light of a lantern, Louise studies his handsome countenance, barely able to take her eyes off him. Shelley disappears for a few minutes, returning with tea and a plate of cakes. He accepts it with a smile of grateful appreciation, jokingly remarking on how his friend can always be relied upon to produce something sweet to tempt his taste buds.

Sporting a tanned complexion, he has a sort of dishevelled look about him due to a head of thick brown hair that reaches well below his ears, a light spattering of grey at his temples. His smile is energetic and friendly, revealing a set of evenly aligned teeth, white and healthy looking. The overall impression on Louise is seductive. Not entirely comprehending why, she suspects the feeling has been aroused from a place deep within her, and suddenly, she feels a strange sense of aliveness.

Finally, they have to say goodnight because Marleen's husband is waiting outside to take them home. As they stand up and prepare to leave, Jeff rises and offers his hand. Walking them to the gate, Shelley thanks them for coming, promising Louise to call soon. She steals a glance back over the garden at the man who sits now in silhouette, enjoying his tea, awaiting his friend's return. Louise has an almost uncanny sense that she has said goodbye for the last time to the lovely garden. As for Jeff, the stranger who has so unexpectedly caught her attention, she wonders if she will see him again.

TWENTY EIGHT

A Brush with Mortality

Though inland far we be, our souls have sight of that immortal sea which brought us hither.

– William Wordsworth

*E*xactly two weeks after the garden party at the British Embassy, Louise finds herself at the centre of a military attack named: 'Operation El Dorado Canyon', code-named by the United States in their air strike against Libya. With the news and media under strict government censorship, nobody expected it to happen and were not prepared.

Just after 2 am on Monday, April 15th, Louise is roused by an unfamiliar sound that seems distant at first. Opening her eyes, she sees Kareem rush onto the balcony. Jumping to her feet, she follows him outside, where things unfold at such an alarming rate that she is unable to process them in real time. It feels as if time has collapsed in on itself in a matter of seconds and together, they look up into the night sky only to see an aircraft approaching with powerful velocity, its landing light flashing red. Suddenly, a high whistling sound assaults her ears, a sound that will stay stuck in her memory forever. Like two crazed individuals, they rush headlong back inside, Kareem moving quickly along the passage with Louise following instinctively behind, hell-bent now on reaching the children's bedroom. Passing the hall window, it shatters in an explosion of glass, sending splinters flying in all directions, but luckily, they manage to clear the space just in time. Entering the room, he grabs Sami out of bed, tossing a blanket over him as he goes while she lifts Tara up, and they exit the house, affording no time for explanation.

They walk hurriedly down the steps to take shelter in the garden at the rear of the building. All at once, the ground beneath them begins to vibrate where the bombs make contact with the earth. Louise has never been so scared, and for a fleeting second, her life flashes before her eyes.

In a near frenzy, they pick their way through the darkness with only a torchlight to illuminate the path in front of them. Amid the deafening noise, another terrible sound reaches her ears, the hysterical screams of a woman's voice. In a wave of silent trauma, she realises they belong to her friend, Safar. Suddenly, her heart begins to pound in her chest, but she manages, somehow, to stay calm, not wanting to frighten the children.

They make it to the far end of the garden, where there is an old, disused gazebo large enough to hold a modest amount of people. The wood is chipped and discoloured, layers of dust have gathered over time, but the roof is intact, and along its outer limits, the seating is dry.

Two men, middle-aged diplomats who are attached to the neighbouring Czech embassy, are already there, leaning against the entrance. They acknowledge each other, and one holds a transistor radio in his hand. At first, Louise hardly notices as he fiddles with it, trying to get a decent reception amidst all the crackling noise. Then, out of nowhere, a voice, vaguely familiar, is speaking, his words clear, without faltering. She can scarcely believe it is the President of the United States, Ronald Reagan, addressing his countrymen, delivering a justifying speech which outlines his reasons for ordering an attack on Libya. He follows it with a clear warning to the Colonel that his government will not be deterred in their intentions to seek justice and avenge the lives of those who have suffered as a result of terrorism.

Louise can hardly believe her own ears. It is far too surreal for her to comprehend that she as an Irish woman and her children are caught up in such a vile political theatre. They are innocents whose fates are to be decided in some dastardly fallout because of a crazy dictator and his quixotic ambitions. As a result, they could all die here, aimlessly and for no purpose.

Without warning, all the lights are extinguished, and they are left in pitch blackness. Louise is sitting tensely on the wooden bench with Sami and Tara held close on either side of her. She gathers them even closer to her while the thundering cacophony of noise ruptures the night stillness, and smoke in the nearby distance billows into the sky like a big mushroom cloud. For Louise, nothing of her past life experience has prepared her for the calamitous night ahead.

Safar appears out of the darkness, shaking with fear, calling on God and the prophets to free them of such a terror. Abu-Bakr, her husband, tries to soothe her with words of calm reassurance as their four children burrow down next to Louise, their blankets clutched tightly about them to provide warmth from the cool night air.

Kareem and Abu-Bakr lend a hand to the old man who lives next door with his daughter Suhailah. Louise hears her voice through a break in the racket, exhorting her father to quit the house for his own safety. Louise knows little about the family except that they live alone, she being the sole carer of her ailing father. Within a few minutes, the men return with father and daughter in tow, urging them to take shelter inside.

The old man grips his beads firmly between crooked fingers, their shrivelled skin worn with age. A look of bewilderment crosses his face to meet his neighbours at such an ungodly hour. With his long cape draped about his shoulders, his daughter urges him to sit, and without protest, he begins to pray quietly, his fingers moving deftly along the beads. Sitting beside her father and looking around nervously, her eyes search the faces of those present, as if they might reveal something to her about this strange, uncanny night. Despite the horror, she is grateful for the company of her neighbours in such a dark hour rather than having to face it alone.

What a piteous community of souls they are, huddled together despite their differences. Separated by lifestyles, nationality, age and culture, they are nonetheless brought together in a time of desperate need, joined by a will to survive and, ultimately, to avoid death. Nobody knows what to expect or what might happen next, painfully aware that each minute may be their last. The terrifying thought brings with it a realisation of human fragility, how quickly a life, all lives, can be snuffed out like a candle.

There is no reference point when one is faced so suddenly, so unexpectedly with the brutal moment of reckoning, when your life flashes before your eyes in milliseconds and time is no longer a tangible measurement, a thing of order, but has instead become an instrument to obscure. Unable to find her voice, trapped in silence, her body motionless, Louise is overwhelmed by fear, terrified at the prospect that they might all die here. Let it be quick, she implores, and if there is a God somewhere, she hopes he is listening to her pleadings so that her children may suffer no pain. Her dearest parents appear before her eyes, and in a moment of abject terror, she realises that she might not see them again in this life.

Fragments of thought begin to float incoherently before her eyes, being numb to all else except the heaving of her own chest. Shadowy thoughts and words that belong to the accursed night burrow deep into her psyche, forming an anatomy of personal trauma, the associations to which would one day suffer an excavation of deep, dark places.

With nothing to cling to but a hope and faith that holds them in the palm of its hand, they keep a lonely vigil together, each with their own thoughts. And so, the night hours grind relentlessly on, and their little company grows steadfast with each passing hour they are alive.

Sharp crackling of anti-aircraft artillery, the roar of rocket launchers and heavy weaponry that have hijacked the night with uncertainty and dread begin to gradually recede, replaced by a deathly silence as the hour of the wolf passes and the first rays of light seep miraculously through on the great wings of dawn.

With it comes a surreal reality, along with a sense that everything is woven together in the tapestry of life, in its totality, a merging of past, present, and future.

They sit quietly until the sun finally appears, its upper limb peeping across the horizon and morning settles uneasily upon the garden. The tense, nervous energy inside the gazebo begins to slowly dissipate as the threat of danger feels less present.

Suhela suggests making coffee for everyone. After the men agree it is safe she steals across the garden, letting herself out through a small opening leading into her backyard. Abu-Bakr signals to his daughter to go and help. Within ten minutes, they return carrying two trays of strong Arabic coffee and tumblers of warm milk for the children. She brings a cloth bag with some bread, still fresh from the previous day. They savour the taste of hot, comforting drinks after such a horrendous night.

Around midday, the neighbouring party tentatively returns to their respective homes. Before they part, it is discussed amongst them that perhaps the wisest thing to do is leave the city without delay and head for less populated, more remote areas on the outskirts or further afield even.

It feels strange to be walking back inside the house and stranger still packing bags with essential clothing for the children and other necessities. Louise tries calling Martha to see if they are ok since their home is close to the military barracks, and Omar would surely have reported for duty. Whilst dashing around, trying to prepare something substantial for the children to eat and trying not to forget the important things, she hears Marleen's voice at the front door, and her heart leaps.

Looking up, she sees her friend walking toward them, Sami and Tara running to meet her halfway. Hugging them to her in a way that touches Louise's heart, without need of words, they both understand in that moment the value of friendship. "Where's everyone? Louise asks, referring to Raabea, Marleen's daughter and son Taher. "They're just in the garden with their dad, speaking to Kareem and your neighbours," she answers.

"Thank god we're all ok," is all Louise can say. About to elaborate, she checks herself, aware of the children's presence. Giving her friend a conspiratorial wink, she beckons her into the next room, leaving them to eat their food.

"What do you think is going to happen next?" Louise asks in a worried voice, "because I don't feel at all safe in this city," she whispers.

"Ach, me neither. What if the regime decides to retaliate and this is only the beginning?" Marleen's Scottish accent sounds even stronger than usual. Louise has no answer for her.

"It was a close shave, Marleen. I thought we were finished, that we were going to die and it's not over yet," Louise remarks solemnly, fighting back the tears.

Her friend goes quiet, and it looks like she is also about to burst into tears. Then they hug each other, and the moment passes.

"We have to try and stay strong, Mar, don't we? For the sake of the children, at least." They both nod in agreement and before they can say anything else, their conversation is interrupted by the sound of men's voices coming from the hall.

"Here they are. Let's see if they have any information." The two women walk purposefully into the living room, eager to know what their husbands have heard.

Word has come that a series of dramatic air strikes intended for some of the city's military installations and other targets have been hit. One of them is the state security compound located at the bottom of their street. Opposite the building, no more than a minute's walk away, there is a small park that Louise and Saoirse often take the children to. Being in the habit of sitting on a bench to chat while the children amuse themselves on see-saws and slides is a way to pass an hour on some afternoons. However, according to a local source who Kareem has briefly spoken to, an entire area of the park is now destroyed, along with damage to several private residences close by.

One of them is the family home of Kareem's good friend. Sadly, he was fatally injured and died shortly after the attack. As he tells them, Louise can barely take it in, especially since she only spoke to him a couple of days previously. He had done a favour for Kareem and called by their house, hoping to find him. She spoke to him briefly from the veranda and felt heartened by his friendly enquiries after her family and how she, herself, was getting on. Leaving a message for her husband, he went on his way but not without an invitation from his family to visit and have dinner with them. He joked with her, saying he had sent the invite through her husband numerous times. He added, laughing, "I can invite you and the children, personally."

The French Embassy was also hit but luckily nobody was injured. Louise walks past it most days, a charming country chateau with its carefully manicured gardens lying tranquilly inside a high gated enclosure. She would marvel at its refined elegance and chic style, wishing she could go inside and see if the interior was as attractive as the exterior. Hit accidentally, the building has sustained quite a bit of damage to its rear, Kareem tells them, lending fresh credence to Louise's worst fear that it is often the innocents who pay the price for political games.

Standing on the front veranda, they look out onto the street where a long line of cars and pick-ups are backed up, moving slowly along the quiet streets to join the main route out of the city. Most vehicles are packed with provisions and all sorts of belongings thrown together in haste to hit the road early. What Louise is witnessing before her eyes is undoubtedly just a small part of a greater movement; nonetheless, it is a weird reality that she too will soon be part of when she joins the mass exodus, leading her away from her home to a remote outpost far from the city.

After a round of tea and sandwiches, they decide to get a move on while the day is still young. In a parting embrace and with a spirit of optimism, the women reassure one another that they will meet again soon while knowing the future was uncertain.

Later that evening, a couple of hundred kilometres away from civilisation of a sort, nightfall is spreading fast across the clear African skies. Louise steps outside the tent to take a stroll and soak up the stillness of the night. She is eager to have even a short respite from the annoyances of her in-laws. The idea of being holed up with them in a confined area is not that appealing to her. Once in her life was enough for that.

Outside, she looks up to see constellations of twinkling stars, like tiny, luminous balls of light beaming down on the earth from a faraway galaxy. Sami and Tara follow her, and together, they stroll along the narrow track that separates the orange groves on their left from the lemon orchards that stretch way off to the right, as far as the eye can see. The light from a nearby dwelling is visible through the trees, the only one for several miles. In the distance, a dog barks, a solitary owl hoots, the sounds blending soothingly into the nightscape. A nocturnal chorus of 'singing' insects signals their hypnotic call, and it seems that all is in perfect harmony, at least in the natural world. In the world of human beings, things are of a different order.

The children have plenty of questions and though Louise attempts to make the answers child-friendly, not to scare them, she also wants to be honest so they know the value of truth. She hopes that by listening and encouraging them to talk about the troublesome events that have unfolded, the world becomes friendlier, and they can feel more content in themselves.

Louise has a flashback to the previous day. It had started off well with the promise of a get-together at Martha's. Tonight, it seems a million miles away, rather than a mere twenty-four hours. So much has happened, too much emotion to process all at once.

A year ago, Diane suggested they each host a monthly coffee afternoon, a kind of social 'gathering' for them all, including the children. It was a good idea, and so far, it has been working out really well. Yesterday, they all turned up, Marleen, Shelley, Saoirse, Magda, a Polish friend, and Diane, an English woman whom she had met through Shelley, and they had since become good pals.

Shortly after arriving at Martha's, the children are preoccupied playing, safely out of earshot. Martha, their hostess, wearing a grave expression, grabs their attention by confiding in hushed tones that a US attack on the city is imminent. Her husband had heard whispers amongst army officials. For a moment, nobody responds because the prospect is too crazy to take seriously, probably little more than the exaggerated ramblings of military men and their war-mongering flights of fancy. At least that is what they chose to believe and to console themselves with.

Despite their scepticism, an atmosphere of foreboding hung about for much of the afternoon but for the most part they had tried to ignore it and chase the disturbing possibility from their thoughts. Loath to spoil their enjoyment, they were also aware that Martha had gone to so much trouble putting on a lovely spread for them so they kept things light-hearted.

Later that same evening, shortly after she arrived home, Louise settled the children into bed and feeling tired, she decided to retire. As she crossed the hall, she heard the sound of heels approaching. Peering out, she caught a glimpse of Marleen by the light of the streetlamp, entering hurriedly. She went swiftly to the hall door to let her in. "Is everything ok Marleen, what's happened?" Ushering her quickly inside, Louise saw she was pale and anxious.

"I just got a call from your sister, Arleen," she blurted out. Pausing to take a quick breath, she continued as her friend began to sense some-thing portentous.

"They're en route, the American bombers. They're coming here, Louise, soon. She saw them refuel, it's on the news there." With a rising and slightly hysterical tone, Marleen slumped into the nearest armchair, inhaling a deep breath.

It took a few seconds for her words to sink in, the very notion too bizarre to imagine. Louise sat down in the chair beside her friend to steady herself before speaking.

"What? I mean, when did she call?" Flustered, she wondered why her sister had not phoned her. After a brief silence, she walked over to a side table where the phone sat and, to her dismay, saw it was accidentally knocked off its cradle.

"Oh no, no wonder she couldn't get me. What a disaster," she exclaimed, and for a second, she felt close to tears. Pulling herself together and doing her best to stay positive, she returned to her seat.

"I explained to her that we were out all day in Martha's. She told me to give you and the children her love and not to call her back tonight. She said it could be dangerous, you know, talking over the phone."

"It sounds like Martha's prediction was right after all and it's more than just 'barrack talk,'" Louise remarked bitterly to her friend.

"I'm scared, Louise and there's not a thing we can do. Marleen said forlornly. As soon as I get half a chance, I'm definitely out of here."

"I know, I'm thinking the same myself, if we get through this. Look, you go home, Marleen. Kareem should be home in about an hour; the sooner the better."

"No, I'll hang on Louise until he arrives, so you're not on your own. Don't worry, Abdul is with the kids," she added reassuringly.

They sat down to drink a cup of mint tea, more a distraction to calm the nerves. Before long, they heard Kareem's car pull up. By now it was close to midnight and Marleen bid her friend goodnight. Meeting Kareem below, they exchanged a few words, and he saw her safely round the corner to the house.

Walking through the door, he displayed nothing unusual in his demeanour. Searching his face for some clue, Louise wondered if he could really be oblivious to the escalating turn of events that was about to threaten their safety. She told him about the phone call from Arleen, and aware of the gravity of his wife's words, he listened attentively, nodding his head in partial disbelief. He assured her he had heard nothing of significance from anyone throughout the day until her latest update. Even if he had heard something, she could understand that he might not want to alarm her. He looked a bit worried, though; she could sense it, along with her own mounting trepidation.

Louise was aware that relations between Libya and other countries had not been good for a while and things had already begun to escalate globally.

Shelley confirmed as much in a conversation they had after the party at the embassy. According to Jeff, her friend, unofficial talks were afoot between the US and England and they were considering their options in relation to Libya. Despite the country's rapidly deteriorating reputation, most people assumed that a military situation would be averted and some agreement could be reached. Like others, she took it for granted without giving it further thought, never believing that events would take such a drastic turn.

Life in Libya was like living in the midst of a political illusion, a false patriotism. In truth, it was a totalitarian state in which the upper political echelons, which existed as a small but all-powerful elite, had their own political agenda: to rule with an iron fist.

Freedom of speech and opinion, the right of any free-thinking individual, did not exist in that regime. Everything was under state control, including television and radio. As for newspapers and reading in general, it was not encouraged, and Louise knew why. Surely, history had taught a valuable lesson: that knowledge is power and therefore something eschewed by an autocratic regime. . Freely given opinion was replaced by an official, sanitised media of mass communications, full of lies and propaganda. She was tired of seeing politically organised rallies regularly broadcast on national television channels.

There was relentless coverage of state-organised demonstrations, massive crowds of so-called supporters, hero-worshippers, stirring up the emotional tempo of the populace, engaging them in a ridiculous spectacle of personality cultism. Louise had found their public displays of hatred and crudity disturbing, especially when they began to burn effigies and gave free rein to their anger and rage.

Notwithstanding all of that, many people were aware at some level that all was not as it should be, and they looked towards the West to compare, sensing there was an insidious, bureaucratic machine at work trying to take over their lives, entrap their thoughts and actions in service of some sinister endgame.

Realistically, there was little or no choice but to get on with life or risk being hailed as subversive. The alternative was too ugly to contemplate. Prisons were overflowing with those who had courageously followed their convictions and met with the executioner's sword.

Those who went in search of education abroad or career advancement at home did better to champion the 'powers that be' rather than seek conflict. After all, one's life depended on it. Louise had heard many a story, disturbing accounts of what happened to those who rebelled against the state system.

Generally, people were extremely wary, afraid to speak freely, sometimes reluctant to confide even in friends unless they could be trusted implicitly. The human condition, being what it is, often finds itself challenged when it comes to loyalty.

Although Louise had never really given the politics of her adopted country much thought, now those politics were impacting her life in a way that she could never have imagined, not even in her wildest dreams. Eventually, the actions of ruthless leaders and murderous dealings began to send shockwaves into the wider world. Louise had no desire to remain in a country that sponsored terrorism. Coming from a completely different political background it felt like living in a parallel universe. She considered herself to be neither expatriate nor native, but just herself. She was not comfortable with the notion that because she had wed a native, her identity might be somehow subsumed under her husband's, which could have implications for her and her children, should she want to leave.

While Louise sits in bed, book in hand, trying to focus on the words in front of her, Kareem lies silently beside her, and though his eyes are closed, she knows he is not asleep.

Everything is quiet in the night outside and it seems there is nothing to be alarmed about, nothing at all. Unusually for Louise, she just cannot bring herself to read this night. Eventually, her eyelids become heavy, so she puts the book down and clicks off the bedside lamp. Soon enough, she sinks into a light, fitful sleep but not for long.

TWENTY NINE

Reinvention

It is never too late to be what you might have been.
— **George Eliot**

Bright rays of sunshine stream in through the window, bathing the hall in a soft morning glow. Nowadays, Louise barely notices the gaping crack in the wall left by the bombs, whereas once she was almost obsessed with studying it, tracing it from ceiling to floor, as if it contained within its structure all the answers to her questions. Not unlike the wall, something inside of her was divided, blown apart, and that summer, when she returned to Ireland, she made the decision to go and talk to someone. After reaching a kind of catharsis, she began to feel somewhat lighter, believing that encounters with darkness enlarge people in ways they could never have imagined.

Today, she feels good about being alive while she contemplates the day ahead. Unusually, she has been left alone in the house without the children since Kareem left early to spend the day at the farm, taking Sami with him. Tara on the other hand, refused to go with her father, preferring to spend the day at Diane's, whose daughter, Nadine is the same age. The eldest girl of nineteen will keep an eye on them while their mothers are out.

It is Shelley's thirty-fifth birthday and they are invited to her house for a celebration. Louise is looking forward to it, especially the rare opportunity to get out by herself. Once in a while, she likes to take time for herself and discuss things with friends that are otherwise off-limits when young ears are listening. Apart from that, she likes to dress up on rare occasions and wear some nice clothes, which makes her feel good.

Saoirse is due any minute. Sadeek is dropping her off so she can go with Louise. She hears the car pull up and, glancing out, spots her getting out of the car, followed by Diane, who is sauntering along from her house across the street.

Within ten minutes, Jabir arrives, punctual as always. He taps gently on the front door, and when she opens it to let him in, his eyes fall appreciatively on Louise as if nobody else exists except her. She greets him with her wide, symmetrical smile that lights up her entire face and unbeknownst to her, she has set his already smitten heart on fire. With their backs to him, Saoirse and Diane look round to say 'hello' and he crosses the hall to shake their hands, politely engaging them in good-natured banter.

Arriving at Shelley's, Louise is last to get out of the car and as she turns to close the door, Jabir goes to say something. A trifle impatiently, she hesitates, looking back at him.

"I, eh, what time did you say this evening to pick you up, Louise?" he asks, looking at her intently. Louise looks back quizzically, having already told him before leaving the house. He sees the look on her face, and before she gets time to answer, he says the thing he wanted to say from the start.

"You look beautiful today."

For a second Louise falters, and can feel her face blush but glances sideways to recover her composure. Looking back at him, she meets his gaze with a shrug of nonchalance and answers him.

"Oh, thanks Jabir, eh see you about eight. Thanks again for taking us."

Without waiting for any further comment, she slams the door shut, turns and walks toward the house, rather flabbergasted at his bluntness and, in that same moment, amused at her own feeling of unease.

The next day she has time to reflect on the compliment Jabir paid her. She knows it was sincere and uncontrived, without an intention to flatter and yet, she cannot imagine why he even bothered to say it.

Suddenly, it dawns on Louise that Jabir might be harbouring secret feelings for her. Maybe it's just a harmless 'crush' she tells herself, though the very notion of it strikes her as pretty outrageous. She tries to expel the thought from her mind and instead apply some rationale. She admits that they have grown close in the past two years and that it seems natural they would develop a companionship. Ironically, the less she sees of her

Kareem, the more she sees of Jabir. Her husband's work takes him away more than ever before, and besides, nothing changes when he is at home. What is more, Louise knows the chance of that happening is very slim. With some reluctance, she acknowledges that she has come to depend on Jabir. They get along well, and if he were to disappear for any reason, she would miss his company a lot.

In the early years of their marriage, Louise struggled when she realised that she was not her husband's priority. Despite endless rows and soul-searching, she has come to realise that what she needs from him has to come freely and not under duress.

One of the many challenges for her is acknowledging her husband's strange relationship with money, the root of which she is convinced belongs to his past. A few years into the marriage, she began to see the extent of it and how impervious it would be to change.

She still has no idea how much her husband earns or any idea about their financial situation because he never discusses it with her. She intuits that he is handsomely rewarded for his work, particularly when he travels abroad.

A case in point is when they had spent a spell in Germany. Out of the blue, Kareem announced his intentions to buy a BMW and have it shipped back to Tripoli. Louise was surprised because there was never a discussion about buying a car, although by then, it was clear to his wife he had a plan. On their arrival back in Tripoli with the new car, Louise's notion of taking a spin in it around Tripoli was quickly put to bed. It was sold almost as suddenly as it had appeared, within a week of their return for a significant profit, according to her husband. She never did have the pleasure of sitting in it. It transpired that the car was bought and sold to finance the purchase of a farm with Kareem's father. The move signalled the beginning of what would become a contentious issue and another big stumbling block in their relationship.

They disagree about money on a regular basis, what she considers to be 'housekeeping' expenses, essentials even and her husband does not. Being more than cautious, he holds onto his money with something approaching a miserly preoccupation. Louise smiles sardonically at the thought and thinks never the twain shall meet.

Meanness is something Louise abhors in others, and yet the irony of discovering it in her own husband is somewhat counterintuitive. She believes that a lack of generosity denotes a deeper meanness of spirit. Such an aversion to parting with money, even to those closest, bears out a humble philosophy. If sharing with others does not provide joy, Louise is convinced there will be no pleasure in withholding it.

His attitude to affairs of money is polarised between extreme parsimony at one end and extravagance at the other, completely lacking balance. To Louise, it seems he is at his most penny-pinching when it comes to her and the children. They have to do without sometimes while he splashes out on half-baked ventures, projects to make money, whimsical ideas which often amount to nothing.

She still remembers how cheated she felt after the German trip, between the secrecy on the one hand and his double standards on the other, along with plenty of other annoyances. A three-day trip to Switzerland, followed by a stay in Paris for three weeks, was a further disappointment, so she vowed not to accompany him on any more trips. Instead, she would travel home to Dublin to enjoy her own time for the duration.

Louise recognises that Kareem is not meeting her needs, and only two choices remain for her: to stay or go. The problem is fear of the unknown, conflicted about making that final, definitive step, and she is not quite ready.

So, she chooses what she believes to be the lesser of two evils, settling for an absent husband she is no longer in love with instead of taking a huge, final step and going it alone.

She wonders about the whole love thing and begins to view it through a different lens. Perhaps what she thought was love was actually something else, a strong attachment or some unconscious force which had driven her into his arms. She can never attest to being bowled over by a great personality, infectious good humour or wondrous charm. What was it about Kareem, then? Something about him had captured her, but she does not know exactly what it was.

She feels pain, fear, dread, rejection and loss to varying degrees and a hurt so overwhelming that she almost loses her zest for life altogether. The despair of loneliness and isolation is the worst, of feeling fragmented, existing in bits and pieces. At times, she feels the life she is living belongs to somebody else and not to her. Over time, she manages somehow, against the odds, to pull herself up and, in getting to know her own strengths, realises she is a fighter.

Nowadays, they live together, are occasionally intimate, share two children and have the name of being married, but in reality, they share very little.

Instead of feeling a strong mutual bond, there is a disconnection. When things are going reasonably well and life is to his liking, Kareem can be warm, even accommodating, up to a point. For all that, it takes very little for him to turn cold and insensitive, moody and bad-tempered for no justifiable reason. She has never forgotten the incident in Germany and the fear it has generated, so vividly etched in her mind. What troubles Louise is his selfishness and refusal to accept accountability for anything he does or says. During these hard times, she refuses to gratify his attempts to control, the need to have his own way, and there is a price to pay for that.

Louise has frequently asked herself, how long can it last?

She has reached an impasse with her husband on the possibility of her driving, amongst other things. Content to let it slide for practical reasons during her second pregnancy, the subject has been raised again and she asks him what needs to be done regarding the necessary paperwork. During her prolonged stay in Ireland, her father had given her driving lessons, but yet again, Kareem continues to play the game of forestall.

One day, feeling really annoyed, she broaches the subject for the umpteenth time and he finally admits to being totally against the idea, protesting that she might be accosted on the road when out alone. She asks him to explain how native women could do what she, a European, cannot, and he reminds her that she is his wife and what others do is not his business. Then she reminds him that he is not in control of her life and that trying to find ways of limiting her freedom will only cause serious problems between them. In his usual dismissive way, he storms out, mumbling obscenities under his breath, leaving her feeling scorned and upset. Henceforth, she drops the subject of driving with him altogether.

Unfortunately for Louise, going it alone is not an option in the culture she is in because a woman can do nothing on her own account without a husband's consent.

When she stops to think about her life and the obstacles to her independence, she cannot ignore the fact that Jabir plays a big part in making it more bearable. From time to time, he travels to neighbouring countries, usually Turkey, on buying trips for his retail business, a man's clothing shop he had opened a couple of years previously. Usually, he is no more than a week or ten days gone, yet it is enough to notice his absence. Besides driving her to where she needs to go when Kareem is away, he occasionally sits with the children, keeping them amused so she can catch up and write her academic assignments without interruption.

Several years have passed since she arrived in Tripoli, and Louise has long since toyed with the notion of creating something new and worthwhile in her life. She decided to turn her attention and energy to study, a kind of antidote to love's failures. She began looking into pursuing studies with the Open University through distance learning. Her research opened up new vistas of interest and enquiry, which excited and surprised her. Once she was set up, all that was required of her was perseverance, and she had plenty of that.

When she first told her parents of her intentions to do a degree, they were pleased and immediately insisted on helping out financially with the fees.

After coming to a suitable arrangement with them, she told Kareem in a phone conversation from Dublin. He sounded pleased but did not comment on her parents' offer of financial support, probably secretly relieved to have no financial responsibility for his wife's studies.

Louise has specific arrangements about assignment submissions, working to her own deadlines which are arranged between her tutor and herself. When she travels home, they have an opportunity to meet and discuss her progress. Already, there is an end in sight and she is studying hard to complete the final part of her degree.

Louise believes her decision to pursue a path in academia is probably the best thing she could ever do for herself. If she had stayed in Ireland, she would have had a similar goal, so she is determined not to allow a missed opportunity to stand in her way; she hopes it will benefit her future in some way. The programme is flexible and blends well with her lifestyle, leaving her ample time to study. Fortunately, she is able to continue giving English lessons to private students, though of late, she is trying to spread them over two afternoons as opposed to four. She thinks about taking a break but she needs the bit of financial independence it offers. Also, she sees it as providing a useful service to students who would be genuinely disappointed if she were to stop.

Life is busy, and outside of her study schedule, the daily routine continues, keeping house and looking after the children who are always with her.

She had hoped that with time and the right circumstances, things would improve, and Kareem might change his ways. It was a hope that sustained her for a long time. Eventually, experience disabuses her of the notion, and she has had to face up to the fact that they are two very different people, incompatible.

When she first set foot on foreign soil, she was a young girl entirely unprepared for what lay ahead. There is a great disparity between the girl she once was and the woman she is now.

It has been a slow burn, pulling away from her husband by degrees. With every slur, ugly pronouncement and minor betrayal, another tiny piece got eroded from the relationship, chipping slowly away to reshape into something where Louise feels more separate, less dependent.

Reflecting on the state of things, Louise tries not to harbour regrets, to resent what has already been done, for to think otherwise is futile and would deny the reality of her two beautiful children. Besides, she is grateful for good friends, Jabir included, and once she can look forward to being reunited with her parents each summer, life will be somewhat bearable. Her new, expanded world presents a solution of sorts, even if it is only a temporary one.

Life marches on, and there are extended windows of peace between them, periods peppered with little harmonies and relative contentment for Louise. She concludes it is because they are not together a lot of the time, so peace is easy enough to achieve. She has also discovered that accepting the reality of how things are has produced a change in her for the better.

Discomfiting as that may be, it is a necessary truth.

THIRTY

A House of Clay

*The people will be a mixture and will not remain united
any more than iron mixes with clay.*

– Daniel 2:43

Some people dream of diamonds, of finding fortunes, of bright lights and treading boards of fame. Some prefer the safety of their own backyards, never venturing too far, whilst others spread their wings and travel to far-flung, exotic places. There are yet others who prefer modest successes and minor triumphs to opulence and grandiosity.

Living in a mansion is something Louise has never thought about. Having lived with her in-laws in overcrowded conditions for a year, she knows what it means to be desperate, to long for a place to call one's own. Finally, when it does happen, she is content, assuming it will be enough to sustain them for several years, at least.

Creating a real home is distinct from merely occupying a space in any house, whether grand or simply a modest place to lay one's head at night. It is more about personality than design.

After spending an extended period in Ireland while Kareem refurbished the new house, Louise is content to return to new surroundings. It had taken a while for her to settle in properly, but she did and was surprised when, within two years, Kareem started talking about building a house. Louise soon realises that he has been playing with the idea all along but has said nothing to her about it. Like most things, it is never a joint decision and Louise is devastated that her husband has allowed such an important decision to ferment in his mind without ever discussing it with her.

205

One day, he mentions rather casually that his father is thinking of buying a farm outside the city in an undeveloped, remote area. Louise is only half listening, mainly through lack of interest and because his family regularly speak about things that never arrive. Now, something in his tone makes her stop and pay attention.

The notion of her father-in-law buying a farm kind of makes sense to Louise because at one time he had a *suk* and perhaps he wants to cultivate his own produce. Of course, he was much younger then and being on in years; it seems a bit late to be taking on such a project. When she says as much to Kareem, he agrees but then states, to her great surprise.

"I'm thinking of building a house there," he says.

She sits up and stares at him in disbelief.

"Build a house on your father's farm?"

"Why not Louise? Do you think we're going to stay here forever? Someone has to think about the future, you know."

She hears the note of defiance in his voice and a hint of caution registers in her head. She begins to see where this might go; it can only be in one direction, like so many other things, except this is potentially life-changing.

She waits to hear more, mindful to keep calm.

"Once we have our own land, Louise, we can build whatever we like to our specifications. I'm not doing this for myself, Louise; it's for you and the children," he insists.

Louise silently notes his remark, and if her husband is to be believed, it surely is reason enough to have consulted with her sooner rather than at the eleventh hour.

Her husband goes on to list all the positives to be gained by such a move. They would have a huge house with a swimming pool and land all around them. Each of them would have a bathroom of their own and Louise an enormous kitchen. Already it sounds a bit too good to be true. Still, she listens without interrupting, resisting the temptation to give an opinion.

"So, if your father buys this farm, have you already spoken to him about building there, and how will that work?"

Louise is beginning to dislike the idea more and more, but better to listen, she figures, and not respond until she finds out exactly what her husband's intentions are. It turns out to be worse than anything she could have imagined.

"We've considered everything, and it's big. There is plenty of room for three or four houses in the future. In a few years' time, it will be built up, though it's quiet now." Louise understands that quiet is code for 'isolated', probably a place in the sticks. She also wonders who the three or four houses might be for. Disregarding anything else, all she can think of is her being stranded there with the children and no car or transport, let alone suitable schools for the children. What of Kareem? Will he miraculously change his lifestyle, stay home longer, and limit his work trips abroad? The whole idea spells disaster for Louise; nothing she imagines could be worse.

"We can go and have a look, then you'll see what I'm talking about," he says persuasively.

"Ok, let us see it and then have a proper discussion about it."

She hopes he can sense the note of caution in her voice, but she refrains from voicing any disapproval.

Louise is already disappointed and annoyed with Kareem, though she remains silent, giving herself time to take it all in. The fact that he has already gone to see the land and spoken about it with his father before mentioning it to her is dismissive, arrogant even. Then, she reminds herself that, for the umpteenth time, her husband is capable of almost anything and true to form, her opinion does not count. A part of her knows he has already made his own decision and telling her now is pure window-dressing.

Building a house around a future that in any way involves her in-laws does not bode well. Instinctively, she knows there is more to it than Kareem is willing to share with her at this juncture.

THIRTY ONE

An Unforgettable Summer

One must maintain a little summer, even in the middle of winter.
— Henry David Thoreau

I t is a sweltering day in late August. The temperatures continue to soar and promise to be like this for weeks, probably into September, before it begins to cool.

This is the first year they are not holidaying in Ireland like they usually do, returning only a few days before Sami and Tara return to school in September. Louise had earlier decided to sit it out for the summer and travel home to Dublin for Christmas with her parents. It seems now like a great sacrifice having to spend a whole summer in Tripoli.

So far, she is finding the experience very trying, principally because of the unbearable heat and a plethora of insects that torment her day and night, especially those horrible, flying cockroaches that cause her body to react with all sorts of strange sensations. Ironically, it is not of that dreaded variety to which Louise succumbs but another, more deadly and dangerous species.

Usually, after noon each day, Louise closes the shutters and turns on the air conditioning to allow the house to cool down before they sit down to eat lunch at around one-thirty. Afterwards, there is little to do except lie down and relax or find something to keep them amused in the house because it is far too hot to venture outdoors. The shops close at one, and outside, a ghost-like quiet descends upon the deserted streets for the entire afternoon until evening.

Naturally, Sami and Tara get restless, being cooped up inside day after day with nothing really to do, no summer camps or activities to keep them occupied. In Dublin, they always have plenty to do during the summer months and now the boredom is getting to them in addition to missing their grandparents. Back in Dublin, Sami loves nothing better than to be out cycling about on his mountain bike, a present from his grandfather. Every year, he has spent his summers there since a small boy and he mingles with friends his own age from around the neighbourhood. Tara, likewise, loves her second home, doing things she enjoys and spending time with her grandmother, both enjoying a really strong bond that was forged from birth. Both Sami and Tara love going on picnics and other excursions with their grandparents and getting treated to all kinds of surprises. They miss all of it desperately, and it is no wonder the hot days seem long and tortuous.

When evening comes, people begin to stir, and traffic starts to move in the streets again. Soon, just after sunset, the *Maghrib,* a summons to prayer, can be heard, the haunting sound of the Imam's voice drowning out all other noise. Even when the sun has disappeared below the horizon, the nights are still warm and muggy, making it impossible to get a comfortable sleep. Frequently, in the middle of the night, feeling sweaty and sticky, a hot and bothered Louise steps underneath the shower and allows the cool water to cascade gloriously over her body, thankful for the partial relief it brings so she can settle a while until the next bout of sickly heat assails her.

The day arrives for the joint marriage of Kareem's two brothers. It has been a long time in the planning, with both men waiting to end a tour of duty, one on land, fighting a war in Chad, and the other at sea, in the Libyan Navy.

Finally, in July, the two brothers marry two cousins in a celebration that lasts for practically ten days. Louise is not looking forward to attending the family wedding and all the drama that accompanies such occasions, but she has to show her face for the main event at least and some celebrations immediately leading up to it. Kareem will hardly be seen for the duration.

It is her first experience of a traditional Arab wedding, and by the end of it, she is a most reluctant participant in the festivities.

Worst of all, the spectacle surrounding its actual consummation is a ritual she can only describe as a medieval practice. For it to be happening in the twentieth century disgusts Louise, and she expresses as much to Kareem, telling him how barbaric and demeaning she considers it to all women. He tries to ameliorate the practice by justifying it, attempting to cast it in a 'softer' light by offering all sorts of reasons, but no matter what he says, Louise is not convinced.

It ends in an argument, and Louise feels genuinely disturbed by the fact that her husband can so vehemently defend something she considers perverse. It is yet another learning curve for Louise, adding further insight into the person she married.

True to Arabic culture, celebrating the nuptials begins on a Monday and by Thursday, things are in full swing. On the night in question, the bride awaits the arrival of the groom, and the atmosphere is truly electric.

Louise finds herself part of an assemblage of women from both families gathered close to the adjoining bedrooms of both brides. Numerous female relatives, neighbours and friends wait in a heightened state of anticipation. Outside, in an enormous tent, the men also wait. Had Louise known what was to follow, she would have found some excuse to slip away. However, it would have proven difficult to avoid being noticed and to find someone to take her home and risk missing the most important moments of the celebration.

The two grooms, dressed impeccably in white suits, finally reach the house where they will unite for the first time with their new wives. Outside, there is a long, drawn-out procession of men which has gathered several streets away. The wedding march stops just shy of the front door and is accompanied by a rising crescendo of voices, beating drums, darbuka, the deafening drone of bagpipes and loud-sounding mizmar. Eventually, as loud cheers go up, both grooms simultaneously enter the bed chambers of their anxiously awaiting brides. The unfortunate women wait with bated breath to receive the husbands they barely know, men to whom they are expected to surrender their unclaimed treasure, whether they feel inclined to or not.

The singing and chanting continue with renewed intensity as each minute passes, and it dawns on a mesmerised Louise what all the hullabaloo is about. She steals a look at the faces of those around her, such jubilant expressions, and she fears her face is no mirror for the jolly revellers.

Without warning, amidst all the noise, a door opens, and out steps Sharif, only to be greeted by a new, more impassioned round of ululations. To Louise, he looks like a deer caught in the headlights. Reaching into his pocket, he pulls something out. Like a magician, in a swift, fluid gesture, he brandishes the thing he holds between two fingers and releases it into the crowd. A woman close by catches it as uproarious cheers rise from the crowd. Short of taking a bow, the proud groom exits after giving the rowdy guests what they want: a pure white handkerchief stained with his bride's blood.

Louise watches aghast, just short of running from the room, feeling a mixture of nausea and disgust rise up in her throat. Taking a couple of deep breaths, she reminds herself, yet again, it is just another aspect of a culture which is completely alien to her but an accepted part of life for those who belong to it. The reality is that many people, including her in-laws, have never progressed beyond an archaic mindset set, and she alone is not going to influence an entire cultural shift just because of her opposing opinions.

The other brother is not so fortunate in his endeavours, however. One can only speculate if his amorous approaches are met with reluctance or that he is not quite up to the task. Unlike his brother, he spends considerably longer with his bride while the guests wait impatiently, and what is more, they make their feelings known with sighs and mumblings about how long things are taking.

Suddenly, a male relative of the groom appeared and stands in front of the bedroom door with his back to the women. Louise can hardly believe her eyes when he proceeds to knock unceremoniously on the door, uttering words she is barely able to catch due to the background palaver. What on earth is he doing? Louise wonders, telling the groom to hurry up? What a performance, a complete farce, Louise thinks. How much worse can this debacle get before the night is over?

After a couple of minutes, the relative disappears, the door eventually opens, and a rather agitated groom emerges from inside. With a shrug of his shoulders, he announces to the entire company, in one single word, the futile result of his efforts in trying to court his new bride.

"Nothing", he shouts, whereupon he walks hurriedly away with a look of exasperation on his swarthy face. His exit leaves the disappointed women free to enter the bridal rooms, and they waste no time doing just that.

Loath to follow them, Louise finds a quiet spot to sit for a while before contemplating a move to offer her customary good wishes. Soon, at a prompt from Zanib, her sister-in-law, she gets up and goes gingerly towards the bedroom.

On entering, she observes a tense-looking Suheir, the new bride, looking hot and bothered. In a state of some undress, the tearful girl is sitting upright in the bed, surrounded by pillows, visibly doing her best to greet the guests, all regarding the event as a 'fait accompli'. The wedding gown Suheir had so recently looked resplendent in lies on the floor in a crumpled heap.

Louise notes with a mixture of horror and disbelief how her neatly coiffured hair is noticeably dishevelled. Moist tears smear down rosy cheeks, leaving a makeup channel running in streaks down her chin. At that moment, Louise wants to scream loudly, demanding to know what manner of violation has taken place here, in so public a setting, to leave a girl so clearly distraught on her wedding night. Instead, she struggles to hold her composure and forces a smile. Taking the girl's hand, she kisses her on both cheeks, sincerely hoping there will be better days ahead for the unfortunate girl with her new husband.

The other bride seems less nervous and more stoic than her unfortunate cousin, only testifying to the likelihood that she is either better at concealing her emotions or has proven to be more stubborn. At any rate, she is still wearing her gown and chatting quietly to some women from her family who are sitting by the bedside. Louise offers her congratulations and makes a hasty retreat from the room. Walking through the courtyard to the front entrance, she feels somewhat traumatised, still smarting from the fiasco she has recently witnessed.

Louise hesitates a few moments until she sees one of Kareem's young nephews exiting the men's tent. Beckoning to him, she insists he go and let Kareem know she is ready to leave. She waits, expecting to see her husband emerge, but is hardly surprised to see Jabir instead, car keys in hand, walking toward her, smiling.

"I'm going to take you home, Louise because Kareem is still chatting to friends and playing cards," he tells her with a laugh, at the same time raising his eyes to heaven in mock impatience.

"Oh, let's go then, no doubt it'll be sometime tomorrow before I see him, and then he'll have to catch up on sleep."

Louise has arranged to have a late breakfast with her friend Kay the following day and pick up the children. They had stayed at her house overnight so she could go to the wedding. They have planned to take the children to the beach, so she prefers not to see her husband if it can be avoided.

"Sorry to drag you away, Jabir, I really am." Walking to the car, she feels the humidity in the night air and can hardly wait to have a cool shower.

"No, don't you mind, I want to get away myself."

On the short journey home, she confides in him her sense of outrage about the bedroom scene she witnessed. He points out that both marriages are arranged, and the practice is dying out. In fact, the more modern families don't do it anymore.

"It was a traditional marriage and the thing is, both brothers agreed!" He informs her with a disapproving look. Louise nods in acknowledgement and decides there is nothing more to say on the subject.

"When it comes to my turn, if it ever happens, things will be completely different," he laughs.

Surprised, Louise turns her head to look at him.

"If ever, you can't be serious."

"I am Louise. Right now, marriage is the last thing I'm thinking about," he replies wholeheartedly.

Soon, they reach home, and on the porch, Louise pauses to remove her gold, high-heeled sandals and relieve her tired feet on the cool, white marble. As they reach the steps that lead to her front door, she gathers the folds of her long evening dress, a shade of cocktail-green chiffon, up above her slim ankles. The dress is figure-flattering and elegant, with a light, matching cape thrown loosely over her bare shoulders. She sighs, so glad to be home, her party piece done.

At the door, she fishes in her purse for the key before turning to Jabir.

"Would you like to drink a cup of tea with me?" she asks.

"Let's do that," he replies without hesitation, and together, they walk silently into the house.

A couple of hours remain until first light, and the fainter stars are beginning to slowly disappear as darkness will soon give way to the dawn light. In the stillness of early morning, there is an unfathomable magic, and it seems that nature has conspired to make it so. Something about it feels compelling and full of mystery, like the energy that flows between like-minded people when they connect on a soul level.

THIRTY TWO

Re-covering

I don't think of all the misery, but of the beauty that still remains.
— Anne Frank

Louise was fourteen when she read Ann Frank's diary. It resonated with her for some reason, evoking her sensibilities in an inexplicable way. A couple of years later, she met Kareem and, in a short space of time, uprooted herself to a part of the world that most people had scarcely ever heard of.

A couple of days after the wedding celebrations of Kareem's two brothers, Louise feels unwell and reckons she may be coming down with something.

By mid-morning, her head hurts, and her body feels heavy and lethargic. When Kareem arrives home at lunchtime, he finds her lying on the couch, with little energy to do anything. Earlier that morning, she had noticed a small lump just below her groin, red and slightly swollen, confirming her suspicions that it was most likely a mosquito bite.

The same afternoon, Kareem has to leave on a VIP trip, destination unknown, for security reasons. It usually works that way since he is flying with a delegation of high-ranking government officials. As he is summoned at short notice, there is time only to eat something and pack a suitcase before his driver arrives to take him to the airport, where he will assemble his team. Once in the air, he will be briefed about the flight plan and itinerary.

"I have to go, Louise, but Jabir will take care of things until I get back. If you don't feel better by tomorrow, go and see the doctor."

"Have you any idea, Kareem, how long you'll be away?" she asks.

"I'm not sure exactly but it could possibly be a week, even more."

At the sound of a car horn, he says goodbye to Sami and Tara. Turning to Louise, he tells her to take care, and without further ado, he walks out the front door.

Only a couple of months earlier, the infamous Colonel had been his most important passenger. He and his entourage were flying to a round of meetings in the East African nations. Muammar, the colourful commander-in-chief, had his own compartment to which none of the crew had access except through his bodyguards, who were mostly women and remained by his side at all times.

Since Kareem's promotion as flight engineer in-chief on board the president's plane, his responsibility has increased considerably. No doubt his financial rewards also, not that Louise has yet sampled the benefits of such an elevation in job status.

Louise can usually follow her husband's whereabouts and progress by seeing brief snatches of the delegation on the local television channel. Reading between the lines of what is alluded to in news reports, it seems probable that the trip will be extended.

Following his departure, Kay, a friend, visits Louise to check if the children would like to take a trip to the seaside. Her husband's family own a chalet on the beach about an hour's drive from the city. She has a boy the same age as Sami and a delightful little girl of four.

Louise has been friends with Kay for a couple of years, having met her through Diane, and she admires her cool, matter-of-fact manner and natural sense of humour. In an environment that does not encourage women to be fully autonomous, Kay manages to carry it off with aplomb, encouraged by her rather forward-thinking husband.

Surprised to find Louise under the weather when she calls, and with genuine concern, she suggests taking Sami and Tara to the beach the following day to give her friend the opportunity to rest and the children a treat. When Sami hears it, he is instantly excited because he loves the beach and has a chance to have fun with Zain.

"If Diane wants to come along and bring Nadine so Tara and herself can be together, there's enough room in the car," she assures Louise whilst looking directly at Tara, whose face lights up at the mention of her friend. Luckily, Kay drives and is able to borrow her husband's Volvo estate, which is roomy enough to accommodate a portable fridge and other beach equipment, as well as seat everyone comfortably.

"Will you be able to manage Kay?" Louise asks. "I'm just a bit worried about the boys in the water, Sami in particular. He knows not to venture out too far in the sea, but you know when they get excited…." her voice trails off as Kay interrupts to reassure her.

"Don't worry, I'll keep him under control," she insists. Looking over at Sami, he looks back at them so contritely that nobody would think him capable of any mischief.

"Well, he knows not to try anything, or he'll not be invited again, don't you Sami?" Kay warns in a good-natured tone.

Louise is grateful to her friend and also pleased that the children have an opportunity to enjoy themselves. Moreover, she trusts her two friends to keep a watchful eye on them even though she is not there herself.

Later that night, Louise begins to feel an increasing stiffness in her joints, aching muscles, and a beating headache. Barely able to move off the couch, she asks Jabir to bring her some painkillers to combat the fever, if nothing else.

The children are in bed early enough, excited about their beach trip the following day, after spending at least an hour putting their towels, swimming gear and other stuff in a bag ready for an early pick-up. Louise asks Jabir to pack some hard-boiled eggs, tomatoes, tuna, and olives to take with them, along with drinks and biscuit packets. Kay always stops to buy fresh, crispy bread on the way and no doubt Diane will also bring food.

Somewhere around 2 am, Louise wakes from a fitful sleep; dripping in perspiration and needing to relieve herself, she gets unsteadily to her feet.

Instantly, a wave of nausea washes over her and she has to sit back down.

Eventually, taking a few deep breaths, she managed to stifle it in time to make it to the bathroom. Oh God, what the hell is wrong with me? She asks herself as another wave threatens. Sinking onto the cool bathroom tiles, she leans over the toilet bowl but only succeeds in bringing up bile because she has eaten nothing except a drink of water and a few sips of weak tea. Catching a glance of herself in the mirror, she looks unusually pale with dark shadows under her eyes. Then, seeing the box of paracetamol in the cupboard, she takes a card and slips it inside the pocket of her robe.

Jabir is standing outside. When he sees her, his face is full of concern.

"Louise, are you ok?" I think we should go to the hospital.

"Not really," she answers. All she wants to do is return to her spot on the couch where she has been lying and flop down. She prefers to lie there rather than in her bedroom because she is close to the veranda and its open door. At least there is an illusion of cooler air coming through from the front of the house.

"Can you get me some cold water and a bowl?"

Reclining in a half-sitting position on the couch, she wonders what she should do, her head throbbing. Jabir reappears with a glass of water, bowl and face cloth. After swallowing the pills, she tries with difficulty to sit up, and as she reaches for the bowl, Jabir goes to catch hold of her wrist. Instead, he catches her hand, and for a brief moment, they look at each other in the semi-darkness. Something unspoken passes between them fleetingly, enough time for Louise to understand something despite her incapacitated state. She gently frees her hand from his and lies back down, allowing him to place the damp cloth on her brow, its coolness offering some comfort.

"You just rest, Louise," he whispers quietly, soaking it again in the bowl.

"It's good", she whispers, closing her eyes and eventually drifts off. When she wakes, it is early morning, and Sami and Tara are beside her, already dressed and chatting about the day ahead. Louise is disappointed she cannot go with them because she loves the beach herself, and it is a rare opportunity not to have to face Kareem and his sulkiness on their return. She had long ago realised that her trips to the beach, occasional as they were, with her friends, ruffled her husband's feathers considerably. He never quite admits it in so many words, but she soon recognises a pattern in his behaviour whenever she mentions 'beach' and, subsequently, his mood when they arrive home at the end of an enjoyable day.

Once, when she challenged him about it, he came close to forbidding her from going, but she told him she would go, irrespective of any objections he might have. From that time, the beach has remained a sore point between them.

By late afternoon, on the third day, Louise's condition has worsened, and she knows that she must seek medical attention. There are only a handful of clinics in the city she would consider going to, so she asks Jabir to take her to one rather than the hospital. Once, Kareem and she had taken Tara with a gastric complaint and had found a doctor who was helpful enough.

After waiting her turn in a hot, stuffy room, she is finally called into the doctor's office. He is a different doctor but pleasant and speaks English quite well. He diagnoses her with food poisoning and prescribes antibiotics to take over a few days, along with advice to drink plenty of fluids. Feeling somewhat relieved but lightheaded and very weak, she walks slowly back to the car where Jabir is waiting. He sees her approaching and jumps out to open the car door.

In the days that follow, she feels little improvement overall, managing the fever and headache with painkillers. She tries to keep hydrated but has no interest whatever in food. As soon as she tries to put something in her mouth, the nausea returns. Also, rather alarmingly, the stiffness in her body is getting worse. She feels so tired and lethargic that she can only move off the couch to go to the bathroom; anything else is too great of an effort.

Safar comes and goes with plates of food for the children, as does Marleen, pausing to chat for a while before leaving her to drift off into another restless sleep. The children hang about, asking questions and not understanding what is ailing their mother. Sometimes they put on a movie and sit watching it beside her.

Louise is ignorant of the malaise that is causing her to feel so bad because the antibiotic seems not to be working. Jabir insists on staying, refusing to leave her alone while she is so unwell. He goes and brings pizza for the children and makes sure they have what they need. Still, there is no sign of Kareem returning.

On the eighth day, Louise is alarmed by the appearance of red blotches on her body and her legs swollen. Marleen calls in the morning and insists on taking Sami and Tara to her house for the day until her friend seeks more medical attention. They are happy to go with Marleen, whom they are very fond of. It is the best thing to do rather than subject them to a round of hospital visits, especially as their father is still away.

Usually, the duration of Kareem's trips is no more than four days but this one seems likely to continue for ten or more. Marleen's husband is able to confirm it from his sources at the airport, and anyway, the progress of their president and his delegation can be tracked on local TV. He has a few more Arab states to visit before returning to Libya.

Jabir has gone to get fresh bread, and on his return, he finds a tearful Louise, uttering things he has never heard her say before. It's obvious to him that things are not well between her and his brother, a fact he has long suspected. She is worried, even afraid, and he tries his best to reassure her.

Putting on a sun dress and light cardigan to cover the rash and her bare shoulders, she scoops up her long hair into a tight clasp to keep cool. She has neither the energy nor inclination to brush it. Then, gathering her wits about her as best she can, she ventures into the mid-morning sunshine with Jabir to drive her to the nearest hospital.

Fortunately for Louise, her decision to seek further advice was a wise one. The doctor explained that had she delayed it for a further forty-eight hours, the result may well have been fatal, with the potential to inflict serious long-term damage to her body.

Once inside the crowded hospital, she can tell at a glance there will be a long wait before she gets to see a doctor. Jabir waits in the car outside and looks in every now and again. The seats are all taken, and some of the women find a space on the tiled floor, so she finds a spot and sits down with her back against a wall.

The hours drag slowly by, and the room is stale, stuffy and like a sweatbox. Jabir appears at one stage, bringing her a flask of cold water. Louise's already aching body is now a myalgia of stiffness and discomfort, worsened by her having to sit on a hard floor for so long.

A small fan twists and turns, a rather pathetic attempt at temperature control since it does nothing except redirect the fetid air around the room.

A myriad of disturbing thoughts enters her mind while she waits. Trying to push them back, she concentrates instead on the children waiting for her to return.

Suddenly, she feels a strong but familiar cramp in her stomach and instantly fears the worst. She wants to avoid using the toilet here if she can. Weak and sweating profusely, she struggles to her feet but never makes it that far because everything around her becomes a blur.

Weak now and sweating profusely, she tries to bring herself to her feet to find a toilet, but she never makes it that far. Suddenly, her head feels light and woozy, and she faints.

Her passing out was probably the fastest way of getting medical attention because the patient is brought immediately into triage for observation following urgent medical assessment. Shortly afterwards, Louise is admitted due to a very high temperature and a significant drop in blood pressure. It turns out she is also severely dehydrated, and following her fainting episode, she lapses into a state of temporary delirium that continues for a number of hours. Throughout the night, it begins to subside as the meds start to take effect and intravenous rehydration begins to restore the loss of fluid to her body.

When a Lebanese doctor pops in to see her the next morning she is awake and partially alert, considering how sick she has been and still is, despite the improvement in her vitals.

"Good morning, I'm Doctor Amin. How are you feeling today?" Glancing quickly at the chart in his hand, he looks down at his confused patient. "Louise, do I have that right?" He waits for her to respond with a friendly smile.

Louise attempts to push herself up in the narrow bed before answering, but finding her body still weak, she relaxes back down.

"Hello, Doctor, yes, you have it right, it's Louise, and I'm from Ireland." Feeling compelled, she adds that important piece of information.

He had realised she was not a native, and at the mention of Ireland, his smile widens.

"Oh, a lovely place; Dublin is, yes, one of my friends is doing his internship there. I've been over to visit him twice."

Pointing to the infusion stand by her bed, he explains to a blinking Louise, eyes drowsy, that she is getting a glucose drip intravenously to get her energy levels back up.

"So, doctor, do you know what the problem is because I was never before as sick as..."

He raises his hand in a gesture of calm, stopping her from speaking further.

"Actually, Louise, I've started to run some tests already, including blood samples we took during the night, and they should be back soon. Can you tell me briefly when you first became ill? Is there anything important I should know?"

Louise begins with the bite and then slowly recounts her symptoms' progression. She adds at the end that her husband is away and it was her brother-in-law who brought her to the hospital.

"Yes, I know, we spoke last night. Now, try to rest and not to worry; I shall be back later on to see you, Louise, ok?"

She nods at him, feeling instantly relieved after speaking to him. His bedside manner is certainly reassuring, and she is grateful to him for it. It is definitely what she needs to help her feel better.

For the first time, she has a chance to survey the room after the curtain is pulled back, but in contrast to Doctor Amin, it does little to boost her mood. Resting her weary head back on the pillow, she wants only to sleep, the comfort of restful sleep.

When Louise opens her eyes next, she sees Kareem standing by the bed. For a few confusing seconds, it feels like a dream until the mental fog clears, and she realises that he is actually present in the flesh. Is it the same day? She wonders with a feeling of confusion. Her husband is speaking, but she is not really listening to his words despite his expression of concern.

Suddenly, Doctor Amin appears, and after greeting Kareem courteously, he turns to his patient with a smile before addressing her in a serious tone.

"Louise, we have the results of your bloods back," he begins. You have a severe infection, and we're going to start you on an intravenous antibiotic straight away."

"What infection are you treating me for, doctor? Do I have to stay here? For how long?" More alert than before, she is thinking about fresh clothes and other stuff she needs.

"Well, for tonight anyway, then you can go home tomorrow when I feel you are out of danger but I want you to come back in here to the hospital just for a couple of follow-up injections. It won't take more than an hour each time."

He turns to Kareem, who is regarding him with a quizzical look.

"What's the problem, doctor?" he asks.

Directing his attention to them both, he explains.

"You managed to contract typhus fever." Aware of the expression of shock on his patient's face, he rushes to console his patient.

"You don't need to worry, Louise, because we caught it in time before you suffered any hypovolemia. That's when the body goes into shock as a result of toxic substances."

"Luckily, you are otherwise healthy and came to us when you did as you were badly dehydrated, too, so all is good."

"How did I get it, doctor? I mean, I'm very careful about hygiene and everything?"

"We live in Africa, a sub-Saharan region," he responds with a chuckle. "We can get pretty much anything here; it's not like Ireland, you can take my word for it," he finishes with a broad smile.

The following day, Louise is discharged from the hospital, but with a stern warning from Doctor Amin that she must rest and do nothing for at least two weeks. After that, she may return to her normal tasks but slowly, he explains, allowing the body to heal. He warns that it could take up to three months or longer. Louise remains silent as Amin addresses Kareem, reiterating how the sickness has depleted his wife's energy. What she needs, he advises, is to eat nutritious food, get fresh air and regular rest.

As Louise descends the hospital steps, she feels so relieved to be going home, to be reunited with her precious children. She is grateful to have found such a good doctor as Amin because, without him, it could have been disastrous. Her friends have been so supportive in many ways, and then there is Jabir. What would she have done without him? As for her husband, now is his time to shine in the days and weeks ahead.

When she is home and settled, later that evening, she has time to reflect and again feels so grateful to be home and over the worst. The children are truly delighted to be reunited with their mother, and there are plenty of hugs all round.

In the days that follow, immediately after her discharge from hospital, she begins to digest the ordeal she has been through. It is hard to believe that she had contracted such a debilitating disease. Suddenly, something is triggered in the deep recesses of her memory, and she is taken back to her youth, to the time she read *The Diary of Anne Frank*. In a moment of sadness, she can still recall the girl's courage and honesty right up to her pitiful demise.

In Belsen, she succumbed to typhus and died at the tender age of fifteen.

THIRTY THREE

A Blissful Escape

Home is a shelter from storms – all sorts of storms.

– William Bennett

After Louise completes a round of injections and her blood is tested, she is finally given a clean bill of health and finishes up with the hospital. She has carefully heeded the advice given to her by Doctor Amin, which is easy enough to follow because of the tiredness and lack of energy she feels.

Throughout the weeks of recuperation, the simple but genuine kindness of friends has aided in her recovery. She greatly values the efforts of Tara and Sami and how attentive they are in their own little ways by keeping the house tidy, bringing her tea and generally being patient with her convalescence. On Fridays, their day off school, they insist on making her breakfast of scrambled eggs on toast. Louise encourages them whenever she can, mindful that her children, Sami in particular, is growing up in a culture where boys grow into men who are unwilling to take on any domestic chores. Therefore, she is adamant that her son's earliest years should be imbued with a balanced attitude. It has been disturbing for her that too many women that she has witnessed are, in her opinion, the equivalent of glorified skivvies for their menfolk.

Every day for two weeks, after she arrives home from hospital, a knock comes on the door, and it is Safar with lunch on a tray. She has gone to so much trouble, preparing food that is tasty, trying to tempt Louise's taste buds back to what they were before she became ill. She knows that Louise is particularly fond of kofta made with minced lamb and spices. Her other favourite dish is falafel, made from ground chickpeas or beans and mixed with herbs and spices, then shaped into small patties or balls and fried. Sometimes, she makes a delicious salad dish called *Tabouleh*, which consists of finely chopped parsley, tomatoes, onion, sweet pepper, and bulgur, seasoned with fresh mint, olive oil, and lemon juice. Louise insists that none other than her friend's cooking has finally brought her appetite back to life.

Marleen also has been a great friend, calling most evenings for supper. They sit and chat, keeping each other company while Kareem is either out or at work.

Kareem's mother, his sisters and the two newlyweds also pay her a visit. She is expecting them because Jabir had told her beforehand. With that in mind, she asks Safar to join them and make traditional tea and without a hesitation, she comes. The 'Hajja' seems to have mellowed somewhat in attitude towards her daughter-in-law, and although Louise has come to regard her with a certain degree of tolerance and understanding, she doubts if there will ever be a bond between them. Louise is not sure if the woman is actually capable of building one, even with her other daughters-in-law, and she can already see that the two latest additions will not put up with any nonsense.

Despite all that had happened in previous years between them, Louise has, after much reflection, come to the realisation that the woman who had caused her no small degree of distress now ceases to affect her in the same way. People might say, 'time is a great healer,' but instead, Louise believes that she has learned to manage things better. Time, by its own measure, provides a passage through which one can find a fresh perspective. In any event, she keeps her distance and they are not a constant in her life.

Ironically, she has a sense that her mother-in-law understands that much.

Alas, summer has passed, and autumn arrives, putting paid mercifully to the intense heat and humidity of previous weeks. The mornings are warm enough with plenty of sunshine, and the daylight hours have grown shorter.

Louise is starting to regain her physical strength and a new lease of life, though it has taken a long time for her energy to return and to feel like herself again. Having slept a great deal, she can attest to the recuperative power of sleep on the body, but despite its benefits, her mood is low. She has a sense that life, as it is, can no longer contain her. Maybe it is just the debilitating effects of the illness still lingering, making her feel restless and mildly agitated.

As winter approaches, Louise finds the November days pleasantly cool and welcomes the occasional heavy downpour. Winters are mild in that part of the world, unlike back home with frost and freezing conditions. The worst she can expect is the tail-end of a sandstorm; it is rare enough, but when it does happen, everything ends up covered in a layer of reddish-brown dust particles, which take days to eradicate.

As for Kareem, his lack of real effort has been disappointing, and Louise feels it, though she carries on without dwelling too much on the fact. He still goes out a lot, true to form, so nothing has changed in that regard. Whenever she suggests going out for fresh air or a drive, she expects to be taken somewhere they can walk, near the beach or along the coast. They could even drive into the town and get something to eat in one of the few cafés along the waterfront and enjoy eating in the car while watching the sun go down. It would be nice for the children and them to do something altogether.

Louise knows she is not asking for much, but for some reason, her husband is still unwilling to do the most basic things she asks. She reminds herself it has been the same for years. Finally, she just stops asking, and as it turns out, she has no desire left to do or go anywhere with her husband. Louise has learnt through painful experience that when something is not given freely, it cannot be forced. That is how he is, and nothing will change him.

As the weeks go by, one day Louise has an unexpected visitor. To her surprise, when she opens the door, her neighbour Suhaila is standing there holding a plate in her hand. After a brief hesitation, Louise remembers her manners and immediately steps back to invite the girl inside.

It is only when she is seated on the sofa that Louise is able to closely observe the girl whom she had first met several years previously at the time of the American attack. The events of that night are still blurred due to the shock and distress they were all in.

The girl before her is small in height, slightly plump around the hips and thighs, but has a slim upper body and a neat waist. Her face is undeniably pretty. Indeed, it is her greatest asset because it features dark, mysterious eyes that seem to dance and sparkle, conveying a sense of vitality and mischief.

Kareem then appears, dressed to go out, with his jacket on and car keys dangling in his hand, but seeing the visitor, he stalls, and they greet one another with the usual customary handshake. He politely asks about her father and his health.

Louise vaguely recalls Kareem telling her that the old man was unwell. It happened one day when Louise was glancing out the window, and she saw the girl standing on the footpath with her father. It was apparent there was some problem or other. Kareem was on his way out the gate at the time and stopped to make conversation. Apparently, her father needed to go to the hospital, but his daughter's car refused to start, so Kareem offered to take them. She remembers seeing Kareem helping the irascible old man into the back seat of his car and Suhaila climbing into the front.

Normally, if Kareem happened to be off, he would be gone by ten, eager to get out early and do things. That morning, however, he had slept in because he was tired, having stayed late at work the night before, sorting a problem until the early hours. Looking at his watch, he seems to have second thoughts about rushing off. Sporting one of his charming smiles, he suggests they drink a coffee before he goes. So, Louise leaves them to chat while she makes the coffee.

Suhaila explains that the treats she brought are a traditional Tunisian sweet called *Bachkoutou*. After tasting one, Louise gives them a thumbs-up.

An hour passes, and neither Kareem nor Suheila seems in any hurry to go about the business of their day. Louise, on the other hand, is eager to get on with stuff she has to do, make lunch and other chores she was interrupted with. Strange, she notes, her husband's sudden reluctance to attend to whatever he had earlier found so pressing.

Rising from her chair, Louise politely announces that she should really set about preparing lunch. The time is running on, and moreover, Sami and Tara are expected in from school. She mentions that she also has an arrangement in the afternoon with friends and should get herself organised.

On cue, the girl stands up, stating rather unconvincingly that she has not noticed the time passing. Kareem rises with her. At the door, she says goodbye and thanks Louise for coffee while Kareem extends an invitation to call again. Turning around, she shoots him a beaming smile and promises to do just that.

In an instant, she is gone, leaving behind a strange sort of energy. Louise barely has time to walk back inside, and her husband rushes past and out the door, mumbling something about coming back for lunch. It strikes her not for the first time that Kareem is being somewhat disingenuous. Try as she might, she cannot put her finger on why she has such a feeling.

As the November days draw to a close, Louise finds herself counting the days until it is time to leave for Ireland, so excited at the prospect of spending Christmas with her family.

She had decided not to tell her family about the illness until she was well on the road to recovery. Even at that, they were horrified when they heard and scolded her for not telling them. Of course, the reason was that they would have worried too much, and there was nothing they could have done at the time.

In mid-December, Sami and Tara are on board a flight to Dublin. She can hardly believe they are sitting on the plane, the children so full of delight at the prospect of seeing their grandparents. Although Kareem may not have welcomed the trip, he seemed to encourage it, wasting no time in approaching the school principal and requesting time off. Whatever he said to her, she was happy enough to agree that the children should have a short break.

Of course, Arleen played her part in speaking directly to Kareem and voicing her concern about her sister's recent illness. In her opinion, it was imperative that her sister have a holiday to lift her spirits. She insisted that her parents needed to see their daughter and be assured she was fully recovered and feeling ok. There was little scope Louise imagined for Kareem but to concur with her sister.

Louise shifts in her seat, trying to get comfortable, not wanting to disturb a still sleeping Tara whose head is resting against her shoulder. She has suffered from travel sickness since her earliest years but seems to be growing out of it. Sami, on the other hand, is a great passenger who loves the whole experience of flying and adventure.

Louise closes her eyes to relax, but disturbing thoughts come stealing into her mind instead. Weeks before, Louise had complained to Marleen about Suhaila's frequent visits to their home. Three times in a week is too much to show up at anyone's door unexpectedly, and her presumptuous manner began to irritate Louise. The girl had shown no awareness of overstaying her welcome, which Louise finds most unusual, considering cultural norms, for a single girl of no family relation to insist on making herself so familiar.

Because Marleen's kitchen window looks directly onto Suhaila's backyard, she is ideally positioned to see and hear what she describes as strange goings-on and constant fighting. By all accounts, the father has a reputation for being quite a cantankerous character. Marleen has heard many angry outbursts, often escalating into full-blown rows that spill out onto the back porch. Doors slamming, screaming women and histrionic scenes are not an unusual occurrence when family members come to call, according to her friend.

Louise tries to imagine what it must be like to take care of a difficult, ageing father and see to his every need. Her parents, originally from Tunisia, had settled in Tripoli when their children were young. Now, they are a divided family, split and separated between two dwelling places. Who could say what the true nature of their family disharmony really is? Louise believes that nobody really knows and, therefore, it is unfair to make judgements.

Outwardly, the picture that everybody sees is of a girl in her late twenties who, for some reason, has decided to stay alone with her father and care for him single-handedly. Yet, according to cultural dictates and the strict societal norms to which she belongs, it is considered highly unusual, even frowned upon without other family support. The locals, not surprisingly, are always ready to indulge in a bit of idle gossip, and Louise senses a general antipathy in people's attitudes towards Tunisians. In truth, anybody who is different is likely fair bait.

What has contributed more so to Louise's annoyance over the past few weeks is Kareem's behaviour concerning the girl, which she can only describe as outright encouraging. She had said very little to her husband regarding her thoughts except that she dislikes the frequent comings and goings. Distracted by the prospect of her trip home, she was determined to allow nothing to overshadow her journey, not even the shifty machinations of her husband.

Louise is once again aware of negative thoughts, but they are easier to discard now that she has more pleasant thoughts to replace them with. All her concerns will be left aside, and for the next two weeks, she intends to make the most of life for herself and the children. No cloud shall cast its shadow on her positively anticipated horizon.

The late afternoon sunshine is shining brightly through the window, bathing everything inside the cabin in a warm glow. Louise guesses it will not be long until the plane begins to navigate its descent.

No sooner have the wheels touched the ground than Louise feels a sudden swell of emotion so intense that it surprises her. She struggles to curb it so she can answer a flood of excited questions from Tara and Sami.

Outside, darkness has already enveloped the December evening, but the lights of the airport buildings illuminate everything within its broad radius. Standing tall and stately atop the entrance building is a giant Christmas tree. Louise is so heartened by the sight of it that she feels like a child again.

The aircraft comes to a halt, and after a short delay, they finally make their way to the exit. Once outside, they can feel the sharpness of the cool night air touching their faces. Louise warms to it instantly because it speaks to her of home and the deepening of past winters. Making their way through the airport building towards the baggage reclaim, passport control, and finally, the arrivals hall, the children quicken their steps. Louise can hardly believe they are finally here and the journey is over.

Racing ahead, the children rush through the doors, their mother behind, pushing the trolley out into a sea of faces. Immediately, she spots them and her heart flutters, skipping a beat. Arleen, unable to stand still, walks briskly forward with her parents in tow. Something about her mother's eager face, her father's gentle smile catches her breath, and her heart swells with love. She is overcome with tears of joy to be back within their precious ambit, enveloped in their loving arms again.

On the road, heading for home, Louise already feels more relaxed and refreshed than she has been for a long time, as if she has shed a heavy coat.

As she steps inside the gate of her parent's house, she immediately sees the holly bush in bloom at the bottom of the garden, its luscious red berries hanging deliciously from their December boughs.

The moment she steps inside the house, her spirit is uplifted, her soul lighter and with every inch of her being, Louise knows where she is meant to be. Home, the perennial sanctuary, where the rags of one's life are turned into cloths of gold, and there is shelter when one is cast adrift on a stormy sea. For Louise, home is a fortress, a state of belonging that provides predictability in an uncertain world.

THIRTY FOUR

A Winter Idyll

Life is lived forwards, understood backwards.

– Søren Kierkegaard

T he streets of Dublin city are thronged with people in earnest preparation for the days ahead, mindless of the freezing temperatures and the promise of snow in the icy air. On the crowded streets and in busy stores, the excitement is palpable, mirrored on the faces of eager shoppers, spilling out of coffee houses and eateries where they pause to savour a brief respite from the world of retail beckoning to them at every corner. Louise is one of them, caught up in the festive mania like no other year. She suspects it is because of where she has just come from, starved of excitement for so long. She might as well be on another planet.

The splendour of Christmas is everywhere, with fairytale lights and the magnificent Christmas tree standing tall at the top of Grafton Street, inviting punters into a magical ambience. Underneath it, on a cold winter's afternoon, committed carol singers belt out their haunting lyrics in a haze of warm, exhaled breath and sweet-sounding melodies. Louise stops to listen to the singing, memories of childhood flooding back from her days in the choir. Their music teacher would insist they begin rehearsals early in November so that their harmonies would be perfect in advance of some special appearances in mid-December.

On Grafton Street, the largest and most prestigious store lends its outer façade to a forest of greenery with suffused twinkling lights. Its window display boasts a cornucopia of iconic Christmas symbols while seasonal birds perch proudly atop branches that glisten with half-formed icicles. Those 'special' birds remind Louise of the gifts given according to the seasonal song, 'The twelve days of Christmas.' Yet, their rich, colourful and exotic plumes seem out of place in the unnatural setting, far from the old midwinter festival of yule.

A showcase of impeccably attired mannequins, dressed to impress, strike a stylish pose, resplendent in a mixture of fur and feathers, satin and sequins, another in velvet and pearls. One leans casually against a fireplace, festooned with festive decorations, champagne flute held delicately in one hand, ready for an evening filled with laughter and merriment. Another reclines elegantly on a plush couch in an exquisite red silk gown and matching cape trimmed with lustrous ermine, the colour of white winter snow. A fine-looking gentleman stands beside her, sleek in an elegant tuxedo of Italian design, finished with a retro-print dinner scarf. Frozen and poised, hand extended, he regards his lady with a cool, confident look as he waits for her to rise in a perfect fusion of sophistication and pizzazz.

There is an abundance of snow, enough to make a handsome snowman who will make his young admirers proud. They gather round in fur-trimmed boots, surveying their handiwork, well-clad in winter woollies of quality and warmth. The playful scene is presided over by a male onlooker out for a leisurely stroll. He cuts a dashing figure, a real fine fish in a jacket of herringbone weave with matching gilet and thick corduroy bottoms. A peaked cap of rich tweed sits at an angle on his aristocratic head, a cashmere scarf wrapped casually around his neck. It looks so perfect, Louise thinks as she stands, taking in the scene.

Gifts, beautifully wrapped, are piled high in a profusion of bows, ribbons and plenitude, waiting to be opened. It seems that nothing is to be spared in the spirit of giving and receiving during the season of goodwill. Those old architects of Christmas, Dickens and Irving, would be proud because they had in many ways romanticised Christmas, steeping it in conviviality and good cheer. The scene before Louise exudes seasonal bliss and sumptuousness, representing an idyllic portrayal of Christmas, starkly removed from the realities lurking in the streets beyond. As sure as holly hangs from the trees in winter, there would be little cheer for some at the close of another year. For many, it would be neither a jolly nor a blessed one, but a cold, lonely and unholy Christmas.

Before Louise begins shopping for Christmas gifts, she decides to stop for a hot beverage. So, she makes for her favourite coffee house on Grafton Street and, once inside, is lucky to find a seat near the blazing fire. The scent of Christmas is everywhere, the fragrance of pine needles and mulled wine mingled with cinnamon sticks and nutmeg, infused with zesty orange and ginger spice. Louise loves ginger, and with a pot of steaming tea and mince pies sprinkled with festive fairy dust and clotted cream, she might as well be in heaven.

Christmas Eve has arrived, and Sami and Tara have gone out with their grandparents. Louise is home alone and takes advantage of their absence to get some gift wrapping done. Once finished, she stands in her bedroom, trying to decide what to wear for a party later at her friend's house.

Suddenly, the sound of the phone ringing in the hall downstairs takes Louise away from her preoccupations. Hurrying down the stairs, half expecting it to stop any second, she makes it in the nick of time, grabbing hold of the receiver.

"Hello, hello," she repeats, only to be met by a crackling sound at the other end. About to replace the receiver, a distant, familiar voice, barely audible but unmistakable, greets her ear.

"Louise, it's Jabir. Can you hear me?" he says in a loud voice.

"Jabir, Oh My God, is it you? I can't believe it, how are you?"

Excited to hear his voice, she can hardly piece the words together.

Suddenly, excitement turns to fear.

"Is everything ok, Jabir? Is something wrong?"

"No, no, there's nothing, everything is fine, Louise, I just phoned to say hello."

"It's great to talk to you, Jabir. I'm, I'm so surprised to hear your voice, it's good, I wasn't expecting it," she laughs.

"Are you having a nice time? How are the children and your parents?"

"Fine, everyone is fine." She pauses, searching for the words.

"The night you left Jabir, it was awful. I'm really sorry about what happened." Her tone reveals her anxiety.

"It's not your problem, Louise, don't worry. I'm sorry I couldn't help you but forget it. Don't talk about it now."

"Ok. How did you know I'm here, in Ireland?"

"Oh, I heard it and decided to call you. I have your number from before when I called your family, remember?"

"Oh yeah, how are things in Tripoli? Is business going well?"

"All is good, Louise, I want to speak to you, to say….to wish you happiness for the New Year."

"I'm so glad you did, Jabir, really. Thanks for thinking of us." Before she has time to utter another word, he comes back.

"Always, I think about you, Louise, you should know that".

Somewhat nonplussed, Louise is unable to fill the brief but awkward silence that follows his remark. Instead, he does.

"I was chatting to a few English people yesterday in Faisal's shop. They were getting ready to celebrate Christmas and it got me thinking."

"Really, how come?" she asks, wondering what will come next.

"I thought about that sweet dish you cooked once; you said it was traditional at Christmas. Remember? It was very good, I don't remember the name."

Louise laughs. "Ah, it must be trifle."

"That's it."

"Oh, I remember now, gosh, you've a great memory, Jabir."

"Are you doing a lot of things there?"

"Yeah, I'm seeing some friends, enjoying time with my family. Only a few days left until Christmas and then we're all spending New Year at my sister's house."

"The line is getting bad again. Louise, I'll leave you to get back to what you were doing. Say hello to Sami and Tara and everyone. Enjoy your holidays."

"Ok, Jabir, thanks for the call, Happy New Year to you."

"Take care of yourself, Louise, bye-for now."

Abruptly, the line goes dead. Louise, still clutching the receiver in her hand, takes a few seconds to distil the brief conversation.

Replacing the receiver on its stand, she sits down on the stairs, grateful for the silence of her parent's house. It is better to be alone so she can gather her thoughts without any disturbance. She realises that she could easily have missed the call but is so pleased she didn't.

For her it seems more than just a simple phone call, a reminder of something she has shrugged off, avoided even, mainly because it presents an inner conflict which could never, except perhaps in her most absurd dreams, be resolved.

What happened prior to her leaving had left a really bad taste in her mouth, the shame of which, even now, she can barely think about. Basically, Kareem threw Jabir out of the house, telling him not to return. Louise cringes with embarrassment as she replays the scene in her mind, so fresh in her memory still.

On the evening in question, Kareem woke up from his afternoon nap in a rather grumpy mood. When Louise reminded him that they were expected that evening at Martha's house for a farewell gathering, he started to grumble and complain about having to go out. At first, she gave him a deaf ear and instead went about getting herself and the children ready. The clock was ticking but there was no sign of him budging to get ready. It was an important occasion for Louise and the children, not to mention Martha and it was unthinkable that she would miss it.

There came a knock on the door and when Louise opened it, she was surprised to see Jabir. After greeting them, he handed Kareem something he needed that he had meant to give him the previous day. Louise offered him tea, and hesitating at first, he glanced at his watch and realised he had a bit of time to spare. Obviously, when he saw Louise dressed to go out, he understood that they had plans.

About fifteen minutes later, Jabir stood up to leave. Kareem, still in a reclining position, made no move, despite a gentle reminder from his wife that they ought to be getting a move on.

From that second, things took a nasty turn. Suddenly, he rouses himself angrily from the sofa, a flurry of curses spewing forth. Passing his wife, he swears rudely at her while Sami and Tara look on in nervous anticipation. Making it very plain that he has no wish to go out or accompany them, Louise quickly decides that the best course of action is to avoid pressing him further but take the children and go to Martha's.

She quickly turns to Jabir at the door and asks if he might drop her and the children off at Martha's if it is not inconvenient for him. She knows he will not refuse.

"No problem, if you're ready to leave."

"Thanks, Jabir, we won't delay you".

Louise reaches for her coat and motions to the children. Nobody is expecting what happens next.

"You're not going anywhere." From the couch, his voice is heard, loud and angry.

Louise stares at him in disbelief, hardly trusting her own ears. Instantly, her natural reaction is to try to defuse the situation, so she tries to speak to her husband in a calm tone.

"Kareem, you know Martha is leaving in a couple of days and this has all been planned. If you're not in the mood, we can go ourselves."

Ignoring his wife completely as if she hasn't spoken, he roughly addresses his brother.

"You go ahead, go on."

Initially, Jabir remains silent, no doubt feeling awkward.

"Kareem, what is the problem? You stay, we go. How complicated is that?"

Louise can feel her anger rising fast but manages to keep it under control for the children's sake and for Jabir, who is still waiting by the door.

"I told you to go. What are you waiting for?" He addresses his brother more aggressively.

"Kareem, Jabir, is only trying to help".

Suddenly, he takes a step towards Louise, uttering an ugly remark under his breath. He comes close, too close, stopping just short of her face, his hand slightly raised. Automatically, Louise recoils, sensing the threat to her person.

Jabir sees the expression of bewilderment on her face and the unmistakable intentions of his brother. At this precise moment, Jabir's voice is heard. "Kareem, that's enough, don't touch her, *haram alek,* shame on you."

No sooner has Jabir uttered the damning words than Kareem spins round, like a man possessed, his attention now focused entirely on his brother. In a rage, he starts spouting unintelligible words and profanities beyond his wife's ability to comprehend, except she can intuit their scalding blow by the look of distaste and disbelief on the face of Jabir. Then, he delivers his crushing ultimatum.

"Get out, get out of the house and don't ever come back." Again, he repeats it, his tone even more aggressive.

"What are you waiting for? Go." He repeats, half crazy.

Jabir looks at Louise, and for a split second, their eyes meet before he turns the handle on the door. In the blink of an eye, he is gone.

Louise stands transfixed, scarcely able to believe what has just happened.

She practically runs from the hall, the children following close behind, up the stairs and away from the obnoxious man below. If she had looked at him a moment longer, stayed in his presence, she fears what she might have said and how he would react. More importantly, the children cannot be subjected to such wrath. Louise has learnt that the safest and smartest thing to do is remove herself from her husband's sight.

Opening the door that leads onto the rooftop garden and stepping outside, she inhales the cool night air, feels it brush against her cheeks until her anger is slowly quelled and panic subsides. After a few moments, her legs cease shaking and her thoughts cohere. Sami and Tara stay close to their mother, waiting patiently and intuitively to ask the question.

"Will we not see Mary again, mam?" Tara asks with tears in her eyes. "I want to say bye to Sabrina and Samantha."

"Don't worry, they're not leaving for a few days. We can go see them tomorrow."

"But we missed the party," Tara reminds her.

"I know, I know, it's a pity but we at least can still get to see them before they leave," she says reassuringly, trying her best to put on a brave face for the children.

"Is Jabir coming back?" Sami asks, with a worried look.

"I'm sure he'll be back, but maybe not for a few days," Louise tries to sound matter of fact.

"Dad told him to go, didn't he, mam? Why, what did he do?" He looks at his mother with an enquiring look.

"Nothing, Sami, he was just trying to help. I don't really understand except that your dad is in a bad mood about something." Louise felt it was better to be truthful with her son rather than disingenuous.

Louise has no rational answer for her young son because she hardly knows herself. It is not the first time he has witnessed his father's moods.

"Let's not think about it anymore tonight. We can talk more tomorrow. Now, go and get ready for bed."

She kisses them both goodnight and sees them off to bed. All sounds quiet downstairs, and thankfully, Kareem seems to have settled himself down.

That night, Louise sleeps in the spare room, avoiding her husband altogether. Although she is extremely angry, she knows it is the best thing for now to try and keep things calm. With their Christmas trip imminent, timing is everything.

In the days that follow, the atmosphere between them is cool and Louise manages with great difficulty to keep things civil. She purposely avoids any mention of the incident with Jabir, and he does too.

They finally get to see Martha and say their goodbyes. Having walked to her house and spent the afternoon, Omar, Martha's husband, drives them home in the evening. It is an emotional parting for the two friends because they know it will be a while before they next meet. Martha is such a special friend for many reasons, but her deep sincerity is what shines through her personality. Louise will miss her dearly.

Since that dreadful evening, Louise had not seen or heard from Jabir until the unexpected phone call. She has thought about it over and over without coming up with an answer to explain what happened. What had prompted such a display of rage from Kareem? Was it the fact that his younger brother had dared to question his actions, confronting him with his own transgression and thereby injuring his pride and sense of importance? Was it something else altogether? Either way, there can be no justification for his bad behaviour, Louise is sure of that. In her mind, it is unresolved, and she intends to tackle her husband about it at the first timely opportunity.

For now, though, Louise feels better for having spoken to Jabir, content in the knowledge that they are still on good terms. She has the distinct impression that he also wants her to know they are still good.

It is undoubtedly the best Christmas present Louise could get.

THIRTY FIVE

A Masquerade

The greatest secrets are always hidden in the most unlikely places.

— Roald Dahl

F our days after their return from Ireland, Safar taps gently on the door. Armed with her mabkhara and a somewhat determined attitude, she asks Louise if they might burn some bakhoor, explaining that it is to ward off any evil spirits that might have been lurking about while she was away.

Amused, Louise reminds her good friend that nobody except her husband has been in the house since she left. Safar makes no comment but remains resolute that the ritual should be done, insisting it is in Louise's best interests.

Not wishing to seem ungrateful or dismissive of her friend's kind intentions, she sits down at the low table on which Safar places the burner and waits for her to strike a match to the oud.

It takes several minutes for a curl of smoke to rise, but when the resin inside begins to heat, the colour of the precious wood chip begins to grow slowly darker and the surface to bubble gently. The smell of smoke starts to fade, replaced by a precious, woody scent that gradually disseminates around them, exuding a sweet but subtle aroma.

Louise was first introduced to bakhoor on a visit to Zanib several years ago. In Bedouin culture and throughout the Middle East, bakhoor, the Arabic equivalent for burning bricks, is an ancient tradition believed to possess certain holistic and medicinal properties. Because it also occupies a unique place in religious belief, it is closely aligned with the spiritual. When receiving visitors, it may be as integral to hospitality as offering coffee and dates. The reason is to refresh and uplift their spirits, but there is also another belief: to dispel any negative or malicious energy, which many hold to be a 'curse' and believed to be brought about by the envy of another.

Bakhoor is basically agarwood or oud, soaked in fragrant oils and mixed with other natural ingredients, like musk and sandalwood. It is regarded as a precious gift of Mother Earth and, therefore, has a distinct place in important rituals and ceremonies.

The two women sit down to drink tea and eat some Egyptian-spiced cookies, better known as *Kahk*. They are a favourite of Louise, and today Safar has made some specially. Presently, they become sensitised to the soft, diffusive scent that fills the space around them while they chat about Louise's holiday and catch up on some local news. Despite herself, Louise feels a sense of calm and peace descending on her. When she says as much to Safar, the woman smiles, a look of deep satisfaction on her face, as if she has rescued her friend from some un-nameable force.

"*Alhamdulillah, ya Louise, barak allah fik.*" "Thanks be to God, Louise and may God bless you," she tells her.

"*Sukran Safar, anti latif jidana,*" "Thank you, Safar, you are kind," she replies and means it with all her heart. When Louise produces the gift she has brought back from Ireland, along with some goodies for the children, Safar is delighted.

When she entered the house on their arrival, it annoyed Louise greatly that Kareem had done nothing to prepare for their homecoming. There was no food in the fridge, not even fresh bread for them to eat after the long journey. Her concern was not so much for herself but for the children. It was so selfish of him.

She says nothing about it to Safar, though she wonders what occupies her husband's thoughts most of the time. There was an accumulation of dust everywhere, on every surface, but more noticeably in the kitchen where a window had been left ajar. Nothing could be cooked or prepared until it was thoroughly cleaned, and he had not bothered himself to do a single thing.

Quietly fuming, she had to roll up her sleeves and start to work immediately, cleaning and scouring until everything was done. She only narrowly resisted an explosive row with Kareem but was glad later that she had. It is enough for the children to cope with being back at school and missing their grandparents without being subjected to more unpleasantness. Still, it takes every ounce of discipline she has left to avoid telling him what she actually thinks. However, what she averts in words is probably shown by her body language. Oftentimes, Louise wonders what the eventual result of all this 'pushing down' will be.

It irritates her further when, on the afternoon of her first day home, Suhaila comes knocking at the door unexpectedly. Kareem is at home looking over some schoolwork with the children and Louise is busy with her chores, so she lets Kareem answer the door. To her annoyance, Louise instantly recognises the voice but ignores it and continues what she is doing. After a few minutes, Kareem calls her. She reluctantly puts aside what she is doing and joins them in the sitting room, ill-prepared to receive visitors and resenting the intrusion.

Comfortably ensconced on the settee, the girl stands up when Louise enters the room, full of smiles and words of welcome. Kissing her on both cheeks, she looks pleased to see her, though Louise is less eager to reciprocate, making no secret that she is busy cleaning and there is a lot more to do before the day ends. Sitting back smugly in the armchair, Kareem suggests she make some coffee. There is an awkward silence for a brief moment, and suddenly, Suhaila fills it by jumping to her feet and offering to make it instead. Louise thinks for a second that the girl has taken the hint, having decided to leave the busy couple to their own devices, but she is wrong. Instead, off she goes to the kitchen, leaving Louise with no choice but to follow.

After coffee, Louise gets up, pleading that she really has to finish her chores before unpacking. Still the girl continues to sit, encouraged by Kareem, who makes no move to bring the conversation to an end. Louise finally leaves the two of them still talking while she returns to her chores. The children have gone to Safar's house to play since their lessons have been interrupted. It is early evening before Suhaila finally leaves. It angers Louise that she has to plunge frantically into housework with little time to unwind after their tiring journey. During these first days, her patience is severely tested, and she feels ill at ease in her own home.

Initially, the girl's visits were sporadic, but of late, they are becoming more frequent and seem to follow a pattern. Louise is determined to nip her visits in the bud, but unless Kareem supports her efforts, it may prove difficult. Nevertheless, she is determined to broach the subject with her husband at the first opportunity.

Unbeknownst to Louise, there are greater influences at work shaping her destiny. In the greater scheme of things, events unfold in a timely way, as they should. If you place your trust in the greater power of providence, you will accept that it is a force that no ordinary skill nor foresight can outmanoeuvre.

THIRTY SIX

A Revelation

Better to be hurt by a truth than comforted with a lie.

— Khaled Hosseini

On a crisp, sunny morning in February, Louise leaves the house early and heads for the local market a few streets away. Dressed in jeans, a t-shirt, a long fitted jacket and mid-calf leather boots, she looks good. Her hair has grown longer than usual, and the large, square frames of her dark ray-bans practically shield her face. Apart from a light coating of pink gloss on her lips, she is otherwise unadorned.

This morning Louise is in no hurry, she might even drop by Marleen on her return since the children are at school until two and Kareem is working away from home for ten days.

Having walked just a short distance, she is suddenly aware of a car slowing behind her and is on her guard. It is a really quiet street where nothing much happens, especially at this time of the morning, and every sound is amplified. The car rolls slowly up beside her at the edge of the narrow footpath and the engine dies. Turning cautiously around, she stops dead in her tracks. Recognising the car and its driver, she can hardly believe her eyes. Through the open window, she hears her name.

"Louise, it's me, get in."

Three hours later, she is dropped off in front of the house with all her groceries and plenty of food for thought. She practically skips up the steps that lead to her front door and once inside the hall after dropping her shopping bags, she realises she is still smiling. In a buoyant mood, she breezes into the kitchen to unload her purchases, but having second thoughts, she abandons them and instead goes into the sitting room and flops into the nearest armchair. In the here-and-now of the moment, Louise feels present and aware of her senses. She wants to savour the moment, as fully as she can, to experience it for what it is because she knows it will be temporary and nothing is going to spoil it for her because she actually feels alive. It is the first time she has laid eyes on Jabir after a long while, too long.

A few days later, Louise has a visit from Zanib, whom she has not seen since the time of her illness. The week before, Faisal had sent word through Kareem to expect her. Although their meetings are infrequent, they have built a close friendship over the years. The strange dynamics of their mutual in-laws and experiences seem to have brought them closer. Zanib usually has a wealth of interesting little anecdotes to recount in addition to the latest titbits of information, so they always manage to have a few laughs when they get together.

Louise is slightly apprehensive in case Suhaila calls unexpectedly, the possibility of which has become a real concern for her these days. Zanib is a private person, reserved in the company of people she does not know. During the time Kareem was away, Louise never saw her, so hopefully, she will have the good sense to stay away for a while. Anyway, if she shows up, Louise decides she has to be polite but honest and ask the girl to give them space rather than jeopardise her sister-in-law's visit. She knows that Zanib would likely find the girl forward and disapprove.

After settling down to drink tea, Louise quickly senses that Zanib is upset about something and sure enough, her face assumes a grave expression. When she speaks, it is to tell her friend that she wishes to confide in her something that is 'heavy' and *haram,* meaning prohibited in the religion. Louise tries to put her mind at rest by reassuring her that whatever it is, she will keep her secret safe. That said, Zanib confides in her some shocking news.

Faisal, her husband, is having a secret affair, which she claims to have discovered by accident. She admits to having suspicions for a long time, even before the birth of her fifth and last child, who has only recently turned three. Louise is temporarily stunned into silence, listening to Zanib elaborate on the unpleasant details. There is a photo, she explains, one she had come across which shows them both reclining cosily on a futon in sumptuous surroundings outside Tripoli, most likely Morocco.

Apparently, Faisal had been to Marrakech on business, or so he said, and Zanib suspects they had gone there together. She guesses the woman in the picture is Lebanese because of her fair complexion. Louise thinks it ironic since Zanib is unusually fair-skinned, which is uncommon compared to native women.

She recalls her first meeting with Faisal several years previously and how struck she was by his appearance and unique style. Over the years, whenever she sees him, he is always dressed to impress, in a suit, collar and tie. Even on isolated occasions when he wears traditional dress, it is of a superior quality, probably made for him specially.

While Zanib pours out her tortured heart, Louise listens, aware that there is very little she can say to alleviate her distress. Privately, she resents her brother-in-law for the pain and hurt he is causing. Louise has always been a bit curious, suspicious even, about her brother-in-law, though he has always been polite to her. For all his surface charm and suaveness, she senses there is much more to his character than what is visible on the surface. He is, undoubtedly, a patriarchal figure, revered by his family, obeyed by his wife and held in great esteem by a community of men. Louise believes he is enjoying the best of both worlds, legal and illicit. She wonders with no small degree of amusement what his mother would make of her son's philanderous pursuits.

She listens intently as Zanib complains that her husband is practically never at home, arriving late into the night hours or worse. Lowering her voice to a whisper as if someone might overhear their conversation, she tells Louise that some nights, her husband does not come home at all.

Then, Zanib confides that she often gets up after her husband has fallen into a deep sleep and taking his shirt in her hand, she sniffs the sweet scent of perfume around the collar and then sees the long, fair hairs that have attached themselves to his jacket. Louise can imagine her standing there, in the solitary night hour, eyeing the offensive strands of hair. Alone with her thoughts, her worst fears are confirmed whilst in the adjacent room, their three young sons are sleeping, oblivious to the secret life of their father. Zanib admits to sleeping in a separate room these days with her youngest daughter, having given up waiting for her husband to return at night to their bedroom.

Looking at her, Louise cannot help but wonder and not for the first time in the past year, if the worry and despair of it all has already begun to erode Zanib's good looks. Her lovely, sleek hair is thinning at the top and her once cheerful disposition is fading. Knowing that she has to say something, she chooses her words carefully, in case she might upset her friend with an unwelcome opinion.

Prior to moving into their new home, they had stayed with Zanib and Faisal for a few weeks. Unfortunately, Louise saw things she would rather not have seen. In her opinion, Zanib is not respected as she should be, and clearly, she is not a priority either. Yet, she answers to her husband's every whim. Louise could hardly wait to leave because she barely trusted herself to keep her mouth quiet.

Faisal is far from being a family man; he makes 'appearances' in his home from time to time as opposed to inhabiting it fully. Actually, it sort of reminds Louise of her own plight.

She had observed, with utter disgust, his extreme laziness while a tired Zanib waited on him hand and foot. Even his children, to avoid being scolded, understood not to disturb him while he took his routine nap.

One day, unable to stop herself, she asked him the question she had been edging towards for so long.

"Faisal, you don't mind if I ask you something? No offence."

"Go ahead," he answered, smiling.

"Would you never think of getting up to get that glass of water yourself, you know, to save Zanib the bother? She does everything herself." Louise tries to sound non-confrontational.

He delivers his answer smugly and with a smile.

"She likes to do these things for me!"

"Does she really?" Louise answered, the smile wiped clean off her face.

Without saying another word, she got up and left the room.

She remembers that during their entire stay, they generally only clapped eyes on Faisal over lunch, and afterwards, he disappeared into the bedroom to sleep for a couple of hours. Like clockwork, he woke and was handed a glass of tea by Zanib. Then, after exchanging a few words, he disappeared into the bedroom, emerging shortly afterwards, dressed and ready to go on his merry way. If they saw him again that night, it was more unusual than commonplace.

Throughout all of this, Louise looked on with an air of detachment since it was not for her to comment on anyone's domestic or personal affairs, much less as a guest in their home. However, she felt real sympathy for Zanib's predicament and understood, without having to be told, that her sister-in-law was in a pretty hopeless situation. She feels empathy for Zanib because, in her opinion, the woman is completely lost on her husband and deserves much better. One thing is clear: she may expect no help, much less understanding from her in-laws down the street, based on personal experience alone.

Louise can hear the anguish as well as the anger in her voice, but underneath it, she believes that a part of Zanib still loves her wayward husband with all her heart. Doubtless, at one point, he managed to capture her with his charm, a charm Louise knows he possesses because she has glimpsed it on occasion, though unfortunately, it is generally lavished on others rather than on his wife and family.

Louise likes Zanib's family and has met them a number of times. They are good people, having an awareness of themselves and a sense of propriety that Kareem's family are sorely lacking.

Before retirement from active duty, Zanib's father held a prominent position in the military during the days of King Idris. His first wife died after only a few short years of marriage. Sometime later, he remarried Zanib's mother, Salma who had three children, a daughter and two sons, both of whom entered the medical profession. The eldest qualified as a dentist, went to America to specialise, married and decided to stay and make his life there.

The other brother, who is still single, stays close to his mother and sister. Naturally, he feels a responsibility towards them, being the only male relative.

According to Zanib, her mother sold their townhouse and relocated to land their father owned outside the city, where they eventually built a villa surrounded by trees and greenery. On the adjacent land, they cultivated their own vegetables and sold the remaining produce to local markets.

Louise remembers the very first time she visited the house with Zanib. Initially, she was overwhelmed by the sheer size of the estate and its verdant, peaceful environs. The contrast between where she had come from and the natural, tranquil place she stood on was staggering, like an experience of heaven after a descent into hell. It was even more heavenly when suddenly she was greeted by the most delightful golden Labrador puppy. He came bounding up to Louise, totally unaware of his part in making her day shine with his friendly, playful temperament. Falling immediately in love with him, she was like a child when it came time to leave, barely able to separate from him and say goodbye. If only she could have taken him with her. That night, while she lay in her uncomfortable bed, she felt sad, remembering the puppy dog. The only way to console herself was by vowing silently that one day she would have her own, just like him.

Zanib's mother is a kind, warm woman, reminding her of Azisa, with a sharp wit and a welcoming attitude.

As it happened, Louise had only to bide her time before a chance conversation arose, which partially solved the marriage puzzle she had wondered about.

It all began a couple of years before Kareem had left to study in Ireland. Suffice it to say that the paths of both fathers had somehow crossed, more than likely through common commerce among men. It was possible since Faisal's father had a busy 'Suk' in the town centre. How Zanib had put it was, "they both knew people." Although the backgrounds of these men were different, one was educated, the other illiterate, they did share something: both were smart and hardworking as well as being 'old-school'.

The common denominator between them was that one had a bright, gregarious son, the other a beautiful daughter of marriageable age. Faisal had graduated top of his class, showing plenty of promise; Zanib was a respectable girl from a good family. It must have seemed like a recipe for marital success.

After a time, the union was agreed between the fathers and the marriage contract signed. Zanib trusted her father to choose an honourable husband for her, so she upheld his decision.

It was not much of a stretch for Louise to form a picture of how things started to unravel after that. All seemed well enough in the beginning, with

Zanib immediately falling pregnant, and within a year of marriage, she gave birth to a daughter and then a son the following year. In the meantime, Zanib's father passed away, and her eldest brother settled in the US.

In their conversations, Zanib complained about her husband's absences and that he behaved as if he were single instead of acting like a married man. As a result of her father's death, her other brother assumed a strong familial role. Along with pursuing his career in veterinary medicine, he took over the management of his late father's affairs, including the care of his widowed mother and, to a lesser degree, looking out for his only sister, whom he had always been close to.

It is not long, however, before he figures out the meanderings of his brother-in-law, much to his chagrin.

Later that night, after she puts the children to bed, Louise starts to think about what Zanib has told her and she wonders what the outcome will be. Faisal and Kareem appear to have a good deal in common; they are both selfish and determined to look after their own interests above all else.

She might as well face up to reality because there is no use in denying it. Things are not getting any better for her either, except she has learnt to manage her life in a way that works much of the time. There is no guarantee, however, that it will continue that way. Besides, is it what she really wants for her future and the children?

Opening the door onto the front veranda, Louise steps outside into the cool night air. Gazing absent-mindedly into the dark vastness of the night sky, faintly lit by a crescent moon, Louise is presented suddenly with a sharp reminder of her place in the inestimable expanse. Drawing her thoughts back to preoccupations in the here-and-now, Louise is a bit unsettled by Zanib's earlier revelation, amongst other things.

Even now, a month later, Louise is feeling a deep sense of indignation and resentment towards her husband and she feels it gradually building without knowing exactly why. Louise is static where her husband is concerned, barely able to raise her temperature beyond lukewarm. If her husband has noticed her lack of excitement, he is silent on the matter. Once his needs are met, nothing else seems to matter and Louise is not bothered. These days she is plagued by migraines, a pretence that serves temporarily to help ward off his unwelcome advances.

After a row, there is a distinct pattern in his behaviour. He lapses into a passive-aggressive silence that can last for days, in which time he is usually unapproachable and unwilling to do anything for them. Even with the children, he is irritable, and they are growing increasingly intimidated by their father's unpredictable moods.

Louise realises she is stuck in a relationship where none of her emotional needs or hunger for intimacy is being met and she has no desire to merely satisfy her husband's libidinous appetite.

She is convinced that one cannot hope to right the emotional shortfalls of a relationship through the sexual act. The waters get muddied and the boundaries between surface and depth become blurred.

Just as she turns to go back inside, she recognises the sound of a car turning into their narrow street. Kareem is home.

Tonight, of all nights, she is not in the mood for conversation or anything else. However, she greets her husband with a smile, asking after his day.

"Busy, busy, two planes are grounded since yesterday and have to be got ready for seven in the morning. We'll get it done."

"Aren't you off tomorrow?" she enquires.

"I am, but I'll have to go in, I'll take the following day or whatever. Did Zanib show up?" He asks.

"Yeah, her brother dropped her. We had a nice, long visit, actually."

"Good, anything interesting? How is she?"

Louise has decided to say nothing to Kareem about her disclosure, not yet.

"Nothing really, you know, just chatting about the usual stuff. She was asking for you. Do you fancy a cup of tea? I made some scones."

"Yeah, go on. Did you see Suhaila?" he asks, laughing.

"No, thankfully," she replies, affecting a laugh but studying her husband's face nonetheless.

"Why do you ask?"

"Oh, no reason, just I wondered if she called, you know the way she usually does," he says with a nonchalant shrug.

"Yeah, well, I want to talk to you about that, Kareem, but not tonight. It can wait." She gives him a friendly smile before going to make the tea.

"I need to get some sleep. I've to be up at six."

Usually, it is his habit to take his tea outside on the veranda and unwind. Sometimes Louise goes and sits with him, but not tonight. He finishes his tea, yawns and stands up, taking a stretch.

"Are you coming to bed, he asks?" with a hint of intention in his tone.

Louise avoids looking at him directly.

"Ah, I was just going to take a shower, Kareem, when you came in. I think I'll sleep better after it. You go ahead. I'll follow you in a bit."

Half an hour later, Louise peeps around the bedroom door; she knows by his stillness that he has already fallen asleep. Pulling the door gently closed, she walks back to the couch and picks up her book where she left off.

Louise is becoming increasingly reliant on a 'sleight of hand' to avoid the lustful attentions of her husband, having no interest in sex with him whatsoever. There is a limit to the amount of headaches, stomach-aches and other subtle ruses one can invent before it begins to sound suspect.

There are diversions that work in her favour some of the time and at other times, they fail miserably.

THIRTY SEVEN

Bittersweet

Bittersweetness is not, as we tend to think, just a momentary feeling or event. It's also a quiet force, a way of being….an authentic and elevating response to the problem of being alive in a deeply flawed yet stubbornly beautiful world.

– Susan Cain

It is mid-morning and Louise is moping about the house, feeling rather miserable. Kareem had left before dawn on a week-long trip bound for somewhere in Eastern Europe.

When the doorbell rings, she freezes, thinking it must be Suhaila. Hesitating, she considers not answering it since she is not in the mood for making trivial conversation or even faking politeness. On the third ring, she takes a breath and walks to the hall door, determined to tell her she is unwell and suggest calling another time.

When she opens it, to her great surprise, Jabir is standing in front of her, a large grin on his handsome face.

Stepping into the hall, she catches a whiff of his cologne, woody and sensual, as she closes the door behind him. It jolts her sharply but deliciously out of her bemusement. Walking into the sitting room, he sits down and beckons Louise to join him.

"Are you surprised to see me here?" he asks, still grinning and looking really pleased.

All Louise can do is look at him and shrug her shoulders in puzzlement.

"Kareem stopped by the house this morning briefly on his way to the airport to tell my mother he would be away. He left a message with her for me to come and see if you need anything or stay if need be."

"What, are you serious? He never mentioned it to me."

Louise gives him her biggest, brightest smile before continuing.

"Remember the last time we met, that morning?"

"Yes, of course, I remember."

"You said you were due to go to Morocco on a buying trip around this time. What happened?"

"Well, I am…. but it doesn't matter. I can put it off for a week or two. It can wait."

"Maybe you should go. I mean, please don't cancel it because… because, of me."

Suddenly, his expression is serious and he looks at Louise rather intensely as he considers her words.

"Is that not a good enough reason?" his tone is soft and measured, his eyes never leaving her face.

"I thought you'd never come back to this house again, Jabir. Why did you?"

Her voice drops to a whisper almost.

"Don't you know?" he ventures.

Louise sits up straight in the chair as if someone has pinched her. Now, it's her turn to look him squarely in the eye.

A moment of tense silence hangs in the air between them until, finally, he speaks.

"I'm here, Louise, because of you, because of our friendship."

"I do know. I'm just…. well, afraid." She admits, rather reluctantly.

"Don't be, I promise, there's nothing to be afraid of."

He smiles, yet Louise is not convinced. Maybe it is herself that she fears, but she keeps it to herself.

Since Jabir's reappearance in her life, she has gained a new understanding of things, bringing with it an entirely new consideration.

"Jabir, I'm sorry if I sounded off-key, but things have been difficult lately." She confesses.

"You don't need to explain, Louise, I know how things are. I've known for a while."

"I just need to talk about it," she insists.

"I understand. You can say anything to me, Louise, anything at all."

He flashes her one of his seductive, melting smiles, revealing an even row of pearly white teeth, which momentarily melts Louise. For a fleeting moment, Louise imagines touching those lips, kissing them hard, but instantly checks herself, chasing the intruding thought from her mind.

"We had a huge argument a few days ago and I said lots of things I have been avoiding for a long time."

Jabir listens without interrupting.

"I can't see us staying together, to be honest," she admits.

"I know exactly what Kareem is like, and I also know it's hard for you. I don't know what else I can say to you, Louise."

Taking a deep breath, he looks away, thinking about what to say next or maybe finding the subject a trifle uncomfortable.

"I'm not the person to advise you about your marriage, Louise. I think you can understand that much."

Rushing in, she is eager to reassure him that she has no such expectations.

"Jabir, of course, I know that, and I understand. He's your brother and I would never want you to feel uncomfortable. I'm sorry, I should never have said anything."

"It's ok, Louise, you don't have to worry." With a big, warm smile, he diffuses the awkward moment.

"You know that any opinion I might have would be biased and that wouldn't be a good thing."

Louise nods, indicating that she understands perfectly.

They chat about other things for a while before he gets up to leave. "I'll see you later on this evening, Louise. Is there anything you need? Maybe Tara and Sami would like to go for a drive, get something to eat outside."

"That would be nice, Jabir. See you later then."

Remembering the last time they met on a nearby street brings a smile to Louise's face. That morning, Jabir had driven them to a quiet boardwalk on the waterfront, where they took a leisurely stroll, surrounded by the calm waters of the lapiz lazuli sea on both sides. They stopped to get warm cinnamon doughnuts and coffee before taking them to a quiet spot so they could eat and chat undisturbed.

True to his word, he returns later on, and they go with Sami and Tara for pizza and ice cream to a new place close to the palm-lined corniche.

Though never named by either of them, the boardwalk is their place, just one of those silently understood things.

During his absence, Louise had missed Jabir quite a bit, only realising it in the weeks following his expulsion from the house. Apparently, he had felt the absence, too.

One day, in a heated exchange, Louise brings it up, reminding her husband that it was a despicable thing to do, throwing his brother out of their home and begrudging her and the children the chance to say their precious goodbyes to friends. She promises Kareem that she will not forget the events of that night.

Kareem reacts in the way he always does, refusing to take responsibility for his behaviour. Instead, he gets angry, loses his temper and begins firing ugly insults at his wife. At one point, he threatens her physically, but anticipating his move, she makes good her escape rather than risk his dire intentions. To avoid things escalating, she thinks it better to remove herself from his presence. The last thing she wants is for the children to find themselves in the middle of an atmosphere on their return from school.

As time passes, Louise is fast approaching a refusal to accommodate her husband's moods, whims and bad manner. She has tolerated it in the hope of achieving a peaceful life and avoiding unpleasantness, but she eventually learns that her efforts are in vain. It is also tedious and counterproductive, so she decides it is time to give up on the strategic, peace-seeking ways.

There was one time she had to leave the house, taking the children with her, chiefly to put a safe distance between him and them. She goes to her friend Diane, whose house is just across the street. Kareem has the audacity to follow, like a crazed person who has lost his mind. By then, Louise and the children are safely inside, but it does not deter him from knocking on the door in a shameless rage, demanding that they come out. However, Diane's husband answers, assuming the role of pacifist, while Louise, mortified, sits with Diane inside. Majeed speaks calmly but firmly to Kareem from inside their gated residence, imploring him to go home, reflect for a while and leave his wife and children to return at their leisure when things have calmed down. He explains that what he is doing is *haram,* imploring him to think about his actions before *Allah* and the holy prophet *Mohammad.*

Eventually, he departs, shamed into capitulation, leaving his family behind with Diane to recover from their unpleasant experience.

The next day, an unexpected knock comes to the door. It is indeed Suheila, and she comes bearing good news about a marriage proposal. Her life has been busy, and that is the reason nobody has seen her lately, she explains. A man had approached her father, expressing an interest in his daughter on behalf of his nephew.

"My father sent him away with a message," she laughs gleefully, an expression of mischief crossing her pretty face.

"This man who is interested in my daughter, let him come to me himself," he tells the representative and, without another word, is sent on his way.

Louise laughs, picturing the old man delivering the message.

The very next day, apparently, the determined beau appears in the flesh, presenting himself to the old man and asking for his daughter's hand in marriage.

"So, have you two spoken then?" Louise asks.

"Not much, just briefly over tea. The three of us chatted a while before he left," She answers, with a look of pride.

To Louise, it sounds civilised, if a little old-fashioned.

"When will you see him again?" Louise enquires curiously.

"He's in the army, stationed in Sirte and only gets back to Tripoli once a month, if he's lucky. His military service finishes in six months and then we can get married in October."

"Congratulations, Suhaila. I hope you'll be happy. Won't you be busy then for the next while?"

"There'll be an engagement party in five or six weeks, whenever Mohammed can arrange leave. His family are so excited to meet me, him being the eldest in a family of six, another brother and four sisters. His father died a few years ago."

"Yes, I can imagine," Louise agrees.

"You and Safar are, of course, invited to the party."

"Thank you for the invitation, Suhaila."

"I'm going to ask Safar if she can help out with the food as well."

"I'm sure she'll be happy to do whatever she can to help".

On her way out the door, she turns off-handedly to ask Louise when Kareem is due back from his trip.

As she closes the door, Louise rejoices in the knowledge that Suhaila is now officially spoken for and will be kept occupied in the following months with wedding preparations. She expects to see very little of the girl, which she thinks is good news for her!

Two days remain before Kareem returns from his extended trip, and Louise has very mixed feelings about his homecoming. Walking into the kitchen to prepare supper for Tara and Sami, she is freshly determined to push negative thoughts from her mind, since they impinge on the here-and-now of what peace remains.

Presently, she summons the children in from playing and sits a while, chatting with them while they eat supper. Bedtime is approaching, and soon enough, quiet descends on the house. Louise then takes a long, luxurious shower to soothe and rinse away the troubles of the day.

As night begins to fall, she listens for the soft, timely knock that will greet her ears like music and a frisson of anticipation begins to spread slowly over her body.

THIRTY EIGHT

Amidst the Sands of Time

In order to understand the world,
one has to turn away from it on occasion.

– Albert Camus

Sami and Tara are excited about the prospect of being away from home for a couple of days. It has come at a good time because Kareem is away again, and Louise feels they need a break. Even a short one will do.

Arianna, a friend of Louise, and her husband Mohammad have invited them on a trip to visit the historic town of Ghadames. She accepts the invitation without a second thought, knowing the opportunity might not come again. The couple have spoken about the place at length, promising Louise she will not be disappointed. Her curiosity is instantly aroused, and she looks forward to seeing the place and spending time with her friends.

Although Kareem had been to Ghadames several times on work-related trips, he hardly said anything about it. Louise figures that a place of such historical and cultural importance deserves more than a passing mention. He knows his wife is interested in history and ancient civilisations, but because it holds no particular interest for him and he has no intention of taking her there, why mention it? She knows Jabir would take them if she asked, but he is already doing enough. As it stands, there are no two people she would rather do the trip with other than Arianna and Mohammad; they are such good company.

Whenever she looks at them, observing their body language, it tells her how at ease they are in each other's company. She cannot help but feel envious in a good way, it is how things ought to be in her view and she wishes her relationship had some of those ingredients. Is it an age thing, she wonders, having met when they were older? Surely, destiny had also played a part in allowing their paths to converge. Against all that, perhaps it is one of the ineffable mysteries of the soul, something inexplicable that cannot be measured by any worldly thing.

Arianna was a Greek historian-turned-archaeologist when she met Mohammad, a practising lawyer with a promising career. After a marriage that lasted two years, followed by divorce, he decided to decamp and seek out a new life in Europe. His heart was set on Italy, but in a change of heart, he travelled to Greece and enrolled in the University of Athens, where he took up international law. Slowly, he began to build a life in his new country and thoughts of Italy faded into the background.

After a couple of years, he grew tired of the law, but his appetite for knowledge remained unsated, so he immersed himself in the study of philosophy and the classics. What better place to do it, he would often say. So, he settled into his studies, believing he had finally found his niche until he stumbled upon something far more rewarding. He found Arianna. From that day forward, they never looked back.

In her own words, Arianna described their courtship simply as "fireworks". They laughed about it sometimes, Louise half-in-jest, insisting hers had been nothing like it.

Her friend is passionate about life, like all Mediterraneans, at times feisty, something Louise admires, and with a man like Mohammad, anything is possible. The adoration on his face whenever he looks at his wife is plain to see. He celebrates her personality in every way.

Arianna has a gentle liveliness, and one could be forgiven for assuming it is all there is to her character, but they would be wrong. Underneath, there is depth, strength and a spirit of generosity that Louise has experienced on many an occasion.

When you ask Arianna for her opinion or advice on something, it is proffered with brutal honesty and objectivity.

She is one of the most striking women Louise has ever seen. Her complexion, like her thick, wavy hair, has subtle Mediterranean tones. The precise jawlines of her well-structured face, accentuated by a long but slim nose, create a rather chiselled look, making the overall effect interesting, even endearing.

When they tied the knot, Arianna, without knowing it, married into an old, distinguished family. Mohammad's father and grandfather before him had held key legal positions in previous governments which existed as part of a constitutional monarchy. One held the post of Justice Minister, the other a prominent judge who presided over the highest court in the land.

Mohammad's mother died when he was still a young boy, leaving him and a sister, five years older, to be raised by their paternal grandmother.

Throughout his time spent in Greece, the family visited him a few times, but he had no intention of returning to Libya. That changed when he and Arianna were blessed with a son they called *Malik,* meaning 'King'.

It was due to a most fortunate coincidence that the two women met. Louise was invited to a neighbour's wedding but had little interest in going except that the bride's mother had been especially welcoming to her when she first arrived.

At the party, Louise was introduced to a woman who she guessed to be in her mid to late fifties, elegantly dressed and modern. Taken aback by her command of English, Louise perked up, eager to engage in her own tongue. Following a polite exchange of conversation, Ethedal told Louise they had recently returned from the United States after a ten-year spell. Her husband, a dentist, had a specialisation in orthodontics and was due to take up a post in the new dental hospital in Benghazi, the second-largest city in Libya. She, too, would take up a lectureship in English at the University. They had come to Tripoli, especially for the wedding, and were to spend two weeks at their house there before returning to Benghazi.

Before Ethedal left, she invited Louise to visit her the following week for afternoon tea, adding there was someone she would like her to meet. Intrigued, Louise accepted the invitation without a second thought.

True to her promise, Ethedal sent a message via her friend Aisha, and the two women went to visit. Once there, Louise was introduced to her sister-in-law, Arianna and her brother Mohammad. It was to be the beginning of a close friendship.

Eventually, after a long but pleasant journey, the little group arrive at their destination. Louise is instantly struck by the sight that meets her eyes on the first approach to the ancient city. She is captivated by the spectacle and unprepared for the visual impact it is to have on her. Standing at a point which had been the crossroads of civilisation and a melting pot of cultures for centuries is nothing short of awe-inspiring for Louise and a victory for her imagination.

Suddenly, Louise gets a sense of the *Arabian Nights,* visions of an exotic, medieval world steeped in fantasy and rich folklore whose desert realms all but set one's imagination on fire.

Beyond the foothills of *Jebel Nefousa* lie the world's best-preserved oasis town, Ghadames, palm-fringed and sheltered in the shadow of the vast mountain range that borders Libya and Tunisia. Located a distance of about 683km from Tripoli, the ancient town was founded by the Romans in the first century BC during the reign of Augustus. In the sixth century, it was a bishopric, converted to Christianity by Byzantine missionaries before the arrival of the MuslimArabs who, over time, built the city edifice which exists today.

The city and its surrounds are true Berber territory. Although the attraction of a more cosmopolitan life beckoned in the capital city, the inhabitants remained loyal to their ethnicity, even speaking their own language.

Ghadames was once a centre of enlightenment as well as a site of pilgrimage. Most significant of all, it played a crucial role in acting as a base for the trans-Saharan trade until the nineteenth century, linking the heart of Africa with various northern empires. It was a treacherous route frequented by smugglers, bandits and snake-oil merchants. Since gold was the main commodity, a constant stream of inbound and outbound caravans rested before continuing their arduous journeys.

"Oh my god, I never imagined," Louise gasps, lost for words, her voice trailing off as she tries to take it all in. Nodding in disbelief, she turns to Sami and Tara, whose eyes are also open and wide in wonderment.

"Isn't it just amazing?"

Both Arianna and Mohammad smile at their reaction.

"We knew you'd love it and at last we're here," Arianna speaks, her eyes sparkling in delight.

Mohammad addresses the children with an encouraging smile and the mischievous sense of fun they have come to expect.

"So, what do you think guys, ready to do some exploring? First, though, let's eat something. Are you hungry?"

They laugh, nodding vigorously at the mention of food. Louise can tell Sami is itching to get out of the jeep and check things out. Without further ado, they finally set their feet down on the reddish sand in a place known as 'the pearl of the desert.'

The small party, led by Mohammad, makes its way toward the outreaches of the ancient city. On approach, its unique architectural style is so different from anything Louise has ever seen. It forms an impression of whitewashed dwellings, intricately decorated and surrounded by beautiful palm gardens.

The oldest part of the enchanting caravan town is flanked by a high wall. For a fleeting moment, she can almost feel the ghostly presence of wealthy, medieval traders sheltering their wares behind its walls whilst others languished beneath the cool pomegranate trees, inhaling deeply from 'shisha' pipes.

As a child, it felt like the Near East held some mysterious allure, and to Louise, now spellbound, it still feels the same, many years and realities later. As an adolescent, she viewed it through a romanticised lens, which stemmed partly from a lack of experience. Knowledge lived is something different. As an adult, it was the unconscious notion that something magical was to be found amidst the faraway, oriental sands. Louise may not have found what she was looking for, whatever she had perceived it to be, but she discovered other, equally worthy things.

Since they are all hungry after the journey, Mohammad deposits them in a shaded spot with a cool drink and leaves them briefly to arrange a place to eat. Having left Tripoli just before dawn, they made two stops. The first was a roadside café for breakfast of coffee and flatbreads, the next to eat sandwiches Arianna had prepared. By the time they hit Ghadames, they are ready for a proper meal.

Glancing about, Louise takes in the slow pace of things, which seems perfectly attuned to the dictates of desert life. Looking out over the old town, she marvels at the medley of mud houses, mosques and minarets that are spread out in front of her.

Lunch is a traditional meal of *ftat,* small pieces of crispy flatbread fried in olive oil and spices, then dipped into bowls of delicious lamb tagine or stew flavoured with freshly sourced mint. There is couscous laden with vegetables and generous chunks of chicken, served in large, pottery bowls. Louise loves their colourful, hand-painted designs, especially the shape of their ornate, conical covers. The pottery is hand-crafted locally and sold in a range of colours and sizes. For dessert, they are treated to a platter of watermelon, dates and figs followed by strong Arabian coffee.

They sit together in a circle on a large hand-woven rug made by the Berbers themselves and partake of the carefully prepared food, which appeals to their eyes first and after their taste buds in a burst of mouth-watering flavours. Louise is fascinated by the colourful world of these indigenous people and how they occupy it with consummate ease. The interior décor is a traditional *Tuareg* wall design, intricately fashioned in a profusion of red and white colour print. The floors are covered in a rich tapestry of hand-woven rugs and carpets, exuding a distinctly cosy feel to the space. There is an amazing wealth of colour and warm, vibrant hues around them that feel soft to the touch of naked feet. Articles of pottery line most of the walls, lending a unique ambience to the space and Louise is immediately enveloped in an atmosphere of tranquillity.

While the men bring their food going to and fro with jugs of water, Louise can hear the low, mellifluous tones of their language, Berber peppered with the odd familiar-sounding Arabic word. Pleasant banter appears to pass so easily between them as they encourage the small party to eat as much as they can whilst staying at a respectful distance to afford them their privacy.

After lunch, they drive a short distance to their accommodation, where they decide to rest briefly before exploring the town proper later. In the evening, the desert temperature drops, and they are able to walk about with ease, taking in all there is to see. Mohammad proves to be an informative guide explaining how the native dwellings serve a mixture of functions.

Pausing to observe one of the houses, he points out how the exterior walls are made of mud, brick, lime and palm tree trunks, which centre around a two-storey main room into which light enters from a grate in the ceiling above. Mirrors hang on most walls to reflect and extend the amount of light in the surrounding areas. It is where visitors sit whenever they come to call, he explains. Next to the room is the *Kubba*, a ceremonial room where a bride awaits her husband on their wedding night. If misfortune should visit, it is also the room in which a grieving widow will mourn her husband's death, according to tradition.

Louise is amazed by the overhanging, covered alleyways, which appear to create an underground labyrinth of passageways. Alleys are characterised by small openings and sharp curves to facilitate ventilation and also to transform a strong desert wind into a gentle breeze. Those passages provide shade and shelter so people can walk and meet more comfortably. It strikes Louise as a rather genius piece of architecture, perfectly adaptable to the region's climatic conditions by keeping its inhabitants cool in summer and warm in winter.

A sea of whitewashed walls offers an effective impression to anyone seeing them for the first time, but Mohammad explains that the real reason is for pragmatic rather than aesthetic considerations. Light colours reflect most of the solar radiation that hits the surface, minimising any thermal load on outside surfaces whilst improving conditions inside the dwellings.

A stairway leads up to a second floor which is reserved for sleeping and storage. From there, a door opens onto an open-air roof terrace where the family and women of the household convene.

Back at the hotel, they watch the sun set from the terrace, where they sit sipping their aromatic tea. Above them, specks of stars twinkle in the black sky, a giant, unfathomable canopy. Despite a sense of desolation, the flat plains, wadis, dry valleys and wavy dunes are not lifeless places. Louise imagines habitats for many organisms that have evolved over time to survive even the harshest conditions.

Mohammed gives the children a brief lesson on the diverse ecosystem that exists there, forming a rich bubble of life. He explains that it is home to gerbils, beetles and snakes. Already, Louise has seen a lizard crawling along the outskirts of the terrace's mud wall, and she shudders at the sight of it. Apart from the occasional loud objection or thundering groan of a disgruntled camel resting nearby, all is quiet as night descends on the serene desert world. A small company of people sit together, unaware of what fate has in store for each of them. No one is thinking about the future, only being present in the moment. Feeling tired after an intense day of activity yet immensely satisfied, it is time to get some sleep before their long drive back to Tripoli the following day.

As Louise and the children prepare for bed, she feels suspended in a different time and, strangely, is in no hurry to leave it for the modern world of civilisation that awaits them beyond the shimmering slopes of *Jebel Nefusa*. It has been a memorable trip, not least of which has been the privilege of spending it in the company of two wonderful people.

Long after, amid the drifting, shifting sands of time, it becomes one of the enduring memories in Louise's mind, tinged with nostalgia. She never forgets her brief sojourn in the enchanting town that stands proudly on the edge of the Sahara Desert.

THIRTY NINE

Bird of Ill Omen

The ultimate value of life depends upon awareness and power of contemplation rather than upon mere survival.

– Aristotle

Several weeks have passed since Kareem's return from an extended trip abroad and life has quickly returned to normal. In those first days, the transition was hard for Louise and the children because they had such fun together with Jabir, and there was lots of laughter, which Louise feels is lacking in their lives.

It seems such a long time ago since she and Kareem first got together. Over the years, Louise has questioned what exactly endeared her to him. She decides that it must have been some wild infatuation that held her in its grip. Falling in love with a mythology built around someone means you may not be able to see the real person. At least not until it is already too late.

In truth, a sliver of doubt had once crept up on her, but she pushed it obstinately away. When the initial fantasy eventually dissolved, she realised there was little chance of achieving anything close to an authentic relationship with Kareem, no matter how hard she tried.

As she continues to mourn the loss of what she believed was love, she realises that its ruptures are as important in developing human understanding as its triumphs. Just deciding where to go from here is fraught with apprehension and uncertainty. She wants to take a plunge, but an overwhelming fear stops her from taking action, and she feels disinclined to muddy the already turbid waters.

Although Louise is grappling with a marriage that is tottering precariously on a cliff edge, she is not completely ready to jump ship, not just yet.

Still only late spring, the promise of summer is in the air. Standing on her front balcony, she feels uplifted by the sound of the early morning birdsong. Lingering there, she enjoys listening to the harmonious chanting of the early singers. Males, proudly perched, proclaim their precious turf and try to attract a mate by showing their prowess in a display of vocal strength. The dawn chorus is at its best in springtime, signalling the hormonal season of courtship.

The air vibrates with the buzzing of bees, and suddenly, her imagination begins to take flight. Before long, it will be that time again, just another five weeks before the three of them travel home to Ireland for the summer. Whenever she thinks about it, she feels the excitement coursing through her veins and visualises being back in her beloved place, waking up in her own bedroom again.

To Louise, it is her sanctuary, a place where imagination, thoughts, and ideas have a chance to flourish, and ruminations about the stuff of life are chewed over with great intensity. It is still a place of secrets and closely held memories to which she regularly returns in her dreams.

From her bed, positioned close to the window, Louise was always able to see the sky above her. She would look up at an expanse of sky, a frame within a frame, in a giant skyscape. Depending on the time of year, it might be a sunless sky, grey and gloomy, with dark clouds gathering. In her mind's eye, she pictures swollen rainclouds, moving in slow motion across a charcoal sky, punctuated by the tall bare branches of winter trees furiously gyrating in the wind. On such mornings, Louise would sink deeper into the warmth and shelter of her cosy bed and close her eyes to the world outside, delaying time until finally, she would force herself to toss the covers aside and leave the comforts behind.

Other times, the canvas would boast a shade of deepest blue, cloudless and calm. Trees, thick with green summer leaves, would swish and sway gently in the whispering breeze. Suddenly, a yellow light would seep through the frame and drench the room in bright, warm sunlight, bathing Louise in a soft, incandescent glow. No time for sleep on those days when everything around her felt infused with life and the world outside was beckoning seductively.

On nights when she felt in a pensive, thoughtful mood and her book lay unopened on the night table, she would lie still and stare at the dark night sky, interspersed with minuscule stars that appeared to twinkle sporadically in the far-off heavens. She knew that beneath the frame, street lamps were lit, but because they were outside her frame of vision, she could be anywhere, looking up at the same magical, mysterious moon. It was a full moon that seemed to arouse her emotions, stirring deep thoughts and questions which would occupy her mind until sleep finally claimed her. For some reason, a crescent moon felt less compelling, creating a calming effect that lulled her gently into a hypnotic sleep.

Between its waxing and waning, a balance of light and shadow, of conscious and unconscious forces, humankind is unknowingly affected by the ebb and flow of the tides within them.

One of her treasured memories relates to her father. She recalls fondly how Saturday mornings throughout her teenage years would begin with a familiar knock on the bedroom door and the sound of his voice behind it.

Louise would wake to the aroma of bacon wafting up from downstairs and she knew that breakfast was on its way. Her father avoided frying, opting instead for grilling everything except the eggs, which he cooked to perfection, sunny side up.

He was always fairly passionate about food, insisting on eating only fresh, quality produce, no canned vegetables or deep-litter eggs for him. From his childhood, he was used to eating good food, most likely from time spent on the farms of his relations in the 'sunny-southeast' of Ireland, a land of fertile, green pasture. His aunts were accomplished cooks along with his mother. Everything was prepared naturally and fresh with great care and attention to detail.

The breakfast ritual was one that Louise learned to appreciate more and more as she got older because it signified more to her than just a meal at the start of her day. There was real thought in it, and nobody since had made her feel special in the way her father had, certainly not her husband.

This morning, Louise has a busy few hours ahead of her in the kitchen. In the afternoon, Safar is having a birthday party for her daughter Ahlam and they are invited. The occasion is special, not only to celebrate her being a year older but to mark the fact that the girl has come through an intense round of medical treatment.

Louise still remembers Ahlam as a pretty, active little girl, full of fun and giggles, quietly mischievous and positively endearing. Her eyes are a shade of the deepest brown with an intelligent sparkle. Depending on where the light falls, they can look black sometimes but are always expressive. Generally, she is to be found following closely on the heels of her older sister Amal, whom she tries to compete with in most things, though there is only a mere two years between them. A younger sister, Afaf and an only boy, Aynaan, are close in age to Tara and Sami, and they get along well.

Within a shockingly short period of time, Ahlam became noticeably thin and sickly, developing an unhealthy pallor. Within a few months, she was afflicted with a debilitating lack of energy and general lethargy.

After much toing and froing to doctors and endless hospital visits, she was finally diagnosed with a rare type of blood cancer. Treatment began, and soon afterwards, she lost her beautiful head of dark, silky hair. It was replaced by a short, somewhat dated and ill-fitting wig hurriedly procured from somewhere. Perched precariously on her head, it was the best they could do so as not to leave the child's head bare. Sadly, it was all that was available at a time when even some basic foodstuffs and other provisions in the country were scarce. Had it not been for the fact that she was living in a developing country, Ahlam might have been able to avail of more advanced medical care for the condition, offering her a better prognosis.

At this point in time, she appears to be enjoying a reasonably good lease of life, but how long it will last, nobody knows. Her mother refuses to speak of it.

Today, she is turning eleven and seems content, all things considered, following a recent bout of chemotherapy.

Louise busies herself in the kitchen, eager to get as much done as she can during the morning before she has to stop and prepare lunch for Sami and Tara when they arrive home from school. She has already made pizza dough and left it to ferment in the bottom of the fridge. Thanks to Martha, Louise learnt how to make the best pizza dough by allowing it to rise gradually as well as some other useful tips. Everyone who eats her pizza likes the earthy, olive-like taste, crusty and flavoursome. It happens as a result of the slowing down of the fermentation process. Jabir is particularly fond of her pizza, so she saves some for him whenever she makes it.

Safar has asked Louise to make pizza for the party and she is eager to help her friend. The actual sauce is easy to prepare, and while she is getting the tomato base ready, she can smell the aroma of vanilla coming from the oven, where the cupcakes and sponges are coming along nicely.

By five in the afternoon, they are dressed and ready to go to the party. A little earlier, Tara and Sami helped carry over the trays of food so her friend could lay them out before the guests arrive, some of whom are neighbours from the immediate locality. Marleen is invited, and so is Suhaila, being a close neighbour.

Just as Louise and the children are leaving, Jabir appears in the doorway.

Clearly expecting him, Louise hesitates for a few moments while Tara and Sami greet their uncle and engage him in a little banter. They have grown quite fond of him, probably because he makes an effort and always has time for them. Louise, assuming an apologetic expression, decides to tease, telling him there is less pizza than she thought and, therefore, not enough for him. Barely concealing his disappointment, he laughs it off, but as Louise walks away down the hall, she turns back, sudden uproarious laughter coming from the kitchen. They leave him to enjoy the pizza, and the three of them set off in the direction of Safar's house.

At the entrance, they can hear the sweet strains of music from within, the sound of Abu-Talib playing his lute, better known in Arabic as *ud*. He is quite an accomplished musician and teaches music at the University of Tripoli. A gregarious character, his choice of career seems to match his personality. He and Safar, his wife, are well suited, both possessing a truly sociable disposition, which is the reason, no doubt, why their home is usually frequented by visitors of all persuasions.

Many of their relatives have already arrived, some of whom Louise is already acquainted with and from whom she receives a warm welcome. As for the new faces, Safar introduces her as a dear friend, warmly complimenting her on a list of positive attributes that Louise waves off with a good-humoured smile.

It is late in the evening when Louise and the children return, and their usual bedtime is long overdue. Still animated and speaking excitedly about the day's events, Louise reminds them that the following morning is a school day and they have an early rise. Soon, they are in bed and sleeping soundly.

The night outside is quiet, and Louise expects any minute to hear the familiar sound of a car engine coming to a halt on the street outside.

Stepping onto the balcony, she pulls up a chair and sits down to savour the stillness. Summoning her thoughts, they come to settle on the enjoyable day that was had by all. The highlight was seeing smiles of joy on Ahlam's face when her birthday cake was brought out. Louise watched with a tear in her eye while her mother lit the candles and exhorted her to make a wish. She wonders what the girl had wished for, suspecting it might be different from other girls her age. It is a poignant reminder of the passing of time, equalled only by the look of pride and love on the face of her mother. Louise is all too aware of her fears because she once confided them to her at a rare moment not long ago. Opening up, she communicated her worst fear: that Ahlam might not survive to see her eleventh birthday, but mercifully, she has. When Safar, with tears of joy, took Louise's hand in hers, clasping it firmly, she understood in that silent moment what no words could convey.

Towards the end of the evening, when most of the visitors had already left, Abu-Talib surprised his wife with airline tickets so they could go visit her family in Alexandria. It has been five painful years since she last saw them, and Louise knows how much Safar missed them. They are just as eager to see their nieces and nephews, especially Ahlam, whom they have not seen since the onset of her illness.

Louise imagines that Abu-Talib has been planning the trip for quite a while and is likely to have made some financial sacrifices in order to make it happen. Because they intend to stretch their trip across the entire summer months, it will be costly, even though Safar's family will accommodate them for the duration of their stay.

Despite his position as a lecturer at the city's university, Abu-Talib is grossly underpaid, like most professionals and academics. In general, the ruling political party are suspicious of the intelligentsia and theoretical learning. Many have already fled the country to seek a better life elsewhere. They are the lucky ones who have the opportunity to decamp with their families to brighter pastures.

Kareem is one of the more fortunate ones, being extremely well-paid and respected in his line of work. He also has the possibility to travel a lot and with that comes extra perks. His wife wonders, if it were not the case, would her husband be content to stay where he is?

Louise hears the car stopping below and Kareem saying goodnight to his driver. Once inside the door, he drops his bag on the floor and looks up, seeing her on the front balcony. He joins her, and they greet one another with a smile before he pulls up a chair and sits down.

"Busy day?" she asks.

"Not really but the next few days will be. How was your afternoon?"

"Do you fancy a cup of tea and a piece of Birthday cake?"

"Yeah, why not, I'll have a piece."

Louise disappears and is back in a jiffy.

While Kareem eats, she begins to fill him in on the day's events and Safar's planned trip home.

"That's good. It'll be very quiet around here for the summer with you, Safar and all the children gone, even Abu-Talib." He laughs.

"I'm sure you'll have plenty to do. You won't be bothered. No noise, nothing to disturb your naps." She says it with a smile, but a touch of sarcasm lurks beneath it.

When he finishes eating, he stands, his expression purposeful and with arms balanced on the railings in front of him, he looks down into the garden and back up at his wife.

"Louise," he begins. Something in his tone alerts her to his next words. She trains her eyes on his face and waits.

"Today, I ran into Sadeek's cousin at the airport. Do you remember him, Amar? Luckily, I wasn't so busy and we had time to drink a coffee together."

"Yeah, I remember him," Louise waits for him to continue.

"He's just back from Ireland, and well, the news from there," he pauses. "It's not good, Louise. I mean about Saoirse."

"What do you mean?"

Immediately, her body tenses, and she senses something ominous.

"She's very sick, Louise."

She looks at him intently before continuing.

"How sick, Kareem, what exactly did Amar tell you? "

"She's been in hospital for the last couple of weeks and the medics haven't been able to do anything for.. For her condition."

Here, he pauses momentarily and shifts his body as if to punctuate his next words.

"She has cancer, Lou, and it's at an advanced stage. It's terrible news".

At the impact of his words, a menacing silence falls upon the night. It takes a few seconds before Louise can form the words to respond.

"Oh God, she told me at Christmas time that she wasn't feeling herself, a bit tired was what she said. I remember thinking, she's just a bit run-down but nothing more."

"You'll be there in Ireland soon. You can see her."

"Jesus, how could things take such a horrible turn?"

"I remember you said that, but her doctor sent her for tests and they discovered something else. Her family and Sadeek are in shock."

"Well, of course, they are. I can't even imagine but surely there is some treatment; she's young".

As Louise speaks the words, thoughts of her sister come to mind. Belle was young too, only a few years older than Saoirse and tragically, age had not spared her. Her youngest child was four years old, and Saoirse's is two; her long-awaited girl after two boys, conceived in Ireland shortly after they went to settle there with the intention of starting a new life.

It was tough in the beginning, Saoirse had admitted, because they had to live with her family while Sadeek established himself in a job, and that took a while. In time, they were able to rent a small place of their own while waiting to find a suitable house. She was happy and relieved when Louise last spoke to her at Christmas because they had just received the good news they had been waiting for all along. Finally, approval came from Dublin City Council and they were offered a house of their own in the location they requested. It was like a dream come true for Saoirse.

Now it looks like her dream might shatter, and after all her patience and perseverance, it seems cruel that she might not be a part of it. The thought is unbearable and Louise looks around in desperation.

"They've sent her home, Louise. She's at home."

"What, she's at home, the hospital sent her home? Is there no possibility of treatment? Is that what you're saying?"

"It seems there's not a lot," Kareem pauses.

"Sadeek told his cousin, it's too far advanced, Louise."

Kareem looks away, and an unspeakable silence follows.

Eventually, Louise breaks the heavy silence.

"How long? Tell me honestly, Kareem." She can hardly believe her own words as she looks piercingly at her husband, waiting for him to answer.

He utters his next words in a measured tone, so quietly as if someone is eavesdropping on their conversation but nobody save the two of them can hear the accursed words.

"She has some time, a couple of months maybe, but they can't be sure. That's all he said, Lou, I swear."

At the delivery of his words, she walks slowly out of the room and down the hall, her bare feet making no sound as they touch the cold marble floor. Her legs feel heavy and there is a choking sensation in her throat as she drags herself sluggishly up the wooden stairs.

She is alone on the roof, encircled by the whitewashed walls that reach just above her head. At her eye level, she can peer out through tiny openings forming part of a narrow, decorative façade. They had sat many times, Saoirse and herself, in this very spot. She can picture it the two of them chatting and sipping peppermint tea in the cool of an evening. She misses her friend.

She recalls when they last met in Dublin at Christmas. Tears gather, eventually spilling onto her cheeks in a steady flow before dropping off her face onto folded arms. She had looked well, a little thinner perhaps, but then Saoirse had always been slender and lithe.

Engrossed in thoughts of that December day, oblivious to all else, the night hours pass unnoticed. Sitting in the café's cosy surroundings, near a glowing fire blazing away in the hearth, time had passed without them noticing. They had time to catch up on all the news; little chats tempered with moments of hearty laughter and multiple cups of coffee. Louise remembers it all so vividly.

After leaving the coffee house, they strolled along Grafton Street, soaking up the atmosphere, the hustle and bustle of their beloved city at Christmas time, its quintessential character, magically reflected in the adage the Irish love to say, even in the face of adversity. "Feck it, sure it'll be grand'. Everything will work itself out!

Eventually, after a long, enjoyable afternoon, they parted company but not before exchanging the gifts they had brought for each other with a mutual promise to park them under the trees until Christmas Eve.

Louise ditched the idea of walking the short distance to her bus stop and opted to take a taxi home instead. It was quicker and there was a biting chill in the air. Her parents knew about her plan to meet Saoirse, but they would soon be expecting her home.

Christmas came, and they kept their word to meet up in the days immediately following the festive period. Actually, it turned out to be twice. Saoirse came to Louise's parents' house, bringing her little daughter, whom she had never seen before. A few days later, prior to Louise's departure, they met again. Only then did she make reference to her state of health, albeit in the vaguest of terms, simply saying that she was feeling very tired and seemed to have lost her appetite for food. Apparently, her doctor had run some blood tests just before Christmas and decided to refer her to the hospital for further tests. She acknowledged that the previous few years had been tough due to the pressures of moving, having another baby and waiting anxiously to get their own place. Having put all of that behind her, she told Louise how grateful she was to finally have a delightful little daughter and a house of their own. She confided that things had been hard on Sadeek, but he was also much relieved, having worked hard to keep things together.

Notwithstanding that, Louise could see that Saoirse was content and that things were finally working out for them. Sure enough, wasn't everything grand they agreed, laughing.

That was what Louise truly believed.

FORTY

One Journey's End

There are many truths of which the full meaning cannot be realised until personal experience has brought it home.

– John Stuart Mill

Louise is sitting on a plane bound for Dublin via Frankfurt a few months after hearing the devastating news about Saoirse. Her view outside the cabin window is partially obscured by the fuselage pushing its way through white, cumulus clouds. Events swirl around inside her head, and nothing seems clear except a sense of relief that she is homebound. It is better, she figures, to be miserable at home rather than anywhere else.

Sami and Tara are excited at the prospect of seeing their grandparents again. Though the children are old enough to understand that their grandfather is very ill and their mother has explained to them, gently, as much as they need to know, the enormity of it is still beyond their grasp, Louise believes. Innocence is a beautiful thing as long as it remains untouched by a cruel nemesis, like the one their mother is grappling with.

Exactly nine days have passed since she got the call from Arleen instructing her to return home without delay. Hearing her sister's voice, she immediately knew something serious was afoot. Her thoughts took her instantly back to a previous time, to a similar call and a tragic ending.

Arleen tried to break the news as gently as she possibly could, but despite her best efforts, Louise was grief-stricken. Later that evening, having composed herself, she sat down with Sami and Tara to explain that their beloved grandad was poorly, trying to make things sound softer. It made no sense to trouble their minds unnecessarily.

Thankfully, Arleen's call came in the morning while the children were at school, so she was able to sit down and quietly process the bad news alone.

For the most part, she spent the following days in a daze, not caring much about anything except the children's basic needs. It felt like a dark shadow had descended on her, and the world was suddenly a dangerous, dismal place. Barely speaking to Kareem, she went about her days, performing the necessary tasks in a purely perfunctory way. At least he appeared to understand that his wife was in a different realm and needed a quiet space. For once, he took Sami and Tara with him on some of his errands.

The very next day, Arleen called Kareem at work, impressing the urgency of the situation and urging to avoid any unnecessary delay with travel preparations. Taking heed, he began making plans for them to leave as soon as the necessary paperwork could be completed.

The days dragged on, and her surrounding world seemed to change, becoming bleak and full of portent. The sole focus obsessively occupying her day was the swift passage of time so she could be reunited with her father without delay; nothing else mattered. Her nights were marked by fitful sleep and distressing dreams. In her nocturnal life, she seemed to make no progress, feeling sluggish and unable to move. Her feet remained firmly soldered to the ground beneath her; other times, she found herself half immersed in stagnant water, motionless and in tears because she couldn't get to where she wished to go. Twice, she awoke in a night sweat, a physiological response to the residual fear left over from her dream. Getting out of bed, she went to the bathroom and splashed cool water on her face. Slowly, she started to feel like herself and decided to read for a couple of hours before eventually returning to sleep. Reading and books kept her calm as they had so often before.

When her in-laws heard the news about her father, they wasted no time in coming to express their concern, a gesture that Louise appreciated. It was Jabir who drove them, and when she opened the door and looked into his face, the concern was evident in his eyes. Hesitating inside the hall, he waited for his mother to greet Louise before he shook her hand. She felt his grip tighten, and as he slowly released his hand, she fought back the tears that threatened to undo her completely. Just the week before, Louise confided in him the distressing news about Saoirse, never imagining there would be yet another horror to follow so soon afterwards.

Louise closes her eyes, hoping to doze for a bit and rest her mind from pestering thoughts. After weighing the quandaries and conundrums of life, wondering about the purpose of it all, she drifts off, lulled into a jaded sleep by the steady humming of the aircraft. Tiredness finally catches up with her.

Time passes, and soon, the lights inside the cabin go dim. Louise is aware of a sudden slowing of acceleration. Rubbing her sleepy eyes, she straightens in her seat and raising her window blind she can make out a range of mountains and some hilly terrain below. She checks her watch, and glancing at Tara, sees that her eyes are still closed, so decides to leave her a little longer before waking her. Sami, on the other hand, is fully alert, viewing the aircraft's progress from his adjacent seat. Before long, they will be gliding over the east coast of Dublin and will be able to watch their final descent.

The captain announces that a mild, clement evening awaits them in Dublin, with weather reports promising sunny conditions over the coming days. Louise feels enormous relief that their journey is approaching its end. The days of worry, emotional exhaustion and pretence are over. Soon, she will come face to face with her father and the unpleasant reality of his condition. She guesses that Arleen has been scant with the details, sparing her the worry until she arrives.

As they descend the steps of the aircraft and walk the short distance along the tarmac and onto the awaiting bus, Louise breathes in deeply the fresh evening air. Instantly, her mind becomes clear and a sense of positivity awakens.

One journey ends as another is about to begin.

FORTY ONE

The Ravage of Loss

❉

Tis better to have loved and lost than never to have loved at all.
– Alfred Lord Tennyson

'My God', he is so thin, is Louise's first thought of her father. She manages to compose herself, holding back a sea of tears that threaten to flow unchecked if not held back. When she hugs him, she can feel his thinness in the hard, sharp edges, where once, not long ago, there was a round softness. His face is paler than usual, and his cheeks are sunken above his jawbone, lending his face a hollowed look. There is little fat on his body anywhere. Louise notes in silent shock and with a carefully concealed sadness, the muscle-wasting, particularly apparent around his shoulder blades and along his throat. Nonetheless, it is her beloved father who stands weakly before her, his flesh fading away in front of her eyes. Yet, it is not his diminished exterior body that she sees, but the core of his nature encased inside it. What captures her heart and speaks to her soul is the essence that lives above and beyond his worldly coat of shrinking flesh.

Observing him closely, Louise is thankful for the one thing that has remained as before. His head of thick, grey hair that he ensures, no matter what, is neatly kept as part of a good grooming routine. It may even be the sole redeeming feature of his terrible illness, outwardly, at least. She imagines it offers some small comfort to her father since, in good health, it has always been a source of pride, one of his minor vanities.

Louise finds it strange to see him sitting quietly in an armchair, frail and inactive, where once he was busy and energetic. His daily routine would begin with a walk to the local shop for a newspaper, and once in the village, he would frequently bump into his neighbours and pause for a chat. He is well-liked and respected for his quiet dignity. Louise thinks how cruel it is that he should so soon be robbed of his life and so much more left to do.

Each morning, he insists on shaving himself, no doubt from sheer habit but Louise is convinced it stems also from a need to hold firmly onto a vestige of independence before it disappears altogether. Regimentally, he carefully lathers his face with cream and slowly applies the razor, his hand still steady enough to perform the task, all the while Louise holding a hand mirror in front of his face. Once the familiar job is done, he appears more relaxed and is able to drink a cup of tea, still one of his great pleasures in life.

Louise smiles wistfully at the disquieting reversal of roles. She remembers only too well her previous visit, the sound of her father's voice calling her from downstairs. On the kitchen table stood a pot of tea, freshly brewed, alongside it, two mugs and a jug of milk. A plate of cream doughnuts was lovingly placed in the middle of the red Formica table, brought fresh from the bakery because they were her favourite.

"Sit down, love and have a cup a tea."

It was as simple as that, and they would sit a while and chat about the affairs of the world; occasionally, matters closer to home or nothing of importance. Usually, Sami would be outside playing, and Tara would go shopping with her grandmother, so there would be just the two of them. The memory would persist ad infinitum.

In many ways, her father is a man of simple tastes and he has shown his daughter a valuable lesson. In the minutiae of everyday life, simplicity is no mean thing but often a place from which more important things take their root and blossom into something much greater.

Now, Louise sits with her father in an entirely different atmosphere, in a way she had never anticipated as a young girl, having assumed in her naivety that he would be around forever, believing in the immortality of the parents, perhaps. Perhaps it is a natural part of our psychological life, particularly when we are still young, to attach a kind of immortality to our parents.

In a room downstairs, they set up a comfortable bed for her father. Sadly, the sight of it reminds Louise that he will never again sleep in the bed upstairs, which he has shared with his wife for over thirty years. Nor will he kneel at the foot of the same bed and address his maker in silent prayer as has been his habit for as long as Louise can remember.

The front-facing room is cosy enough, with an artificial log fire set in the centre of a small marble fireplace against the far wall. The summer days are warm, but the temperature grows cool at night, and the constant low heat absorbs the chill from the surrounding air.

Most nights, Louise occupies an armchair, staying close to her father, keeping him company through the dark hours. He has trouble sleeping because of a persistent cough, and whenever he manages to doze off, his sleep is soon interrupted. She makes sure to arrange his pillows so that his head is elevated to facilitate the passage of phlegm to exit his mouth without getting caught in his throat.

With the daylight hours comes a degree of optimism that fosters an illusion of hope, reflected in her mood. The very sounds, movements and routine habits that constitute the pattern of daily business and necessity are intrinsic to the order of life. Is it any wonder one could forget that death is close at hand? Would there be better days ahead still?

The dark night hours are of a different order, and Louise finds it hard to keep sinister thoughts from slipping in. Perhaps it is her imagination, but she reckons that during those nocturnal hours, her father's anxiety is aroused, although he never says. While the rest of the house tries to get some sleep, he struggles with wakeful episodes, trying to clear his throat, to struggle through another night and hang on at the edge of life without complaint. There is little Louise can do to alleviate her father's symptoms except hold a plastic cup to his mouth and be there, beside him, a presence in the room. In time, she would come to realise that it was enough.

With the passing of weeks, the bright summer nights start to wane, twilight arrives earlier, and the nights seem longer. Autumn is painfully approaching and winter cannot be far behind. The children have enjoyed the summer, taking advantage of the long daylight hours. Between bouts of play, they sit by their grandfather, regaling him with little anecdotes of their latest escapades. Other times, they just sit quietly and watch television together.

Louise's sisters come and go rather sporadically from distances outside Dublin. Juliette stays for two or three days at a time, arriving fully laden with apple pies, scones and fairy buns. The visiting parish priest, whom she is usually on hand to greet, certainly appreciates her homemade treats. It is a small return for his pastoral ministrations and what little spiritual comfort he brings to her father in his final days on earth, being a man of some faith.

In the background, there are quiet rumblings of sibling discontent. Occupying centre stage in their grievances is their mother. Louise has come to realise that the intricacies and nuances of their convoluted relations formed long before her birth are still evolving. Those maternal entanglements are well crystalised and predate her unexpected arrival into the fold. She is mindful that her sister Marianne is a mischief-maker. Nothing much has changed since Louise was a child and her sister was already a young woman. Thankfully, more important things in life had distracted Marianne, her boyfriends, a career and a busy social life, shifting her focus temporarily away from her 'baby' sister for several years. Until, one day her interest was reawakened. By then, Louise was a fifteen-year-old adolescent and Marianne a woman of twenty-six.

Louise has picked up on the disparaging glances and contentious remarks that pass between her sisters. Marianne is barely able to conceal the true nature of her feelings. Either she concerns herself with the business of others, or she complains about the injustices of her own life. as she sees them.Everyone is subjectedto her sanctimonious ramblings.

Juliet likes to control situations and is obsessed with tidiness, to the point of annoyance. She is more subtle, whereas Marianneis brash, generous; the other is tight-fisted. Juliette is smart, sharp and not without charm but craves approval. Marianne seeks recompense because, after all, the world owes her something, or so she believes. Both are argumentative but in very different ways.

Arleen, being the eldest, is highly favoured by their mother and can do no wrong, it seems. That fact is a source of rivalry among the siblings. Louise feels that Juliette works hard to earn her mother's approval and, despite her best efforts, seldom achieves it, whilst Arleen has to do very little. She is seen as the shining star in the family constellation.

Juliet is particularly fond of her father despite having a complicated relationship with her mother. As for Marianne, she is rather more successful in knowing how to ingratiate herself with her mother's affections. Louise thinks that she is a bit spoilt by her mother, but in an unobtrusive sort of way.

Marianne was eleven when Louise was born, and perhaps she felt intruded upon by an unexpected baby sister who claimed her parents' affections.

Louise notices how her sister frequently succeeds in influencing their mother and how adept she is at turning things to her advantage. Some of the things she says are often downright silly, totally without foundation, and Louise suspects calculated to offend and defame. She is in no doubt that her sister is a rabble-rouser, plain and simple, something her mother very likely knows, but she seems bent on appeasing her daughter no matter what, much to Louise's growing distaste. Unfortunately, Louise had fallen prey to her sister's manoeuvrings and manipulation at a time when she could have done with her support. Alas, she was too young and inexperienced, waking up to her sister's subterfuge only when it was too late.

One could be forgiven for thinking that while their father sits quietly, waiting for death to come knocking his daughters would be consumed with grief and sadness at the prospect of losing him. Surely, they would know how to conduct themselves in a manner that is respectful of that fact. On the contrary, it may be that the threat of losing their father acts as a catalyst, unleashing some powerful negative emotions. Louise is, therefore aghast when she sees her sisters, ostensibly mature women, behave like children.

Then, one afternoon, the pot boils over, reminding Louise of a Shakespearean tragedy. For days afterwards, she cannot believe the foolishness and malice of her sisters who, between them, fail to regulate their emotions despite the gravity of their father's illness. Sadly, a wall in the house is all that separates him from their misplaced grievances.

As the argument becomes heated, it spills out into the garden, ending with their mother, who is now distraught and reacting completely out of character. Louise has never seen her mother cry, much less sob, believing her to be unemotive and stoic since she has never seen her behave in any other way. The pitiful sight completely unnerves her, made worse by the picture of Tara innocently kneeling beside her grandmother, confused and full of fear, trying to offer what consolation she can.

Louise, feeling like a bystander somewhat removed from the high drama that unfolds before her eyes, is no less affected by it. Hardly able to believe what is happening and not fully understanding why, she is more aware that her family dynamics are complex, the roots of which were sown long before she had any influence. She understands that all combined, they represent a history of fraught relationships and minor power struggles that have been allowed to build up over time and remain unresolved. It occurs to Louise that her mother has created her own monster.

Not for the first time, Louise is reminded of Regan and Goneril, brought to life between the pages of Shakespeare's *King Lear*. Those two infamous sisters of literature bear a resemblance to her misguided siblings, albeit with a slight twist. Nevertheless, both are overcome by their desires, unable to control their petty jealousies and sense of entitlement, even in the face of death. Not unlike Cordelia, Lear's youngest and most devoted daughter, Louise later on becomes the ultimate scapegoat for her sibling's grievances and her mother's ineffectuality.

As her father's condition worsens, Louise plunges into a darkness of her own. Now, he barely sleeps at all, his nights fiercely interrupted by a raspy cough and a foul, black sputum that he spews relentlessly into a plastic cup that she holds up to his mouth. Louise knows instinctively that the days, nights, moments are ticking agonisingly towards her father's eventual demise. Being with him there in those final hours causes her to question many things, mostly incomprehensible musings. What strikes her with a harsh, stark clarity is that even love is not enough because it offers no protection from the inevitable. The sad reality is that the business of death is solitary. You come into this world alone, and you leave it alone.

Finally, those dreaded last hours arrive. For Louise, it is signalled by the arrival of the palliative care nurse and the composed but gentle expression of resignation on her face. A kind of numbness descends on the sorrowful group as they assemble around her father's still body.

His beloved wife, daughters, grandson Sami and only nephew, to whom he has always been close, are present. The priest is there to say the final prayer, to announce the passage of his humble soul into the next world, just as her father would have wished.

Upstairs, Tara wakes anxiously from her sleep to enquire about her grandad. By now, his breathing is shallow, his pulse slowing as the last dose of morphine does its work.

Just after midnight, in early September, as the season is turning, her dear father leaves the world peacefully behind. If there is ever an ideal way to die, Louise believes, in her humble estimation, that her father's death is the closest approximation.

Mercifully, her father never had to leave his home for an unfamiliar and isolated stay in one of the city's residential homes. Nobody, except his family, administered his personal care. No stranger washed, undressed, pulled or poked at him while he lay helplessly at the mercy of some unfriendly, uncaring individual or worse. He wore his own clothes and was spared the indignity of any toilet-assisted intervention, at least while he could still do for himself, rather than by default. He remained in control of his mental faculties without medication to calm or make him clinically pliable. Instead, he was blessed to hold onto his own agency. Perhaps his prayers were answered after all.

Louise wonders if somebody, anybody, a spirit will greet him at the other side, beyond, whatever that might be. It seems so unspeakably inhuman to have to let go of someone you love. Louise knows it is just the beginning and will take time to process such a monumental loss. She has no idea how it will be even though she had experienced a hint of it before when her sister died. The loss of a parent is different.

The brutal severing of a life and pure finality of death are forces to be reckoned with, and when she ponders over it, she feels the depth of it is unfathomable. The utter powerlessness of the human condition over death may leave one feeling that they have been duped, deprived, or even beguiled. What or who is responsible for it is a question Louise cannot answer. In her scepticism, she realises that the most frustrating questions are posed repeatedly through the very pain and suffering of life.

Rationality has its limits and Louise finds no refuge in its cold comfort. Instead, her vain attempts to make some sense of irrationality and non-meaning reveal that her efforts at understanding will never be absolute. In any case, she comes to recognise that the ontological questions she poses for herself, despite the unique circumstances and personal terms in which she asks them, far exceed the scope and understanding of the individuals who ask them.

In a world where you have to confront what the great psychologist Carl Jung named "the terrible ambiguity of immediate experience", without logical belief systems, human beings have no choice but to strive and suffer. One day, they may hopefully arrive at a state of radical acceptance for what befalls them in the world and ultimately be responsible for creating their own meaning. Until then, Louise is pushed and steered involuntarily to the very limits of existence, and maybe on these outer perimeters, she will find the best of all possibilities.

FORTY TWO

Heartless

*The broken heart. You think you will die, but you keep living,
day after day after terrible day.*

– *Great Expectations,* Charles Dickens

Under a burning sun, its rays dazzlingly bright and intense, Kareem drives the pick-up through the Libyan Desert, part of which stretches across the northeastern Sahara. Its name is derived from the Arabic word for desert, *Sahra,* a land whose sandy plains are arid and inhospitable, where often, no rain falls for years at a time.

The terrain is bumpy and uneven, making for an uncomfortable ride, but that is the least of Louise's problems. Though it is mid-September and temperatures are lower than in high summer, the heat of the sun is scorching. Here and there, Louise can see an area of sparse vegetation, but very little grows due to the harsh environment.

The unpleasant conditions of the journey seem to be matched only by her husband's mood, which is volatile, ready to erupt at the slightest provocation.

He had picked them up from Carthage International Airport in Tunis, once an ancient city, now a wealthy suburb. From the little she can see, it is a city Louise would love to explore sometime if she ever has the opportunity. Passing through, she marvels at its beautiful villas surrounded by gardens, filled with red hibiscus blossoms and rich, purple bougainvillea.

As soon as she sees her husband, it is apparent that he is not looking forward to the journey ahead, exchanging but a few words with his wife and children despite not having seen them for several months. When she asks him if anything is the matter, he ignores the question, immediately understanding that her question was not well received.

It is a hellish journey, compounded by intense heat, buzzing mosquitoes and ill-temper. After driving for roughly four hours, they come upon a small clearing in the sandy wilderness. Positioned conspicuously in the middle is a tin-roofed shed. Outside stand two Berber men, clothed in traditional dress, looking eagerly towards them as they approach.

Kareem stops his old pick-up at the edge of the camp and, alighting, issues a sharp-sounding greeting to his native countrymen. Deeply bronzed and desert-worn, they respond with warm smiles and piercing black eyes. With arms outstretched, they invite the incongruous little party to partake of their modest provisions. Stacked under a worn-looking, patched tarpaulin canopy are crates piled one on top of the other and filled with bottled water and Fanta, brought from nearby Tunisia. Without refrigeration, they will have to quench their thirst with liquid, warmed by the temperature, rather than savour the sensation of cold liquid against a dry palate. On a nearby stand, pieces of raw meat are randomly arranged, ready to cook on what appears to be an old, makeshift grill of sorts, its bars bent on one side.

At a word from Kareem, it is lowered on top of a low flaming fire and sprinkled with salt. Louise imagines it has not seen water or soap for the duration of its use. Looking on with mild distaste, she observes a swarm of gorging blowflies hovering around it, which is the deciding factor. Despite feeling hungry, she suddenly has no appetite, at least not for what is on offer. Likewise, Tara declines to sample it, causing her father to swear angrily and issue a stern warning that there would be nothing better on offer before they reach home. Sami is slightly more accommodating, joining his father in a sandwich of dry bread, roughly broken with the charred meat inside. His mother can only hope he will not suffer any consequences from eating it. At the same time, she curses herself for not being sufficiently prepared in bringing her own snacks, especially for the children, but Kareem neglected to tell her about the journey that they faced. Normally, they could fly to Tripoli, but unfortunately, the flight was not in service. She had no idea of the route Kareem planned or the length of the ghastly trip.

They had eaten a good breakfast that morning, and during the short flight from Malta, they ate a light snack. Louise assumed they would find a café or restaurant on the return journey to have a proper meal. She smiles wryly to herself, realising that you could assume nothing when it concerns her husband. She had better muster all her strength until they arrive in Tripoli, where she will undoubtedly face the next hurdle.

After a brief and frugal encampment, they take to the road again or rather, the sandy plains and plateaus.

It is another three hours before they stop for a toilet break. On the edge of the desert, one can not expect luxury, and the conditions were primitive.

Fortunately, Louise is more prepared this time, with a stock of wipes and tissues in her bag to see them right. During the short stop, Kareem drinks a glass of strong black tea, and they are on their way again.

Night has fallen as they reach the outer limits of the city. Earlier on, Tara and Sami had drifted off to sleep for the last leg of what turned out to be a ten-hour, gruelling journey and one Louise is not likely to forget.

Finally, when they pull up outside the house, relieved as she is to have survived the journey on several levels, she braces herself before going inside. Though travel-weary, hungry, and exhausted from the effects of the heat on her body, it is not that alone that holds her back.

Her heart becomes suddenly heavy in her chest, her legs feel like jelly and she has to force herself to move in a forward direction. Momentarily distracted by her thoughts and feelings, she turns to Tara and Sami, realising how they must be feeling. It seems all so strange and unfamiliar to be back after four months away.

When she enters the house that has been her home for nearly eleven years, it feels empty and unwelcoming. Glancing around her, she takes in the state of things. Dust is everywhere, and it is obvious that nobody has bothered to clean or do anything with it for a while. In the kitchen, the fridge is empty, and there is nothing in any of the cupboards for them to eat.

Suddenly, Louise feels an uncontrollable urge to scream loudly and, at the same time, burst into a fit of crying to relieve her frustrations. Fighting off the urge, she stops herself and instead turns her attention to the children who are looking expectantly at their mother.

"C'mon you two, let's get ready for bed. I'll make you some Ovaltine and we can chat for a bit before you fall asleep." Fortunately, it is all she finds in the cupboard, and she sets about boiling water to fill two mugs of the nutritious drink that will have to suffice for the moment.

The next morning, their first day back in Tripoli, the sun shines brightly, illuminating every nook and cranny of the house. What was partially unseen the previous night, under cover of darkness, appears unsparingly clear in the early morning light, much to Louise's annoyance. Standing in the middle of the kitchen, she looks at the worktops and counters in dismay, covered in a heavy layer of dust, making it impossible to prepare any food, even supposing there was any to eat. At that precise moment, Kareem appears in the doorway, mumbling something about making him a coffee. She ignores his request and looking into the empty fridge for a second time, turns to her husband.

"Kareem, there's absolutely nothing to eat in the house, not even eggs or bread for the children to have breakfast."

He looks completely undisturbed by the fact as he already knows it.

"It's our first day back after so long." She looks at him with an expression of distaste.

"I'll go to the market in a while, just make some coffee for now," he repeats, looking unperturbed by his wife's remark. Suddenly, Louise decides she has had enough.

"Kareem, I don't know what you were doing or thinking about before we arrived back but there are two children and there should be something to eat in the house." Louise can see he is getting annoyed but keeps going regardless.

"As for the house, you couldn't even run a cloth around, take the thick dust away. Even if you didn't want to do it, I'm sure your sisters would have obliged, had you thought to ask them. A great welcome home. To be honest, the place is a disgrace and you don't give a damn. You expect a lot, don't you?"

Louise looks at her husband with contempt and he is angry. The usual cursing and swearing will begin any second, but she cannot stop now.

"You know what we've been through, Kareem, for God's sake, my father is only dead a week, it's been tough on all of us. I really thought you'd be more considerate in the circumstances."

As soon as Sami and Tara hear the angry voices, they appear in the kitchen.

With shocking suddenness and ear-shattering sound in the small kitchen, he unleashes his foul temper. Louise can hardly believe her eyes as a torrent of glass and crockery comes crashing to the floor where she and the children are standing. In a moment, all the contents of her kitchen cupboard lie in shattered pieces at their feet. It happens so fast, in the blink of an eye but with such force that Louise never even sees it coming. Then, he opens the lid of their chest freezer that stands in the far corner of the kitchen and, grabbing several sticks of frozen bread from inside, he empties them onto the floor in such derision whilst mumbling obscenities at his wife. In a flash, before she has a chance to react or utter a single word, he turns and walks out of the kitchen, leaving his long-suffering family and a trail of destruction behind him.

A transfixed Louise stares in partial disbelief at the old, rustic dresser made of solid pine, standing empty, its doors swinging open. It had originally belonged to a French couple who worked with Shelley at the embassy. When given a new posting, they were eager to find a good home for their precious antique cabinet, and Louise fit the bill. Until a few moments ago, it was her statement piece in an otherwise ordinary kitchen, reigning tall over things of a lesser beauty. Now, it is forever tarnished with an unpleasant memory.

Stripped bare of its beautiful, ornate glass, the old dresser looks exposed, just as Louise feels. Pieces of her delicate porcelain tea set, a vintage red with gold trim, lie in smithereens. It was a special gift from a close friend. Beside it, similarly destroyed, is a floral, nineteenth-century Victorian jug and a very old and beautiful teapot which had been in her family a long time, a gift when she got married.

Weeks later, with the benefit of hindsight, she gains some insight into what had likely sparked off his foul mood that first day. It was not as if the scales had finally fallen from her eyes; she knew what her husband was capable of. Convinced that she had said nothing in particular to set him off, his behaviour seemed completely disproportionate.

In the months they were away, her husband had no responsibilities and was entirely free to come and go as he pleased, without having to think about anyone else. In fact, it was obvious, he had hardly been in the house except perhaps to shower, dress and sleep. He never cooks, so his meals were also taken outside. Louise wonders if there was another 'distraction' she has not considered, but she prefers not to focus on things she can only speculate about. Perhaps he has grown accustomed to his own company.

The prospect of their homecoming, coupled with the inconvenience of having to travel to Tunis to collect them, likely irritated him no small amount. Finally, when his wife expressed her annoyance and disappointment at his lack of care, he lost control like a child unable to regulate his emotions and threw a tantrum instead. For Louise, it was a step too far.

As the days pass and the horror of what happened begins to recede, not from her mind or memory but from the immediacy of the moment, Louise feels an increasing repugnance towards her husband. At the same time, she gains a deeper perspective, the impact of which hits her like a sharp object, all the more because it is directly related to the death of her beloved father and the loss of her dear friend Saoirse.

Louise reasons that if her husband cannot show compassion, empathy and generosity of spirit at such a time when his wife is grieving the monumental loss of a parent, his children's grandfather, then when will he show it?

FORTY THREE

Epiphany

※

As you sow, so shall you reap.

– Galatians 6:7

Louise is adamant that her marriage is over. The relief that follows the wake of such a resolution brings a new determination to her days. Five long weeks have passed and the children are settled at school, challenged by new lessons and enough homework in the evenings to keep them occupied. Still, they are always glad when Friday arrives so they can rest and enjoy a day off. It has taken them all their time to adjust after their long break away, not an easy transition for them, having to deal with the loss of one grandparent whilst desperately missing the other.

They have loved Ireland from the time they were babies and hated leaving. When they arrived back in Tripoli, they had to cope with a father completely unaware of his role as a parent and what it entails. He only seemed interested in his own affairs. Approaching eleven and twelve on their next birthday and growing up fast, Louise is very aware that they have an acute understanding of their parents' troubled relationship.

On that first awful day, after their arrival, Louise sat them down to try and explain a few things honestly and with a degree of sensitivity to their developing emotional lives. She chose her words prudently in her humble attempts to soften the blow, but her aim was more about giving them a chance to say how they felt. Saddened by the scale of their observations, she was surprised by some of their cogent remarks, but relieved they felt at ease sharing them with her.

She discovers that Tara, with her keen intellect, is much less forgiving of her father than her brother. Then again, it comes as no surprise to Louise since she has long suspected her son to be more conflicted when it comes to his father. Perhaps it is simply a boy-father thing, further influenced by the culture and approaching adolescence or maybe even a combination of all three.

Notwithstanding that, Louise is not wholly convinced because she knows her husband has instilled fear in her son around all things to do with school and studying, like his father before him: a case of history being repeated. Sami is aware that his father has high expectations of him, something she does not support. Kareem's continual berating of his son, forever pushing and applying pressure on the young boy to excel, has been, in her opinion, counterproductive, having the opposite effect, serving instead to switch off any potential regarding academic interests that he might otherwise have.

Kareem's insistence has been the source of many arguments in the house. There were times when she had to intervene to protect Sami from the physical threats of his father. Alarmed by the wrath of her husband and a cruel rage that seems to come out of nowhere, she found herself shielding her young son more than once, telling him to pick up his books and leave the room to put distance between them. The situation never ended well, often turning into a full-blown row between her and Kareem. There are times when her husband's nastiness knows no bounds. He becomes obsessed with getting his own way, a kind of self-gratification where the other person's needs are frequently ignored, right-minded decency and empathy being way out of sight. Recently, Louise has sensed an anxiety in Sami whenever his father enters the house and she finds that worrying.

Nearly six weeks have passed and it has taken her until now to even begin to process her father's death, having no idea how complex it would prove to be. It has been made worse by the terrible reception she and the children have received coming home.

Events surrounding their arrival still feel surreal, and she has propelled herself through the motions of what needed to be done at the time, without pausing to think. There is still a feeling of numbness, a complete separation of her inner world from the outer sphere, the one she moves in like a robot. It is for the sake of her two children and how they might be feeling that drives her on, feigning a show of strength that she does not feel.

In those first days following their arrival, as she cleaned and scrubbed, she thought about a lot of things, stuff that had not occurred to her before, imagining scenarios to the extent that she surprised even herself. Despite sleep disturbances, she felt sharp and alert, as if the body's adrenalin had triggered her into a 'fight-or-flight' mode, providing her with the energy to see things through. Maybe her efforts to restore things and reclaim a level of orderliness acted as a vital catalyst before arranging the more complex things into some kind of order.

She realised, too, that there was nowhere she could run since escape was not an option. In the days that followed, it did occur to her that it was not the only option. Patience would have to be her stalwart friend.

Late one evening, as sleep eludes her yet again, she sits down with a glass of peppermint tea clasped between both hands. Nothing stirs in the house and the children are sleeping soundly after a busy day. The only noise to disrupt the stillness of the night is the tuneless whine of caterwauling in the street below.

Stealing a glance at the picture frame that holds a photograph of her father, she finds it deeply provoking, giving reign to her persistent thoughts.

It is as if he intends to speak to her from some far away, nondescript place. In answer to the temptation, something inside her seems to fall away. Alas, the unspeakable grief, sorrow and despair rise up in her, sitting heavily on her chest, forcing her breath to come in short, uneven gasps. She swallows hard to stifle a loud, uncontrollable sob from escaping her mouth whilst simultaneously forcing herself to stand and rise from the chair.

Suddenly, feeling very tired, she moves automatically, as fast as her legs will transport her, down the hall and up the stairs, nearly tripping halfway. Completely overwhelmed by a rush of emotions, her vision begins to blur and by the time she reaches the top of the stairs and lets herself out onto the roof, her eyes are drowning and visceral emotions begin to erupt, unchecked.

She has held it all together admirably without understanding how trauma disrupts the body's natural equilibrium as well as the mind. It is time to finally 'let go', to open the floodgates. Like a great dam that holds the water back until one day it becomes necessary to release it from a reservoir, to preserve its structural integrity and avoid a catastrophe, Louise gives way. Desperately needing to give free rein to her latent grief, which has been slowly building over months, even years, Louise succumbs.

She feels the dis-ease assaulting her physical body as well as her spirit. A myriad of unacknowledged thoughts and fears lie constricted in a tangle of stubborn knots at the pit of her stomach. Her head begins to pound and suddenly, it feels as if a great pressure is rising in her throat, pressing forward to dislodge. Unbeknownst to her, it is a perfect culmination of psychosomatic forces and for a brief moment, it feels to Louise as if she is losing her grip on sanity itself.

She does nothing to stop the abundant stream of salty tears from flowing freely down her face. She cries unreservedly for her beloved father and for the loss of a unique bond that was so untimely ruptured. Like a person cast adrift on a captainless ship, Louise feels exposed and vulnerable. Unable to comprehend the raw fact that she will never again see him in this life causes fresh tears to spill onto her warm, blotchy cheeks. She feels anger for the snatching of a life in such a short space of time, but despite it all, Louise takes comfort in the privilege of having sat with him during those long summer nights.

Gathering up her t-shirt, Louise wipes her eyes roughly, and after taking a deep breath, her focus begins to shift. Surrounding the void left behind by his death, there are other losses that need to be mourned. There was time to acknowledge the death of Saoirse but not to process it, at least not in any real way, because her father's illness had overtaken everything.

Her friend's funeral was a harrowing experience, one she is loath to think about even several months on. Standing alone on the roof, a cascade of unwanted memories come flooding back. It strikes her for the first time how removed she had been from what was happening, like someone having an out-of-body experience. For days afterwards, she felt numb, suspended between precious moments in their friendship and a refusal to believe she was gone forever.

Forgetting about time, Louise sits on a low mattress and leans her back against the wall, allowing the thoughts to crowd in, and instead of feeling like a massive storm is gathering in her brain, an unusual calmness suddenly washes over her in a rather uncanny way and suddenly, for the first time, she can actually 'sit' with her own emotions, allow them to surface, rather than resist and push them down here.

She can even weep for the life she did not have, the one she would have liked, imagined and still hopes for. Those shattered assumptions, toppled by traumatic events, cannot now be assimilated into her previously held worldview. For Louise, the world she thinks she knew has ceased to be an entirely benevolent place but is a more hostile one in which she feels undermined. Nothing is certain. Nothing can ever again be taken for granted.

She knows from that moment forward, she will never again be quite the same person she has been. Her relationship with her 'self' is utterly changed.

With the fading of the Imam's soulful voice, still ringing in her ears, the first rays of light slowly steal across the eastern sky, reminding her that it is time to face a new day.

Closing the door quietly behind her, she leaves the rooftop and descends the stairs. Kareem meets her halfway between the hallway and the kitchen. He mumbles some remark in passing about having to stay on late at work that day. Louise simply nods, having no words to add. From behind the window curtain, she watches him go. Leaning against the pillar, he stands waiting for his driver to arrive, cigarette in hand. As the car pulls away, breaking the quiet of the early morning, Louise feels an enormous relief. She knows instinctively it is not due solely to her cathartic, therapeutic experience on the rooftop. It is something more.

She feels nothing, certainly not love, not even its close companion, friendship. It comes as a great release for her, a kind of permission to stop trying, to let go.

From that moment on, despite her fairly recent return from Ireland, her focus turns immediately to how she will return there. In the meantime, she resigns herself with some reluctance to the fact that life must continue irrespectively. A large part of that involves doing her best, no matter what, to avoid or ignore any potential conflict in the house for the sake of the children. Knowing it will require some sacrifice on her part and a great deal of patience, she is committed, nonetheless. If it means finding a way, a skill to 'manage' her husband in order to achieve it, so be it. Louise is all too aware that impulsive actions and angry words will get her nowhere and could ultimately cost her and the children dearly.

There is wisdom in waiting for the right moment to act.

FORTY FOUR

The Ambiguity of Loss

Heaven has no rage like love to hatred turned,
nor hell a fury like a woman scorned.

— William Congreve

Louise hears the scream through the open window and instantly freezes. Something about it is chilling. Followed immediately by another, equally terrifying, she recognises it as coming from Safar's house just across the way. Puzzled but alarmed, she has no clue what could be amiss since her friend is not due to return from Egypt for another four days. Her husband had returned only a couple of weeks previously with the girls and their son. According to her eldest daughter, Amal, whom she had spoken to on their return, her mother stayed on in Alexandria to attend the wedding celebrations of her younger brother.

The day before her trip to Ghadames, Louise heard from a neighbour that Ahlam was in hospital but understood it was nothing more than a routine check.

Louise hurries to the front door and finds Sami and Tara already there. By their worried expressions, they, too, have heard the sound. Quietly, she tells them to go back inside and wait until she returns. Lifting up her keys, she slips out with a feeling of unease, sensing instinctively that something grave is afoot.

She barely reaches their gate when she sees Safar's husband walk hurriedly out and into his car. Something is definitely wrong; she can tell by his demeanour.

With each step that brings her closer to the front door, the crying and sobbing from inside grows louder still, and the heavy atmosphere is palpable. Finding the door ajar, she pauses momentarily and, gathering her wits about her, sets her foot tentatively inside the darkened hallway.

It is Amal she sees first, distraught beyond belief, pale and grief-stricken as she comes towards her, weeping uncontrollably. Louise catches hold of her flailing arms, eyeing her pitiful state and in an effort to console her, she gathers the girl in her arms and holds her tightly.

"She's dead, Ahlam is dead." The words pour out of her mouth between anguished sobs.

"My sister is dead."

Their eyes meet, and, in that moment, a moment that no words could possibly fill, Louise feels utterly powerless. It is then that confused thoughts fly to her dear friend whose beloved daughter would be likely laid to rest by the time she returns from Egypt.

The Islamic faith dictates that people bury their dead without delay, a practice Louise experiences as alien to what she knows. After mourning the death of her father, sister, and friend, she feels that time is needed for the bereaved to absorb the sheer enormity of death before their loved ones are committed to their final resting place.

On an overhead balcony of the Dublin Mosque, reserved for women only, Louise had stood with a small gathering of women, amongst them Saoirse's grieving sisters. Below them, the men stood at the front in lines of even formation. It is a scene Louise would never erase from memory because foremost in her thoughts were Saoirse's heartbroken parents, their absence communicating a poignant message. She knew them as decent, humble people who were entirely unprepared for the cruel fate that had robbed them of their eldest daughter. On that same morning, her thoughts went to Azisa, the woman who would always occupy a special place in Louise's heart. Far away, she was undoubtedly suffering her own loss and grief, bereft of a daughter-in-law, unable to be with her eldest son and longing to comfort her grandchildren who had lost their mother.

Louise thinks of her own parents and the loss of Bella, reminded again that it is not in the natural order of things for a child to die before a parent and their progression into old age would indeed be swift.

The day after Ahlam passed away, her body is taken to the burial site in a silent procession led by Abu-Talib, his many relatives and members of the community at large, all of whom are male. Certain Muslim communities encourage women to attend the burial, but traditionally, it is only the male mourners who are attendant. Kareem is part of the procession that makes its way to the mosque, where they separate into lines, preparing to turn their faces towards Mecca. Finally, with outstretched hands, they bow their heads reverently and wait for the Imam to lead them in the *Salat-al-Janazah,* or funeral prayer.

Louise, like everyone else, is in shock at the suddenness of the young girl's death, and there is a desperate fear in people's hearts at how her mother will receive the dreaded news.

Her reaction is visceral, like nothing Louise had ever witnessed. Her dear friend, the woman she has known for many years, is so utterly broken by the untimely death of her beloved daughter that she completely shuts down, her mind and body going into a freeze in an attempt to protect the psyche. It is heartbreaking to watch her collapse into an incoherent state where she appears not to be present for considerable stretches of time. Louise tries to say some comforting words to her friend, but nothing registers, so she is obviously disconnected from reality. For days on end, she slips temporarily into repeated swoons and stupors. In between, she sits solemnly still, her eyes open and fixed but unseeing. The women attempt to lay her gently down, placing a pillow under her head and wait until she closes her eyes and rests. When she wakes, someone is on hand to hold a jug of water to her lips, urging her to drink. Despite their exhortations to eat the food they prepare, she refuses, waving it silently away.

Louise cannot even begin to imagine how traumatic an event, the loss of her daughter must be for Safar. There is no doubt in her mind that such a psychic injury will stay lodged in her friend's body and mind forever.

Louise feels helpless, and at one point, her sorrow turns to anger at the displays of uncontrolled weeping and loud wailing amongst a few older women present. She believes it will not help the one who is really suffering. Looking on aghast, as they tear at their faces, leaving angry red marks on their skin, she begins to understand the reason why such histrionics would not be welcomed at a graveside. She had once been to another funeral with Kareem's family and witnessed the same spectacle, which seems to be common amongst more traditional women. Loud, induced wailing is strongly discouraged and deemed 'haram', meaning that which is contrary according to Koranic teaching. A calm dignity, showing a degree of stoicism, is considered more worthy. Louise wonders where the displays of unchecked emotion stem from and why some women indulge in it while others do not.

Several weeks pass before the women stop coming, close relatives return home and finally, they leave Safar and her family to contemplate their own private grief. Louise stays away for a few days, allowing her friend some space but not without her offers of help if she needs it. Naturally, there is a deep sadness about her that has not been seen before and is so out of character, so tragically different to the person Louise has known. Zest for life and effervescence, once such a natural and delightful part of her spirit, has been crushed. For the rest of her life, she will likely associate her long-awaited journey home to Egypt with tragedy instead of joy.

During those sorrowful weeks, Louise never quite knows what to say to Safar. Although she has started to speak after a long silence, her words are few. A lot of the time, they sit in silence, drinking tea, watching their daughters and relying on them to lighten up the room. Louise is patient with her friend, sensing that death and its painful loss hold her firmly within its grip. It will be long before those life-affirming smiles are seen again on her friend's face.

Several weeks later, plans for a party are underway in another house nearby. The day has finally arrived when Suheila will celebrate her betrothal to the man who had asked for her hand several months previously. Traditionally, the engagement celebrations are marked with a visit from the groom's parents to the home of the bride. Family relatives, friends and neighbours are all invited.

Custom dictates that the groom's family come, bearing gifts, great and small but usually expensive. Gold jewellery represents the most important part of the dowry and it is commonplace for the bride and her family to request specific items. The husband-to-be is expected to deliver, and no expense should be spared for his future bride.

Guests are generally unabashed in their comparisons and opinions on what they see. Gifts arrive in large round baskets, beautifully decorative and lined inside in velvet. There could easily be ten or more baskets, depending on the size and quantity of the gifts they hold. A large sheep or more is customarily presented to the bride's family to symbolise a blessing from God and to give thanks and help feed the guests who will attend the wedding feast.

Suhaila had called on Louise a week before the party to invite her personally. She seemed genuinely happy and chattered excitedly about her special day. Her brother and sister-in-law, who live in Tunis, had been given the task of finding a dress for her, and they were to deliver it in advance. She rarely spoke about her mother, and when she did, it was usually only a passing mention, so it was a surprise to hear her say, with a broad smile, that her mother would oversee the preparation of the food along with a couple of helping hands who had volunteered to assist her. Of course, Safar is in mourning and will not be going, but nevertheless, she sends word, insisting she will prepare some food and send it on the day.

According to Suhaila, the house was to be given a thorough scouring, and she had taken it upon herself to give the two main rooms and entrance a fresh coat of paint. Louise offered her coffee, but she declined, saying there was an errand she had to do for her father. With a promise to be part of her celebrations, Louise wished her well and stood watching as she tripped lightly down the steps.

The weeks trudged on, and with a little over a month to go before Christmas, Louise is already thinking about the year ahead. While silently contemplating her own crisis of faith, Kareem is already planning a pilgrimage to the holy city of Mecca the following summer. Work will take him to Saudi Arabia, and once there, it is unthinkable that he will return without undertaking one of the six pillars of the Islamic faith. Louise hopes her husband can gain some humility from tending to his spiritual needs otherwise, it strikes her as a wasted exercise. She is not inclined to object because, in theory, it is an admirable thing to undertake, but at the same time, she wishes he would attend to the little things before the great. The words of Van Gogh steal into her thoughts.

"Great things are done by a series of small things brought together."

By the time Kareem embarks on his spiritual journey, Louise hopes to be back in Ireland with the children. She decides that there is no purpose to be served by rocking her husband's boat or her own ahead of time.

The afternoon of Suhaila's party arrives, and Louise, dressed for the occasion, waits for Marleen and together they walk the short distance to the party.

On arrival, they are given a warm welcome by Suhaila's sister, along with an introduction to their mother. A folding partition between the two main rooms had been removed to create more space for the guests. Louise gets the clean scent of fresh paint hovering in the air, a smell she loves because it brings back memories of childhood, whenever her father decided to paint the house.

Plenty of guests have already arrived and are seated along the walls. Louise recognises some neighbours, and they enquire about Safar, eager to show their concern because she is so well-liked and respected by everyone who knows her.

Everyone's attention is directed towards the far end of the room to a small, raised platform where the bride-to-be would eventually sit.

The level of chatter is loud, lively and convivial, with an air of excited expectancy as all present await the appearance of Suhaila.

The food is already laid out on a long table, ready to be served after the groom's family arrive. Shortly after the guests arrive and are settled, they are offered a drink made from crushed almonds, customarily served as an accompaniment to *amaretti* or almond cookies, crispy on the outside and deliciously soft on the inside. The famous almond biscuits from the region of Emilia-Romgna were adopted by the natives, who at some point had acquired the recipe from their Italian colonists. Fortunately for them, the Mediterranean basin is the perfect habitat for cultivating almonds, which have grown in the region since ancient times.

The food is plentiful and appetising, with different varieties of Brik, a typical, savoury dish of Tunisia, resembling a triangular envelope of thin, crispy filo pastry packed with filling and lightly fried, a favourite of Louise's. There are homemade sesame rolls filled with tuna, falafel made from ground hummus and kufta stuffed with minced lamb, flavoured with herbs. They are just some of the culinary delights on display. Louise suspects that Safar has sent other food as a neighbourly gesture, as she is not there.

Presently, when everyone is settled, Suhaila makes her entrance.

From the moment she steps into the room, all eyes are drawn to the girl who appears in front of them transformed. It is not the ball gown, though

Louise has to admit, it was well chosen. Something seems to radiate from inside Suhaila because she is truly glowing. Smiling warmly at everyone, she walks, with measured steps, to the far end of the room, the gentle swish of her skirts audible as she passes and takes her seat on the throne-like chair. It sits at the far end of the room on a raised platform made by joining a couple of wooden pallets together and covering them with a carpet.

There she sits, rather demurely, in her lovely ball gown, its puffball skirts spread out around her, commanding the room with her presence. The dress is a delicate shade of pale pink chiffon with a fitted bodice that clings flatteringly to her slim waistline. Its bouffant sleeves are delicate lace trimmed with velvet and finish just above her elbows. A row of tiny pearl buttons run midway down her upper back, adding a distinct but soft embellishment to the gown. Whether chosen by coincidence or with intent, the colour accentuates her natural olive skin tone. Her jet-black hair is loosely arranged in a bun, held in place with a white, floral clasp. On a small table to the side of her chair stands a large vase of white, jasmine flowers, symbolically positioned. Louise can get the rich, heady fragrance that hangs sensually in the air around them. Amongst the flower's many attributes is its association with purity and love, a chance to send a message of affection to someone you care about. The word itself, Jasminus, is a derivative of its Persian equivalent, *Yasmin,* meaning 'Gift from God'. In the palatial gardens of the Middle East and beyond, gardeners were known to plant jasmine outside the bed chambers of their masters' windows, hoping to bestow on them good health and fortune that they might be more kindly disposed towards them.

The level of anticipation in the room is palpable, everybody waiting for the moment when Suhaila's in-laws arrive. Guests speak openly amongst themselves, expressions of curiosity transparent on their faces. Will the groom be making a brief appearance? Are the family local or from further afield? What does the groom do for a living? Louise knows he is in the military because Suhaila told her. Apart from that, she knows little else of significance.

Two hours turn into three, and the much-awaited guests are still nowhere to be seen. A quiet tenseness creeps into the room, creating a tiny dint in the celebratory atmosphere of the occasion. Suhaila's mother invites everyone to partake in the food, but some of the visitors protest, albeit good-naturedly, saying they would prefer to wait for the groom's family to arrive. The others agree, insisting it is improper to eat without them. With an air of nonchalance that appears rather unconvincing, Suhaila's sister remarks that their guests are unavoidably delayed and will arrive shortly. Louise steals a look across the room at Suhaila, sitting patiently in her chair and wonders what thoughts are going through her mind.

Night is falling fast, and there is still no sign of the groom or his family. Loud chatter has turned to hushed tones, and guests are becoming visibly uneasy. Finally, three relatives of Suhaila make a move, one pleading a distance to travel home and a reluctance to delay her husband, the driver, any longer.

Announcing their departure, they extend good wishes to all before taking their leave. As discreetly as she can, Louise glances across the room to where Suhaila sits and on her face, she reads her biggest fear. By now, Marleen has quietly voiced her own reservations to Louise, who agrees that things are not looking good for Suhaila or her family.

More guests follow in dribs and drabs until only a few remain. As Louise and Marleen attempt to make a quick but polite exit without drawing attention to the obvious, a small group of older women from the surrounding neighbourhood are less discreet. Whilst donning their hijab in readiness to leave, they cast disapproving glances in the direction of the mortified bride and her family.

Mumbling to one another as they walk out the door, Louise is sure she overhears one of them remark how shameful it is to keep a bride waiting so long.

"There are things more shameful than waiting," is the response from the other.

FORTY FIVE

À Bittersweet Christmas

I will honour Christmas in my heart and try to keep it all the year.
– Charles Dickens

N obody would ever know it is the eve of Christmas because there is
nothing, not a vestige of festive sparkle, to be seen outdoors. A humble
tree stands in a corner of Louise's living room in stark contrast to
what she would like to have. Sparsely decorated but adequate nonetheless,
it is her own personal nod to a tradition she has observed since childhood.

It is the first Christmas Eve since her father's death, and they are at
home watching a Christmas movie, having spent the afternoon at Marleen's
playing board games and eating delicious mince pies. Louise has developed
an appreciation for life's smaller pleasures, things she had once taken for
granted, but some things have changed.

It is no surprise when a gentle knock comes to the door, a sound Louise
has been waiting for. Suddenly, she is filled with nervous excitement at the
prospect of seeing him again.

Over two months have passed since they last saw one another, although
they have kept in touch on the phone. He had left exactly a week after
Louise returned from Ireland, and their parting words had stuck in her
mind. His trip to Istanbul was a business venture to buy and source different
ranges of merchandise for his newly acquired shop.

Louise missed him while he was away, and it scared her a little to realise
that she had come to depend on him a great deal.

When he steps into the hallway, every impulse inside her is screaming
and clamouring to open her arms wide and welcome him back in the way
she would like. Instead, she has to be content with a warm smile. In his

deep brown, nearly black eyes lurk the darker secrets of his heart, and in them, she sees the penetrating reflection of truth. It is a moment of blissful terror, and she looks hurriedly away.

Tara and Sami are genuinely pleased to see their uncle after such a long spell, and they have plenty of questions to keep him busy while she makes some tea.

Jabir has brought gifts for them as well as some delicious Turkish treats. There is a large, attractively wrapped box full of assorted cakes and sweets from an artisan confectioner, just in time to be enjoyed by all on Christmas day. Louise compliments him on such a good choice. With a satisfied smile, he admits he purposely wanted to bring something festive.

The children eventually head off to bed, leaving the two of them to chat, and Louise finds herself opening up to Jabir about her deepest thoughts, just as she has always done.

"I feel really sad inside Jabir, but I'm trying hard not to show it in front of Tara and Sami, it wouldn't be fair because it hasn't been easy for them."

"I do understand, it's too soon. I know you're thinking about your father, especially today and tomorrow. I'm sorry, I can't do more but..."

Rather abruptly, his words trail off, and Louise thinks she sees a pained look cross his face. There is no doubt, but she hears a note of frustration.

Quickly, she responds.

"No, Jabir, you have always been here for me. I know that and so do you." They look at each other for a long moment and smile.

"It won't always be like this." He utters the words with a conviction that Louise does not feel, but she wants to believe him all the same.

Getting late, he stands up to leave, finally. Moving towards the door, he reaches into his pocket and gently pulls something out. He hesitates before placing the small box in the palm of her hand and gently closes her fingers around it.

"Goodnight, Louise and enjoy tomorrow. Happy Christmas."

Before she can say a single word, he opens the door and disappears into the night outside, leaving her only with the sound of his footsteps on the stone path as they recede into the distance.

She walks slowly to the kitchen and immediately sets about doing some last minute preparations for the following day. Not ready to open the tiny box, she places it carefully in a safe place until later. Turning her attention to the cooked, stuffed potatoes, she lines them up uniformly in a large roasting dish, one layer on top of another, before pouring the spicy tomato sauce on top and setting them aside to absorb overnight. The next day, they can be heated in the oven before serving. Adding the finishing touches to her trifle takes hardly any time at all. Next, she sets out a row of decorative paper cases, into which she puts small, rounded balls of chocolate flavoured with the essence of crushed almonds and rolled in coconut.

It is the early hours when Kareem gets home after a long flight from Delhi to Tripoli. Louise is in bed but not asleep, a myriad of bittersweet thoughts keeping her awake. She hears her husband's approaching footsteps in the hall, but when he opens the bedroom door and finds his wife's eyes closed, he decides not to disturb her. Discarding his clothes, he takes a blanket with him and goes to lie on the couch in the living room.

The following morning, Sami and Tara are pleased to see their father after his short absence. Finding their modest but well-selected gifts under the Christmas tree, they chat excitedly about the day ahead and the plans their mother and Marleen have made. Louise had managed to bring their gifts from Ireland without being discovered, making it possible to capture the element of surprise. They would have so much more if they were in Dublin, but Louise could only do her best in the circumstances.

Listening to Tara and Sami, Louise feels something tugging at her heartstrings and realises with nostalgia and relief that the simplest of things can make a difference. Perhaps her children would do better in the long run by not acquiring things too easily and having to wait for certain things in life to come their way. It will surely have advantages for them later on. Appreciation and gratitude are valuable lessons for young people, and it is better to learn them early.

Louise cooks breakfast, and they all sit down to eat together, a rare but welcome occurrence considering the day it is. Kareem talks to them about his trip to India and some of the places he visited when not working.

Opening one of his suitcases, he takes out the presents he brought for the children. For Tara, there is a white, porcelain elephant encased in a lovely ornate box, a souvenir to keep in her bedroom. Also, there is a cute silicone 'Bunny Lamp' to position beside her bed. For Sami, there is a giant jigsaw of the Asian continent featuring the Himalayas, challenging enough for him to do. He also gets a couple of sweaters and a winter jacket. What Louise likes most is a charming audiobook named 'Good Night, India', which is for Tara, who likes to read. It is so beautifully bound for a children's book, with eye-catching artwork, vibrant colours and overall aesthetic appeal. Inside it features some of India's most important cultural landmarks, wonderfully demonstrated: the golden temple, valley of flowers, the Himalayas, tigers in the Sundarbans, blue train and much more — a really educational book. Kareem presents his wife with an ornate jewellery box, hand carved in wood and gold-leaf. Beautifully wrapped in a gift box labelled 'The silk house' are two scarves, one long, the other large and square, in neutral colours of black and cream. Louise accepts her gifts graciously, thanking her husband for his tasteful choice.

It is two in the afternoon when they sit down to eat Christmas lunch. It feels good to have everyone assembled at the long table, which Louise has taken time to dress to create a festive atmosphere. She wants to create a festive mood for the guests who, like her, are far from home. They need to feel the day is special.

Louise had brought a large tablecloth with placemats and accessories, all the way from Dublin, symbolic of the yuletide season. She even managed some candles. An excited Tara, eager to help, dresses the table with her mother.

It is truly gratifying to behold her guests, Marleen, with her husband and two children, Shelley, Arianna and Mohammad, joining them at her Christmas table. Fortunately, Kareem is in rare, good spirits, a bonus for Louise, and it seems his return from abroad has been a timely one, which happens to facilitate her plans perfectly.

For the first time in her life Louise cooks a fresh turkey, delivered to her by one of Kareem's friends from his family's farm. It has been a steep learning curve for her since she had to feather the large bird before cleaning him, and it had proven to be quite a task. Eventually, it is stuffed with her mother's recipe and laid out on a roasting tray. After all her labours, she holds her breath for a brief moment, afraid he might not fit inside her oven, but luckily, there is just enough space. Having achieved that much, she worries that her culinary skills might be found wanting, but on the contrary, everyone enjoys the food immensely.

As she modestly accepts the repeated compliments of her guests, she privately thanks her lucky stars that the day is shaping up well and all that matters for now is to be present in the moment and enjoy the festivities. She is aware that days such as this do not come often. Who knows, it might be the last time Kareem and she sit together at the same table.

By early evening, the satisfied company disperse — a good day had by all. The children help their mother clear up and soon everything is back in its place.

Marleen has invited them over to hers for a special Christmas supper to be followed by charades and board games. Kareem decides to stay home, pleading tiredness after his long journey, and Louise has no doubt they will enjoy the night without him. In any event, they have only to walk around the corner.

When they arrive, Marleen gives them their gifts, thoughtful and well chosen as always. Then, they are treated to a delicious supper with all the trimmings and soon after, the fun starts. Beginning with charades, they progress on to board games that go on late into the night. Eventually, it is time to say goodnight, and Christmas is over for another year.

They steal quietly into the house, not wanting to wake Kareem. The children bid their mother goodnight, and Louise, feeling suddenly tired after an active but fun-packed day, is ready for sleep.

For several weeks after her return from Ireland, their relationship was perfunctory. Following the episode in the kitchen when the dresser got smashed up, they communicated on a surface level. Then, little by little, they began speaking again, albeit with a reserve and guardedness on Louise's part. Moreover, Kareem failed to apologise for his behaviour.

At the same time, she began to process the death of her father, and held fast in the grips of a great loss, she was emotionally stretched, sometimes to the point that reaching the end of a day was a challenge.

Her father's death is still very raw, and it has been hard to properly mourn, much less heal in the circumstances she finds herself in. Not a day has passed in three months, since her return but she replays that first day. It feels unbelievable, yet with the passing of time, resentment towards her husband continues to build.

She misses Saoirse, too, especially at this time of year. Strangely, Louise thinks she can sense her spirit hovering about her at certain times, and it feels kind of comforting.

During the past months, whenever she considers her husband, it is with a strong distaste and the notion of him touching her is completely blocked off in her mind.

After being away for a week in December and returning on the eve of Christmas to find his wife's mood somewhat lighter the following morning, he may have misread the situation. Of course, being the opportunist that her husband is, Louise knows there is likely no other way would he see it. He gives her gifts, which she accepts and they pass an enjoyable day even though it is in the company of friends.

Louise is sure her husband is sleeping soundly, and perhaps he is, until Louise creeps quietly between the sheets. Just as she begins to settle, sleep about to overtake her, she feels the caress. After such a good day, Louise is loath to end it in negativity of any sort. Even though every bone in her body, every shred of flesh, is resisting his touch, Louise knows what she has to do. Forced to make a quick calculation, a judgement call, she can either spurn his unwanted attentions or give in to his desire. Louise knows that withholding sex from him will come at a cost and she has the following day to consider. The last thing she needs, the children need, is a sulking man with injured pride, creating an atmosphere in the house on her birthday, spoiling their plans. It happened before, and Louise knows from past experience that it could happen again.

She grudgingly but convincingly gives him what he wants, and it is all over before she knows it. In his egotism, he mistakenly believes her enthusiasm stems from pleasure at satisfying her desire. In reality, it could not have been further from the truth.

Louise wakes with the first rays of dawn and gently rouses herself, mindful not to disturb her husband and risk a repeat performance. She need not worry since he is sleeping soundly. Slipping quietly out of bed, she walks barefoot down the hall and into the living room. With a careful movement of her hand, she adjusts a couple of hardbacks, and reaching into the space behind, she retrieves a small box.

It alone is beautiful to look at, carved out of burl walnut, and Louise can feel the smooth, polished surface between her fingers. Opening the lid for a second time, she admires the gold locket, a tiny emerald stone set in its centre. She has never seen anything quite like it before. Not daring to remove it from its secure place, she looks at it a while longer before closing the lid and returning it to the empty space behind her books, where it will remain.

Louise stretches herself out on the couch to rest a while before the children wake and to plan what she will wear later on. She has a perfect outfit in mind, a real showstopper and today, she is determined to look her best. They have a busy day ahead, and she is looking forward to spending the afternoon with Shelley, who is hosting a tea party for a few friends at the embassy. Of course, Sami and Tara are also invited, and it happens to be Louise's birthday.

There is an unexpected surprise awaiting her at the Ambassador's Residence.

FORTY SIX

A House of Hollow

Better than a thousand hollow words, is one word that brings peace.
— The Buddha

It is barely a week into the New Year when Kareem announces he is going to be away for a few days on a work-related trip. Before heading off, he suggests to Louise that they take a drive to his father's farm. Louise is surprised and has no desire whatsoever to accompany her husband there. She is surprised that he has even asked. The fact is, several years have passed, and along with them, some deeply hurtful associations that Louise does not wish to revisit. However, she has promised herself to appear agreeable; at least that is what she wants her husband to think. So, she makes the decision to go with the flow and go with him.

Kareem has continued, all this time, undeterred with his project, whilst Louise has refused to support it. She made that decision long ago for reasons she believes are in the best interests of her and the children. Why now, she wonders?

Kareem had planned to build a house on his father's farm at one stage but Louise was totally against the idea. However, he ignored his wife's opinion and the reasons she put forward and forged ahead without her knowledge or approval. She discovered it when the foundations were already laid on her return from Ireland one summer. The whole business caused her a great deal of upset, and they rowed bitterly about it for months until, eventually, Louise decided to give up on it altogether. She had enough to worry about, and she knew Kareem would never see her point because he simply did not want to. It was not going to serve his personal cause, and as Louise learned, it was always about Kareem. Apart from this, she figured it would take years to reach fruition.

No matter what Louise said, Kareem refused to take her concerns seriously on such an important decision concerning their future and how it could impact her and the children. It occurred to Louise more than once that the build was more about gratifying her husband's personal ambitions than anything else. In the seven years since the foundations were laid, Louise had not changed her mind, and despite her initial reaction, it did not deter her husband one iota from pushing ahead with his plans. Being totally dismissive of her concerns at the start, Louise wonders why he would care about them at the end.

From then onwards, Louise refused to have anything to do with the build, never talking about it or showing interest. She learned about its progress indirectly from other people or Sami, who sometimes went there with his father.

She knew skilled workers and manual labourers were brought from outside the country to work on the construction, and she guessed the cost was substantial, though her husband never discussed that aspect of it either. In truth, the entire situation and everything associated with it had left a very sour taste in her mouth.

As far as Louise is concerned, it is Kareem's project and his alone. It began that way and nothing has changed since. Except, now that the house is near completion, he wants to show Louise the fruit of his labours, hoping that it will cancel out everything that has gone wrong before. While he may assume that what he has achieved should be enough to appease his wife, her position has not changed. She is adamant that because her opinion was not valued at the outset, it is not relevant now. For Louise, time has changed nothing.

The farm, as it is so-called, is more of a small plantation with fields of olive groves, oranges and lemon trees. Scattered amongst them here and there is the odd fig tree, which, in full sun, bears large, succulent fruit. At the far end, where nothing of particular value grows, lies the spot on which Kareem had marked out to build his house.

Today, he appears in unusually good spirits, and Louise cannot help but wonder if it has anything to do with the events of the previous evening. Although her suspicions are aroused, she has no way of knowing if they are justified, so she tries to banish any such thoughts from her mind.

When they arrive, some Sudanese labourers are on site, working on the inside of the house. At a word from Kareem, they down their tools and retire to a makeshift hut he had erected for them, where they can eat, sleep, and rest.

Alas, the great house comes into view a short walking distance from where they park the car. It stands imposingly on a slight elevation, its superior vantage point adding to its general advantage. At first sight, it deserves to be named a mansion, a most impressive-looking structure from the outside, and Louise cannot help but be in awe at what she sees.

Walking slowly towards the house, it seems to beckon invitingly and for a split second, she can hardly believe her eyes. Yet, it is not a figment of her imagination but reality.

Her feet leave soft prints in the sandy earth, and soon, she arrives in a clearing at the centre of which there is a wide entrance. Double gates are flanked on both sides by tall sandstone pillars, announcing an entry with a powerful statement. Inside the gates, Louise can see that work is underway in the courtyard garden. A winding, flagstone pathway leads to a series of wide, sweeping steps that gradually narrow out on approach to the main entryway. The front façade of the house boasts an attractive portico with columns and a roofed veranda that wraps around the front of the house, boasting an ornamental balustrade that lends a beautiful finish to its exterior. Louise pauses, observing the steps that sweep rather dramatically up to a heavy oak door with a palm tree carved vertically into its entire length. On either side of the impressive door stand two large Anatolian urns. Louise can see they are beautifully fashioned and handmade with the greatest care.

After climbing the last few steps, she closes her hand over the shiny, round doorhandle, at once feeling the cool, smooth brass against her skin. Ever so gently, she turns it, eager but cautious, wondering what she will find within, having left the grand entrance behind.

On entering, she steps into a large, square hall, much like the reception area of a classy hotel, fine and elegant. The floors are polished-white Italian marble, the ceilings high and handsomely decorated with an ornamental finish, its edges in gold-leaf trim. In the centre, a wide, stately staircase leads upstairs to a landing awash with natural light as it comes pouring in through a long, oval-shaped window of stained glass. Louise falls instantly in love with it the second she lays eyes on it, thinking it is the loveliest feature in the entire house. Agog at the sheer size of things, Louise looks around incredulous at the design and spaciousness of the house's interior.

Undeniably, it represents a huge achievement for Kareem, his personal 'magnum opus'. Louise acknowledges the fact ungrudgingly, feeling somewhat proud of what her husband has accomplished. His ability to create something original and elegant is undisputable, and she remembers that he always had a good eye for interiors, even clothes, putting unusual things together and making them work.

Although she has been silent and largely invisible throughout the construction, she recognises how challenging a project it has been for him, the amount of work and mental planning that has gone into the build, and, not least, the expense. That much acknowledged, Louise then thinks about a cost that cannot be calculated, that is, in monetary terms alone. Whereas she assesses the psychological cost, Kareem calculates the financial. While she and the children endured the tears and absences, her husband will undoubtedly accept the compliments and prestige it will bring since there is surely nothing to rival his house in the entire city.

Kareem waits purposely outside with Sami and Tara, allowing Louise to go inside for the first time, alone.

"Well, what do you think, do you like it?"

"She responds to his question with a big, sincere smile.

"It's the first time you've seen it. A lot of work was done in the summer while you were in Ireland." Kareem leans casually against a wall in the entrance hall, waiting for his wife to speak.

Standing back, she casts her eyes in all directions, making a gesture with both hands. Finally, she answers, intent on putting everything aside so she can answer honestly and fairly.

"What can I say, Kareem, really? You've done an amazing job and built a fantastic house, the design, everything about it. I love the marble interior, the staircase, especially the stained-glass window. She looks up to the first landing.

"It has to be my favourite. What more can I say?"

He laughs loudly and a look of triumph crosses his face. Better if he had let it rest there and be prudent with his words, but Kareem could not. That was his mistake.

"It's for you, Louise, I built this house. I told you it's for you and the children."

Louise smiles but declines any engagement with her husband's remarks. Instead, she sidesteps, steering the conversation back to the house itself.

"The doors are exquisite, Kareem. You had them specially crafted in Ghana, wasn't it? I remember you mentioned it at one point."

"Yeah, that's right." He looks pleased that she remembers.

"They're specialist carpenters over there and so cheap for their excellent workmanship. I managed to bring one at a time on the aircraft over a few months."

Louise is not surprised because West Africa is one of the poorer countries on the continent, and labour is cheap. She points out to Kareem that despite it being the work of a master craftsman, there is very little opportunity to have his work rewarded as it deserves to be except outside his country.

"C'mon inside, I want to show you a few things while you're here." At his suggestion, they take a look inside.

He begins by pointing out some interior features, like the eight-arm crystal chandelier hanging over the stairs. Others, slightly different in design, adorn the other main rooms, all transported with great care from Czechoslovakia. As she pauses to admire the magnificent light fittings, she suddenly remembers hearing about the trip some years ago but nothing about the lights.

In some of the rooms, Kareem had installed rotating fans mounted on the ceilings. He explains to her how they are designed to cool the air underneath them by turning in a particular direction. They remind Louise of the spinning blades on a helicopter, except they are much smaller.

There are five bathrooms in the house, four upstairs and two downstairs, one of which Louise is particularly keen on because of its unusual shade of ivory and its gold-coloured fittings.

The stately staircase finishes on the top landing, which is long and wide, displaying an ornate balustrade fashionably embellished in quality steel. It runs its entire length, leading to the primary bedrooms and a roof garden.

"You have always said that you'd love a big kitchen. Is this one big enough for you?"

Standing in the centre of an enormous space that features a white marble island, Kareem can now afford to set a challenge.

However, Louise gives another one of her non-committal smiles but passes no remark in answer to her husband's question.

"You'll never again complain about a small kitchen, will you?"

Actually, it has never been the size of their kitchen that bothers Louise but the never-ending plumbing issues, so he has got that wrong for a start, she notes. Within a relatively short time of moving into and renovating their home, Kareem suddenly lost interest in it, becoming firmly focused instead on his new build. So, any troubleshooting with the waterworks or other necessary DIY was deemed a wasted effort. He never admitted to it, but Louise sensed it, nonetheless. A few things around the house needed attention but were always met with excuses. Chief amongst them was the fact that he was away a lot. Louise thought it might also be a kind of revenge for not supporting his new project. Besides, Kareem knew his wife depended on him for repairs, and sometimes, she had to just make do.

Several hours have passed, and it is time to head back for supper, back to the house that Louise feels comfortable in despite its imperfections. Having listened to her husband wax lyrical about the new house and his plans for the furnishings, she grows weary and begins to feel a slight stirring of past conflict rising in her. As evening begins to fall and shadows lengthen on the remote, quiet fields, Louise is only too glad to leave, having finally seen the 'great' house. She feels slightly agitated all the way home in the car, resisting an urge to snap at her husband, who is unusually nice to her.

Kareem drops them off in front of the house, announcing he would return in a while. They shower and then eat a light supper together. When Sami and Tara are finally in bed asleep, Louise picks up her book to read a bit but soon finds herself distracted. Her thoughts turn to events of the previous evening.

Later that night, Louise lies awake in bed, churning the events of the day back and forth in her mind. What Kareem has done is unmistakably great, but it is, after all, his creation, not theirs. She wishes she could feel differently that the house he built would fill her heart full of joy. The prospect of ever living in it should surely make her happy, but in reality, it only provokes fear and uncertainty.

Years have passed, and with it, the best of her children's precious childhood. Beautiful though it is, bricks and stones tell one tale while hearts and minds tell another. Her husband would undoubtedly say it was all worth the sacrifice, but whose sacrifice was it?

When she voiced her well-founded fears about the remoteness of the site, Kareem shut her down, dismissing her concerns and fobbing her off with some half-baked excuses. It was like he had already made up his mind, fixed certain plans firmly in his head, and with time, he became even more intransigent.

From the moment Kareem first introduced Louise to the idea of building a house, an alarm bell sounded in her mind. Initially, he told her that his father had decided to buy a farm outside the city. Soon afterwards, he got the idea to section off a site with the intention of building a house there. According to his narrative, he reached a financial agreement with his father, the details of which Louise was never told. She has always suspected her husband of being deliberately vague and had reason enough to wonder if he was truthful about much of what he told her.

Then, to her surprise, there came a mention of Kareem's brothers also building houses on the farm. Faisal was the first likely candidate to build a bigger home for his increasing family. It was put to the Hajja that she should consider relocating, but the suggestion was not well received. In fact it sparked quite a bit of conflict over weeks, ending in a vicious row between her and her husband. Like Louise, the Hajja was never keen on the farm; ironically, it was the one thing on which they shared some common ground. Their reasons, however, were very different.

Neither woman wanted to be stuck 'in the sticks', isolated from their community of people, dependent on others to take them where they needed to go. At least, on foot, one has access to their neighbour. Where the farm is located, a car is the only means of transport.

There were other disagreements between family members that Louise had no way of knowing about, and had it not been for Zanib's young son, who conveniently carried stories from his grandparents' house, she would have remained in the dark.

Apparently, the Haj wanted his younger sons to spend their leisure time at the farm, planting and working the land, but they had no interest. That angered their father but found sympathy with their mother for no reason other than favouring her sons. Faisal was keen on building a house on his father's land, but being the eldest, he felt a sense of entitlement, which his father did not share. That led to further conflict.

As far as Louise is concerned, her husband could well have afforded to purchase a plot of prime land close to the city, like others of her friends. She never warmed to the notion of living on shared land or in the pockets of family members, and that is how it would be, she was sure of it, if they lived in such close proximity. She always wished to be entirely independent and separate from the family. The kind of commune she visualised was out of the question because it would leave her with no privacy. The idea of them knowing her every move, a target of their inquisitiveness, made her uneasy and all the more determined. There were so many downsides to consider if Louise was ever to entertain the possibility of living in the house her husband built. Perhaps if he had approached it differently and handled things more sensitively, he might have found his wife more willing to compromise.

One thing of which Louise is certain is that Kareem's lifestyle is not going to change, and if he expects his wife and children to be stranded in some remote outpost while he is absent most of the time, he has gravely miscalculated.

FORTY SEVEN

Chicanery

Oh, what a tangled web we weave, when first we practice to deceive.

– Sir Walter Scott

L ouise and the children have spent the afternoon at Arianna's house. Usually, they return late in the evening after supper, but today they leave early because something unexpected has come up for Arianna. She drops them home, and as the car turns into their street, Louise is just in the nick of time to catch a glimpse of Suhaila exiting her house from the side gate. The evening is still bright, affording a clear view, so there is no mistaking the fact it is her.

Louise is more than surprised at the sight of her after such a long, unexplained absence. Naturally, Louise wonders what is of such importance that it brings her to their home in the evening.

Nobody had seen Suhaila for weeks after the engagement party, the one that never quite materialised, and Louise had heard whispers that neighbours were still talking about the debacle.

Thinking back to the events of that night, Louise recalls Suhaila's outward show of composure while inwardly, she must have been dying at being jilted most capriciously. Nothing, after all, could be more dishonourable than such a cowardly form of rejection for any human being in front of their family and friends.

As the evening wore on, things began to take on a surreal quality, and Louise, like everyone, began to suspect that something was very wrong. She and Marleen were amongst the last guests to leave; mindful not to linger, they said goodnight diplomatically without inviting further conversation.

Sure enough, late that night, the raised voices of her father and brother were heard. They sounded angry, and according to those who heard it, a disturbing chain of events was set in motion. The sound of a woman's voice was also heard, most likely Suhaila's mother. It was followed apparently by a series of high-pitched screeches that pierced the night air. The screams rang out, described by those who heard them as desperate and alarming.

The same sound brought Marlene to her kitchen window, which overlooked the back porch of Suhaila's house. Unable to understand what transpired exactly, her husband translated from behind the partially closed shutter. Other neighbours were also brought to attention by the unfolding drama.

Suhaila, so the story goes, appeared in a fit of rage, wielding a kitchen knife, and it was obvious to all present that she intended to do herself a grave injury. Her sister, taking a step forward, pleaded with her to put the knife down but was forced backwards with threats and a half-crazed expression. The sight of Suhaila brandishing a knife was enough to deter anyone who dared to get close.

At the same time, she began tugging fiercely at her ball gown as if her skin was reacting to a severe irritation that she was trying desperately to divest herself of. When the material refused to give way, she ripped it from her shoulders with a force driven solely by anger and frustration. Completely mindless of the two men standing by, she used the knife to make a tear down the middle of the skirts. It fell in a heap to the ground, leaving her standing in her underslip, still clutching the knife firmly in her hand.

A shriek of fear went up from her mother as she bore witness to her daughter's dishevelled state. She could then be heard invoking *Allah* in a 'Dua', a special prayer where one asks directly for divine assistance. There was little anyone could do except resort to prayer, and her distraught mother was heard to pray, beseeching the Lord above to look kindly on her unfortunate daughter.

Soon after, a flash of lucidity must have entered Suhaila's disturbed thoughts because she glanced at herself in partial disbelief and rushed hurriedly into the house as if pursued by some evil force.

A door slammed loudly shut somewhere inside, followed by another, more alarming sound. Suddenly, Suhaila gave way to uncontrollable sobbing that filled the night with an eerie gloom.

When Louise first heard about these events, her thoughts flew to the iconic Dickensian character of Miss Havisham. Elements of the gothic tale seemed to be mirrored in hers, mainly secrecy and betrayal. Both women were burned by their expectations of love and romance: one literally, the other figuratively.

By all accounts, Suhaila's mother, at one point, turned on her son, accusing him of 'mischief-making', and warned him that if any harm should come to his sister, she would hold him accountable. Meanwhile, his father shuffled quietly away to a corner where he sat in shock, calling for someone to bring him his beads.

After several attempts on the part of Suhaila's sister to enter the room and offer some consolation, she found the door still locked and Suhaila unresponsive. Nobody slept that night, kept awake and alert by episodes of intermittent sobbing. Then, sometime before dawn, they heard the sound of heavy furniture being moved and positioned against the door. Eventually, the sobbing stopped, and all went deathly quiet.

Later that day the beleaguered girl emerged briefly from her room, to answer a call of nature. Refusing to speak or to eat anything, she retreated to her room once again.

Marleen kept Louise informed whenever she heard something, but it is common knowledge that the girl had not been seen out for several weeks and was in isolation. As far as Louise understood from local commentary that reached her via the grapevine, nobody really understood what had gone wrong for Suhaila and why the proposed marriage never materialised. Much speculation and rumour was circulating, lending weight to the old adage, "no smoke without fire." Despite all the gossip, nobody could be certain about anything, so it remains a mystery.

As Louise says goodbye to Arianna and walks the short distance to her front door, she experiences a strange sense of foreboding. Stepping into the hall, she is surprised to find Kareem since he rarely arrives home before her. He immediately greets Sami with questions about his schoolwork, and Louise follows Tara into her bedroom to help her get stuff ready for school the following day. Louise decides to wait until the children are tucked safely in bed before addressing any questions about the recent, unexpected visitor.

Two hours or more have elapsed, and she waits, giving her husband an opportunity to mention it if he is so inclined. They chat about the day's events and drink tea until close to bedtime. Still there is no mention of a caller. Louise decides to take the bull by the horns.

"I saw Suhaila earlier this evening, walking out of here through the side gate." She looks intently at Kareem, her eyes never leaving his face. He looks back at her unflinchingly.

"Really?" his reply is non-committal, spoken quickly and almost too casually. He knits his eyebrows together in surprise.

"She might have knocked on the door, but I never heard. I was sleeping in the far room and woke just as you and the children arrived."

It strikes Louise as a strange coincidence, and the timing seems off, but she merely nods in agreement.

"Ah, ok, well it's odd, to say the least, because nobody has seen or heard of her since the engagement."

He shrugs his shoulders and makes a face indicating that he has no answer. Touching his wife's shoulder as he passes, Kareem announces he is off to bed.

"Are you coming to bed, Lou?"

"I just have a few things to do here before I go. You go ahead. You're up at five."

Even as she says the words, she knows they sound hollow, but she wants to be alone. In any event, if Suhaila wishes to see her for any reason, she will call another day.

FORTY EIGHT

A Dangerous Liaison

It is easier to forgive an enemy than a friend.
— **William Blake**

As Louise turns the key in the lock and lets herself in, the only thing on her mind is the bag containing a gift she had forgotten to take with her earlier that morning. It is the reason for her unplanned return. Standing in the hallway, the aroma of freshly brewed coffee lingers in the air. Distracted, she thinks nothing of it; she better be quick because Arianna is waiting in her car to drive them to a friend's.

There is nobody at home; the children are at a birthday party for the afternoon and are to be picked up later. She wonders how she forgot the bag, after going to the trouble of wrapping and writing a card. Anyway, no harm done, she reminds herself as she starts down the hall to retrieve it. Suddenly, she is stopped in her tracks.

From somewhere inside, she hears a giggle, a sound she immediately recognises as female and all at once, she forgets about the gift for a second time.

What follows next is unmistakable: a long, low moan, the language of sexual pleasure. While she stands there in complete confusion, it suddenly increases in intensity. Aware of a sudden, crawling sensation down her back, Louise recognises, to her dismay, the voice of her husband.

Rooted to the spot, she holds her breath a moment before daring to breathe again while straining her ears to listen. Then, as if some unknown entity is propelling her forward, she moves barefoot along the hallway with measured steps and wobbly legs that barely manage to hold her upright. Outside the kitchen door, she stops and, making no sound, hides behind the dresser where she can peer in unseen at a safe distance.

The shutters are pulled shut, and despite adjusting her vision to the darkened room, it is plain to Louise what is happening. Transfixed, she stares wide-eyed in disbelief as she struggles to comprehend the scene unfolding before her very eyes.

Her husband stands naked, his taut buttocks facing her as they move back and forth rhythmically. Their clothes, hurriedly discarded, are strewn about the kitchen floor. Suhaila, her back leaning into Kareem, is partially covered by his body as she bends slightly forward over the kitchen table. Her hands, small but visible, are spread flat on either side to steady herself. It is the same table on which Louise prepares the family meals. Her husband's two hands are firmly placed on the girl's narrow waist, and as he reaches a hand slowly up to caress her breast, she emits a soft moan of pleasure. Grasping his other hand, she guides it down to fondle her nether regions and thereupon produces an immediate reaction. Mounting an unrestrained response to her arousal, he mumbles something in her ear and in an instant, she is flat on the table, he on top of her. In their excited passion, the tiny coffee cups are swept off the table, making a loud noise as they hit the floor but they are too far gone in the throes of passion to pay any attention.

Nor do they notice the figure that lurks quietly concealed behind the hall cupboard that faces into the kitchen at a particular angle, making it possible for Louise to have an ample view of her husband making love to another woman.

The last image in Louise's mind as she turns away is of Suhaila wrapping her legs around her husband's torso. Stealing hurriedly away, she hears Kareem's short gasps of breath, his grunts of pleasure and Suhaila's groans, deep and visceral, the sound of total abandonment.

Outside, the late afternoon sun is still shining when Louise emerges from the house, and only then does she remember Arianna, who is parked and waiting. Struggling to regain her composure before approaching her friend, she knows the painful truth cannot be hidden. Putting her sunglasses on, she takes a deep breath and opens the car door to get in, mustering as much courage as she can.

Back in the house, Kareem and his paramour might have remained ignorant of her presence had it not been for Louise neglecting to close the main door when she flees. After a few minutes, it slams shut, and a startled Kareem, alert to the noise, peers out. From the rear balcony, he would have spotted Arianna's car below and his wife inside before it pulled away from the kerb.

Once they had disentangled themselves, it must have come as quite a shock to Kareem because he never expected his wife to return when she did. He had neglected to lock the door from inside. One thing is for certain, it makes for a disastrous ending to an otherwise exciting rendezvous.

While the fiasco is taking place, Arianna sits waiting in the car, wondering what on earth is keeping her friend. When she sees her coming through the gate, carrying nothing in her hand, she guesses something has gone awry.

"Is everything ok?" She asks as a pale-looking Louise gets into the car.

"Just drive the car away from here, Arianna, please." She asks in a pleading tone, most unusual for Louise.

Something about the tone of her friend's voice makes her refrain from further questioning. Turning the key in the ignition, she drives off without a word in the direction of her home. Within a few minutes, they pull into Arianna's driveway, the plans they had initially made for the afternoon suitably shelved.

"C'mon, Louise, let's go inside, and I'll make some coffee. Then you can tell me what the hell's going on."

Without a word, Louise follows her friend somberly into the house.

It is later that evening before Louise returns to the house, having collected Sami and Tara. As she suspects Kareem is not there, thankfully, because she could not bear to look at his face. Being able to confide in Arianna has helped take the edge off things so when she faces the children, she is able to maintain a semblance of normality, for their sakes.

When Kareem finally returns, it is past midnight. The children have long gone to bed, and Louise is in the upstairs bedroom when she hears the sound of his car. Downstairs, the door closes gently, and to her absolute chagrin, she hears his footsteps climbing the stairs. Louise immediately gets off the bed and stands facing him as he appears in the doorway, wearing a somewhat bold but wary expression. He opens his mouth to speak but she stops him straight away with a firm gesture of her hand. He seems undeterred despite his wife's angry demeanour.

"I want to speak to you, Louise, about today, to explain, you have to listen to me."

Struggling hard to keep calm instead of screaming an obscenity, what she really wants to do takes every ounce of restraint she possesses. But she manages, just about, on account of the children sleeping downstairs.

"No, you listen to me," she whispers between clenched teeth. "I don't have to listen to anything, nothing at all from you, Kareem. Do you understand?"

He goes to speak, but she moves closer to him with an expression he has never seen before. It catches him off guard.

"How dare you come up here," she whispers. "If you think I want to speak with you after what happened in this house, you must be mad, do you understand, MAD."

He takes a step backwards, staring at her in silence, getting the message along with her expression of disgust.

"I just want to tell you, Louise. It's not what you think......believe me, I mean, I know it looked......he breaks off, I need to explain how it happened."

He is almost beginning to sound desperate, but it makes no difference to her.

Throwing her head back, she laughs sardonically, and then, in an instant, her tone changes, becoming measured and caustic, before she utters her ultimatum.

"There's nothing to say here, nothing at all, so don't even try. If you want your affair to stay secret, don't annoy me, or I promise I'll make things very embarrassing for you and your lover."

He looks at her, nostrils flaring, eyes wide, about to say something but relents.

"Don't push me, Kareem. I swear I will… if you annoy me anymore. Go downstairs and leave me. Don't dare talk to me until I ask you to… it won't be anytime soon. For the sake of the children, let's try to act normal for now, so you know. I don't want them upset by your shenanigans and wondering what's happening."

Louise can only imagine how horrible that would be.

Observing her husband, she sees that he looks the most uncomfortable she has ever seen him, but she is not foolish enough to believe it is her feelings that he is worried about.

Leaving him standing there, she walks into the bathroom and closes the door, relieved to finally hear his footsteps descending the stairs.

In the days that follow, Louise tosses every minute detail over in her mind, and she has no doubt that the affair between her husband and Suhaila has been going on for quite some time. Unfortunately for them, they just got careless, eventually resulting in their little tryst being discovered.

She thinks about the frequent, unannounced visits and how she politely tried to discourage them. It was the over-familiarity that first struck Louise as odd. From the start, it seemed Suhaila wanted nothing more than to befriend a new family who had come to settle in her neighbourhood. Perhaps she was lonely, in need of distraction and liked the idea of making friends with a Western woman. Whatever way Louise looks at it, given how well she understands the customs of society, the girl's behaviour has been far outside the norm. Perhaps the girl underestimated Louise's deep grasp of their culture, and that was her mistake. In any event, certain boundaries apply universally, and Suhaila has neglected to respect even those.

Louise is by nature a private person, friendly but reserved with people she does not know. Looking back, she is certain of one thing. It was her husband who encouraged relations to develop and ultimately seduced the girl next door. Meanwhile, Louise welcomed the girl into their home, showing her kindness and hospitality without ever thinking for a moment that something sinister was afoot.

As time passed, Louise began to wonder about the supposedly shy but affable girl who, almost overnight, became a regular caller to their home. After a while, she found her forwardness irritating and inconvenient because she was likely to arrive at the most unsuitable times.

Kareem was loath to see things the way his wife did and was unsupportive of her efforts in trying to curb the visits, not surprisingly! At one point, he even went as far as provoking an argument, accusing his wife of having an overactive imagination.

How right she had been. Smiling knowingly to herself, she recalls the summers she was absent, holidaying in Ireland. Three months of unmitigated opportunity for Kareem to have free rein. Oh, if only she had known.

She now sees the red flags that had been waving alarmingly in front of her from time to time. How often her gut feeling spoke to her until finally, she took heed, rather late, but some things are hard learned and happen with good reason.

Of all things, it was a home video Kareem made that was the clincher. He had decided to try out his new camera on the occasion of the children's birthdays since both fell in November. Louise always celebrated them jointly, organising a party and going to quite a bit of preparation to make the day special for them.

A few days after the party, Louise watched the video and remembers feeling excited by the images of everyone, including herself, moving across the screen.

All her friends were invited with their children of course. Maybe she was simply too fussed to notice, so busy attending to her guests. Shortly after everyone had arrived and the party got underway, Suhaila showed up, looking pretty, in a cream, knee-length dress and kitten heels. Her hair was loose for a change, as opposed to being tied up and on her lips she wore a shade of blush-pink that complemented her skin tone.

At some point during the evening, after the birthday cake was cut, they moved upstairs to the roof garden. It was really for the children to have a bit of fun enjoying some music and dancing with the adults. Kareem was there too with his camera.

Up to that point, there was nothing unusual about the footage. Her husband's skill using a video camera, though amateur, was able to capture the general atmosphere of the occasion. Plus, everyone, including the children, was treated to a 'spotlight moment', something to look back at and laugh. There was one person, however, for whom the camera's gaze was long and persistent, drawn to again and again, like a magnet. No matter where the camera's focus went, it was brief, compelled to return and rest again on its favoured target, its object of desire. As for its subject, she surely knew she was being observed, and she persisted in smiling seductively at the camera. Of course, it was the person behind the lens who commanded her attention as he continued to film, enjoying himself unabashedly. Such daring body language as hers was not lost on Louise, though she ignored it at the time.

Sitting comfortably in Arianna's house, sipping a cup of chamomile tea, Louise calmly tells her friend what she had witnessed. Arianna listens in disbelief, amazed at Louise and how she had left the house without going crazy. In the spirit of her 'Greek' temper, she displays enough anger for them both, feeling the pain of betrayal on her friend's behalf.

Much later, Louise is to look back on the events of that afternoon and ask herself a question. Why did she turn on her heel and walk silently away without a word? There were no angry screams or ugly scenes, just denial, disbelief and disconnection. Louise felt those emotions in her subjective experience of what she saw and stoically suffered humiliation and deep disappointment. For it was not her husband's nor his lover's dignity that she wished to preserve but her own.

Later, when time and distance separates her from the event, she is truly glad she acted as she did.

One of the first things Louise does when she returns home on that fateful evening is to throw out the *dallah,* a traditional Arabic coffee pot used for centuries to brew *gawha,* or coffee.

Thereafter, the boosting aroma of freshly brewed coffee harbours an unwelcome association in her mind. Louise wonders how a harmless thing can produce such a distasteful reaction.

Strangely, by a process of complex mental phenomena, certain things, including smells, can attach themselves to memories and produce affects, sensations and emotions. It would be a while before Louise could enjoy the aroma of roasted coffee beans again.

FORTY NINE

A Strange Disappearance

Lying to ourselves is more deeply ingrained than lying to others.
– Fyodor Dostoevsky

Louise presses a buzzer on the outside wall, and an automatic side gate immediately opens to admit her inside the embassy compound. Before entering, she gives Shelley a wave as the car pulls off, having agreed to meet back in a couple of hours.

In spite of herself, she is consumed by the beauty of spring, and though it is early, she can already feel the gentle warmth of sunshine on her face. Walking along the tree-lined path that opens onto the flowering gardens, a chorus of chirping birds keeps her company along the way. There is such a feeling of tranquillity inside the high walls, cut off as it is from any noise or traffic outside its boundary. Louise finds it hard to believe that beyond it lies a bustling city that is well awake and going about its business. Passing the grand pavilion, tennis courts, and general recreational area, she arrives at the consulate building. It looks even more impressive at this time of day with its elegant, arched portico, supported by double columns so finely embellished in frieze. The entire façade faces out onto perfectly manicured lawns and Louise imagines herself spreading a crisp, white tablecloth on the lush grass to empty her picnic basket. How nice that would be, she thinks, but then she reminds herself that the purpose of her visit is not a frivolous one.

Notwithstanding that, she had dressed carefully and decided on her navy, three-quarter length trousers, tapered just above her slim ankles and a toile de Jouy pattern silk blouse. On her feet, she wears white leather espadrilles. Her long hair, its natural waves made lighter by the sun, hangs loosely about her face, occasionally held back by sunglasses positioned on top of her head. Louise would be pleased to learn how elegant and attractive she looks.

One of the most arresting things is her radiant smile, a captivating smile revealing a perfect row of pearly, white teeth. Put that with a natural, friendly disposition, and it could melt hearts. It is likely the first thing Jeff notices when he comes forward to greet her.

At once, her rambling mind is brought sharply back to reality by the sight of him approaching, dressed casually in a white linen shirt, jeans and a pair of loafers.

"Louise, good morning. It's nice to see you again."

Extending his hand, he then kisses her lightly on the cheek, much to her surprise, and she notes the Duchenne smile that reaches up to the corners of his eyes, a mixture of blues, sparkling and intelligent.

"Morning Jeff, thanks for taking the time to meet with me, I really appreciate it."

"Don't mention it. Anything at all I can do to help. Let's go round to the sunroom and sit down, shall we? It's better than my office, much brighter. I think you'll like the view over the gardens."

They make small talk as they walk, and Jeff is right, the sunroom has an air of calm and relaxation with lots of natural sunlight pouring in. Louise is put at ease straight away, and she guesses he knows that.

After settling into a stylish rattan armchair, Jeff leaves her in silent contemplation while he goes off to bring the coffee. Over the previous days, Louise had rehearsed the conversation she would have with him over and over. Now that she is actually sitting here it feels like she has overthought things, worried unduly, in her desire to sound less urgent. Why dress it up in the first place? Undeniably, Louise finds the whole thing embarrassing, having to seek personal advice from a man she barely knows, no matter how willing he is to help. Nevertheless, she feels somewhat relieved, remembering what Shelley said about trusting Jeff and being honest about things; the circumstances which she has no control over.

Soon, he returns with a pot of coffee and biscuits, setting the tray down on a table between them. Louise is aware of how handsome he is, not in a classical sense but in a more rugged, unconventional way, making him all the more arresting.

In stature, he is easily six feet tall with a lean but well-toned physique, typical of a seasoned swimmer. She knows because Shelley had mentioned he swims in the residency pool every morning. Apparently, he has a chalet on the beach, a short drive from the city where he spends his free time, swimming and reading mostly. It would account for his tanned skin and hair fading from the sun to a sandy shade of brown.

"I'm a bit worried, Jeff, because my, em, our passports are missing, and I'm not sure what to do about it."

Louise chooses the very moment he begins pouring the coffee to make her disclosure. Nodding first to indicate that he is listening, he looks at her with probing, blue eyes, taking his time before answering. Then he speaks in that deep, almost hypnotic voice that Louise has only recently come to know. For a split second, Louise feels he can see right through her, but she is spared from answering the obvious question regarding their whereabouts.

"You're absolutely sure, Louise? I mean, they've not been mislaid somewhere in the house or got thrown out in error, have they?"

He laughs, dispelling any tension in the air. "Forgive me, a stupid question. I presume you've already searched."

"It's fine, Jeff, a perfectly reasonable question." She smiles, beginning to appreciate his deliberate line of enquiry.

"What do you think the chances are that they might show up somewhere in the coming weeks?"

"To be perfectly honest, Jeff, I'm not so sure. One thing is for certain: they've vanished from where I left them, in a very secure place."

"Ok, right, that's good enough for me. The important thing for you to know is that we can assist you and the children with replacement passports."

"Well, that's a huge relief because it's been a nightmare, Jeff, over the past week, thinking about it. So, you're sure it won't be a big problem." Louise can hardly believe her own ears, but she has to be certain.

Immediately, he puts her at ease with his broad, warm smile as he lifts the coffee pot to replenish their cups.

"I promise you, and I never break my promises." He laughs.

She nods with a sigh of relief.

"We can work with Irish interests on your behalf, Louise. Even in extreme situations, which I don't believe yours is, arrangements can be made for you and the children to leave if that is what you wish."

Louise listens attentively to what he says, making sure she understands the import of his words. Before responding, she hesitates a moment, and he fills the space by removing the coffee tray, allowing her to gather her thoughts and the awkward moment to pass.

"That's great to know, Jeff. I can't thank you enough for all your help. Hopefully, it won't come to that. Maybe they will turn up somewhere."

"Let's give it two weeks, shall we? Can you spare that?

Louise nods in acquiescence.

Then he pauses a moment in reflection, a thoughtful expression fixed firmly on his face.

"If it were to become known that new passports could be issued, for example, might that make a difference to…let's say their disappearance or appearance, as the case may be?"

Without waiting for her to answer, he laughs, instantly diffusing any tension attached to the question. Louise finds herself laughing, too, the mood in the room growing lighter.

"Do we understand each other?" He looks at Louise directly with a mischievous smile.

She pauses a moment. "I think we do, Jeff, yes we do."

Shelley has arranged with Louise to come and take her home after their meeting. When she arrives, Jeff makes fresh coffee, and they chat briefly before going their separate ways. Jeff walks them both to the main gate, where Shelley's car is parked just inside. There, he bids them adieu with a final word to Louise.

"Let me know if there's any change, just keep in touch, ok." He hands her a card with his direct phone contact.

"Thanks again, Jeff, for taking the time to see me."

"My pleasure."

His words ring in Louise's ears on the short journey home and Shelley notices she is already in better spirits than earlier. "Feel better now after getting some advice, Louise?"

"Definitely, at least now I know I'm not stuck. That would be the worst thing possible and Shelley, thanks for encouraging me to go and talk to Jeff and for asking him to see me."

Shelley rolls her eyes and sighs in mock impatience.

"I told you already, I did nothing, nothing at all, but you don't believe me. All I did was introduce you both."

Louise is quiet, waiting for her friend to finish speaking.

"Look, I've known Jeff for a long time, and apart from working with him, I know him as a friend. He's a serious person, despite his witticisms and keen sense of humour.

"I get that, but I still appreciate it, Shelley, and he didn't have to see me."

"The thing is, Louise, Jeff likes you a lot. Don't laugh, really; I'm not joking or trying to flatter you."

"It's nice to hear, and I'll take the compliment, though I can't imagine that I've done anything to earn it," Louise laughs.

"You don't have to do anything, Louise, except be yourself."

Again, Louise laughs, highly amused by her friend's vote of confidence.

Suddenly, without quite knowing why, she surprises herself by asking Shelley questions she never intended to.

"I like Jeff too. There's something about him, I don't know, captivating maybe; he's certainly a handsome guy and has the personality to match."

"Well, he wouldn't hold the position he has if he wasn't smart and intuitive." "I imagine so," Louise replies.

"Yeah, but apart from that, he's affable and good-natured, but you're right, he has a charisma that's very appealing."

There's a momentary pause before either of them speaks.

"You two had lots to talk about at the Christmas party, Louise, remember? You both appeared to be enjoying yourselves immensely."

Shelley turns and winks at her friend, giving her a wide smile.

"We did, didn't we?" She agrees, an expression of immense satisfaction crossing her face.

"By the way, you looked stunning in that ivory silk dress."

"Ah, thanks, Shelley, it's nice to get dressed up once in a while. Actually, I discovered Jeff and I have some common interests, and it was so refreshing just talking to him. I suppose it's been a while since I enjoyed such stimulating conversation," she adds with a meaningful smile.

"Absolutely, you won't find much of that here." Shelley raises her eyebrows in a gesture of frustration.

Suddenly, Louise feels slightly emboldened.

"Does he go home to England often to see his family?"

"I only know that he's an only child. Apparently, his mother died when he was young, but his father is still alive. He doesn't really talk much about his family."

Presently, they arrive at Louise's house, and Shelley pulls over.

"Will you come in, Shelley, have lunch with us? Kareem is working late, and the kids are due in shortly from school."

"I'd love to, but Hussein is flying this afternoon, and he'll want to see the twins. I've got to go pick them up at his family."

Shelley's husband is a pilot, working for the same national airline as Kareem, so they know each other slightly. Louise met him once, briefly, and got the impression that he was more liberal-minded than Kareem.

Back in the house, Louise sits down to evaluate the events of the morning, and once again, she is relieved to have spoken with Jeff. Perhaps he is right about one thing: the passports might just show up. He was so diplomatic, saving her the embarrassment of going into precise detail that she really wanted to avoid.

Suddenly, she begins to feel more empowered, like she is taking back some control of her own life. Perhaps things are playing out in a particular way for good reason. Not so long ago, she had entrusted the momentous and uncertain meanderings of her life to fate and time. Now, Louise feels like that the time has finally arrived, and she is facing a watershed moment in her life. She decides to take a risk.

Rising confidently from her chair, she vows that when her husband returns, she will be ready for him.

FIFTY

A Turning

Yet knowing how way leads on to way,
I doubted if ever I should come back... I took the one less travelled by.
And it has made all the difference.

– Robert Frost

"**K**areem, we need to talk."

Kareem looks at his wife calmly, and if he feels any trepidation at all, it is not apparent in his demeanour. In the circumstances, some humility is called for but in this instance, it is absent.

"I'm ready, Louise when you are, " he replies a little too quickly.

She crosses the room and sits opposite her husband, who immediately reaches for his Marlboro cigarettes. Lighting one, he straightens himself on the couch and regards his wife curiously. Having had over a week to think about their brief conversation, he has undoubtedly racked his brain to come up with some sort of credible explanation to exonerate him from the web of deceit he has spun.

Louise has arranged with Marleen to have Sami and Tara for the evening. Naturally, she wants them out of the house while they discuss things.

Surprisingly, he is the first one to speak.

"Louise, I want to say something about what you saw that day in the kitchen. Can you listen, please?"

Looking at her husband steadily, without flinching, she listens, her expression inscrutable as a dark hole.

"It was never meant to happen. I swear to you, I lost control of myself. You have to believe me".

He pulls hard on his cigarette, shaking his head in apparent disbelief at his own actions.

Perhaps he takes some degree of encouragement from his wife's silence, allowing him to press on.

"I'll make it up to you, I promise, whatever I can do." He insists.

Perchance, he might be able to sway her with his protestations of human weakness and by owning up to his mistake.

Had he been smart enough, he should have left it at that, but he goes a step further in his shallow attempts to soften his wife.

"It was her who.... I mean.... she offered to make some coffee and, and then called me to the kitchen. I thought something was the matter, so I followed her."

He pauses for a breath.

Louise waits, remaining totally sceptical of his flimsy story.

"It was clear to me, I... I knew what she... what her intentions were and without any warning, she kissed me. I... I was shocked, and I just, I guess I lost control in that moment. I didn't think and it just happened."

Louise sits, motionless, having uttered not a single word. Studying her husband, she notes how he creates quite a convincing performance, but she is not to be swayed. There is little to say as far as she is concerned because her mind is already made up.

"Actually, what you're really saying, Kareem, is she seduced you, that's it, isn't it?"

He stays silent, hearing the note of sarcasm in his wife's tone, which unnerves him momentarily.

He holds his head dramatically in both hands, making a display of some remorse for his transgression, suddenly calling on *Allah* and the prophets to have mercy and give him strength against temptation.

"She came to me and put her arms..."

"Kareem," Louise abruptly interrupts his flow in a sharp tone that stops him instantly.

"I doubt *Allah* will hear you, and I certainly don't want to hear any more of your pathetic story."

He protests, about to continue, but she manages for the second time to halt his drivelous flow.

"KAREEM, I think you've said enough. Do you understand me?"

He stops talking, and for a few moments, silence takes over.

"The talking is over, Kareem, and so are we, so let's not pretend. Let's agree to be civilized in front of the children, ok?"

Looking across at his wife, he is suddenly aware of her composure and, for the first time, seems taken aback by her calm, detached manner. He is expecting an angry outburst, but it never comes. She is about to add even more to his frustrations, and he is unprepared for it.

Casting his adulterous affair to one side now, she addresses him in a matter of fact tone, switching the direction of the conversation altogether.

"Kareem, my passports have disappeared; I've searched for them all over the house."

She meets his eyes, making it hard for him to look away while he is nonchalant.

"Surely, they must be somewhere in the house, did you move them and can't remember?"

Louise ignores his deceitful comment and focuses instead on what she is about to say next. She guesses he had never expected her to go looking for the passports, and had it not been for her checking something else, their absence would have passed unnoticed.

He begins to relax a bit but is confused as he tries to gauge his wife's unpredictable mood. As for Louise, there is nothing more to say except wait, be patient a while longer, and see how things pan out. She has but one thing on her mind since her untimely return the previous autumn following her father's death; that is, to go back.

Taking a deep breath, she regards her husband with a derisive expression whilst struggling to conceal the contempt she now feels for him.

"Kareem, I know you have the passports. You know where they are."

Unsurprisingly, his initial reaction is to laugh dismissively and look away.

"Kareem." addressing him again, there is a note of warning in her tone.

"I'm serious, and you need to listen to what I have to say."

Shifting slightly in his chair, he looks directly at his wife like he is ready to meet the challenge. At the same time, he can feel the energy in the room about to turn.

"If your intention, Kareem, is to hold us here against my will, I'm not going to make things easy for you."

A flash of anger crosses his face for a fleeting second, but he holds his tongue.

"If we have to endure the summer here alone while you are away because of something you did, then you will have to also suffer the consequences— I promise you."

Suddenly, he is off his seat, his anger now clearly apparent. Louise knows from experience what is coming, what to expect. It is like a volcano about to erupt. With only a small window to make her point, she casts caution and her apprehensions aside. Rising from her chair, she walks over to her husband, and, standing in front of him, speaks her ultimatum clearly and distinctly.

"Here it is, very simple. Get me our passports, or I swear I will tell everyone about what I saw, about your betrayal. I am not going to beg you to do the right thing."

Kareem glares at his wife like a man demented, and in his rage, he comes too close, alarmingly close, to making his intentions violently clear.

Anticipating his move, she steps to one side, away from him, edging closer to the hallway.

"Do not attempt to come near me, or I will go right now to Suheila's home to confront her and her father. Do you understand? You will not be able to stop me. Is this what you really want?"

"You are crazy."

She ignores the idiocy of his remark; instead, she musters a strength she never knew she possessed.

"How do you think it will sound? A respectable Muslim man, married with a family, carrying on an illicit relationship with a young, single girl. Who is crazy now?"

Undoubtedly, he is caught off guard as he tries to gauge his wife's unpredictable mood.

In truth, Louise has no appetite for revenge because, contrary to common thought, it is never sweet, but rather tends to leave a sour taste in one's mouth. Besides it goes against her very nature, being more of a pacifist.

At the mention of Suheila, Kareem sits back down on the couch, lights up a cigarette and continues to mutter obscenities under his breath.

Louise waits in silent triumph before continuing, though she suspects a chord has been struck. Still, she has no trust in her husband whatsoever, and she believes that *'one swallow does not make a summer'*. The battle is not yet won.

"Your family, Kareem, will want to know why we are not travelling home as usual. Do you think I am going to lie on your behalf?"

She laughs derisively.

"Seriously, after you tried to trap me and the children, why would I?"

There is a moment of silence before her final word.

"Think about it, Kareem and make the right decision for both our sakes, but mostly for yourself."

She doubts if he gets the intended jibe. At that, she leaves the room to allow the dust to settle.

Later that night, Louise lies in her bed, turning things over and over in her mind. Kareem is sleeping downstairs, and the children are peaceful. Not a sound is to be heard that might disturb the stillness of the night outside except the distant hoot of an owl.

Louise is convinced that with a little time on his side, Kareem may believe that she will forgive his infidelity and have things patched up between them. He may now feel that hope has been upscuttled. She knows, too, that her husband is arrogant and narcissistic enough to believe she will never leave him. It may be that very assumption that could lead to his downfall.

Louise has decided to withhold her visit to the embassy from her husband, at least for the time being. She prefers to remain wary of her husband's intentions.

Louise no longer cares about staying married to Kareem, but there is still a way to go. Despite all that has happened, she knows she has to tread really carefully and not alienate him entirely. The missing passports are proof enough of the possible lengths he might go to if he feels sufficiently threatened. Although she suspects it to be a knee-jerk reaction on his part, a stalling device, she is not completely certain. He may fear that she intends to leave with the children and not return. Once she leaves the country, he has no recourse to bring them back, so withholding their passports gives him control over the possibility of that very thing happening.

The next day, the children are off school and Louise slips out, leaving them to have a late breakfast with their father. She calls at Marleen's, and together, they walk to the market. The temperatures are climbing steadily in early May. Usually, at this time of year, Louise has 'itchy' feet and is ready to 'fly the coop' and head for green pastures. Marleen, too, is preparing to leave for England, so they have plenty to chat about, not least the latest situation with Louise.

Back in the house, a surprise awaits her. As she opens the front door, Tara is there, barely able to contain her excitement.

"Mom, we found the passports," she yells with delight. Holding them firmly in her hand, she gives them to her mother, so happy to be the one delivering the missing goods.

"How did you find them?" Louise asks her daughter with a big, great smile, hardly able to believe it.

"Dad went upstairs to get one of his manuals, I think. I was tidying up my room after you left, and he called me upstairs to help him search."

"Where was Sami?"

"Oh, he was outside playing."

"So, we were looking everywhere, Mum, in the same places, and I knew we wouldn't find them. I kept telling Dad we had already checked, but he kept looking. Then, in between two big rugs, he found them."

"Huh, um, so he found them there." Louise allows herself a wry smile. The expression on Tara's face is one of disbelief, but she waits for her mother to comment first.

"It's odd, how on earth the passports should end up there?"

Tara looks back at her mother blankly, realising it is not a question but more of a statement.

"I think Dad knew they were there, Mum, and he doesn't want us to go to Ireland." She whispers the words with conviction, real fear written on her innocent face.

"Well, we don't know that for sure, Tara, but at least we have them now, and that's all that matters, so don't worry, love."

She hugs her daughter tightly and kisses her on the cheek to offer reassurance.

"Only a few weeks left to go, and we'll be off."

Tara smiles back at her mother; the mere mention of their upcoming trip and the prospect of being reunited with her grandmother is enough to chase her fears away.

A little later, when Kareem arrives home for lunch, Louise is in the kitchen about to dish up the food, and she hears him ask Tara if her mother has heard the good news.

"You'll be able to go and see your grandmother now in Ireland."

"She'll be waiting for us, Dad because she's by herself in the house, and I bet she's feeling lonely."

Louise walks into the sitting room carrying Kareem's dinner on a tray. Hearing her daughter's words, she feels a pang of sadness. Tara is such a caring, empathetic child, always sensitive to other people's feelings. The bond she has with her grandmother is strong, as Sami had with his grandad before he died. They will surely miss his presence in the house when they return.

Apart from a fleeting mention of their recovery, neither of them mentions the passport situation again. Nonetheless, Kareem understood that his wife knew he had hidden them and why.

Later that afternoon, Louise is alone in the house. Kareem is at work, and the children have been invited to a birthday party at Kay's.

Reaching into the back of the cupboard, Louise accidentally topples her favourite, much-loved ornament, and to her utter dismay, it comes crashing to the ground, shattering into hundreds of tiny fragments. The crystal mermaid was a wedding gift given to her by a special friend. For Louise, it is an object of great sentimental value. Aghast, Louise looks at her precious object scattered about her feet and knows instinctively that it can never be replaced. Even if she were to find something similar, it would not have the same symbolic worth.

Without warning, the tears begin to flow unchecked, streaming down her cheeks leaving rivulets of warm, salty liquid. She was not expecting to have a meltdown, not today of all days but it happens nevertheless, and she cannot halt the onslaught of emotions once the floodgates are open.

With the shattering of the mermaid, something shifts deep inside Louise, and she experiences some kind of an epiphany. It brings with it a striking clarity, the beginning of an understanding of what had brought her to this place and moreover, why she has stayed so long, too long. That knowledge brings its own relief, bringing a cathartic effect. She gets lost in her own thoughts, travelling back in time, she sees herself as a young girl. Sensing now the relentless desire that had driven her passionately on, a desire which had finally duped her and determined her destiny.

It was a fantasy that seemed to promise such sweet satisfaction when reality became too much to bear, so she began searching for something different. Therein lies the paradox. Fantasy life continues to sustain us yet simultaneously eludes us. It arranges a pleasurable framework in which to experience reality, locked into the imagination, but the reality perceived is already compromised by individual subjectivity. Humans guard this intimate, secret world of their fantasies, and it becomes the driving force of life. While it cannot promise to get them what they want, it can secure something of equal consequence. In Louise's case, it was a short-lived satisfaction.

Louise could not have known all this at the time, but whatever she was lacking provided the staging for her own trap.

Now her desire is seeking something else, something more meaningful, and it is centered around an entirely different thing.

The next day, Kareem takes their passports so he can begin the paperwork, which will enable them to travel to Dublin without delays. She hands them over with a degree of reluctance. She can only hope there will be no unpleasant surprises and things will go to plan, her plan that is. With that thought in mind, she has now to play her part.

Louise has never considered herself to be hypocritical or deceitful, but extreme circumstances call for equal measures, and she knows what she has to do.

Despite holding the firm belief that permanent solutions to relationship problems are never found in the bedroom, she is prepared to make an exception. Since she is not looking to mend things, it will be the only time.

It is late when Kareem gets home, but Louise is prepared when she hears him turn the key in the lock. Closing the door quietly behind him, he heads directly for the bedroom as she knew he would. On entering, he finds her already there, waiting, an expression of pleasant surprise crossing his face. He pauses for a split second, a sparkle of anticipation in his eyes and the next moment, he crosses the room to where she stands in silhouette against the partial moonlight that seeps in from the night outside. Wearing only a light chemise, her hair falls loosely around her face, her lips a vibrant shade of red. In the dark stillness, Louise radiates a sultry, sensuous charm that has an immediate effect on her husband.

As they kiss, Louise closes her eyes, not that she is in any way enraptured but rather to blot out the sight of her husband. Intent on avoiding a full congress, she wants to hasten a 'happy ending' for him, so she brings all her feminine wiles to bear to make it happen. She can only stretch herself so far before her distaste for him and everything he represents threatens to rise up and engulf her.

Sure enough, the reward of instant gratification is enough to quell Kareem's sexual appetite and, more importantly, is enough for Louise to have made her point.

Afterwards, they lie on the bed and talk about nothing in particular until Kareem surprises her with a question.

"Do you still think our marriage is over?" He asks.

Louise is not sure if it is a trick question or an unconscious slip, and she takes her time to answer. When she does, it is with a question of her own.

"Will you see her again when I'm gone? Continue the affair?"

Now, he is the one surprised, and his answer is instantaneous.

"What are you talking about, Louise? Don't you know the answer? Of course not; it's finished, over, never to be repeated."

Her response is calm and measured.

"Ok, I believe you, but you know Kareem, I have no way of knowing that, especially when I'm not here. If I hadn't seen you together, it would still be going on, I'm sure of it."

He makes no attempt to challenge her proposition. Balancing on her elbow, she looks at her husband for a long moment before continuing.

"It means I have to trust you, trust in your word, so in the same way, you have to trust me, trust that I'll come back."

Within a couple of days, Kareem hands them their tickets, and the travel arrangements are in place. It will not be long now.

Louise is relieved that a matrimonial implosion has been averted only by her skillful manoeuvrings and a belief that her cause is better served by following her gut instinct and throwing water on the fire instead of petrol. It is a fear of being trapped, even temporarily, that has allowed her to curb her anger and impulses, enabling her to focus and avoid a tempest although at times it has been difficult and painful.

By avoiding one route, she has succeeded in offsetting another, more dangerous one.

FIFTY ONE

A Poignant Reminder

Whom the gods love, die young.

– Herodotus

The two women stand together with palms open in silent prayer, their body language conveying a trust and surrender to something much greater than themselves. The sight of Safar is a sobering one, tearful but bearing the loss of her beloved child stoically and with dignity.

The surroundings are stark, and Louise is further deflated by the dry and derelict look of the place. Beneath the parching sun, the ground is barren and completely untended, with loose stones strewn about everywhere. Scattered all round are boulders and large fragments of jagged rock, making it impossible to walk with any ease. Instead, they pick their way through dilapidated graves, barely recognisable, until they reach one with fresh earth, the one they are looking for. Nothing else distinguishes it; no symbolic markers, headstones, or aesthetic touches can be seen anywhere.

On death, the Muslim rite of passage is that the corpse be wrapped in a shroud and committed directly to the earth, flush to the ground and at right angles, toward Mecca. It is believed there is no use for either casket or coffin, and Louise finds it all too grim for comfort.

Looking round, she takes in the desolation; not a single tree, flower or shrub to break the depressive monotony of the godforsaken place. No sign of life, colour or beauty to contrast with the finality of death.

Louise feels like she has a mountain of grief inside her, a towering edifice of lost love and ghosts pervading her very existence in the world of living, breathing things. Through the loss of Belle, her sister, Saoirse, her dear friend and her beloved father, she is, in some obscure way, more aware of her own mortality.

However, reflecting on death is only a study in ignorance, an exhaustive meditation yielding very little. All humans stand on a level of equality with respect to understanding its empty content. Despite the wonders of the universe, it seems to withhold from us mortals more than it is ready or able to give. As the great philosopher Wittgenstein once put it, *"Death is not an experience of life."* Yet, in that, there is a great paradox. It is precisely through death and because of death that we cherish life, for only death can give life its meaning.

After a few minutes of silence, Safar turns to Louise.

"Barakallahu feek, ya rouhi", "Jazak, Allahu khayran". 'God bless you my soul, may God reward you for the good.'

As Safar utters the words, she takes Louise's hand in hers.

For all these years, they have remained friends, and Louise feels so fortunate to have known this kind-hearted soul. In the future, wherever destiny may lead them, Louise will never forget her dear Egyptian friend.

There, in the solemnity of their surroundings, a pact is forever sealed between the two grieving women. Louise is silent, too overwhelmed to speak, and her friend senses it.

"Yalla, habibti, " Safar beckons. Let's go, dear.

Together, they make their way slowly out onto the sandy track, leaving the burial ground behind, but death, a silent companion, continues to shadow their movements through life.

FIFTY TWO

Nemesis

Narcissus does not fall in love with his reflection because it is beautiful but because it is his.

– W. H. Auden

I nside the cabin, they settle themselves comfortably into their seats. Kareem boards the plane with them, and after introducing his family to the cabin crew, they make a bit of small talk before saying their final goodbyes. Sami and Tara get a hug from their father before he makes his way to the cockpit to exchange a few words with the captain and first officer before disembarking. Once back on the ground, he gives them a final wave and then turns to chat with the baggage handlers.

As Louise looks down at her husband through the window, she is aware of a genuine sadness descending on her, but she also knows that she has reached her limit. It seems to her that the thing we human beings long for psychologically and emotionally is often more adventurous than what the human psyche can sustain. Although she was totally unprepared for the emotional havoc her marriage and relationship had wreaked upon her, she is nevertheless grateful to have withstood the pain and hurt of it all. At least she can pick up the shattered pieces of her life, begin healing the broken memories, and move forward.

Smiling wistfully, Louise is convinced there is really no logic or practical solution to help solve matters of the heart. Entangled as they are in family histories and bound up in illusive, fantastical moments, they are certain to spark a bittersweet clash of two conflicting worlds, the inner, secret one and the other occupied by reality as we know it.

Cupid can be a capricious and fickle fellow, leaving his victims wounded and bearing invisible scars which may take a lifetime to heal. Louise has learned the hard way that the forbidden, sweetest-tasting fruit can end up leaving the sourest taste.

The engines have started up, and Louise is holding her breath, ready for an imminent ascent. Soon, the aircraft will be climbing high in the sky, enveloped in fast-moving clouds. Then, once the aircraft has exited Libyan airspace, it should follow a flight path to its destination in Malta, which is the first leg of Louise's journey home.

Looking out of the tiny window, she sees the plane begin to make the slow turn that will angle the nose of its massive body towards the runway. Her gaze comes to settle on the figure of Kareem still standing by the hangar, talking with the handlers. As Louise continues to stare at her husband, she searches her heart for a sign, some semblance of emotion, anything which might still be lurking there, but instead, she feels nothing, nothing at all.

Once in the air, Sami and Tara fall asleep after their early morning rise, plus the previous night when they hardly slept with excitement. Louise finds herself alone and undisturbed with her thoughts.

Reaching for her shoulder bag on the seat, she takes out her wallet and carefully extracts a piece of folded paper from its inner compartment.

Opening it for the second time, she stares incredulously at the message, which is short and succinctly written but rich in meaning. Three simple words, *I love you,* yet they present her with a myriad of complexity. What is she to do with them? The answer springs from somewhere deep inside her, an inner voice that speaks to her.

"Absolutely nothing," it says.

Pondering over the note, she realises that Jabir must have understood she would not be returning. How could he presume to know her mind? she wonders. It was nothing she had said, at least not definitively. Yet, it seems that he has drawn his own conclusions. When she last saw him, only days ago, she sensed he was slightly distant. When she suggested he stay for coffee, he declined, making some excuse about having to meet someone. However, the following morning, much to her surprise, he returned.

In the hallway, their suitcases were lined up in readiness for their departure the following morning. Standing in the doorway, she caught him casting a wistful glance in their direction. Suddenly, in what felt like a long, awkward moment, their eyes locked and coming toward her, he took something from his pocket. Thrusting it into the palm of her hand, he closed her fingers over it and with one final squeeze, he walked swiftly and silently away without as much as a backward glance. Louise opened her mouth to say something but swallowed her words, hesitating at the door before finally stepping back inside.

At thirty-thousand feet and well above the clouds, Louise allows herself, for the first time, to feel the full weight of his words and to acknowledge how much it had taken for him to own them. To actually verbalise them would have been too much, and besides, she believes he wanted to avoid her feeling compromised by those very words.

Her ponderous thoughts are broken by the sound of the refreshment cart approaching. She gently rouses the children so they can eat some breakfast. Sure enough, they eat heartily despite their tiredness, and soon, they chatter about everything they mean to do once they arrive in Ireland.

Before long, they touch down in Malta, and Martha is waiting for them in the arrival hall. There is great excitement at being reunited and they set off to spend a couple of nights at their friend's before continuing their onward journey.

A further surprise awaits Louise before she embarks on the final leg of her journey home to Dublin.

FIFTY THREE

A Sublime Sunset

Of all that is good, sublimity is supreme.

– Lao Tzu

The sun is beginning to set over St Paul's Bay, where they sit on the terrace overlooking the shingle beach below. Louise can see the children having fun with Martha, throwing pebbles into the calm waters and waiting for them to plop, sending ripples out to form small circular waves. Looking around to take in the greater sweep of the bay, Louise experiences a sense of peace, something she has not felt for a long time. If this is as close to heaven as she can get, so be it.

Saint Paul's Bay or San Pawl-il Bahar, as it is known by the locals, is a small seaside village. Once a place of summer residences for the native

Maltese, it has metamorphosed into a melting pot of eastern Europeans, Middle Eastern Arabs and Italians who all call it their home. The placename owes its origins to the shipwreck of Saint Paul, a voyage from Caesarea to Rome as documented in the Acts of the Apostles at the very foundations of Christianity.

Louise stands against the balcony railings, staring pensively out at the ocean, barely able to grasp the fact that she is here on this beautiful little Island in the centre of the Mediterranean. Jeff comes to join her, and she can catch the scent of his aftershave lingering in the light, balmy breeze.

"A penny for your thoughts, Louise or can I ask?"

He speaks without looking at her directly; his head inclined outwards to the sparkling sea. She knows all the same, from his tone, that it is a meaningful enquiry.

"No, not at all, it's hardly a secret."

He turns to look at her, and she smiles warmly at him.

"I'm just so glad to be here, and I have to thank you, Jeff; you've been so good."

"Don't mention it," with a wave of his hand, he dismisses her remark. "It was nothing, really. I'm delighted to be here and enjoying myself immensely."

"It's nice to have the opportunity to see Martha because we won't meet again for at least another year." Louise speaks her thoughts out loud.

"You had time to catch up then, after you arrived yesterday?"

"We did, Jeff, after a delicious supper. The chat went on into the late-night hours."

Early that morning, Louise was summoned to the phone and she assumed it to be Arleen, her sister, checking on their travel arrangements. It came as quite a shock to hear Jeff's voice on the other end, explaining that Shelley had given him the number so he could get in contact.

He invited them all for dinner in the evening and insisted on sending a private taxi to take them from Martha's home in Marsaskala to a quaint, little eatery situated on the north coast of the Island, famous for its seafood.

Whenever he visits Malta, he eats at the same restaurant and stays at a nearby hotel, so he is well acquainted with the area.

It all feels a little surreal to Louise, especially Jeff's unexpected appearance, but she has not dared to ask what brings him to Valetta, whether it is consular business or something else.

After dinner, Martha suggests taking the children for a stroll along the beach. Because Sami and Tara have grown up with Martha's two daughters and are similar in age, they get along well together. Leaving Louise and Jeff on the terrace to enjoy the tranquil atmosphere of the evening, they head off down the beach.

Absentmindedly, they watch the children make their way leisurely along the shoreline toward the promenade, pausing every now and then to examine seashells and gather pebbles for throwing in the water. Suddenly, Jeff breaks the silence with a question Louise is unprepared for.

"Will you let me take you to the airport tomorrow, Louise?"

Despite being caught off guard, her smile is spontaneous, and she accepts without a second thought. Jeff appears genuinely pleased that his offer is accepted. He orders two Aperol spritzes, and they sip on them as the sun begins to sink. Louise feels herself relax into the evening, captivated by the layers of cloud, red and orange hues reflected on the horizon, a giant canvas of vibrant colour splashed across the sky. Her cares and worries seem to melt into the night atmosphere and she has a feeling of being connected to nature and to herself. There is nothing like a beautiful sunset and good company to end a perfect day.

She is content to ignore her troubles for the little time she is here. Overwhelmed by a failed marriage, amongst other things, the most she can think about now is planting her two feet firmly on familiar ground in the place she loves so well.

Jeff tells her about the many interesting places to see in Malta. She has already told him of her deep interest in ancient history and her wish to see the great Caravaggio paintings housed in the Baroque cathedral in Valetta. He has explored the ancient capital at length, explaining how it was first established during the Middle Ages by the Knights of Saint John. His favourite place, by far, is the Island of Camino, which is renowned for its beautiful clear waters and considered a nature reserve and bird sanctuary. Adding to this, he finds the native Maltese to be among the friendliest people he has come across on his travels.

"You can go by ferry or hire a private boat to take you around the islands in a day," Jeff says.

"Yeah, I'd love to see it; I intend to, at some point," Louise replies.

"Well, you've got a guide here waiting whenever you're ready."

"I'll hold you to that, though it could be a while," she laughs.

"I'm a patient sort of guy, I can wait." The reply comes swift and clear without a shred of ambiguity.

"That's nice to know Jeff, I'm flattered."

"Don't be, I'm serious. I have friends that I sail with now and then. I can use their boat any time to show you the Islands."

They look at each other for a long moment before Jeff finally speaks.

"Let's join the others, shall we?"

Reluctantly, Louise rises out of her seat, thinking she could stay for longer and listen to him talk about his travels. Then she remembers they have an early start the next day so better to say goodnight.

Leaving behind the magical setting, they walk through a charming little garden and exit via a side gate to descend the steps which lead directly onto the beach. There, mingled with the gentle sound of lapping waves, is laughter, a sound she has heard too little of. When Louise calls their names, they seem slow to answer, still full of fun and playfulness.

And so, the little company gather, bound by ties of friendship and love, together under a moonlit sky, not knowing where the future will lead them or how their destinies will entwine with each other.

FIFTY FOUR

Inception

One day in retrospect the years of struggle will strike you
as the most beautiful.

– Sigmund Freud

Less than seventy-two hours later, they are sitting on another plane, the one that will take them home to Ireland, where they belong. Once they are air-bound, Sami and Tara take out their new games, leaving their mother to indulge her latest thoughts.

Louise closes her eyes and allows thoughts of Jeff to come rushing in. Their parting seemed a little surreal and not what she was expecting. He had picked them up early that morning, so when they arrived at the airport there was enough time to sit and drink a coffee. Then he disappeared for a few minutes and returned with gifts for Sami and Tara, something to occupy them on the journey, he insisted. Louise was touched by his generosity and also by the fact that the children appeared to genuinely like him, probably because of his easy-going, jocular way of relating to them.

In her mind's eye, Louise re-enacts their parting scene, his final words after taking a card from his pocket and handing it to her.

"As soon as you get settled, Louise, call me."

She thanks him for everything, and offering him her hand, he clasps it with both of his.

"Promise you'll call," he repeats, looking at her fixedly but with a roguish smile.

"I Promise."

At those parting words, she turns and walks a few paces to join Sami and Tara, who are waiting for her.

Glancing back over her shoulder, she sees Jeff still watching them and suddenly, on impulse, she turns. With an urgency that neither of them expects, she closes the gap between them in a few short steps. Moving forward, he seems to read her intentions. In a heartbeat, he opens his arms and embraces Louise tightly in a bear hug. For anyone who cares to notice, it is entirely spontaneous, a fluid motion that is raw and emotionally charged. At that same moment, they exchange an unspoken look of understanding before Louise turns on her heel and walks hurriedly back. At the security gate, the children stand waiting for their mother and together, they give a final wave before disappearing into the crowd.

Louise has to admit that she felt a rush of attraction to Jeff the first time she saw him in the embassy gardens. There was something about him she found immediately arresting, not only his looks, though he is undeniably handsome, but maybe his kindness. In the short time they have known each other, he made her feel special on every occasion. Now she is ready to recognise the strong connection between them.

From a state of reverie, Louise drops into a contented slumber. She sees herself, with her father, strolling carelessly in a meadow whose lush green fields appear to rise out of a pasture that is partially covered in a blanket of mist. Barely visible but nonetheless distinctive is the bluish-black and white colouring of dairy, Friesian cattle lounging languidly in the hazy afternoon sun. The sound of silence is comforting, and in those precious moments of quietude, she escapes the madness, finding some reprieve from a busy mind and a weary soul.

She awakes as the plane is beginning its gradual descent and seeing that the children too have fallen asleep, she takes some moments just to gaze lovingly on them a while before they wake. Smiling to herself, she turns and raises the blind so as to look out and feel the thrill of knowing that very soon her beloved destination will come into sight. Looking out of the small window, she is met by rays of bright afternoon sunlight, and suddenly, a displaced thought enters her mind. It brings her back, way back to a different time and another plane journey where she could see only darkness. Dismissing the memory, she turns her attention back to the children, whose eyes open wide with delight as they realise they will be landing very soon. Today is a day for positive, life-affirming thoughts, and Louise is hopeful that she will have many more.

Descending slowly beneath the clouds, Louise looks out eagerly onto a familiar landscape below, and the sight of it brings immediate tears of relief to her eyes. She savours the moment, pushing away any thoughts of the future that lie ahead, open and unfathomable. There is only now, and she wants nothing more than to bask in the security of the present.

On life's journey, we often feel cheated by the entanglements of time and space and we succumb to its games of chance and treachery as it measures out painstakingly what has already been ordained for us elsewhere.

Looking down, Louise sees a tapestry of soft, green hues, shades of emerald, olive, sage and moss, all blending into a lushly woven blanket. It instantly warms her senses and wraps her in a deep, verdant calm.

She feels a loosening of threads, threads which have so far bound a life so tentatively together. Soon, they are bound to unravel, revealing past mysteries and brutally exposing the present. Armed with a quiet determination and strength of spirit, Louise is ready to move forward.

Epilogue

Life is no fairy tale and the world can be a cruel place.

Some find out too late, even the realists amongst us
fall prey to its evil charms.

For everyone has a fundamental fantasy that becomes a shelter
from too much reality until it shatters into a million pieces around us.

We engage in self-sabotage, unknowingly,

Trading simplicity for complexity,

Spiritual richness for materialism,

Human flaws and frailty for perfection,

Depth of meaning for shallowness,

The morals of Finch for the spoils of Faust,

A right to be sad for pseudo-happiness,

And still, the world can be a beautiful place
but we have to look for beauty, know how and where to find it,
often in the most unlikely places, sometimes in obscurity
but always within ourselves,

Search well, my friends.

About the Author

Oasis is Millie Blackwood's first novel. Her love of storytelling was fostered in childhood and later nurtured by a passion for books and reading. As an adult it grew into a deep curiosity about the human spirit in all its vicissitudes. She has a fascination with the stories we tell ourselves.

Millie is a Psychoanalytic Psychotherapist and a Clinical Supervisor. She has a love of the natural world and unspoilt places, and going for long country rambles in the company of her dogs is always a joy.

Her interests include reading medieval history, philosophy and epistemology. She also loves music and poetry. Millie is currently working on her next book. She lives with her family in Dublin.